FEAR OF THE BEAST

"Come on up," Sam shouted. "Let me see you!"

And one Beast did just that. A young Beast, lacking the caution of age, leaned forward, just a few feet from the cave opening. It roared at the young man, its breath stinking. Sam shot it between the eyes, then stood smiling as the dead creature tumbled backward. It would not be wasted. Its relatives would feast on the cooling flesh and still-warm blood, sucking marrow from the bones.

"One less," Sam said, spitting contemptuously on the ground. After he walked away from the rancid hole, a huge old Beast stuck its head out of the den. He had been on this earth for many hundreds of years, and was old and wise, as Beasts go. He had never known a human without fear—until now.

Growling, the Beast slipped back into the earth to warn the others of this human; tell them to stay away. For he was not like the other humans: He had been touched . . . by the Other Side.

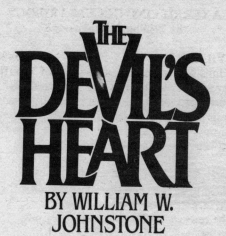

THE DEVIL'S HEART

BY WILLIAM W. JOHNSTONE

ZEBRA BOOKS
KENSINGTON PUBLISHING CORP.

ZEBRA BOOKS

are published by

KENSINGTON PUBLISHING CORP.
475 Park Avenue South
New York, N.Y. 10016

Second printing: December 1984

Printed in the United States of America

To A.E.J. and C.W.J.

Stay with me God. The night is dark,
The night is cold: my little spark
of courage dies. The night is long;
be with me God, and make me strong.

—Poem found on a scrap of
paper in a slit trench in
Tunisia during the battle of
El Agheila—1944.

December

The town of Whitfield no longer exists. Very little of the northwestern part of Fork County exists, except in the memories of those who might once have lived there and were fortunate enough to be gone when the great fireball struck, searing the land for miles.

Scientists were stunned by the suddenness of the huge fireball, for it seemed to materialize out of the heavens, traveling at such a tremendous speed it was almost beyond calculation.

Where had it come from? the scientists were asked by a stunned population.

From straight out of the sun was the reply.

And you could not have predicted it?

No.

Why?

The scientists hedged that question, for many of them were sworn, avowed atheists. But finally, one man from an observatory in California who was not an unbeliever did reply, although not to the satisfaction of all his colleagues. His reply brought laughter from more than a few of his fellow scientists.

"How does one predict when the hand of God will fall? And how hard the blow will be?"

If indeed it had been, as the scientist said, "the hand of

God," it had been a mighty slap from Him.

By the time various Spies in the Skies satellites picked up on the cannonading mass of fiery destruction, it was already on top of the satellites, through them, burning them before they could photograph more than a one-second shot at best, and transmit that to earth. Those pictures that did make it back to earth were immediately ordered seized by presidential order. They would be released for public viewing . . . sometime. At a date that would be set . . . sometime.

"Why?" came the immediate one-word question from the press.

The president did not tell them the real reason for his order. He did not tell them because he did not want them to think he was nuts. He did not tell them for a number of reasons, but chiefly because he could not think of a reasonable way to tell people that he had been visited by someone . . . or something . . . in a dream (or was it a dream?) who had forewarned him of the terrible, cataclysmic fireball of death. So he put the monkey on the backs of the military, telling the press it was in the best interest of the nation that the matter not be discussed for a time. It had to be studied and all that. Probably for a very long time.

And the president warned that should there be any leaks—any leaks at all—the leakee would spend the rest of his lengthy tour of duty attempting to hand-carry snowballs between Fort Myers and Miami, along the Tamiami Trail, without benefit of insect repellent.

There were no leaks.

The ball of fire that leveled Whitfield and parts of Fork County was, some scientists said, more than a mile wide and about three miles deep. Some said it was shaped like a

Star of David. Others said it looked like an artist's conception of God's face; a striking resemblance. The president told the scientists to shut their damned mouths, too, or face the prospects of never receiving another dime of government money—for anything.

But many people witnessed the strange blue lights that preceded the crash of the . . . whatever the hell it was, and they asked about those lights.

But suddenly, all was quiet about the mighty ball of fire, except for speculation, and that soon began to fade as other news pushed the holocaust out of the headlines. Only the insurance companies were left to ponder over the crash and dole out large sums of money to the relatives of those who had been killed.

An astronomer in California thought he knew what had happened. But he kept his mouth shut. Not out of any fear of the government, but because he felt it was the right thing to do.

One investigative fellow did put some rather interesting and curious events together after a bit of prowling. But since he was a career army reservist and did not wish to spend his summer obligations to Uncle Sam cleaning up gooney bird shit on Guam, he kept his mouth shut. Someday, maybe, he'd write a book about it. Maybe. But only if he could be assured the protection of the Dalai Lama in some cave in Tibet.

What he had pieced together was this: at almost the precise moment of fiery impact with earth, a series of fires leveled a huge mansion in Canada. And just before that, something had been seen leaving earth, moving toward the heavens, traveling at tremendous speed. No one knew what that thing was. Or if they did, they weren't talking. And there were people who still remained unaccounted for after the fire at the mansion. One of them was a young man named Sam Balon King, whose stepfather had been a doctor in Whitfield, and whose mother had once been married to a minister . . . in Whitfield. And that minister had died under very mysterious circumstances, back in 1958, when another disaster had befallen that tragedy-ridden community.

But the investigative reporter wisely closed his journal on both disasters . . . for a time, at least.

PROLOGUE

It had been abnormally hot for this late in the season. By this time in northwestern Nebraska there was usually a lash of winter's approach in the air, a bite that brought color to the cheeks of pedestrians, urgently but softly speaking of the harsh winter just ahead.

But the winds that blew across the plains and rolling sand hills had a torrid touch, oppressively so, bringing a sudden surliness to the people of this sparsely populated county, turning most tempers raw and confusing a few as to why.

The many knew why. The few would learn too late.

And out in the badlands, some miles from Whitfield, inside a fenced-in area where horror sprang to life back in the late 1950s . . . something stirred. A creature cautiously stuck its head out of a hidden cave and looked around, viewing its surroundings through evil, red eyes. The Beast had felt the hot fingers of the wind pushing through the cave entrance as a probing hand might do, signaling those which serve another Master that it was time.

The Dark One was near.

The wind grew in strength and heat, the Beast snarling in reply. The manlike creature rose from its sentry position to crawl out of the filthy hole, rising to stand like

11

a human, bits of dust and twigs and blowing sand striking its hairy body. But to the Beast, it was a signal of love, a gesture of welcome. The Beast roared, its breath foul. It held its huge arms upward and shook its fists toward the sky, roaring its contempt for that God who occupies a more lofty position than the Master of the Beast. For the creature knew but one God: the Prince of Darkness; the Lord of Flies; Ruler of all that is Evil.

From behind the sentry came a guttural sound, as other Beasts rose from their long sleep, surly and hungry. They craved meat, and the sweet taste of blood.

But the sentry again tested the wind, and the wind spoke its reply: wait. The sentry held up one warning paw to those below it, holding them at bay. He growled, and the others drew back into the darkness of the evil-smelling hole in the earth. They knew they must obey.

Wait, the growling sentry told them. The Master will tell us when we may move. Be patient, for you have waited more than twenty years, a few more weeks won't matter. Wait.

ONE

"You're late getting home," the woman said, a flatness to her voice, as if she knew the reason for his tardiness.

"Yes. Very difficult labor," the man lied.

Jane Ann King smiled ruefully, but kept her thoughts to herself.

"Is that a letter from Sam?" Doctor King asked his wife. He really didn't give a damn, but anything was better than having to listen to her run her mouth asking endless questions and not believing anything he told her.

Jane Ann nodded.

"What does he say?"

She shrugged. "I haven't opened it."

Tony laughed. "Why the hell not?"

His laughter infuriated her. She sighed, rising from her chair, walking to a corner table. "Let me show you something, Tony." A Bible rested on the table. Sam Balon's Bible. The Sam her son was named after. The son who did not yet know how and why his real father had died. But that time of unawareness was rapidly coming to a close.

Jane Ann said, "When I got the letter this morning, I was just about to open it when the phone rang. I put the letter on the Bible on my way to the phone."

Oh, fuck! Tony thought. Who in the hell cares? He

13

held up a hand. "Wait a minute, baby. I can sense this is going to take half the night. It's been a long day. I'm beat. Let me fix a drink." He smiled. "You want one, baby?"

"You know I don't, Tony. But you fix yourself one. Fix yourself a strong one." She could smell the odor of sex in his clothing, and wondered which female he had serviced this time. She realized she hated her husband. And had for a long time. No, she amended that . . . not hate. Rather—she searched for the right word—I loathe not him, but what he has become.

"Thanks a lot." Tony walked to the wet bar, fixing a strong drink. "Go on, tell your story," he said. But goddamn, keep it short.

"I'll skip the details, since I realize you aren't particularly interested in them . . . and not much of anything else that lives in this house. The letter won't stay on the Bible, near the Bible, or on the bookcase next to the Bible. It won't stay . . . on a level with the Bible." She did not tell him she had called Wade, telling him about it first.

Tony looked at the Bible. How he hated that book; he didn't like to get too close to the offensive book. But he took the letter from his wife's hand and placed it on the Bible. It flipped off onto the floor. Tony took a large gulp of whiskey and again took the letter, placing it back on the Bible. Again, the letter was propelled off the Word of God. No matter where Tony placed the letter—on a level with the Bible—it would not stay.

He silently rejoiced, keeping his face passive. He had an idea what was happening, and thought Jane Ann did, too. She was beginning to suspect.

Outside, the wind picked up in strength, tossing bits of

rock and twigs against the house. The hot wind seemed almost to be a signal.

Tony placed the letter under the front cover of the Bible. The small table began to shake as the Bible seemed to press against the letter. The table suddenly collapsed, sending Bible and letter to the floor. Jane Ann picked up the Bible and placed it on a shelf. Tony grabbed the letter, looked at it, then shook his head. When he spoke, his voice was full of shock and awe . . . and something else Jane Ann could not understand.

"Goddamn!" Tony swore.

Reverend Sam Balon had written his name in that Bible when he had first received it, back in the late forties. But such pressure had been placed on the letter that the name Sam Balon was now clearly visible upon the white of the envelope. Tony quickly placed the letter on a low coffee table.

Jane Ann was watching him closely. She thought she could see pleasure in his eyes. And something else: evil.

"Impossible," Tony said. "Unless . . ." His words trailed it off as he realized that the Master of Darkness was truly coming. Perhaps he was already here! He had to get to Jean Zagone. Had to tell the Coven Leader of this. She would be pleased at this astuteness. Perhaps reward him with some nice, young girl.

"Unless what, Tony?" His wife's hated voice brought him back to his surroundings. He glanced at her. Her face was pale, eyes calm, hands clenched into fists at her side.

"Nothing," he said.

"Well . . . I think Sam is trying to tell us something."

"Oh, shit! Sam is dead, Jane Ann. More than twenty years dead." Tony hoped Balon wasn't trying to tell

15

anybody anything.

"As we knew him, yes, he is dead. But his soul is alive. We're mortals, Tony. We don't know what is behind the veil. And remember, Sam was touched by Him—chosen by Him, if you will."

"I don't believe that crap anymore," he said, the words tumbling hatefully from his mouth.

And Jane Ann's worst suspicions were now corroborated. She wanted to slap her husband.

His mood shifted as he forced himself to put his arms around her. He kissed her cheek and found it cool to his lips, very unresponsive. "Honey, we're the youngest of the survivors of that . . . incident. And we're not kids." He grinned down at her. "But you're sure sexy enough to be a kid."

She pushed him away from her. His body odor was awful. She could not remember the last time Tony had showered. More evidence against him. She walked swiftly from the room, returning in a moment with an 8 x 10 glossy of the late Sam Balon. The picture was in a frame with a glass front.

Tony's eyes narrowed at the sight of the minister. He hated that bastard. He reached out to take the picture from her.

"No!" She spun away from his hand.

"You think your precious Sam Balon is some kind of fucking saint? That he's sending you messages? Hell, baby, maybe he just wants some pussy."

"Pick up the letter!" she said, speaking through gritted teeth.

For some reason, unexplained in his mind, Tony was suddenly afraid of his wife. He picked up the letter without questioning her.

"Hold it against the glass," she said, lifting the framed photograph. There was a knowing smile on her lips that angered the man.

Tony pressed the letter against the glass. Within seconds, the envelope began to smoke. She jerked the letter from his hands before the smoke turned into a blaze. The front of the envelope was slightly charred.

She looked up at her husband, a smile on her lips. "Yes, Tony, I believe Sam is trying to tell me something. What's the matter, darling? You seem . . . afraid."

On Friday nights, the chanting would begin as no more than a low murmur in the hot night, then grow as the winds picked up in heat and velocity. The chanting would become as profane as it was evil.

The participants in this macabre chanting would gather around a huge stone circle, miles from Whitfield. There were carvings in the stones. On one stone, two figures were depicted: a saintly looking man and a beastly man-creature with hooved feet. The creature and the saint have been there for thousands of years, locked in silent combat, with no apparent winner.

This area was known as The Digging, the ruins of equipment and rusting old mobile homes still evident. The entire area is enclosed within a tall chainlink fence. Roads to the area were destroyed in the fall of 1958. Only in the last few years have they been quietly reopened by some local people. The state bought the land and condemned it because of the dangerous caves in the area. So they said.

This was the area where, for centuries, sightings of

monsters have been reported: hairy, ugly beasts with red eyes and huge clawed hands and large yellow, dripping fangs.

All nonsense, of course.

Suddenly the chanting would cease. The silence would grow heavy. The wind ceased its hot push.

And the screaming would begin, the agonizing, wailing pushing past lips, tearing out from a human whose skin was being slowly ripped from its body; who was undergoing more sexual depravity than was ever thought of by de Sade . . . in his blackest moments. The shrieking would continue for hours, the torches of the now silent witnesses to evil flickering in the night, turning the blood-stained altar dripping a slippery black.

The screaming would gradually change into a madness-induced moan, then into a low sob. And then silence. And then one by one the torches would cease their flickering fiery quiver, and the area known as The Digging would become as black as the Devil's heart.

And as still as a musty grave.

Dear Mom and Dad:

Sure is a change from the sand hills where I grew up, but I love it here at Nelson College. And guess what?: I'm rooming with a guy whose name is Sam B. Williams.

"I wonder what the B stands for?" Jane Ann asked.

"I don't give a damn what it stands for," Tony said. "Just read the damn letter."

Sam B. (he's called Black) has a really super-fine

18

*sister; she's going to school at Carrington College—
that's just upriver from us. Black is going to fix me
up with her soon; said he told her all about me and
she's really anxious to meet me.*

"I wonder what her name is?" Jane Ann asked. The
name Black had triggered an old alarm within her.
Tony wished she would just toss the letter in the
garbage and shut her fucking mouth.

*I'm going home with them over the Thanksgiving
holiday to meet their parents. They live up in
Canada, right on the edge of Province Park—really
wild and beautiful. Black said it's miles from any
neighbors. I'm really looking forward to it. Black
and I have a lot in common: we both spent three
years in the military. He was in some Canadian
outfit, paratroop-commando, and, of course, you all
remember me: Ranger Sam. Black and I have done
some skydiving together, and we've talked about a
long camp-out this spring. Maybe his good-looking
sister will go along, keep me warm? (Just a joke,
Mom.)*

Got to go. Will call later.

*Love,
Sam*

Tony stood up. "Very interesting letter. I have to go,
Jane Ann."

"I want to know who this Black fellow is," Jane Ann
said. "And I'd like to know more about his sister."

"I'm not going to sit here and argue with you, Janey. I don't give a damn what you do."

"I've realized that for a number of years, Tony. What did you mean about us being the youngest of the survivors?"

He shrugged. "Well . . . Miles and Doris, Wade and Anita . . . they're all in their sixties—all retired. Neither man is in good health. And for the last few weeks . . . neither Wade nor Miles has acted . . . well, friendly toward me."

"Since the hot wind began blowing?"

"Yeah, if you just have to connect it that way."

Across town a phone rang. Wade Thomas quickly silenced the jangling. "All right, Doris. Sure, I can come over. I know, I'll be careful. Miles wants to build a what? What the hell is a golem? Are you serious! Okay, I'll be right over." He hung up, his face holding an odd look.

"What's wrong with Miles?" Anita asked.

"Doris says he's cracked. Says the old *momzer*'s nuts."

"What's a momzer?"

"I have no idea. But I'll bet you it isn't complimentary."

"Well, what's a golem?"

"Ah . . . well, Doris says it's a kind of monster made out of clay, endowed with life. A protector, sort of."

The man and wife exchanged glances. Anita shrugged.

Wade came to her, putting his arm around her shoulders. "Honey . . . ?"

"No, Wade." She was firm. "I don't believe it's happening. Not again. I will not leave our home."

"It is happening, Anita. And you know it."

20

"You go see Miles. I'll be all right."

Tony lit a cigarette, ignoring Jane Ann's shocked look. "Tony, you haven't smoked in years!"

"Well, I started again. It's my business, not yours."

"How is your practice, Tony?"

He shrugged. "You've been seeing a lot of Wade and Anita lately, haven't you. And that damned ol' Jew."

And with that remark about Miles, she knew all pretense had been ripped away. "You want me to leave this house, Tony?"

"I don't give a damn what you do."

"I see."

"Look, Janey . . ."

"Don't say another word, Tony." The warning was softly spoken, but it held firm conviction.

"I may or may not return this evening."

"Your choice, Tony. But I think you've already made the most important choice."

He looked at her, his eyes hooded and evil. He nodded his head and walked out into the night.

Across the street, at the Cleveland home, eyes watched his movements, then lifted to the woman standing in the door. In her mid-forties, Jane Ann was still a very beautiful and shapely woman, with the ability to turn men's heads as she walked past.

Jane Ann lifted her eyes as the feeling of being watched touched her. The Cleveland family—father, mother, and three children—stood behind the huge picture window, all of them staring at her. She stepped quickly back into the house, picked up Balon's old Bible and returned to the porch. She held up the Bible, the dull gold cross on

21

the leather shining in the glow of streetlights.

The Cleveland family pulled the drapes.

Jane Ann stood for a moment on the steps, the hot winds blowing around her. "I won't run," she whispered, clutching the Word of God to her breast. "I won't run, and you can't make me run."

The wind sighed around her. And had she looked closely at the invisible wind, she could have seen a light mist forming where the wind touched the corner of the house.

"Miles, this is foolish," Wade pleaded with the man. "It's . . . folklore; myths. Hell, man, you haven't been in a synagogue in fifty years! You sure haven't been kosher in all the years I've known you."

"I'm a Jew," Miles said stubbornly. "My God will not forsake me."

"*Bubbemysah!*" Doris said.

Wade looked up. "What?"

"Old wives' tale," Miles translated. "It is not. Just ask the people of Prague."

"Ask the people of Prague," Doris said sarcastically. "What ask? That happened—supposedly—in the sixteenth century. I'm sure there are thousands still around who witnessed it."

"It happened," Miles insisted, looking at her. "I know, my grandfather was a cabalist. He told me it did."

"Your grandfather was a *meshuggener*," she replied. "All this foolish stuff. I'll go make coffee."

Miles shook his head and grinned. "She just called my grandfather a crazy old man. Wade, my God won't let me down. I know it."

"Seems like He did a pretty good job of it at Dachau, Buchenwald, and Auschwitz. To mention but a few."

"Don't blaspheme, Wade. Now is not the time. Ah . . . who am I trying to kid? Me! that's who. I'm talking in one breath about something I was taught not to believe in, and in the next breath talking about being a Jew. Then I talk about a golem. Used to listen to my grandfather talk about golems. Ah," he sighed heavily, "takes a rabbi to build one anyway. I think. I'm an old man, Wade. Sixty-eight next month. You wanna know what I think, Wade—I'll tell you: I think it's too late. That's what I think. For all of us. We should have left this place that summer . . . after we . . . did it." He thumped the arm of his chair. "Pulled out. But no, we were full of piss and courage . . . so we stayed. Like fools. Well, whatever it was, it's back. And you know it. I'm glad our kids have all gone away." He waved a hand, thin and heavily veined. "But I'm just too old to run. Wade, you go back and get Anita. The two of you, get Jane Ann . . . and run."

"Anita won't run, Miles. I can't convince her it's happening all over again. And Jane Ann is beginning to suspect more each day. She told me she wasn't running."

"Sam is not here to protect us now, Wade. And I don't mean no slight against you in saying that."

"I know you don't. Miles . . . I believe Sam is here." He told him about the letter.

"My old rabbi should hear this story. He'd crap on himself. May I be forgiven for saying that. Yeah, Sam was a wild one. If there was a way back, he'd find it. I hope he's here. Oh, Wade! What are we saying? Foolishness. Sam is dead. So let's have some coffee and cakes and talk

23

about all the good times."

An hour later, Wade stepped out of the Lansky house. The hot winds still blew. He walked to his car, pausing with his hand on the door. He looked up. "Sam, Jane Ann is not going to run. But if we stay here, they'll kill us, and do much worse to Jane Ann before she dies."

But the wind still blew hot, and Wade received no reply to his statement.

And the clay that Miles had painfully, slowly dug from the banks of a river—several hundred pounds of it—and had carefully shaped into the form of a man, with arms and legs and a featureless face, lay in the basement, in a huge packing crate.

It appeared lifeless.

It was in the summer of 1958 the horror finally surfaced, erupting like a too-long festering boil, spewing its corruption over all those near it. Specifically, the town of Whitfield and part of Fork County.

Those who survived the terror remember it as the summer of The Digging. And not many of the town's 2,500 residents did survive. Only a few. A few believers. More than a few unbelievers.

Whitfield was destroyed. At the end of that week of devil-induced terror, the town was a broken, burned-out, still-smoking ruin.

An archaeological team (they said) had come to Whitfield, ostensibly to investigate a huge stone circle, its interior barren of life. But what they were really doing was searching for a stone tablet. Satan's tablet, upon which were carved these words: HE WALKS AMONG YOU. THE MARK OF THE BEAST IS PLAIN. BELIEVE IN HIM. ONCE

TOUCHED, FOREVER HIS. THE KISS OF LIFE AND DEATH.

And the tablet had been found.

After that, the town's fall into the blackest depths of sin and depravity had been swift, with only a few resisting: the minister, Sam Balon, whose own wife, Michelle, was part of the Devil's team, as old and as evil as time. Father Dubois, a Catholic priest, had driven a stake into her heart, then stood by the bed with Sam, watching her metamorphosis through centuries of evil, and finally, her death.

The old priest was killed a short time later. Then the horror unfolded in Fork County.

The Undead walking. The Beasts of the devil prowling.

Sam Balon had pulled together a handful of people, true believers in the Lord God. They fought the horror with everything they could find and with every ounce of strength and faith they possessed. Sam had acted as the right hand of God.

It was a week of mind-tearing horror and days and nights of fear; of seeking out and killing those who worshiped the Devil. Finally, to save the few friends who remained, and to save his new wife, Jane Ann, Sam agreed to fight off the advances of Mephistopheles' witch, Nydia, a beautiful woman whose soul had been given to the Prince of Filth centuries before, in return for everlasting youth and unbelievable beauty.

Sam Balon had sent the Devil's agent, Black Wilder, tumbling back to Hell with a stake through his dark heart. All part of the bargain. Then the witch, Nydia, took Balon into the spinning darkness of trackless time. And the man of God and the Witch of Hell fought for Sam's seed of life. In the end, Nydia beat him and Balon was killed, his naked body found by the survivors. Cut into the earth beside the body, this message: HE MET ME—AND I DO RESPECT COURAGE.

It was signed by Satan.

The young doctor, Tony King, took Jane Ann as his wife, and the son of Sam Balon would not learn of his true father's fate for years—until it was almost too late.

TWO

"We'll leave the main highway at St. Gervais," Black said. "Then drive northeast until we come to where mother owns some property. We'll pick up a four-wheel drive there; sometimes you can't even make it to the house in a four-wheel. It can get rough."

Sam nodded, not really paying much attention to the words of his friend and soon-to-be-host. Since the moment he and Black had picked up Black's sister, Nydia, Sam had sat in a near state of shock, overwhelmed by her beauty. He did not believe he had ever seen a more beautiful woman, and when she told him that no, she didn't have a steady boyfriend, and that really she hardly dated at all, Sam began counting his lucky stars.

Nydia was five feet seven, she told him. She did not volunteer her weight, and Sam tactfully didn't ask. But whatever her weight, it was distributed in a most delightful manner. Her hair was as black as the darkest night, her eyes a deep blue. Her skin was flawless, with just a hint of the long-ago Mediterranean ancestry. Her designer jeans were filled out perfectly (Sam could only guess at her shapely legs, and his guesses would later prove one hundred percent accurate), and her breasts were full.

Nydia was as taken with Sam as he with her, looking

him over very carefully, and liking everything she saw. Sam was well over six feet and muscular, with big shoulders and arms, a narrow waist. He had his late father's unruly mop of thick, dark-brown hair, and since leaving the army, had allowed it to grow a bit longer than the service likes. Sam's handsomeness was not of the pretty-boy type, Nydia concluded. He was . . . rugged-looking, with a solid, square jaw. And she had never before in her life been so drawn to a member of the opposite sex. She did not—at least up until now—believe in love at first sight. Now she was not so sure.

But she was certain of one thing: she was going to get to know Sam B. King very well. Just about as well as any woman can know a man.

And that shocked her, for she was a virgin in an age of overt promiscuity.

"How do you get out if you can't use a four-wheel drive?" Sam asked.

"Oh . . . snowmobiles, helicopters. We have them all at Falcon House," Black replied with the ease of a person born into great wealth.

"Must be nice," Sam mused. "How did your father get his name?" he asked Nydia. "I've never heard of a person named Falcon."

"His name is really Falkner," she replied, her voice touching Sam in some very intimate places, producing some uplifting results. Uncomfortable if one is wearing jeans. "And he isn't really our father. Our real father is, well . . . either dead or gone someplace; we don't know, since mother refuses to discuss him. The only time she ever mentioned him she flew into a rage."

"We don't have to hang dirty linen in public, dear,"

Black said. "Besides, you are digressing from the question."

"Forgive me, brother dear," Nydia said, her eyes narrowing in sudden anger.

Quick temper, Sam noted, filling that away in the back of his mind.

"Falkner means," she continued, "or so I'm told, Falcon hunter. His father began calling him Falcon when he was just a baby. It's been Falcon ever since. Truth or fiction, it's an interesting story."

"Your mother's name?"

Black smiled, the smile not going unnoticed by Sam, who chose to ignore it, but he filed that away, too. The smile had seemed . . . odd.

"Roma," Nydia said. "Means the wanderer. My mother has . . . seen most of the world during her life. But despite her age—which by the way, she will not reveal—she is still the most beautiful woman I have ever seen."

"Even more beautiful than you?" Sam said, the words popping from his mouth.

Black laughed and so did his sister. "Thank you," she said. "But in answer to your question: yes, she is. You'll see. Roma is beautiful."

"Falcon and Roma," Sam mused. "Fascinating names."

"We are an unusual family," she replied. "I believe after you've spent some time with us you'll agree with that."

More than you realize, sister, Black thought. And soon it will be time for you to know just who you are. And what you were born to do—and become.

29

The trio had flown into Montreal, picked up one of the family's fleet of cars, and now, at St. Gervais, they all helped transfer the gear, then clamored noisily into the four-wheel for the eighty-mile trip into what Black called Canada's near outback.

A thought popped into Sam's brain, the thought becoming vocal before he knew why he said it, "You guys go to church?"

"No," Black said, trying to keep his reply from being too short. "We were taught to believe in God . . . and especially," he fought a smile, "the Devil. But we practice no form of . . . popularly organized religion."

"I've gone to a church several times since I've been at Carrington," Nydia said. "I found it most interesting. I plan to keep on attending."

Black almost lost the big four-wheel. He wanted to scream at his sister, but instead bit his lip so hard he brought a drop of blood. Stupid bitch! he silently cursed her.

"Do you go to church, Sam?" she asked.

"Not as often as I should. I kind of got away from it in the service. I've got to start back, though. Nydia? How come you didn't go on to college when you got out of high school? I mean, I don't mean to be nosy; you can tell me to go to hell if you want."

Precisely where you are going, Sam, Black thought. In time.

Again, that lovely laughter from the backseat. "Don't be silly, Sam. No, mother asked if I wanted to go straight to school, or see the world with her and wait for Black to complete his stint in the service. Mother wanted him to go into the military. A real tough branch of the service.

30

Said in the years to come, the training would do him a lot of good. She said she once knew a man whom she admired greatly; she wanted Black to be like him in some ways. I think she said this man was a guerrilla fighter of some type; Special Forces, maybe."

"Sounds like my dad," Sam said, gazing out the window.

If the communiques could have been heard by human ears, they would have sounded like the rolling of enormous thunder splitting the heavens.

"How about it, Mighty One?" the dark voice ripped through the heavens. "A wager, perhaps?"

The replying voice was calm and assured. "Don't tempt me, Beelzebub. I might decide to end it all. I did once before, remember?"

"Bah! You won't. Not for this inconsequential bit of rabble. Your team against mine, like in the old days. If you win, I'll give you a million whimpering souls from the pits—so to speak."

"I could take them if I so desired. It was their choice. It always is. You should know. Remember: Thou shalt have no other God . . ."

"Oh, shut up! Don't bore me with that drivel! I had quite enough of that claptrap infinities ago."

"Why do I waste my time talking with you?"

"Because I'm interesting, and despite what you lead others to believe, you haven't yet given up on me, that's why."

"All right, proud one: I'll wager."

"I don't believe it!"

"If my team wins, you convert to my side."

"In a nun's cunt! Judas Priest, when you make up your mind to play, you really want to be a high roller, don't you?"

"Take it or leave it."

"I'll . . . leave it."

"I thought you would. No, Prince of Rats, I don't like this game of yours. I thought we settled all this a blink or two ago?"

The reply was slyly made. "Balon made a bargain."

"And it was kept, was it not?"

No reply.

"No, Filthy One, I won't interfere . . . directly. But I might, and I stress *might*, make the teams a bit more even."

"You wouldn't dare! That's against the rules."

"Oh?"

The voice that was laced with venom and evil howled and flung curses and spat ribbons of filth into the Heavens, attempting to penetrate the firmament. But the Mighty Voice chose not to reply.

Conversations with inferiors tended to bore Him . . . rather quickly.

"Your dad?" Nydia asked. Her ears had been listening, but her eyes had been fixed on a strange occurrence in the eastern sky. She had never seen anything quite like it: streaks of pure white darting down to almost touch upward thrusts of the ugliest yellow she had ever seen.

God rules the Heavens, she thought. But the Devil rules the earth.

And that sudden thought puzzled her, for she had only been to church a few times in her entire life. She did not remember ever hearing it before.

And what did that narrow plume of white and yellow have to do with religion?

She pushed the confusion from her brain. "I thought your dad was a doctor, Sam?"

"Not my real dad. He was a minister. But from what mother has told me, he was a real rounder. Back during the Korean War, he was a guerrilla fighter; one of the first of the Special Forces. He was a boxer, worked in a carnival, too, I think. Did all sorts of things. He was a real hell-raiser, though, before he became a minister."

"What happened to him?" she asked.

"He was killed before I was born. I never really knew exactly what happened. Mother has always kind of evaded that question whenever I brought it up. Said I would know someday. But I really want to know. It kind of bugs me."

"Were you in Special Forces, Sam?"

"No. I was a Ranger, out in Washington State. Real good outfit. You never hear much about the Rangers."

"Black was a Commando," she said, but there was not one note of pride in her voice, and Sam wondered about that.

"Yes," Sam replied. "That's a good outfit, too."

"Did you see combat, Sam?" she asked.

"Not . . . that I can talk about, Nydia."

"In other words," she grinned, "drop the subject?"

"That's about it," Sam agreed.

The three of them laughed about that.

"Men!" she said with false disgust. "But I know more about you than you think, Sam," she said mysteriously.

Sam did not ask what she knew about him, or how she had learned it. When he did remember to ask, he didn't, figuring Black had told her.

33

The conversation lightened, and they sang songs and told jokes and the miles seemed to fly past; three young people having fun. And then suddenly, out of the deep timber, just at that time when night reared up to touch and alter day, the massive house came into view.

Falcon House.

One could almost touch the evil that hung over the small town of Whitfield, and one could certainly see it in the eyes of the townspeople as they moved slowly up and down the streets. Just as it had happened in the 1950s, the evil had approached the people slowly, as a languoring sickness, sluggish in its growth, but deadly when it reached the brain or the heart.

Now many in that doomed town huddled in their homes, not understanding what was happening around them. The phones would not work; their neighbors were turning against them; their cars and trucks disabled . . . deliberately, and they were afraid.

Whitfield never regained its population total of 1958; fewer than 800 men, women and children now resided in the small town; perhaps 250 people in this part of Fork County, on the ranches and the farms.

But the Master of Darkness had taken note of his mistakes in the past, and did not intend to repeat them this time: no sudden departure from the churches—let that be a very gradual thing; no open rebellion; no mysterious disappearances or suspicious deaths; no closing of roads and sealing off this part of the county. There was no need for that now. Of the 1,050 residents in this part of Fork County, 850 had been inducted into the Coven of the Hooved One. More than enough.

The Lord of Flies felt that a handful of aging Christians

could do little to halt his movement in Whitfield, and that silly old Jew with his golem that would never be anything more than several hundred pounds of clay, immobile in a box, gave the Prince of Filth several moments of high humor.

His followers would have several hundred people to test their mettle upon. An ample number to produce days of screaming and nights of sexual depravity. Depravity being one of those Christian words, of course.

The King of Evil had moved slowly this time . . . no need for rushing; no need for panic; no need for elaborate schemes. The old Jew and Jewess would be no problem, and the aging newspaper man and his silly wife would meet the same fate. The doctor had been easy: the Prince of Darkness had had a high time playing with the good doctor over the years, tempting him, luring him, teasing him, and then, finally breaking him.

But Balon's widow, mother of that boy-child who was blessed by that accursed meddler in the Heavens . . . she was another matter. A very strong Christian type. Prissy little thing. Goody-goody. She had resisted all of his subtle and not-so-subtle advances; just couldn't shake her faith in Him. She was still a very attractive woman—beautiful, in fact. It would be very interesting finding her breaking point: mentally, sexually, physically.

Yes, very interesting. Quite.

But the Master of All Things did not share the Dark One's sense of humor. And while there were limits beyond which He could not go—directly—in dealing with the problems facing humankind—on earth—He could take a hand indirectly. Other than the ultimate warning He had given, so many years before.

And in His kingdom, spanning worlds and creatures and living things as yet unknown by anyone outside of the firmament, all under His never closing eyes, He brooded and sighed, knowing Sam Balon had slipped out—again. And also knowing He was hard-pressed to contain His personal bodyguard from following.

And a smile as bright as a thousand sunrises touched the face of the Universal Life Force of good.

"Good Lord, what a house!" Sam breathed. "In the middle of natures' beauty . . . this."

"Quite a pad, huh, Sam?" Black smiled.

"But . . . how?" Sam asked. "I mean . . . why here?"

"How was easy when one is as rich as Roma and Falcon," Nydia said from the backseat. Sam thought he detected just a hint of irritability in her voice; a touch of maybe-this-is-just-a-bit-too-much, too big, too pretentious. "Why? It was originally built, or someone began it as an inn, a hotel. They ran out of money. That's when Mother and Falcon stepped in. They had money from both sides of the family, and they retired young enough to really enjoy it. And they enjoy solitude."

"They can sure have that up here," Sam observed.

"The nearest neighbor is thirty-five miles away," Black informed him. "Two of the servants are trained paramedics in case of any medical emergencies that might arise, and the house has a huge generator and several smaller back-up units. As you can see, Sam, solar energy is used to help cool and heat the home. We'll give you the grand tour, don't worry."

The massive house was two full floors, running east and west, with another single floor rising up from the center of the home, starkly commanding the second and first floor wings beneath it.

"Your parents must employ a full-time grounds-keeper," Sam said.

"Several," Black told him. "Come on, Sam—meet the folks."

Falcon was tall and well built, a very handsome and athletic-appearing man. Age indeterminable. His hair was very black, with gray at the temples. It did not appear to have been touched with dye. His handshake was firm and his smile friendly, although his eyes were so dark Sam could not tell if the friendliness touched them or not.

But it was Roma who literally took Sam's breath away. He was very conscious of Nydia's eyes on him when the older woman appeared in the foyer of the great house.

She was the most magnificent woman Sam had ever seen.

He has his father's eyes, Roma thought. And his father's build and hair. I wonder if he has his father's cock?

"Mrs. Williams," Sam said, taking her offered hand.

"Roma," she corrected with a smile, her hand soft and warm in his. "I am so very happy to have the opportunity to meet you at last. Black has written much about you. But we'll have time to chat later. Lots of time. I know you all must be weary from your journey. Sam . . . Black will show you to your quarters. Rest for a time. We have drinks at seven, dinner is at eight-thirty. Informal, of course."

The woman before Sam was as tall as her daughter, with the same midnight-black hair and full, sensuous lips, her lipstick a slash of dark red. Her skin was that of her daughter's, touched with the same tint. Her figure was flawless; for her age, breathtaking, with full, heavy breasts and under her gown, long, shapely legs. Had Sam known exactly how old the woman who was once known as Nydia the Witch really was, he would have passed out on the floor.

Sam was very conscious of the woman's frankly sexual gaze. Then, as abruptly as the gaze was heated, it cooled, and a smile crossed her lips.

"I . . . have the strangest sensation, Mrs. Williams," Sam said.

"Oh?" The smile did not leave her mouth.

"I feel as if I know you; as if we'd met before."

"Oh, I rather doubt it, Sam. You're such a handsome young . . . devil," she said laughing, "I would surely remember the event. We'll chat over drinks in a few hours. We have days to get acquainted." She turned and walked from the foyer, knowing full well Sam's eyes were on her body. Roma knew many things. Her mind was a storehouse of information—all evil.

Brazen witch! Nydia thought, fuming as she watched her mother parade from the room, hips slightly swaying. The contempt she felt for her mother almost boiled to the surface.

Careful, Mother, Black projected. Your cunt captured Sam Balon, but it failed to conquer him. And young Sam is truly his father's son. It is not worth losing a daughter to gain another conquest.

I know both your thoughts, Roma thrust to her son, the waves stopping Sam cold in his tracks, suspending him momentarily. And I know my daughter has begun to hate me. And I know why. He is interfering. He is breaking the rules of the game. I will have to speak with the Master.

The projections ceased. Sam shook his head. "Boy . . .

38

that trip must have been more tiring than I thought. I was out of it for a few seconds. I felt . . . strange."

"It's the excitement," Black said. "New people, new places—kind of a strain, that's all. Come on, I'll show you where to bunk."

Where to bunk! Sam thought, after Black had escorted him to his rooms. It was a suite, consisting of a large bedroom, a sitting room, a huge bathroom, and a large walk-in closet. Sam looked for a radio. None. TV? None. Come to think of it, he mused, he had seen no TV antenna on Falcon House. Only the shortwave antenna for communication. It was almost as if they wished to be cut off from the outside as much as possible.

Turning to unpack his suitcase, Sam could not shake the feeling of foreboding that hung about him, and could not understand why he should feel that way.

His peripheral vision saw the doorknob slowly turning, the door easing open. Sam tensed.

THREE

"Sam?" Nydia called.

The young man grinned, expelling air from his lungs. "Here, Nydia."

She stepped inside, closing the door behind her. "You're really very special company, Sam." She smiled, aware of their being alone together. "This is the first time Mother has ever let a guest stay in this wing. Especially," her dark eyes sparkled with mischief, "in the room next to mine." She pointed to a closed door on the far side of the room.

Sam returned the grin. "Well . . . I'll have to keep my door locked then. I know how difficult it is to be a sex symbol—been one all my life."

Nydia rolled her eyes in mock awe. "Oh, my! I didn't know I was in such celebrated company. Perhaps you'd better keep your door locked. I might try to break it down, lusting after your body."

"In that case," Sam feigned great haste in digging into his jeans pocket, "let me give you the key."

Laughing, they stepped closer to each other. They stood for a moment, content to look into the other's eyes. Finally, Sam said, "I certainly am glad Black invited me up here."

"I certainly am glad you came." Something clouded

40

her dark eyes. "Sam? Be careful in this house."

"What do you mean?"

"I . . . don't know how to explain it. But," she bit at her lower lip, "sometimes guests are . . . changed, sort of. In a very strange kind of way. Spooky. I've seen it happen many times over the years. Watch out for the unexpected."

That feeling of foreboding suddenly became much more intense.

Both the young people whirled as the door opened behind them. Roma stood looking at them. "I could not help overhearing," she said. "You will find, Sam, that my daughter has a very active imagination. She desires to become a fiction writer, and I think she sometimes has difficulty separating fact from fiction." She held out a hand to her daughter. "Come, dear. Let's not be rude and prevent our guest from taking his rest."

Sam caught a flicker of something very close to contempt in Nydia's eyes. "Of course, Mother." She glanced at Sam. "See you in an hour or so. Perhaps you'd enjoy a swim before cocktails? We have an indoor pool and a selection of trunks in case Black forgot to tell you to bring a suit."

"He did. And I'd love a swim."

"I'll tap on your door in about an hour. That door." She pointed to the connecting door between their rooms, then glared openly and defiantly at her mother.

The woman left, with Roma closing the door, flashing a brief smile at Sam. A smile that left Sam guessing at its true content. But Sam, like his father, although not to the degree of the elder Balon, was worldly, and he thought he knew what was behind that smile.

Should be an interesting week, he thought. He

stretched out on the bed and was asleep in three minutes, sleeping the deep sleep of a young person at the very pinnacle of health and physical conditioning.

He dreamed of a strange-looking medallion but could not bring the relief of the medal into clear focus. In his dream, Sam questioned where he had seen the medallion. Then it came to him: around the necks of Black and his mother. Some sort of family crest, he imagined. And he pushed the dream from him and slept.

And as he slept, the cross around his neck, the cross that had belonged to his father, began to glow in the darkness of the room. It seemed to pulse with life.

Roma and Nydia in bikinis was just about more than Sam could take. Several times the young man had to hit the water of the pool to cool his emotions, throttling an uncomfortable stiffness.

Roma (she had to be in her mid to late forties, at least, Sam thought) had the body of a twenty-year-old, without any sign of aging, no sagging, no marks of age. She was truly astonishing. Both mother and daughter were absolute, sheer, flawless, physical perfection, and Sam's eyes greedily drank in their beauty whenever he felt it was safe to do so without being obvious. Although several times he got the impression they were both parading for his benefit. Neither Black nor Falcon were poolside, and Sam asked Roma about that while Nydia lapped the pool.

"Oh, they're discussing some . . . financial matters, I'm sure," she said, smiling. "Unearthly as far as I'm concerned. Neither of them care for swimming; they prefer riding or fencing. Both are quite good with the rapier. Do you fence, Sam?"

"No, ma'am."

She laughed. "Ma'am? Really, Sam. That makes me feel positively ancient. Roma, please." She cut her eyes and visually traveled over the young man's body, lingering at his crotch. Yes, she thought, just like his father: amply endowed.

Sam felt he was being mentally raped.

He was.

Sam cleared his throat. "May I ask a personal question, Roma?"

"You may ask anything you wish, Sam."

Okay, lady, he thought. How about you and me finding the nearest bed and getting it on?

Then he was aware of a burning sensation in the center of his chest, right where his cross usually lay.

Roma smiled. "I'm also mildly psychic, young man."

"Oh, boy," Sam muttered.

"Really, I'm flattered, Sam. It's quite nice that a handsome young man—certainly young enough to be my son—would desire me."

"You're not angry with me for thinking that?" Again, that strange burning sensation in the center of his chest.

"Don't be silly. I can't imagine a woman who would be angry."

"How do you do that? I mean, read people's minds?"

"Was that the personal question you were going to ask?"

"No, ma'am. I mean, Roma."

"You were going to ask how I managed to stay so young-looking."

"Damn," he muttered. "I'm really going to have to control my thoughts."

"I was born in Rumania, Sam. A . . . well, a few years ago," she laughed. "I have a mixture of races in me, and

43

my mother was astonishingly beautiful." (She was, five hundred years ago, when Roma, christened Nydia, was born). "My mother was over a hundred years old when she died. And still quite attractive." (And begging for her life while Nydia the Witch bludgeoned her to death, laughing as she did so). "I really take no special care of my body, other than to exercise daily and watch my diet."

With that, she rose from the poolside lounger and executed a clean, graceful dive into the water just as her daughter was walking toward them, rubbing her hair with a thick towel. Sam watched her stride toward him: like her mother, ripe perfection. And, like her mother, dressed in a bikini that scarcely covered all the essentials.

"My mother is quite a woman, isn't she?" Nydia asked, sitting down and catching her breath from her laps in the huge pool. Steam rose in light upward exhalations from the heated water.

"At least that, Nydia. I would think Falcon would be extremely jealous of her."

"Did she come on to you, Sam? Sure, she did," she said, not giving him time to answer the question. "Oh, they both do what they want to do. Have their little affairs. I've known about them both for years."

"Why do I get the feeling you and your mother don't get along?"

"Because it's true. We're civil to each other—most of the time—but we stopped being friends a long time ago."

"Care to talk about it?"

"Later. Here comes the never-aging sexpot."

Sam shook his head at the acid in Nydia's remark.

"Nydia's been going to a church," Black said to Falcon.

The men sat in the study, the heavy doors closed.

"I know it, so does Roma. There is nothing we can do about it. For several reasons. But we know He has been meddling."

"But why? I thought the rules . . ."

Falcon cut him off with a wave of his hand; a curt slash of impatience. "The Masters make the rules, each knowing they can break them at will. If, really, any rules do exist, which I more and more doubt. But nevertheless, we are required to follow what our individual Master dictates. And don't ask questions. What goes on in the minds of the two Supreme Beings is beyond the grasp of even us. When are the others arriving?"

"Tomorrow. Noon. I arranged for a helicopter to bring them in."

"Balon's bastard know of their coming?"

"No. Neither does Nydia."

Falcon brooded for a time, his dark features unreadable. "You feel . . . how many to be ready converts?"

"Ten. Five young men, five young women. The others are for our mutual enjoyment. Two young men, four young women."

"Leave the men for Roma. We'll share the women. They are young?"

"And tender."

"Lovely?"

"Beautiful."

"Virgins?"

"I think . . . possibly three. Susan is curious of our Master. She will be an easy convert, and an easier fuck. But one of them I know is pure. She is the one I picked for you."

Both men laughed, the chuckling evil. "Problems

should they vanish?"

"By that time it will be over and done with, *bon?*"

"*Oui.* Balon's bastard is to be Roma's . . . exclusively. You understand that?"

"Yes, Falcon. Unless she tells me differently."

"You may have to kill your sister, Black. Or, on a more pleasant note, plant your seed within her. Does either prospect disturb you?"

The young warlock shrugged his reply.

"Good. You are your mother's child. Well, now . . . a full nine days." He smiled, the smile as corrupt as his heart was dark. "I am looking forward to the time."

The hot wind picked up, rousing Jane Ann from a fitful sleep. Tony had not returned. She opened her eyes and gasped in fright when she saw the mist at the foot of the bed.

The mist began to change, to take some shape, and her fright turned into a mixture of relief and joy. Jane Ann smiled.

"I will do what I can to help," the voice said, beating a silent message inside her head. "But I don't know how much He will allow me to do. I am rather a maverick within the Kingdom."

"Oh, Sam!"

"Let me finish. You have lost half of all you once loved, Balon flung his message. And I can tell you no more than that. Help Miles and Wade while you can. In the end, it will be up to you and the clay man. But more weight will be put on your shoulders, your faith."

She did not understand. "Tony? He is the half I have lost?"

"I can tell you no more at this time."

46

Jane Ann knew then that her suspicions had been correct. Tony had gone to the other side. "Our son?"

"He will be tempted, and he will fall from grace more than once during the next nine days. But I can do little to help. I will attempt to see him, perhaps attempt to write to him. I . . . think he will find an unexpected ally coming forward. But my place is with you, and at the end, you will have a choice to make."

And Jane Ann knew what that choice would be.

"Don't be too hasty in your decision." Balon hurled the warning. "You have many, many good years ahead of you. You don't have to do this."

"I must."

"Once you have decided, the only alternative is to accept the Dark One's offer."

"I will never do that. I love you, Sam. I want to be with you."

"I must go now," Balon projected. "Be careful."

The mist began to disperse, becoming shapeless, formless. Then one slim tentacle of mist broke from the vapor and moved down the side of the bed to touch Jane Ann on the cheek. Then the mist was gone. She put her hand to her cheek: the spot was damp. Soon her tears had kissed the touch of love that endured . . . of life after death.

Dinner had been quite an event, the setting something Sam had heretofore witnessed only in the movies. The meal had been served in courses, and the coffee the best he had ever tasted.

"Mother owns land in Columbia," Black explained. "We have the beans flown in and grind them ourselves."

Falcon was very polite throughout the meal, but not

47

given to much conversation. He and Black excused themselves after dinner and went into the study, closing the door. Nydia said she was going to bed and would see Sam in the morning.

The look Nydia fired at Sam was full of warning. And Sam did not really understand it . . . at least he tried to convince himself of that.

Roma rose from her chair and held out her hand. "Come, Sam, walk with me. The night air will do us good."

He held her wrap and was conscious of the heady perfume wafting into his nostrils. He was grateful when they stepped out into the cold night air of the terrace.

"Tell me about yourself, Sam," she said, standing very close to him.

"Not that much to tell. I'm twenty-one. Went right into the army out of high school. Did my time, and glad I did. Here I am."

"You and Black have a lot in common. Black and Nydia were born in March 1959."

"So was I. Where were they born, Roma?"

"Rumania."

"I thought that country was under communist control."

"I travel wherever and whenever I choose, Sam. My investments are worldwide. Tell me about your father."

"I never knew him. He died before I was born. My mother married a doctor before I was born. He delivered me. Doctor Tony King."

"But you always knew this King person was not your father?"

"Oh, yes. They made that clear when I was old enough

to understand. My dad was a minister. Big man."

In more ways than one, she thought. "But you never had the calling?"

"Me?" Sam laughed. "Oh, no. But I have worn dad's cross around my neck—all my life." He touched the center of his chest, feeling the outline of the cross.

Roma fought to keep herself from recoiling away from the young man. She remembered that cross very well: it had burned her several times while she and Sam Balon were grappling for control, prior to mating as they fought in circles through timeless, trackless space, neutral ground, ruled by no Master.

Roma shivered.

"Cold?" Sam touched her arm instinctively, protectively. At the touch, his chest began that strange burning, now much more intense.

"No," she said shortly. The mention of that damned cross driving all thoughts of sex from her. She moved away from his touch; the burning in the center of his chest ceased. "I must go," she moved toward the house. "I'll see you in the morning, Sam. Sleep well."

She was gone, the darkness of her gown fading into the night.

Footsteps echoed hollowly on the stone walkway leading from the yard. Sam turned. A tall, almost emaciated-looking man slowly made his way up to the terrace.

"Best you go in the house now, sir." The man spoke slowly, as if the act of speaking was painful.

"Why?"

"Because it is going to rain, and you are not dressed for the elements."

49

Sam looked up into the sky. Thousands of stars twinkled down at him. "But there isn't a cloud in the sky!"

"It will rain," the man insisted. "Soon."

"What's your name?" Sam asked.

"Perkins. Jimmy Perkins."

"Have you worked for the Williams long?"

"Years. Go in the house now." The man turned, and the night seemed to dissolve him.

Sam listened for the sound of fading footsteps. But none could be heard. The man appeared to have vanished.

Perkins? Sam thought. Now . . . where have I heard that name before?

Lying in his bed, conscious of Nydia in the next room, near but so far, just before sleep spread its gentle blanket over him, Sam was still musing over the tall man with the somehow familiar name.

And on the dresser, the cross glowed dully.

"Meddling!" Satan fired a dirty salvo into the Heavens. "Always meddling. Why can't you abide by the rules?"

"You are complaining about rules being broken, Asmodeus? How droll."

"We made an agreement—aeons ago. You rule the Heavens; I rule the earth."

"I don't recall any hard and fast set of rules." The Master of All chuckled, and the Heavens rumbled with thunder. "Hooved one, you amuse me. Your mind, what there is of it, is open for inspection. My maverick resident returned to earth by his own volition—not with my permission."

50

"You lifted the veil."

"Not necessarily. Balon is a curious one, and a brave one. He takes chances; he pries; he investigates. Besides, the boundaries that divide life from death are at best shadowy and vague. Who shall say where the one ends and the other begins?"

Satan howled his laughter, the foulness stinking the air. "That is not very original of you, Thunder-Breath. Have you taken to spending your time reading Poe?"

"Idiot! Who do you suppose put the thought in his mind?"

"I was under the impression it was I."

"That says a great deal for your intelligence."

"I don't have to stand here and be insulted."

"Anywhere you go is an insult to someone."

"Bah!"

And the Heavens became silent as a gentle rain began falling over Falcon House and the grounds surrounding it.

"Miles!" The mist formed at the foot of the Jew's bed. "Open your eyes. Look at me."

Miles fearfully opened his eyes, looking at the mist. He began silently reciting prayers, recalling them as if he had just stepped out of the synagogue.

Miles tried to speak but found he was voiceless.

"Don't be alarmed." The mist thrust its silent projection as it began to take shape. "I can hear your thoughts."

"Go away!" Miles said. "Sam? My God—my God! Oh! I think I'm having a heart attack."

"And I think you're as full of it now as when I knew you years ago."

51

"Don't think ugly!" Miles sat up in bed. "You're too close to Him to take chances."

"Miles?" Doris stirred by his side. "What's wrong?"

I should tell you and you'd have an accident in your gown. "Nothing," his voice popped from his throat. "A little gas, is all."

"Umm," she said, and then fell into a deep sleep.

"She won't wake up again until I leave," Sam projected. "You may speak normally."

"I wish you had taught me how to do that years ago."

"I didn't know how years ago."

"Sam—I'm dreaming all this, right?"

"It is not a dream."

"I was afraid you'd say that. Sam, I'm an old man, with more than my share of aches and pains: bad circulation . . . and that other thing, too. Arteriosclerosis. And I got . . ."

"Not anymore, Miles."

"What do you mean, Sam?"

"Do your legs hurt you, Miles?"

Miles thought about that for a moment, his hands feeling his thin legs. His legs were not cold, nor did they ache. He looked at the mist and said: "What did you do, Sam?"

"Corrected a few physical problems. You and Wade will have to be strong, mentally and physically, to make it through this upcoming ordeal."

"Why am I experiencing this feeling that I am about to get the shitty—excuse me, Sam—end of this handel?"

"I don't speak Hebrew, Miles."

"Bargain. You really don't? That seems odd."

"All languages are as one there, Miles. Miles? Am I your friend?"

"Oy! Here it comes; I knew it."

"Wouldn't you rather go out in a blaze of glory, Miles?"

"If it's all the same with you, Sam, I would rather not go out at all! Sam, old friend, do you realize what you're doing to me? You turned my head all cockeyed more than twenty years ago. I'm a Jew—I don't believe in all this crazy stuff. Now here you come again—no offense meant. Sam, please, it's good to see you; what there is of you. But . . . oh, Sam! What do you want from this old man? Let me rephrase that: What's gonna happen to me?"

"You're going to meet The Man in nine days."

"Some friend you are! You fix my legs all up where they don't hurt—first time in five years—then you tell me I'm gonna die in nine days!" He lay back, his head on the pillow. He closed his eyes. "If I don't see you, don't talk to you, you'll go away."

He was still for a few moments, until curiosity got the best of him. He opened his eyes. The mist that was Sam Balon was still there, looking at him.

Miles sighed, then said: "Well, sometimes it works. Okay, Sam . . . I never could win an argument with you. What do you want me to do?"

"Finish the Clay Man."

"I knew that was coming, too."

"I will speak with Wade and Anita. Perhaps Wade only. They will come to stay with you and Doris. The Clay Man will have power for nine days only; for the duration of the siege. When life leaves him, the four of you will go home."

"How is it, Sam? I mean . . . where you are. Were. Where you stay."

53

"Different. But I don't stay there often. When I'm there, I'm usually in trouble with Him."

"That, I can believe. Sam? What does this make me? This flies in the face of all that I was taught as a child. Everything I was taught to believe."

"I cannot say what it makes you. That will be your choice at the end."

"Wonderful," Miles said dryly. "I love a mystery."

The mist began to fade.

"Sam?" Miles cried. "What about Jane Ann?"

The mist projected its reply, and Miles was saddened.

Breakfast at the mansion was served buffet style, with Sam and Nydia eating together.

"Did you sleep well?" she asked.

"Passed out," Sam said, buttering a piece of toast. "I don't recall ever sleeping so soundly."

"It's the silence of the woods. But sometimes it can be . . . well, frightening."

"How?"

Her eyes were serious as they fixed their beauty on Sam's face. "Do you believe in the Devil, Sam?"

"Of course."

"Do you believe in possession?"

Sam chewed thoughtfully for a few seconds. "Yes, I do, Nydia. Even though most Protestants don't. But my father did. My real father. Mother told me he did. My stepfather was raised in the Catholic Church, but he broke from it when I was about ten . . . just a kid. Tony stopped worshiping God. Just quit. I don't know what happened. But mother taught me the Bible, and to believe in demonic possession. One thing she stressed was that the Devil walks the earth. Yeah . . . it was about that

54

time I started hearing whispers about Tony running around on Mother. But," he shrugged, "his loss. Mother is beautiful. I don't understand men who run around on their wives. Sorry, I'm digressing. Why do you ask about possession?"

"Are you a Christian, Sam?"

"Well . . . technically, yes, I suppose I am. I'm not very pure at heart at times, though."

"Christians aren't supposed to be perfectly pure—I don't believe that's possible for a human."

"Sounds like you're really serious about religion, Nydia. I mean, don't take that the wrong way . . . so am I. It's serious business."

"I . . . would like to know more about it, yes. Tell me, Sam: can you still be a Christian and lust after someone?"

"I don't know, Nydia. That's a human trait, isn't it? Yes, I think you can, if you recognize the fault and try to do something about it. I think being a Christian means believing in God, trying to do right by his Commandments. I think it all depends on how a person lives his or her total life: do you help others in need; try to think good thoughts; do the best you can? Those types of things." He smiled. "Are you lusting after someone, Nydia?"

"Yes." She put her hand on his and squeezed gently.

Sam returned the gentle caress. "I couldn't take my eyes off you after we met."

"I felt the same. And . . . Sam? It's funny, sort of. I got the feeling that it was . . . right. You know what I mean?"

"Yes. It was . . . odd. I've never felt anything like it. You know, we're going to have to be careful: your mother reads thoughts."

"What do you mean, Sam?"

He told her of the events poolside.

Her expression was one of confusion. "I wonder why she kept that from me all these years?" She shyly rubbed her fingertips on the back of his hand. "Roma is also lusting after you—and she'll have you, Sam."

He shook his head.

"Yes, she will. Roma always gets what she wants. One way or the other. Don't anger her, Sam—please. I'm afraid of her; always have been. I . . . can't say more. Not until I'm more certain of the thoughts in my mind."

"Hey," Sam said. "Let's not get heavy with this, Nydia. I have an idea. Let's go exploring this afternoon. Hike in the woods. You want to do that?"

"Yes," she said, her voice a caress.

"Hey, you lovebirds!" Black called from the door. Sam and Nydia looked up, both slightly embarrassed. "Just call me the little ole matchmaker, huh?"

He walked to the buffet line and fixed a plate, sitting down at the table.

"Really, Black," Sam smiled, "you can't blame me, can you? She's positively gorgeous."

"Really?" the brother questioned. "I always thought she was rather plain."

Nydia stuck out her tongue at him and rose from the table.

"Sis?" Black caught her arm. "Sit down for a second, will you? I owe you both an apology." They looked at him. "Yeah, I forgot to tell you: I invited some others up here."

"Who?" Nydia's tone was sharp.

"Oh, you know them all, sis: Lana, Linda, Carol,

Susan—a few more. Then there's Adam, Chad, Burt, Mac . . . some others. I was going to tell you both, but it just slipped my mind."

"Thanks, brother," Nydia said, fire flickering in her eyes. "A couple of those you named are okay; the rest are creeps. I cannot tolerate them."

"Give them a chance, sis. That's all I ask. You just don't know them."

"That's the problem, brother dear: I *do* know them. I'll get the cook to pack us a lunch, Sam. Let's go as quickly as possible." She whirled and left the room, her anger evident in her step.

"You and sis have plans, Sam?"

"Hiking, exploring some."

"Be careful, and don't get lost," Black cautioned with a grin. "It's pretty wild out there."

"Oh, I'll be careful, Black. Like you, I've had some pretty extensive training in staying alive."

The young men locked glances, Black finally saying, "Yes, that's true. I've often wondered just which one of us is the tougher."

Sam's smile was tight. "I hope you never have to find out, Black."

Sam left it at that.

Sam had more of his father in him than even his mother suspected, for he never traveled unprepared. In his rooms, after dressing in jeans, heavy shirt, and jump boots, Sam slid a heavy-bladed knife, in its leather sheath, onto his belt. And he had brought with him— quite illegally—a snub-nosed .38 pistol. He slipped that into a pocket of his jacket and then knocked on Nydia's door.

"You ready, Nydia?"

The door opened and she stood before him, a young lady just as beautiful in jeans and rough shirt as in a ballroom gown.

"You look good enough to eat," Sam told her.

"I've thought about that, too," she said, a smile on her lips.

Sam cleared his throat and decided to shift gears and head in another direction. "Nydia? Why don't you like those people Black invited up here?"

"You don't know?" she seemed surprised. "I guess not. They have a . . . cult at Nelson and Carrington. They've tried several times to get me to join. I refused."

"What kind of cult?"

"They practice Devil worship."

FOUR

Sam did not realize just how isolated they were until he and Nydia got into the deep timber on the edge of the big park just north of the Williams' home. The dark timber closed around them about 500 meters from the edge of the estate.

"Beautiful," Sam said. "So beautiful and peaceful."

Nydia started to reply when three shots cut through the crisp air. Sam instinctively grabbed for the pistol in his coat, checking his movement just before touching the inner pocket. Nydia caught the quick movement and smiled.

"It's a signal to return to Falcon House," she said. "Come on. It might be important."

"Sir," Perkins said, "there was a radio message for you just moments after you left. In the communications room. Mr. Falcon is waiting."

"The message is rather terse, Sam." Falcon handed him a slip of paper. "I do hope this will not alter your plans to visit with us."

Sam did not reply until he had read the message: MONTREAL FLIGHT 127 1922-58 J.A. He looked into Falcon's dark, unreadable eyes. "This is it?"

"That was the entire message, Sam. I asked for a

59

repeat, and that was it."

"Well, I guess I have to get to Montreal somehow."

"We'll take the Rover," Nydia said. "Go together."

"Now, dear . . ." Roma opened her mouth to protest.

Daughter met mother, head to head, with an unwavering look. "I know the roads, Mother. Sam doesn't. So I'm going with him." There was a firmness to her voice that said she would brook no more objections.

Roma smiled. "Of course, dear. I was only going to suggest you change into something more suitable for the trip."

"Certainly you were, Mother." Nydia's smile and tone were just short of condescending. "But we'll go as we are. Come on, Sam." She pulled at his arm. "We'll be there in a few hours."

Driving away from the estate, Nydia asked, "Sam, what does 1922-58 mean? The time?"

"I don't think so. Could be, but I doubt it. 1922 was the year my dad was born. '58 was when he died."

"J.A.?"

"My mother's initials."

Nydia shuddered beside him.

"Cold?" Sam asked.

"No. Suddenly frightened. For some reason. I just got the worst feeling of . . . I don't know: foreboding, I guess I'd call it."

"Nydia?"

She glanced at him.

"I have the same feeling."

Flight 127 came in and emptied its load of passengers. Sam knew no one on the flight. Sam and Nydia sat in the now deserted arrival area, looking at each other, questions unspoken in their eyes.

"Son?" the disembodied-sounding voice came from behind the young couple. Sam was conscious of a burning sensation in the center of his chest.

They turned, looking around. No one was in sight. Nydia dug nervous fingers into Sam's forearm. "Son? Was that what that voice said?"

"Easy now," Sam attempted to calm her. His own nerves were rattled.

"Sam?" she said. "Look on the table in front of us."

Sam slowly, almost reluctantly pulled his gaze to the front. A manila envelope lay on the low table. "That . . . wasn't there a second ago."

"I know."

Again, they looked around them: the arrival area and the corridor were deserted. They both stared at the envelope.

Sam touched the packet. It was cold to the touch. He picked it up and carefully opened it. A picture and several sheets of paper. The picture was of his father. Sam looked at the 8 x 10 for a long moment, then handed it to Nydia. "My dad," his words were charged with emotion, spoken in a husky tone.

"I can see where you got your good looks," she said. "He was a rugged, handsome man. Sam? Who put the envelope on the table, and who was that who spoke to you? And where did he go? Sam, there was no one within shouting distance."

There was a slight grimace of pain on Sam's face.

"Sam?"

"I don't know the answer to any of those questions,

61

Nydia. But I'll tell you this: when that voice spoke, my chest started burning. It's just now going away, but man, did it hurt for a few seconds."

"Your chest?"

"The skin on my chest. Right in the center." He looked around them: no one in sight. Sam unbuttoned his shirt, hearing Nydia's gasp as his T-shirt came into view. "Relax, I'm not going to strip." He tried a grin. "At least not here."

"That's not it, Sam," she said, her voice tiny. "Look at your T-shirt; the center of your chest."

He looked down: the fabric was burned brown. In the shape of a cross. The cross Sam wore. His father's cross.

Nydia reached out, pulling up his T-shirt. The cross had burned his skin, leaving a scar in the shape of a cross. Sam touched the red scar; it was no longer painful, even though he could see it was burned deeply.

Sam unfolded the pages and almost became physically ill. The handwriting was unmistakably his father's scrawl. Sam had seen it many times on old sermons.

"Sam? You're as white as a ghost!"

"I . . . think that's what just spoke to me. My father wrote this."

The young man wiped his suddenly blurry eyes and once more looked at the writing, reading slowly, Nydia silently reading with him.

> Son—Writing is difficult for me, in my condition. Want to keep this as brief as possible, but yet, there are so many things I must say to you and the girl.

"How . . . ?" Nydia said, then shook her head, not

62

believing any of this.

I have watched you, son—whenever possible—grow through the years. Tried to guide you—help you—as best I could, Nydia, too. The girl beside you, not the Nydia I . . . knew. Like that time you got drunk in your mother's car and passed out at the wheel. That was a close one, boy.

"I'm the only person in this world who knew about that," Sam said.

Nydia said, "In this world, yes." She looked at the young man, wondering why she said that.

Give the cross you wear around your neck to the girl. Do it, son, without delay. Time is of the essence.

Sam removed the cross from his neck and handed it to Nydia. "Put it on," he said. He could see she was, for some reason, softly crying.

No one will be able to remove that cross from her. No one. I cannot guarantee she will not be hurt, but . . . well, you must have faith.

Now then, a cruel blow for each of you, for I know your thoughts: Nydia is your half sister.

"Oh, my God!" Sam said.

When I knew her mother, Roma was not her name. Her name was Nydia. She is of and for the Devil. She is a witch. After the hooved one attempted to take over the

63

town of Whitfield—and failed, then—during which
Wade, Anita, Chester, Tony, Jane Ann, Miles, Doris,
and myself killed hundreds of Coven members, I made
a bargain with our God to save your mother and what
few Christians remained. I won, in a sense. But so did
the woman you know as Roma. I killed, or at least sent
back to Hell, Black Wilder, the Devil's representative.
Your half brother, son, Black, is named for Wilder.
And like that spawn of Hell, he is a warlock.

   When you leave this terminal, the both of you must
go to a Catholic church; get as much holy water as you
can. You will need it.

   I must rest for a moment. Writing is not something
one does where I reside.

Sam glanced at Nydia. Half sister?
She met his eyes, read his thoughts. "I don't care."
Sam shook his head in confusion and returned to the
letter.

   It would be wrong, son, to say the Devil is back, for
that one never leaves the earth; so I'll simply say he has
returned to Whitfield. There will soon be a great
tragedy in Whitfield, and I must be there to help your
mother, for her ordeal involves both of us . . . and the
girl. There will be no survivors from Whitfield. None.

"Mother . . . ?" Sam whispered.
And as if Balon had anticipated the question, the letter
continued:

   She has made her choice. Tony has gone over to the

other side. He has done so willingly; indeed, a long time ago. I could not stop him, for his faith is weak, as is his flesh. And that is something you will have to deal with as well.

You have a mission, Sam, and I do not envy you your task, for it may destroy you . . . not necessarily physically, and I can say no more about that. But you are as surely set to this mission as I was, years ago. You will be tempted, and you will fall to some of those temptations, for you are a mortal, blessed, in a manner of speaking, but still a mortal.

A Coven is being established at Falcon House. It is a house of evil, and you must return there. Your job is there. You will not be able to contact anyone in Whitfield. Whitfield is dead; past saving. But your mother will speak to you—in some way—before she slips through the painful darkness to the other side and to peace and blue and light.

We will meet someday, son. I am certain of that and can tell you no more about my surety.

The feelings you and the girl share is something that you both must cope with. I cannot help you, and will not lecture you. But I will say this: the union that produced Nydia was not a holy union. If anything, it was blessed by the Dark One.

"Riddles," Sam said. "The letter is filled with riddles, and I don't know what they mean."

I love you deeply, Sam, and wish I could be of more help to you in your task. But I have said too much already.

Now . . . I must go. Place the picture of me in the envelope, for that is all of me I can give you that will remain tangible. Put the letter on the table and do not touch it again.

Love, Father

Sam placed the picture in the envelope, the letter on the table. Together, still in mild shock, not knowing what to believe, the young man and young woman watched the pages dissolve into nothing. Then they were alone.

Nydia put her head on Sam's shoulder and wept.

"I have done all I can do to help Sam," said the silent voice as it pushed out of the mist and into the sleeping brain of Jane Ann.

She sat up on the couch, rubbing her eyes. "When did you see Sam?"

"About a minute ago, in Montreal."

"Neat trick, since you're in front of me at this moment. I won't pursue how you managed that."

"That would be best. You will understand soon enough."

"A time warp?"

"There is no time in my world. A year is the blink of an eye. Drop it, Janey."

"All right." She stared hard at the misty face of the only man she had ever loved. "Tell me this: how did our son look?"

"Considering the circumstances, well . . . and confused, upset." The misty face smiled, then projected, "bewitched, bothered, and bewildered."

"Oh, Sam!"

"Now you see why He is constantly calling me on the carpet . . . so to speak. Our son is falling deeply in love."

Jane Ann smiled. "How wonderful."

"With his half sister."

"You were a rounder before you came to Whitfield, weren't you?"

"Yes, but . . . well, I'll explain at a later date."

"I'm not sure I want to hear about it."

"As you wish. But don't jump to conclusions."

She glanced at the clock on the fireplace mantel. "Tony might be back for lunch any moment."

"Tony will never again set foot in this house, Jane Ann. Not for any decent purposes, that is."

"I don't understand."

"You will."

"Miles?" Doris called down the basement steps. "What are you doing?"

"I keep telling you and telling you: I am building a golem. So stay out of here. No telling what this thing might get in its head to do."

"How can a thing with clay for brains get something into its head?"

"I don't care to argue with you."

A moment of heavy silence. Miles looked up. She was still standing in the doorway.

"I believe you, Miles," she said quietly.

"Oh?" his voice drifted up, full of disbelief. "So what changed your mind?"

"You remember me saying you were as crazy as a *vontz*—after you told me about speaking with Sam Balon?"

"How could I forget being called a bedbug? So?"

67

"He's . . . it's in the kitchen, now!"

"So ask him to take a seat. I'll be right up."

"Wade? I cannot believe you are seriously considering taking part in this insanity!"

"Honey, you didn't see Sam last night, either."

"Well, honey," she mimicked him, "neither did you. I warned you about that second piece of pie."

"Babe," he was very patient with her, "we've been through a lot together. I've tried to bring you along easy this time. But time is up. Look around you, honey—look at the houses we're passing, the people sitting on the porches. Any of them waving at us? Any of them calling for us to stop, have a cup of coffee, like they used to do?"

She looked straight ahead, refusing to speak.

"He's here, Anita. He's back. The Dark One. Sam says this time Whitfield is through. He . . ."

"If your friend, the spirit man, is so all-fired blessed, why doesn't he just wave his hand and make all this . . ." Tears sprang into her eyes. ". . . hatefulness go away?"

"Did you pack like I asked you?"

She sighed. "Yes, Wade. I'll humor you until we can get you to a mental hospital."

"Anita, old gal," he spoke softly. "My wife of so many very good years, listen to me. We're not going to make it out of this. We're going to die, and Sam says the only thing he can do is make it as easy for us as possible."

"How considerate of him."

Wade turned into the drive, parking by the corner street lamp. "We're here, honey."

"Oh, goody!" she clapped her hands. "Do I get to see the monster man *and* Sam Balon? A double treat? Oooh, I

68

can hardly wait. This is better than the county fair."

Wade held her hand as they walked up the sidewalk and up the steps to the porch. Doris opened the door.

"Thank God!" Anita cried. "A face I know is normal and a mouth that is not raving about things that go bump in the night."

"I'll get the luggage out of the car," Wade said.

Anita stepped into the house and stopped dead still in the living room. A huge gray object, in the shape of a man, a giant man, stood against the wall across the room. It was at least eight and a half feet tall. It was faceless.

She turned to ask Doris what that thing was, was this some kind of a joke and what's the occasion for a party? She dropped her purse on the carpet as her eyes found the mist hovering just above the carpet by a chair.

"I believe you know Reverend Sam Balon," Doris said.

Anita fainted.

They had gone to a hardware store and bought several containers, then went to half a dozen Catholic churches seeking holy water. The priests, once they saw the young couple was sincere, asked no questions but merely gave them as much holy water as they wished.

"I just don't know . . . if my mind can . . . accept all that's been thrown at me this day," Nydia said. "But a lot of things are beginning to fall into place."

"Explain that?" Sam asked. They were halfway back to the Williams' mansion, eating a mid-afternoon lunch by the side of the road. The lunch they were supposed to have eaten while exploring the woods.

"Well . . . this is only a small part of it, Sam, but have you ever been in a home that didn't have some religious

69

paraphernalia . . . somewhere? A painting, a cross, a Bible . . . something? I haven't. Our house is bare of anything religious. But . . . that could be explained away by the fact that Roma and Falcon don't go to church. But I know what an upside down cross means, and both Roma and Falcon have those in their rooms. Roma, Falcon, and Black always go somewhere on Friday nights—they stay all night—always returning just before dawn. And they all wear the same kind of medallion."

"I'm surprised they haven't tried to make you wear one."

"Oh, they have, dozens of times, beginning when I was just a small child. But it always irritated my neck; caused great ugly rashes; made me sick, very sick. The last time, just a couple of years ago, Roma threw the medallion away. It was gold, Sam! Worth hundreds of dollars, and she just tossed it into the garbage. She flew into a screaming rage and kept saying: 'Damn that son of a bitch! Black Wilder, you knew this was going to happen. And damn that bastard preacher.' I didn't know what she was talking about, Sam. Raving was more like it. And I didn't ask."

"Dad wrote about Black Wilder. The Devil's represen- tative. The preacher must have been Dad."

She covered his hand with hers. "Sam? For years they've kept it from me—or tried to—but they practice evil. I can't prove it, for they're very careful. But I know they do. That house is evil. The people who work for them are evil. And Jimmy Perkins . . . the way he looks at me. Something about him frightens me."

"I wish I could recall where I've heard that name."

They looked up as a huge Sikorsky helicopter flapped and roared overhead. The helicopter, capable of carrying

70

sixteen passengers, was soon out of sight.

"Heading for the house," Nydia said glumly. "Poor Lana and the others. They don't have any idea what they're getting into."

"Lana?"

"Lana McBay. Small, blond, and very pretty. Doesn't date much. Word is . . . around the school . . . she's a virgin." Nydia paused for a moment, a reflective look on her face. "Come to think of it, the word is that several of those girls Black mentioned are supposed to be virgins. Linda, for sure, so the talk goes. But . . . I don't much like her."

"Why?"

Her reply was a noncommittal shrug.

"Does Falcon like his women young?"

"Oh, yes," she quickly replied. "For a fact. I've seen him looking at me in a way that makes me very uncomfortable. Just like Jimmy."

"Have either of them ever tried anything with you?"

"Oh, no. Never."

"Tell me about Falcon. You know he isn't your real father. Has he been around long?"

"For as long as I can remember. There isn't much else to tell. I . . . really don't know where they get their money—either of them. I was told they both owned interests in a number of factories and businesses, and that this is where they got their money. I do know mother owns a company that makes wine and perfume, another company that makes clothing for women. I've seen those businesses."

"Tell me about the people who run them. Those you had a chance to meet."

She was again reflective for a moment. "Yes, I see

71

what you mean. They . . . seemed to be afraid of Roma, but yet . . ." The sentence trailed into silence. ". . . The medallions. The top people all wore medallions, like mother and Falcon and Black."

"And the one your mother tried to make you wear?"

"Just like it."

"And did they ever meet on a Friday. Friday seems to hold some special significance."

"Yes. Several times. And it was just like I told you before: they would all disappear about dark and not return until almost dawn. Mother said it was business, and not to worry. I always had someone staying with me, a sitter or companion. Sam? I'm frightened. I *don't* want to go back to that house."

"We have to go back, Nydia. I don't believe we could do anything else."

"Sam, let's try. Let's see if we can just run away—go back to New York State. Please? Let's try."

Sam hesitated, not wanting to risk angering his father—if any of this was real, and not a dream. He wavered, sensing that Nydia's fear was very close to overwhelming her.

"We'll try," he said.

But the four-wheel would not start. Sam complained of his chest burning, and the cross around Nydia's neck had begun to glow.

"All right, Dad," Sam said. "We get the message."

The four-wheel started; the burning and the glowing ceased.

"All that could have been a fluke," Nydia suggested.

Sam turned around, heading back to Montreal. The four-wheel died in the middle of the road. The burning and the glowing began again.

Nydia said, "All right, Mr. Balon—no more. We'll go back."

The four-wheel started; the glowing and the burning faded.

"Any doubts now?" Sam asked.

She shook her head. "But where do we start, Sam?"

"At Falcon House."

FIVE

"What do we do?" Anita asked. She had recovered from her shocked state and sat sipping tea, her gaze alternating between the mute huge, motionless clay man and the mist that was Balon.

"Wait," Balon projected. "None of you can start it. The golem will not kill without some overt provocation toward one of you."

"What . . . can that thing do?" Wade asked.

"It has the strength of twenty men. It cannot be stopped by anything mortal. A golem is all things of earth. But none of you need concern yourself with the mysteries of the cosmos. The golem will have no will other than what I give it."

Outside, although the day was bright and clear and warm, thunder rattled the windows of the house.

"Excuse me," Balon said. "No will except that which *we* give it."

The thunder ceased.

Miles said a very quick and fervent prayer, while Anita clutched at a small Bible.

Wade seemed amused. Doris looked at him and said, "You find this amusing?"

"He's still a reporter at heart," Sam said.

"I have personally witnessed one of the greatest

74

stories a reporter could possibly witness, back in 1958," Wade replied. "And am about to witness another. And I am unable to write about either. Pity."

"The whole town—all our friends—have turned against us," Anita said bitterly. "And all you can think about is reporting a story."

"Our friends are dead," Wade replied. "Just like before. They have rejected the teaching of the Almighty and of His Son, Jesus Christ. They have made their choice. So be it."

"I'll go along with the Almighty part," Miles said. "The bit about His Son . . . ?" He waggled his hand. "I got to see it to believe it."

Sam Balon seemed amused by the exchange.

"Him, now," Doris said, looking at the misty form. "He could clear it all up . . . if he would."

"He can't even clear himself up so we can get a look at him." Miles grinned.

"STOP IT!" Anita screamed. "It isn't a joke, my God! I can't take this joking about . . . our deaths!"

Wade put an arm around her, pulling her to him. "I think it's the best way to hide our fears, honey. But you're right; it is no joking matter."

"Everything mortals question will be explained," Balon projected. "In time."

Anita pushed her husband from her, took a deep breath, and glared at the mist form that was once her minister. "I believed in you with all my heart and faith twenty years ago, Brother Balon. I'll do the same now."

"Good," Balon said.

"Someone's walking up the sidewalk," Miles said.

"Jane Ann," Balon projected. "I asked her to come over for a time."

"She is going to stay with us, isn't she?" Doris asked.

"No. The Clay Man will protect you. I will stay with Jane Ann. You will all know why that must be at a later time."

Miles laughed. "See, momma—who says there ain't sex after life?"

"Miles!" she whirled around, glaring at him. "You shut your mouth with talk like that." Her face suddenly split into a wide grin. "Besides, for the past five years that's all you've been able to do: talk!"

Miles reddened, then grinned. He leaned back in his chair and folded his arms across his thin chest. He had a retort, but thought it best to keep it to himself.

"I agree," Balon said to him.

Miles looked startled for a few seconds, then smiled. "No bad jokes up . . . there, huh?" He pointed upward.

"You'll see," Balon said.

A cup of Doris's good tea beside her, Jane Ann looked at the small gathering. "Out of the entire town, all this part of Fork, this is it, Sam?"

"Yes. There were those who felt they were Christians. But as they are soon to learn, they were only fooling themselves. And they knew it all along."

"How sad," Anita said.

"It will be the end of Whitfield and this part of Fork County. There will be no more Beasts, no more black masses—there will be nothing."

"Do you mean," Wade asked, "this time we'll really beat the Devil?"

"No!" Balon's reply was emphatic. "No mortal can ever beat the Devil. Only God. And only when He is ready. The Prince of Darkness will just be through here, that's all. And hopefully in a certain part of Canada, as

76

well. And do not ask me questions about that."

"When does God plan on beating the Devil, Sam?" Wade asked.

Balon said nothing.

"Strong silent type," Miles said.

"Shut up," his wife told him.

Miles sighed.

"I don't know if I'll be able to lie to Roma," Sam said. "She'll see I'm lying."

"About what we . . . saw, and heard?"

"Yes."

"Then . . . ?"

"I don't know. I don't know what to do, how to start, or even where to start, really. This is all so mind-boggling. Dad said the cross would protect us . . . but how much protection will it offer? So much of what he said was . . . unclear. How about the way I feel about you? Will . . . God," he stumbled over the word, "condone my lying? My feelings? I just don't know."

She moved her gaze from Sam's face to the road ahead. Falcon House reared up. "We're about to find out," she said tensely.

"A joke?" Roma said. "What a very bad joke to play." She could not read his thoughts, and that told her Sam was lying. It also told her that someone . . . probably Balon, was interfering; that he had been in some sort of communication with his son. That was nothing new to her: people could and did move quite freely from either side of the death line . . . providing one had the right connections with the Master of whatever world.

She peered hard at Sam. But she could not read his

77

thoughts. She looked at her daughter, and for the first time since Nydia's birth, her mother could not read her.

And Nydia realized she had blocked her mother out. "Don't look so upset, Mother," she said innocently, the double meaning not lost on Roma.

Roma's returning gaze was tight. She managed a small smile. "A joke? Who would play such a crude joke on you? Bring you all the way to Montreal for a joke?"

"Kids back at Nelson, I suppose," Sam said.

"Well," Roma said, "it's over. You have both returned. And we have more guests. We'll have such a gala time this week. Both the east and the west wings are alive with young people."

And the Devil, Sam thought. He looked hard at Roma, thinking: Fuck you, bitch!

She merely smiled.

Ugly, Sam fired his thoughts. Ugly and old and vain and stupid.

The smile remained fixed, even softened just a bit.

And I'll bet you're a sorry screw!

Her expression did not change. "You both must be tired from the hurried drive," Roma said. "Why don't you have a bit of a rest and get cleaned up; join your friends later?"

"They *are not* my friends," Nydia said. "A very few I get along with; the rest are creeps."

"They are our guests!" Her mother's tone was sharp. "And *you will* be civil to them."

"I will ignore them whenever possible." Nydia stood her ground, facing up to her mother for the first time in her life.

High color rose to Roma's cheeks. "We shall discuss

78

this later."

"No need for that, Mother." The reply was calmly stated. "I've said what I plan to do, and that is that."

Roma was inwardly fuming, but she managed a slight smile. Balon has worked his crappy Christian magic on my daughter, she thought. I wonder how many times over the years that sanctimonious stud has meddled in Nydia's affairs—and mine? No matter, for this time I have him boxed: he cannot be in two places at once, no matter if he is as obstinate as that warrior Michael, and just as militant.

"As you wish, Nydia," Roma said. "I must admit, you do have a great deal of your . . . father in you at times."

"Yes." Nydia smiled. "And I cannot tell you how proud that makes me."

I'll break you. Roma stared hard at the young woman. She shifted her gaze to Sam. And I'll break you as well. And when you are both mine, I'll breed you and have a grandchild that will make the Master proud. And if I can't do that, young people, then I'll give Nydia to Falcon to do with as he pleases. And I assure you, daughter, that will be an experience you *will not* savor.

"We'll see you at dinner, Roma," Sam said, taking Nydia's hand. The gesture did not go unnoticed by the mother.

Roma nodded her head only slightly, her eyes unreadable. "Yes," she said. She turned and walked away.

"She is very angry," Nydia said.

"Not nearly as angry as she'll be when she sees that cross around your neck."

"Or the burn on your chest."

"Probably be best if we don't swim after this."

"That was to be my next suggestion." She squeezed his hand as they walked down the hall to their rooms. "Sam? I'm not afraid any longer."

"I don't know whether that's good or bad. But neither am I."

"Wonder why?"

"I don't know. And I'll tell you something else: I cannot think of you as my half sister."

"Then don't."

"How come," Sam said, his grin identical to his father's mischievous grin, "if I'm supposed to be so holy all of a sudden, my thoughts are so sexy?"

"I don't know about that." Her hips brushed his, the touch charged with wanton longing. "But mine aren't exactly pristine."

"Are we both awful?" Sam's question was spoken in all seriousness.

"No." The young woman's reply held the same weighty tone. "I think we're just being honest."

"What . . . do we do about it?"

They walked slowly through the great house.

"Give it some time," she said. They were at her door. She lifted her eyes to his. "I'll keep the door between our rooms unlocked."

"It's to be my decision alone?"

She said, "My mind is already made up." She opened the door and stepped into her room. The door closed softly behind her.

Sam showered quickly and dried off, stepping into underwear shorts. He padded barefoot into his bedroom to stand in front of the floor-to-ceiling mirror. The dark, thick mat of hair on his chest looked strange with the burned-on scar of the cross directly in the center. He wondered if the hair would ever grow back.

He gazed into his mirrored reflection. "I have a mission." He repeated his father's words, speaking in a whisper. "And it may destroy me. I will be tempted, and fall to some of those temptations."

He wondered if his father had been writing of Nydia or Roma, or both? Then he decided his father had been referring to Roma.

He stepped away from the mirror and carefully hid the containers of holy water. He opened the manila envelope and sat on the edge of the bed, studying the 8 x 10 of his father. He was still gazing at the 8 x 10 when the knock sounded on the hall door.

Slipping into a robe, Sam opened the door. Adam Benning stood in the hall, smiling at him.

"Sam." Adam stuck out his hand. "Bet you're surprised to see me?" It was spoken in a greasy manner.

The two young men did not get along well. Although the same age, Adam was a senior while Sam was a freshman. And Adam was a sly, sneaky type . . . the type Sam didn't like.

Sam shook the offered hand. It was clammy and soft. Sam resisted the urge to wipe his hand on his robe. "Yes, I am. Black didn't tell us he had invited others."

Adam grinned lewdly. "Thought you'd have Nydia all to yourself, huh?"

Sam stared at him just long enough for Adam to begin to feel uncomfortable under the unblinking gaze. "I think I'll lie down for a time, Adam. So if you'll excuse me . . . ?"

81

Adam flushed hotly, clenching his hands into fists at his side. "Well, there's always one, I guess; always one person that has to screw up a good thing."

"Meaning me, Adam?"

"You might learn a thing or two up here, Sam. It should be interesting."

"Maybe more than you realize," Sam replied.

Adam's smile was ugly. He stalked away without shutting the door. Sam turned at a slight noise behind, tensing, then relaxing as the connecting door to Nydia's room opened. She stepped into the room and Sam closed the hall door, locking it.

"I've got an idea, Sam," she said, moving closer to him. He could smell the clean scent of bath soap, and the ends of her raven hair were slightly damp from the shower. A pulse beat strongly in her throat.

It was not a holy union, his father's words returned to him.

Sam could see she was wearing nothing under her robe, from the waist up. He could but guess about from the waist down.

If anything, it was blessed by the Dark One.

Sam pushed his father's words from his mind. "I'll be glad to hear your ideas, Nydia." His voice was husky. "I sure don't have any." Boy, what a lie!

"Your dad may not like this," she warned, taking another step closer to him.

"My dad dumped this . . . mission in my lap." Sam's tone was a bit sarcastic. "And if you're listening, Dad, I'm sorry. But I don't know what to do."

"Let's play along for a time," she suggested. "I mean . . . can we leave? I don't think so. I found out my

82

mother can't read me as before, and I suspect your dad had something to do with that. But the strangest thing has happened, Sam . . ."

He arched an eyebrow at her pause, very much aware that that was not the only part of him that was beginning to arch upward. He resisted an impulse to fold his hands over his crotch.

"I can pick up on your thoughts, now," she said, smiling. "And yes, Sam, I am wearing panties."

And she deliberately chose not to wear a bra. The thought popped into Sam's mind.

"You see?" she said. "It's not exactly reading a mind as much as just guessing accurately what the other has done or is about to do."

She wants me to kiss her. Sam sensed that mental push very strongly.

"So do it, Sam. Before I change my mind."

He stepped off the short distance between them with as much mixed emotion as when he first hurled himself out the open door of a plane, back in jump school. The one main difference being, he recalled, he did not have a hard-on back then.

"How crude," Nydia whispered. She was slightly tense as his hands cupped her face.

"We're going to have to do something about this new power of ours."

"First things first," she said, her lips trembling as her hands found his lean waist and pulled him to her.

Sam kissed her mouth, her throat, her neck, as their hips met in a frontal assault, as frenzied an attack as storming a beachhead.

And then, as they both would later recall, events began

happening as if they were really above it all, watching two distinctly different beings in the room.

Her gown dropped to the carpet in a silken rustle of fabric, and his eyes became as greedy as his searching mouth. She pulled the waistcord to his robe and it parted. One touch from her hand and a shrug of his shoulders and robe made contact with gown on the floor.

Her pantie was no more than a thin strip of almost diaphanous silk, the lushness of womanhood vividly outlined, a perfumed jungle resting at the completion of gently curving belly.

"I am not perfection," she told him, thoughts mingling and meeting invisibly.

"You are to me," he replied.

She wore nothing except the gold cross, nestling between her breasts.

His shorts joined her panties on the floor and they were content to stand naked in the center of the room, their lips touching gently, minds speaking volumes of silent words.

"I can't believe it's wrong," she said.

"Nor I."

She ran her hand down his flat, ridged belly to grasp his maleness, fingers encircling the thickness. "Will it hurt me?" she asked, her voice throaty with passion and trembly from anticipation.

And he knew she was telling him she was a virgin. "I . . . don't know."

The bed seemed the most logical place to answer any number of questions, and they were soon there, without either of them realizing they had traversed the short distance.

His lips found the hardness of nipple and his tongue brought them to jutting nubs of excitement, while his hand traveled over the silkiness of belly to touch the edge of pubic hair and beyond: touching, lingering, fondling the wet lips and extended clitoris, finally moving to caress and part the folds of her, entering the soul of womanhood while she breathed words into his mouth as they clung to each other, joined at the lips.

She found his maleness, hard and eager, and with a knowledge that is inbred, began stroking him, finding to her astonishment and delight, the muscle of love thickening and hardening even more under her soft hand.

She clutched almost frantically at him, whispering, "Now, Sam! Now!"

He shifted on the bed and was between her legs, positioning himself. He gently placed the source of his manhood against the outer fold of woman and gently pushed, penetrating only a bit. She sighed under him, arching her hips upward, willingly asking for and receiving more of what she had desired since the moment of introduction only a few hours before.

Sam slowly and with a tiny bit of pain pushed the length of him into the hot wetness of woman, then slowly withdrew. And from that moment on, it was a battle with no losers; a war of silk and fire and passion; an ageless confrontation between man and woman . . . but it was more than that. It was a time of pain and pleasure for the both of them as they dueled on the bed, turning the sheets into a satiny battleground, a mixture of scents, a tangle of flesh. It seemed to them to stop time, to halt the forward movement of that which is unstoppable except for that brief time between the cessation of the heart and the soul exiting the cooling flesh.

Nydia began low whimpering sounds, shedding a few hot tears, not from pain or guilt, although one of those would come later, but from the knowledge, the signals her body was sending to her brain, that this deliciousness, this first time that would never again be the same, was about to end. Several small orgasms had shaken her, wavering almost sinfully through her, but as that one huge climax began its grip on her, she fought to hold on. But it was not to be. She grabbed almost too tightly at Sam's shoulders, pulling his mouth to hers as a feeling unlike anything she had ever before experienced ripped through her like the bow of an ice cutter charging through thick ice.

Sam exploded within her, his juices mingling with hers, a volcanic eruption of fluid that spread its warmth around the silken walls of the ultimate entrapment of male and female.

Nydia wrapped her legs around his and pulled him to her until it seemed there was only one person on the bed: a huge double-headed, many limbed creature. She shivered slightly as he softened within her, and she sighed as he withdrew from this battle. Not retreating, merely recouping resources. She kissed him, and he returned the touching of lips with a gentleness that was almost sad.

And they slept. Together. And the two were not alone.

Sam awakened once at the sound of a gentle knocking on the door. He fumbled for his clothes and padded barefoot to the door. The hall was empty, but two trays of food were beside the door. He took the trays in and placed them on the dresser. He wasn't hungry, and Nydia was deep in sleep. He crawled back into bed, and she nestled her warmth against him.

The food was forgotten.

"I have been blocked," Falcon said to Roma. "I cannot tell what is happening with Balon's son and Nydia. Is He interfering?"

"Indirectly, I believe. Through Balon, I am sure. My daughter and Sam now have powers even they do not realize they possess. And I do not understand that. I have attempted to speak with the Master, but I have been unable to do so. *That* distresses me."

"Roma?" Falcon lingered over the word, drawing it out as his mind raced. "Perhaps . . . yes! I sense the battleground has been marked; the Master of Light and the Prince of Darkness have finally agreed on something."

"*They* haven't agreed on anything for thousands of years. Except Their mutual dislike of each other." She was silent as the implication of his words struck home. "You mean . . . you believe we are alone in this? That neither Master will interfere any further?"

"For now, yes, I do. For how long . . . ?" He shrugged eloquently, then put a finger to Roma's lips, a gesture of caution. "But I believe this, darling: should we fail here, we are through on earth."

She thought about that for a moment, her beauty marred by the ugliness of her deliberations. She laughed nastily. "Things seem to be repeating themselves. I'm beginning to believe our Master's sense of humor is equalled only by his lack of trustworthiness and loyalty."

87

"I hope you know what you are saying, for I surely don't."

"My sins—I *hate* that word!—have come home to roost." She smiled. "Isn't that a quaint expression? A colloquialism, really. I picked it up in Alabama, right after the American Civil War. Excuse me, the War Between the States. I plotted against Black Wilder more than twenty years ago. Someone in this house is plotting against me."

"Not I!" Falcon drew himself to his full height, indignant that she would even think him guilty of such treason.

She laughed darkly. "No," she said patting his arm, "not you, Falcon. Even for a warlock you have an inordinate sense of honor and loyalty. And we have known and liked each other for too many centuries."

"Then . . . that leaves only . . ." He refused to speak the name.

But Roma had no such reluctance. "Yes. My son. Black. He is . . . strange, even for us. And he is also young, ambitious, and, I have to admit it: he possesses my genes and none of his father's."

"But surely the young man realizes his power is not yet equal to yours; will not be until he leaves this life and assumes his true role in the ways of the arts." Falcon shook his head. "But . . . you are right. Black is . . . odd, even for us."

Her gaze silenced him. "I don't wish to discuss my son's pederastic tendencies. It is not forbidden by our Master." She sighed and waved her hand. "But you are correct, of course. He does go too far at times. But I have had many offspring—some good, some bad." A thought sprang into her mind; a thought she did not share with Falcon.

"If we are alone here," Falcon mused. "I wonder if the same applies in Whitfield?"

"Probably. I feel Balon is there, looking after his precious Jane Ann. I never could understand what he saw in her. No tits."

SIX

"Explain a golem to me, Sam," Jane Ann said.

They were in her home, after having spent hours with Miles and Doris, Wade and Anita. Tony and some of his friends from the Coven had been to the house, and had, in the vernacular of the young, trashed it, writing filthy sentences on the walls, stating plainly what they were going to do with Jane Ann.

But Balon's Bible had not been touched. It sat on the small table like a sentry on duty.

Jane Ann had cleaned up the house and painted over the nasty words and obscene drawings.

"There is no such thing as a golem," Balon thrust his reply.

"But that . . . creature standing in the corner in Miles's living room!"

"Yes."

"Then it is real?"

"All things are real. Mythology is real. Dreams are real. Evil is real."

"Sam . . . you're being vague."

"In a sense. But really, I am telling you all that I can."

"All right," she said after a time. "I think I see. If we believe in it, it is real. But if someone does not, it doesn't exist." She waved her hand toward the outside.

"But . . . will they believe in it?"

"Oh, yes. Be assured of that."

"God must have a sense of humor."

"He created humans, didn't He?"

And the clock in the hall chimed its message: it was Friday. The horror was about to begin.

Sam awakened with his arms full of soft, warm nakedness and his heart pounding. But he did not awaken with a start. He wondered why his heart was hammering so violently in his chest? He opened his eyes, looking around the dimly lit room. He saw the trays of food on the dresser and remembered bringing them in. Nothing else was disturbed. He listened but could hear nothing. He glanced at his watch on the nightstand and knew then what had awakened him. It was just past midnight. Friday. But what was so special about that? Friday? The day Satan is worshiped, of course.

He gently brought Nydia out of sleep.

"I love you," she whispered. "And I don't think it is wrong." She smiled. "And I must look awful."

"No, you're beautiful." He picked up his watch. "Look at the time."

"Oh, God! No wonder no one checked on us."

"What do you mean?"

"It's Friday. They would all probably be at the circle of stones, behind the house. I used to ask them what they did out there, but I would get such silly answers I finally quit asking. Something about star-gazing was what they finally settled on. I never did believe it."

"Nydia? You're holding something back from me."

"Yes."

"Tell me?"

91

"It . . . isn't time, Sam. I will. I promise."

He thought of her statement in the four-wheel about knowing a lot about him. He shrugged it off. "You mentioned something about that circle of stones this afternoon while we were eating at the park. It triggered something in me then; the same thing happened now. There is something about a circle that is whispered about back in Whitfield—used to be, anyway." He paused. "Sure. Now I remember. Kids used to say that was where the Devil lived. That must be where Dad met the Devil. Oh, damn, Nydia! How much of this is real and how much is not? What in God's name are we supposed to believe and do? I don't know. I do know this: I want to see this circle of stones. We'll go out there tomorrow."

"Are you out of your mind?"

He ignored that, for he believed he just might be . . . for a number of reasons. "Can we see it from the house?"

"Faintly. From that window." She pointed. "But you can't see it at night."

He slipped from her warmth and blew out the small lamp, plunging the room into darkness. He opened the drapes. "Nydia," he called. "We can see it."

"What do you mean?" She crawled from the big bed and came to his side, pressing against him. She gasped at the sight in the small clearing behind the mansion.

It was torch-lit.

"I've never seen that before," she said.

"It's begun," Sam said flatly, without fear. And Nydia picked up on the firmness in his voice. "The nine days have begun."

"Sam, what are you talking about? What nine days?"

He looked at her in the darkness of the room. "Nine

days, honey. We have . . . they have, nine days. Don't ask me how I know. I just know. And I'll tell you something else: my knowing scares the shit out of me!"

In Whitfield, around the circle of stones, as behind Falcon House, the pledge was being chanted: "I renounce God the Father, God the Son, and God the Holy Ghost."

And in both places, the Beasts growled their approval.

"I renounce and deny my Creator, the Holy Virgin, the Saints, Baptism, Father, Mother, Relations, Heaven, Earth, and all this world contains that is good, pure, and sacred."

They lifted their arms straight out in front of them and screamed: "Praise the power of the Prince of Darkness. For only he is the true Master.

"I give my body and mind to Satan. Praise be his name. My Master. None other than him. This I swear by all that is unholy."

And the Beasts of Satan howled their agreement, their eyes wild, jaws leaking drool. The Beasts began dancing: an obscene hunching and howling, dancing to the beat of music they alone could hear.

"Is there a gun room in this house?" Sam asked as they dressed. The drapes were closed, the room lighted. Somehow they both felt much more comfortable with the lights on.

"Yes. Falcon enjoys shooting." She grimaced a sudden distaste.

"What's wrong?"

"He likes to see animals suffer. He's an expert shot, but I've overheard servants talking—down through the years—that he'll deliberately shoot an animal where it will take it the longest to die. He likes to listen to a wounded animal scream."

"Nice fellow," Sam muttered. "The servants?"

"You mean can we trust them? No, I don't think so. They have all been with Roma for as long as I can remember. Especially Jimmy Perkins. He's a sneak. That's not the right word. He's a zombie."

"You may be more right than you think about that," Sam told her. "Come on—let's see this gun room. I want to see what Falcon has in stock."

They walked down the dimly lit hall, walking quietly but not stealthily, in case they met someone unexpectedly and aroused suspicion. Nydia stopped him at a doorway.

"The first of the guest rooms in this wing," she whispered. "This would be Adam's room. All the boys' rooms are on the left, girls' rooms on the right."

Sam cautiously opened the door and looked in. The room was deserted. "You take the girls' rooms," he told Nydia.

Only Mac and Howard were in their beds. When Sam tried to wake them, he could not. They were sleeping as if drugged. Which, he concluded, they probably were. Across the hall, four young women were in their beds: Judy, Lana, Linda, and Susan. Sleeping soundly. Too soundly. Sam shook Lana gently, then roughly. She could not be roused. He did the same with each of them; they could not be awakened. He noticed the heavy gold medallion on a chain around Susan's neck.

"They're all drugged," he told Nydia. "I guess. From now on we'd better be careful what we eat and drink. I'll

94

bet you those trays of food I found outside the door to our rooms were drugged; that's why no one checked on us."

"Mother always uses the buffet line when we have this many guests. At least that's been her routine in the past."

"Routine can be dangerous," Sam said, remembering his training. "Lulls one into a false sense of security."

Nydia smiled. "Yes, Sergeant."

Sam slipped his arm around her waist and let his hand slip down to the curve of her buttocks. He gently caressed her.

"Don't start something you can't finish," she said. "And here in the hall would be a perfectly dreadful place to be caught making love."

Sam removed his hand.

She stopped them before they entered the foyer they had to cross to get to the gun room on the second floor. "I just remembered something: Falcon has a reject room in the basement. He spends hundreds of dollars—maybe thousands—on guns every year. If there is the slightest flaw: a scratch on the stock, a tiny bit of bluing that's wrong, anything . . . he won't have it. Just throws it in the reject room and forgets it."

"He doesn't return them?"

"No, never."

"That's the place for us, then. Take one of his favorite guns and he'd probably miss it. Where are the servants' quarters?"

"That way," she said, pointing. "First floor, in the back."

"Come on. I want to check there, too."

The servants' quarters were all empty.

"That answers another question," Sam said. "Come on, we'd better hurry." He wondered how long the ceremony at the circle of stones would last.

"It breaks up just before dawn," she said, reading his thoughts.

"Pretty good gimmick we have going," Sam said with a grin. "It may really come in handy before all this is over. I wonder how far we can project and read each other's thoughts?"

"We'll try tomorrow." She tugged at his arm. "Today, I mean. Come on, let's get to the reject room."

Sam selected a good shotgun and a high-powered rifle, then picked a pistol for Nydia. The weapons were all in good condition, except for needing cleaning and oiling. They were fine weapons, from old and skilled manufacturers. He stuffed his pockets with cartridges and had Nydia do the same. She was nervous, wanting to leave, but Sam wanted to prowl. He found a tarp-covered cache of camping equipment, loading them both down with shelter halves and blankets, rope and tent pegs. They filled two packs, then filled two smaller knapsacks. Finally Sam picked up two pairs of binoculars and steered Nydia toward the door.

"I feel like a beast of burden," she complained on the way back to their rooms. "Why do we need all these coils and coils of rope?"

Sam stopped in the dimly lit hall.

"What's wrong, Sam?"

"Beast. Why did that word spark something in me?"

"Black hasn't been trying to frighten you, has he?"

"What do you mean?"

"He likes to tell people about monsters that roam the

96

timber in back of the house. No, he wouldn't tell you. He likes to tell girls, frighten them."

"No, it's more than that. Has something to do with Whitfield. Rumors of Beasts—Devil creatures. Are there beasts in the timber?"

"I . . . don't know, Sam. I've seen . . . something. Heard noises and sounds that . . . were not human, but yet, really not animal, either. But more animal than human. If that makes any sense. And once, when I was about, oh, twelve or thirteen, I suppose, I went walking one afternoon, back where Mother had told me never to go. The smell that came out of that hole in the ground was hideous. When I walked closer . . . I don't know how to explain this . . . the growl that came out of the hole was . . . not menacing as much as it sounded like a warning. To me. As if whatever it was in there was telling me to stay away. This sounds funny—odd, I mean—but it seemed to me like it was saying it didn't want to hurt me."

"Your mother, Falcon, Black . . . do they ever go back there?"

"Sure! It's just in back of the circle of stones. Big hole in the ground. I've been to the circle dozens of times since then. But no farther."

Sam thought of the tales the kids used to tell back in Whitfield: stories about monsters and Devil-Beasts, and about what happened to cause the state to fence off the area known as The Digging. And he remembered stories about deep holes in the ground: holes that emit a very foul odor. A hideous odor.

Just as they began walking the hall, a door slammed in the house. "Run!" Sam whispered, and they raced down the hallway, up the steps, and to their rooms. In their haste, neither noticed the cartridge fall from Nydia's pocket, the brass gleaming dully on the dark carpet.

Footsteps slowly tracked them, shuffling up the steps, down the hallway. They stopped, a hand reaching down, long, bony, pale fingers closing around the brass. Jimmy Perkins looked at the cartridge, grinning grotesquely. He put the cartridge in his pocket, then shuffled down the hall to Nydia's room. He stood for a moment, listening, his ear to the door.

Had to be that young man that Sam Balon fathered, he thought. Snooping with Nydia. Found Mr. Falcon's gun room. Both up to something. But, he grinned, almost chuckling, I won't tell Mr. Falcon. His smile grew more obscene. Maybe Miss Nydia would give him some of that tight young pussy in return for keeping his mouth shut? It was worth a try. He'd see about that if he didn't forget. He turned away to get the silver goblet he'd been sent to fetch. The thought of fucking Miss Nydia burned in his tormented mind. The front of his pants bulged.

"Jimmy Perkins," Nydia whispered. "He's the only one who walks with a shuffle. He's horrible!"

They flushed the food on the trays down the toilet, leaving just enough on the plates to satisfy any curious minds, then Sam began cleaning the guns, inspecting them, hiding them. He horseshoed the shelter halves, blankets inside the horseshoes, and fastened them to the backpacks after he and Nydia packed a few items of clothing, the ammunition, and most of the rope. They stowed the packs in the closet, behind some luggage. It was the best they could do, knowing it would not fool any thorough search.

"Tomorrow," Sam said, "we swipe some food from the kitchen: canned goods, anything that will keep without refrigeration. A sack full, at least. It'll be heavy, but it has to be."

"Are you planning on us running, Sam? Into the timber?"

"I . . . guess so, eventually." He looked into her serious eyes. "Nydia . . . I don't really know what we're going to do. I don't know what I'm supposed to do. I just wish Dad had been more specific. If that was my dad. I guess it was," he added lamely, and with a heavy sigh. "If he had told me: Sam, I want you to destroy that house and everyone in it—I would do it. Be doing it right now. But, Nydia, I just don't know what I'm supposed to do!"

"I know, Sam." She took his hands in hers. "I've been kind of . . . blocking everything out. That your dad said, I mean. Mother a witch. Falcon and Black warlocks." She tried a laugh that didn't come across. "It's something out of a very bad movie script. I want to believe—and do, in part, I guess—but another part of me says . . . Oh, Sam—I don't know. I'm like you: I'm so confused." She leaned forward and kissed his mouth. "But whatever happens, Sam, I know you'll take care of me." She said it confidently, with all the love and trust in her.

Sam put his arms around her, savoring the scent of her hair. He had to fight to keep his thoughts from becoming too negative.

Dad? Sam flung the plea into the darkness. Please tell me what I'm supposed to do.

Roma met them in the hall at midmorning. "Did you young people sleep well?" The question was asked with

99

a smile.

Nydia returned the smile. "Almost as if we were drugged, Mother."

A pulse surged heavily in the older woman's neck, but her smile remained fixed. "I'm so glad you both rested well." She searched them both for thoughts, but as she suspected, she was blocked from their minds. "What do you two have planned for today?"

Plotting your total destruction, I suppose, Sam thought. "Nothing special. Might take a walk in the timber. It looks beautiful."

"Oh, but it is. Do return in time for a rest this afternoon," Roma said. "Falcon and I have such a gala evening planned."

Like what? Sam thought. Drinking human blood? "I promise we'll be in attendance, Roma."

"And you don't even know what we have planned," Roma said, smiling.

"Oh . . . I imagine something novel," Sam said dryly.

"At least that." Roma patted his cheek, her fingers warm on his flesh. She shifted her gaze to Nydia as her fingers lingered on Sam's cheek. "You're a lucky girl, Nydia. I hope you realize that."

"I know, Mother." The reply was softly stated. And you should see him with a full erection, she thought.

Crude, Nydia! Sam flung his thoughts.

Couldn't resist it.

The women smiled and purred at each other, their claws barely concealed, until Sam pulled Nydia away, toward the dining area. The large room was empty except for Lana and Susan. Linda and Judy had been sleeping when Nydia looked in on them before coming downstairs.

100

The rest of Black's young guests had not gotten in until just before dawn. They were still sleeping.

Sam and Nydia had no choice but to eat, for they were ravenous, not having eaten for eighteen hours. They would have to take a chance on the purity of the food. They filled their plates and joined the two young women.

"Hey, you two!" Lana beamed up at them. "We missed you yesterday. Heard you had to go into Montreal. Oh, Nydia, this home is so beautiful. Like something in a grand movie."

"It is that," Nydia said. A horror movie. But . . . how do I warn you?

We don't! Sam flung the thought into her brain. She has to find the true course herself.

How do you know that? she silently asked, calmly eating her breakfast.

I just do. Someone . . . or something is telling me. Perhaps later they will tell me differently.

And Sam counted Susan as among the lost when she said: "Black is taking me on a hike this afternoon. Says he wants to show me some ancient stones. He gave me this." She pulled at the gold chain and medallion Sam had noticed her wearing when he saw her sleeping. "Mr. Falcon offered one just like it to Lana and Linda and Judy."

The medallion of the damned. Of the Devil.

"Stupid Lana refused hers," Susan said. "So did Linda and Judy. I just cannot believe you did that! How rude."

"It's just too expensive a gift, Susan. I . . . just don't think it's right to take something that expensive."

Susan's eyes glittered as dangerously as a snake before striking. The venomous look faded, and she returned to

101

her breakfast. Eating in silence for a moment, she abruptly left the table without saying another word.

Lana's going to be all right, Nydia fired the thought.

I don't know, Sam disagreed. I don't think so. She's playing some sort of game.

"I think I just lost a friend," Lana said glumly. She was a small, very petite blond, with delicate features, deep blue eyes, and a lush little figure.

"Then she wasn't much of a friend to begin with," Sam told her.

"I . . . really don't . . . well, don't take this the wrong way, Nydia," Lana said. "And I don't believe you will, but I am . . . kind of sorry I came up here."

She's lying! Sam projected.

Nydia ignored the thought. "I know, Lana. I don't like most of my brother's friends, either. And neither does Sam." She started to warn the blond about her mother, the house, but the words would not form on her lips. She struggled to speak the warning but remained mute. She shut her mouth.

You see? Sam silently scolded her.

You can't know for a fact that she is lying!

I know only the words that come into my head.

But I thought your God was a just God? Nydia flung the challenging question.

He is. But He also helps those who help themselves. And He cannot tolerate a liar.

I don't understand, but I will accept what you say.

That's half the battle, honey.

Sam then remembered something, the recollection coming so strongly it hit his mental processes with the impact of a tidal wave: His Bible. He had never unpacked it from his luggage; it had remained in the bag since his arrival at Nelson College. And it was still there, in the bag, in his room . . . at Falcon House.

An unexpected ally.

"We have an excellent library here," Nydia was telling Lana. "All the latest novels. I'll show you where it is, and maybe you can find something you'd like to read."

"Oh, I'd love that. Could I . . . maybe dine with you two all the time—if it's okay?"

"Sure," Sam said. That way maybe I can figure out what you're scheming. "Sure, you can eat with us."

She squeezed his hand. "Thanks, Sam. You're the nicest guy I know."

She was gone from the table before Sam could reply.

"Umm!" Nydia said, humor creeping into her eyes. "I have some competition."

"Nah." Sam brushed it off. He leaned close and whispered: "Besides, I like girls with big tits."

The silence that hung over Whitfield was heavy and evil. Like a hot, humid day, it clung to people, enveloping them in a stinking shroud.

Those who thought they had fooled the Almighty as easily as they deceived their friends now found themselves caught in the middle of something they could not understand. They prayed to God, but they had lied in their hearts too many times, and even now, their prayers were insincere. They watched as phone company personnel pulled the plugs to their phones, cutting them off from the outside world. They sensed evil and danger all around them and tried to flee in their cars and trucks. But they could not get out of town. They returned to their homes and waited in fear for the unknown to occur. And they prayed, but the prayers fell on deaf ears.

They called their pastors, but the church pulpits had long ago been filled with those who worship another God. And the preachers laughed at them, some of them making evil deals with the husbands.

"Save you?" the preachers questioned. "All right. Your life for your wife."

"It's a deal," many husbands cried, pushing their wives into the arms of the ungodly.

The wives were taken and raped . . . among other acts committed against them.

But the husbands found that to bargain with the Devil is a fool's game. And they would learn that very painfully.

In the Lansky house, the golem stirred as invisible life was breathed into it. Wade watched it slowly shuffle across the floor, its ponderous legs and massive arms moving like some primal creature just awakened from a million years of ice-locked sleep. It bumped its head on an archway and stopped, looking almost stupidly around the room, the slits that were its eyes having no expression.

Miles came into the room and took the huge clay man's hand as one might take the hand of a child. "Is it time?" he asked.

The golem nodded, gaining balance and understanding with each second.

"What do I call you? You gotta have a name."

The golem shrugged its solid shoulders.

"I think I'll call you Hershel."

The golem lifted its hands in a gesture of acquiescence as Doris and Anita huddled together against a far wall.

Wade sat with a faint smile on his lips.

"That thing really understand what you're saying?" Doris asked.

"I suppose," Miles said. "Sure, it does."

She walked from the corner of the room to look up at the huge clay man. "You can't walk around with no clothes on. You look . . . indecent."

The golem gazed down at the woman.

"So I made you some pants. You wait where you are." She left the room, returning with a large pair of trousers. "Denim," she said, holding out the jeans. "Difficult material to sew. But I did it."

The golem looked at the offered jeans, then looked at Miles.

Miles wore an exasperated look. "Momma, a golem don't know from pants. What's he gotta have pants for?"

"Because I said he's gotta, that's why. If he's gonna be our *shtarker** he's gonna look nice, at least."

The four of them managed to get the jeans on the golem, and, surprisingly, the jeans fit well.

Miles patted the golem on the arm. "Joe E. Lewis, you ain't, Hershel, but you got class."

The golem lumbered out of the room, bumping his head as he went out the door. He sat down on the porch, waiting.

Wade picked up his shotgun, checking the loads. Miles did the same. The four of them sat in the living room. Waiting. Waiting for the evil to begin. Waiting for the horror they knew was coming.

Waiting for the night.

Waiting and praying they had enough faith to get them

*strong man

105

through it.

"Did you have anything to do with my friends' decision to remain in Whitfield?" Jane Ann asked Balon.

"Their final decision . . . no. That was something they decided upon a long time ago. Unknowingly. Wade made his decision when he shut down the newspaper. Miles when he sold his store."

"Tony?"

"He lost his faith years ago. Young Sam was only a child. Tony is evil."

"The world is a pretty crappy place, isn't it, Sam?"

"Father Dubois and I discuss that same topic from time to time."

"You make it sound like old home week."

The misty face smiled. "Heaven is not what most mortals envision, I can assure you of that. But I can tell you no more."

"I wish this was over."

"Yes."

"I want to go home."

"You will."

"Is it lovely . . . there?"

"It is different."

"Peaceful?"

"Quite."

"Am I going to suffer before I . . . go?"

"I cannot lie. Yes."

"Miles and Doris? Wade and Anita? Anita is not very strong."

"They will suffer to a degree."

"But mine will be physical." It was not spoken as a question.

106

Balon projected no reply.

"Your silence tells me I'm right."

The mist thrust no mental response.

Jane Ann sighed. "I will endure it."

"Yes," the thought pushed into her brain. "And so must I."

SEVEN

"They're leaving," Roma said to Falcon. "Heading into the east woods." She swore, a venomous string of profanities. "It is difficult for me to believe I have birthed a Christian. It's disgusting! Where did we fail, Falcon?"

He laughed. "*We* didn't, Roma. Put such thoughts aside. Balon interfered, that's all. His seed must have been strong."

"Like a hot river."

"You still remember?"

"I shall never forget it. I mounted him a half dozen times before he lost the battle and I could keep him inside me."

"Tell me, Roma: Did you cheat?"

She seemed astonished he would even ask such a foolish question. "Of course!"

"Then there is the answer to your question, and many more unasked questions. Why Black is deceitful and plotting, for one. Balon's seeds were many. Pure and strong, with most of them forming Nydia. Black is weak and scheming. Weak in many areas; I've known that for years. We must not lean too heavily upon him. You know, of course, he cheated taking his difficult military training?"

She whirled about, her face flushed. "He swore to me he would not."

"But he did. I wanted to tell you . . . wanted to see how that deception affected him. I will tell you this, and you know I am a warrior: Black will be no match for young Sam. I . . . sensed something else, as well, Roma: the young man has killed, and not just in the heat of open battle. I sense . . . he has killed, once, at least, probably several times, on orders from his government."

"Covertly and cold-bloodedly?"

"Yes."

"When you were able to see his thoughts, study his innermost character, how had the killing affected him?"

Falcon paused, lighting his pipe, sending billowing clouds of fragrant smoke swirling about him. The silence only heightened the moment. "Not at all," he finally said. "The young man is a true warrior. And you know how He," Falcon cast his eyes upward, "feels about warriors."

"Young Sam is his father's son." Roma smiled.

"Entirely."

Her smile grew wicked.

Falcon read her thoughts. "Roma . . . ?"

She met his eyes, dark evil gazing into dark evil. "Yes, Falcon?"

"It's too dangerous. You're much too old for that nonsense. Birthing the twins almost killed you. Or have you forgotten?"

"No, but I failed with them. And now—if your deductions are correct, and I believe they are—I know why. It would not be that way with young Sam."

"*You* would not cheat? *You*, my dear?" He chuckled. "Anyway, Roma, it's out of the question for a number of reasons, paramount among them the fact young Sam is in love with his half sister, and she with him. They're practically nauseating with it. Besides, I forbid you to take the chance." He turned his head, smiling as he spoke the last, knowing what her reaction would be. He was not disappointed.

She gave him a look that would have stopped a runaway truck dead in the road. "You FORBID it!" she screamed at him. "Forbid! *You* do not forbid *me* to do a fucking thing!"

Falcon sighed. "And I worked so hard improving your vocabulary, taking it from the gutter. Now you revert."

"Forbid me! Are you forgetting who is in command here?"

"Not at all, my dear. Calm yourself. I was merely attempting to be practical about this matter. Roma, consider the risk factor. One: even should you seduce the young man without cheating, having a demon child would kill you. That is written. Secondly: the Master would surely void your plan. Oh, Roma . . . go fuck the young man, anyway you can, and get it out of—or in your case—into your system. Then forget it. We have matters of much greater urgency here."

She whirled and stalked from the room, cursing under her breath. Falcon watched her leave, slamming the door. He stood and slowly shook his head. A pity, he thought, to be so obsessed by the memory of Balon. She fell in love with a Man of God.

He shuddered at the thought. How degrading!

"They stopped watching us," Nydia said. "I could feel her eyes when they left me. They're planning something, Sam."

"Sure they are. Evil. I just wish I knew what I—we—are supposed to do about it. Do I have a free hand? I don't know. Nydia? I . . . we're stumbling around in the dark with this thing. I don't know what to do. Yes, all right, my dad appeared and wrote me a letter. I've convinced myself we didn't dream it. A sign of the cross is burned—burned—into my chest. Okay, I'll accept that I've been chosen . . . but, damn it, honey . . . chosen to do what? I have to assume that I am to follow in my dad's footsteps; do what he did back in Whitfield in the fifties." He stopped at the edge of the deep timber and sat down on a large rock, Nydia beside him.

"Dad was trying to tell us something about our being related. But what? He said it wasn't a holy union. Does that make our feelings all right? I'm going to say it does. I can't help the way I feel about you. We were drawn together from the moment we met. You felt it, I felt it. And we'll just leave it at that.

"Mother always said I was just like my dad. I guess the service proved it: it . . . really doesn't bother me to kill. I can't say much about it, although I don't know what it would matter now, to you, I mean, but sometimes Special Troops have to kill. Cold-bloodedly. A very few get picked to do that. I got picked. I did my job. I came back to base. I did that several times. No guilt feelings. None at all. No remorse. No nothing. I think Dad must have been like that.

"Okay, then. I'll do whatever in the hell—that's an odd word to pick, isn't it—I'm supposed to do. I'm hearing voices in my head; words pop out of my mouth that are alien to me; I know things that mortals aren't

111

supposed to know—and don't ask me to explain any of it. I can't. So I'll just have to wait until someone, or something, gives me the green light with instructions."

She put her arms around him and held him. And as has been the case for thousands of years, woman gave her strength to man through her touch, her gentleness, her understanding . . . and the fact that women are the more mercenary of the species.

"We'll both know when it's time, Sam," she told him, holding him. "I believe that. And I believe that our feelings for each other are right. And you must believe it."

Holding hands, they walked into the timber, and the silence of God's free nature seemed to make them stronger, and draw them closer. The mood was almost religious, the towering trees a nondenominational cathedral silently growing around the young couple. They came to a small, rushing creek and sat on a log by the bubbling waters.

"Tell me more about being a Christian, Sam."

"I don't know that much about it, Nydia. I . . . sometimes think it's a . . . feeling one must have. And I don't have it very often."

"I think you're a better person than you will admit to being, Sam."

"I've killed in cold blood," he said softly. "Before I was twenty years old."

"Yet you've been chosen by a higher power to do . . . something good here on earth."

He looked at her. "Killing your mother and brother, probably. Have you thought about that, Nydia?"

"Yes. But I have no feelings of love or affection for

112

either of them, Sam. I don't recall the last time I felt anything for them. I've always felt like a stranger around them . . . out of place . . . unwanted and really unloved. I don't believe they know love. I'll put it stronger than that: they worship Satan, so how can they know love?"

His smile was gentle, full of admiration for her. And love.

"Do you believe in baptizing or sprinkling, Sam?"

"I was baptized when I was just a kid. Too young, really. You don't really understand what it's all about at twelve or thirteen. It's exciting . . . the thing to do. Yeah, I guess either one would do. I'm not even sure it's necessary. How about the thief on the cross?"

"I know that story. I want to be a Christian, Sam."

He looked at her. "I really hope the thoughts I'm picking up from you aren't correct."

"They are."

"I'm not a minister, Nydia. I'm not even a very good Christian. How can I baptize you?"

"Do you remember the words, Sam?"

"No. I really don't." He searched his memory. "Well . . . I remember what Jesus said to the eleven disciples after the rock had rolled away . . . or something like that."

"Oh, Sam!" She laughed at him, her laughter tinkling bells in the forest. "All right, that will have to do. So say them. Do it."

"Do it? You mean . . . here? Nydia, I don't have the . . . uh, authority."

"What authority does it take?"

"Well, I don't know, exactly."

"Then how do you know you don't have it? I mean,

113

you're a baptized Christian, aren't you? Can't a Christian baptize somebody?"

"I . . . guess so, Nydia. But I'm not about to stick you in that water," he said pointing to the creek. "You'd turn blue!"

"Then put your fingers in the creek and do that other thing."

He grinned at her, the grin fading when he saw she was serious. Feeling very much like a fool, Sam kneeled by the fast-rushing creek and wet his fingers. He touched his fingers to her forehead and said, "Jesus said this, Nydia, and I really hope someone is listening who knows what this is all about. 'All power is given unto me in Heaven and on earth.

"'Go ye therefore, and teach all nations, baptizing them in the name of the Father, and of the Son, and of the Holy Ghost.

"'Teaching them to observe all things whatsoever I have commanded you: and lo, I am with you always, even unto the end of the world.'"

And Sam knew something all powerful had been guiding his voice, for he had not read that passage since he was a child.

He kissed her lips and said, "I feel kind of like an idiot, Nydia."

"I really hope Jesus didn't add that," she said dryly.

"What do they represent?" Susan asked, her eyes on the circle of stones.

Black moved closer to her, standing just behind the young woman. She could smell the musk of his cologne and it was rich and heady, arousing some heretofore hidden urge deep within her. Black breathed deeply of her perfume and placed his hands on her shoulders.

"It is said that here is where ancient ceremonies were held," he told her. He now stood with his groin pushing against her buttocks, knowing she could feel his slight erection. He pushed against her. She made no effort to move away.

"What kind of ceremonies?" she asked, her voice low.

"The people who worship here, Susan, worship a Master who allows them supreme pleasures in life. Their Master knows that mortals are susceptible beings, and to place too many restrictions upon them is not wise. Are you a Christian, Susan?"

"I was baptized as a child, but I don't attend church."

"Why not?"

"I just got away from it, that's all."

"The talk at school is you're untouchable. That Susan is super-cool. All ice."

"You're touching me, so the talk must be wrong."

"They say you don't smoke grass, don't drink . . . nothing."

"Like I said, Black: the talk is wrong." She pushed her buttocks against his heating, swelling groin.

He moved his hands from her shoulders to her slim waist.

She said, "Tell me more about this religion, Black. It sounds very intriguing."

"What would you like to know about it?" His hands were gently caressing her denim-clad hips.

"Oh . . . like what is your church called? And I assume you belong to it."

"Yes. Many names. Depending on the locale."

"Have I ever been to one of your churches?"

"I doubt it." He buried his face in the lushness of her hair and breathed the scent of her.

"Why all this sudden attention to me, Black? I've seen you looking at me at dances, but you never asked me out."

"I didn't believe you'd go out with me."

"Why?"

"Because of the talk."

"But I'm here, aren't I?"

"And we're alone."

She turned in his arms and kissed him, running her tongue over his lips, pushing against him, working her hips against his. "Did you bring blankets so we could fuck, Black?"

He laughed, his lips still on hers. "I have to admit I did, Susan."

"All right," she said softly, then added, "Lana and the others are so stupid they don't realize what happened, Black. But my father was a doctor—the research kind. I know when I've been drugged. Besides, I'm a light sleeper; not like I slept last night. You didn't have to do that, Black."

He said nothing.

She pulled away, opening her jacket, then removing it. Black gazed hungrily at the swell of her breasts pushing against her shirt. She lifted the heavy gold medallion. "Seems to be a great many of these, Black."

"But I gave only one—to you."

Her eyes were serious as they gazed into the darkness of his eyes. His were unreadable. "I studied this medal-

116

lion quite closely this morning. Under a magnifying glass."

"And?"

"It was . . . unusual. I found myself captivated by the detail."

"But not offended?"

"Oh no."

"Some people are offended by the scene."

And she sealed her fate when she said, "I found myself wishing I was a participant."

"Did you now?"

"Yes."

"You could be."

"Tell me what I would gain."

"If you're one of the lucky ones accepted by our Master—really accepted by him—everlasting beauty and life."

"I'm a virgin, Black. I really am."

"Why? Saving yourself for the right man?"

"Something like that. But I think I've found him."

"It would be an honor for me."

A thin line of sweat formed on her upper lip, although the northern air was cool. "I think I like your god, Black. And I'm not a fool: I know what Adam and the others practice."

"Do you now?"

"Yes. Black magic. Voodoo. Devil worship."

"It doesn't frighten you?"

"It fascinates me."

He took her hand and placed it on his swelling crotch. "Does that fascinate you?"

She gently squeezed. "I'd like to see more before I

commit myself."

"You know the way."

She nodded and drew back, spreading the blankets away from the circle of stones, on a thick mattress of pine needles. She kneeled down, slowly wriggling out of her jeans. She patted the space beside her.

Naked from the waist down, but with their shirts open, they lay under the blankets beneath the trees. She gripped his penis and worked the foreskin back, the angry red glans glistening.

"It's big," was all she said.

There was no need for foreplay; her juices were wetting the insides of her thighs.

"Think you can get that in your mouth?" Black asked.

"It's real big," she repeated.

"Try."

Without hesitation she bent her head and took him, while his fingers worked at the wetness between her legs. He pulled her mouth from him and positioned himself between her legs, inserting only a small portion of himself inside her.

"More," she groaned.

"First you tell me your God is shit," he said.

She hesitated, then complied, uttering the blasphemy. And the medallion around her neck began to glow.

He slid another inch inside her and said, "Praise the Master of Darkness, Susan."

"Yes," she whispered in passion. "I do praise Him."

He moved between her legs and she screamed in pleasure and pain. Black said, "If this feels so good, Susan, why then does your God deny this pleasure to his subjects, whenever they choose to partake of it?"

"I don't know!" she wailed, struggled to get more of him inside her.

"Because your God is shit!"

"Yes. My God is shit!"

At his urgings, blasphemous words rolled from her mouth, leaking like filth from a broken sewage line.

And God must have frowned as the Devil laughed when Black shoved his manhood into the laughing, screaming, corruption-spouting young woman. His newest convert. By the circle of stones. Not too far from a reaking hole in the ground.

"Susan screaming," Nydia said, her lips tight as the wails of pleasure drifted through the timber.

"But not in pain," Sam observed.

"No, I guess not. My brother is . . . amply endowed. Like you," she said, glancing at him.

"My father must have been hung like a bull."

She laughed. "What a marvelously elegant expression."

"Shall we hike through the timber and see what's happening?" Sam suggested with a grin.

"What is this, another side to you? The voyeur?"

"I just want to see if Dad gave him the same equipment."

"You're awful. You and Black are . . . about the same, in that department."

"How would you know?"

"I'm his sister, remember? I've seen my brother naked on numerous occasions. None recently, thank God." She was gently leading him in the opposite direction of the wailing pleasure sounds.

119

"Must be gettin' good," Sam drawled.

"You're incorrigible! Remember, Sam: He has His eye on you."

"Before you get too pious, honey, remember the same applies to you."

She looked horrified. "I forgot about that."

They walked a full mile from the circle of stones before they spread the ground sheet Sam carried. He said, "We'll give them time to get it done, then wander down that way. I want to see this circle of stones and the hole in the ground."

She lay back on the ground sheet, her hands behind her head. Sam's eyes began wandering. "Don't get any ideas," she cautioned him, pointing upward. "He's watching."

A half continent away, many of the residents of Whitfield began answering the call of their Chosen Master, gathering in a huge clearing on the Zagone Ranch, whose eastern range bordered on the fenced-in area known as The Digging. While God did not interfere—directly—into the affairs on earth, at least not too often, and certainly never in any obvious manner, Satan was bound by no rules on earth, and could do anything the Dark One chose to do. And did—often.

There would be no interference from anyone in this part of Fork County. The Devil had seen to that. Should anyone travel through, all would appear normal, and no one would have any desire whatsoever to stop—for anything.

But the Dark One did not know that God also had plans for this part of Whitfield, and was already working.

This time, if all went according to Satan's plans—and the Prince of Darkness saw no reason why they should not—there would be no great billowing plumes of smoke from burning, exploding buildings; no racing about the county blowing up ranch houses and shooting people— none of that business this time. No, all would be handled a bit more sedately this time around. His followers could, of course, have a bit of fun: dance, sing, engage in their heretofore forbidden open orgies, all that type of mortal frivolity. Perhaps some human offerings would be fun. Certainly the Jew and Jewess and that idiot aging reporter and his simpering wife would die . . . and then . . . the Master of Grotesqueness would have his fun with Balon's bitch. *That* would be worth the waiting.

He pondered his options: whether to pass her around among the men until she died from exhaustion, or let the women have her. Perhaps have a pony mount her. That would certainly be an interesting sight. There were so many things to do with Balon's bitch.

Well, he had time to think things through. But . . . behind all his smugness, all his confidence that, at last, he would finally beat that Ageless Cosmic Meddler in the firmament . . . was the thought of that maverick resident of that miserable place: Balon.

Why did He allow Balon such liberties? That puzzled Beelzebub. Balon was not like many of the others; Balon was a relative newcomer. Of course, there had been many others before Balon, hundreds down through the years, but with few exceptions they had been such wimps, such a praying bunch of hand-wringing, psalm-singing sisters.

But not Balon. Balon, Mephistopheles concluded— had concluded, years ago—was a mother-fucker. And one fine warrior. It just wouldn't do to have many like him wandering about.

Perhaps, Satan thought . . . yes! Yes, there was a way. Maybe Balon would take it.

"Not a chance," the words ripped into Satan's thoughts.

"You have already extended yourself too much here on earth, Star-Wart," Satan replied. "Don't press your luck."

"You cannot tempt Balon."

"How do you know?"

"I know Balon."

"Bah! I think perhaps you have grown a bit too cocky of late. You forget, *I* know your limitations here on earth. *I* know exactly what you can and cannot do. *I* . . ."

"If you mention *I* one more time, Scratch . . . *I* will certainly interfere with your plans. Directly."

"You wouldn't dare!"

"Try me."

Satan was silent for a moment, smarting under the lash of words from the only thing in the universe he feared. "You will leave us alone here in Whitfield?"

"I didn't say that."

"I must have some agreement from you."

"I don't bargain with you."

"Not good enough."

"I will never bargain with you, Belial. You should know that by now."

"Afraid I might beat you, eh?"

The Heavens were silent.

"Oh, all right!" the Tempter pouted. "But you have to give me something to seal the bargain."

122

"I told you, Hooved-One: I do not bargain with you. Your slyness with words will not work with me."

"What is so special about Balon. You can tell me that, at least."

The Heavens were again silent.

"Ah! Of course!" the Mephistophelian voice cracked. "I see. Balon. Yes. You rather like him, don't you? You don't have to reply—I know. Yes, while your pet, Michael, is out flitting about the heavens, you'd like Balon sitting with you, eh? You do like your pet dogs, don't you? Is Michael there now?"

The Heavens rumbled as the archangel voiced his objection to being called a dog.

Satan laughed, and lightning licked across the sky. "Turn your militant maverick loose, Thunderer; let him face me. Let us see if his powers are as great as mine."

That was the wrong thing for the Dark One to suggest.

The Heavens were calm, even while Satan howled and cursed and called down malisons on all the residents of the firmament. He received no reply.

That enraged the ruler of filth. Satan fired his thoughts into the head of Jean Zagone. "You have sampled nearly all the men around you, bitch!" he said, still smarting from his conversation with the Holy One. "Pick five of the most virile and have them ready to receive Balon's pious whore."

And on the Zagone ranch, on the plains, the dancing began, preparatory to the Friday night sacrifice. The Coven members danced lewdly, hunching obscenely as they shouted filth to the Heavens. They were not afraid in their vocal and physical defilements, for the Prince of Evil had assured them his protection; guaranteed them a

123

long and lustful life on earth.

These Coven members, these worshipers of Darkness, these students of Bell, Book, and Candle . . . they had made any number of mistakes in their evil lives. But paramount among them was believing anything the Devil said, while forgetting that the one True God is a vengeful God.

EIGHT

"Let's see how far our thoughts will carry," Sam suggested. "We'd better know, 'cause I think things are going to get down to the nut-cuttin' pretty quick."

"I do love your expressions, Sam," Nydia said, smiling. "I wonder if your father used the same colloquialisms? Bearing in mind he was a minister."

"Probably so. Mother often said he was a real character. Would speak his mind whenever and wherever."

"And yet, he has God's favor. I don't understand that. From what little I know of God's Word, I always thought of Christians as rather meek and mild types."

"Oh, I think that's a dangerous misconception, Nydia. God loves His warriors. I think Michael sits at God's side. Some even think he is God's bodyguard. Others think of him as the hand of retribution."

She glanced at him, thinking: Yes, I believe God does love His warriors.

They separated in the timber, walking first a few hundred yards apart, testing their ability to project and receive thoughts. They found that distance did make a difference in the receiving and sending.

"Let's go see this circle of stones," Sam said.

"What if we run into Black and Susan?"

He grinned at her, thinking how beautiful she was in the light filtering through the timber. "We'll just ask them how it was."

She playfully pushed him away. "Sam, you're impossible."

But the circle of stones was deserted when they got there. They looked for Black and Susan, finding only the still-pressed-down blanket of pine needles where they had lain.

Sam kneeled down, studying closely the stones of the huge circle; he studied with great interest the largest stone, which depicted scenes of great depravity: of men with huge jutting phalluses; of women with their legs spread wide, exposing the genitalia; scenes of mass orgies: men with men, women with women, men with small children; scenes of hideous torture; of grotesque creatures, monsters, leaping and snarling. And finally, on the east side of the boulder, a scene depicting a saintly looking man who was locked in some sort of combat with a beastly appearing creature.

Sam looked up from his studying. "You didn't tell me about this."

Her face was pale. "That was . . . never there before, Sam. I mean, the rocks, yes, but not all those carvings."

"Nydia . . ." he let his statement drift away. "No . . . I imagine the carvings were always here; you just couldn't see them. They are probably exposed only when Satan wants them to be." And how do you know all that? he silently questioned his mind.

"Or when he is near," she said tightly.

"Yes." Sam rose from his squat position and put his arms around her. She was trembling.

"I'm scared, Sam. For the first time, I'm really

126

frightened. Now I know what you meant when you said you didn't know what to do—where to start."

Sam comforted her as best he could, for he, too, was frightened. "Come on. Let's see this hole in the ground."

They smelled the stench long before they came to the hole, both their noses wrinkling at the foul odor. "Can you imagine what it's like deep in that hole?" Sam tried a grin, unaware that his father had said almost the same thing to a couple of friends back in '58, standing near The Digging.

"Gross!" Nydia said. She watched as Sam reached into his jacket pocket. His face paled. He jerked his hand from the pocket as if he had touched a snake.

"What's wrong, Sam?"

His face regained a bit of color after his initial shock. "That . . . that's not my pistol in there."

"What!"

"I . . . thought just a moment ago, when I was kneeling down by that boulder there was too much weight in my pocket. But I shrugged it off. That's not a .38 revolver. That's an . . . automatic."

"Let's see, Sam."

He looked at her for a long moment and then put his hand into his jacket pocket. With his hand still in his pocket, he said, "Oh, my God!"

"Sam!"

He pulled out his hand, the hand containing three fully loaded clips for a .45 automatic pistol.

"What kind of gun did your father carry . . . back in Whitfield?"

"I don't know."

"Take out the pistol, Sam."

The young man hesitantly put his hand back into his

pocket, gingerly pulling out the big automatic. He checked it. A full clip in the butt. He turned the weapon and saw a brass nameplate embedded and riveted into the handle. SGT SAM BALON KOREA 1953

"It's . . . it belonged to my father," he choked out the words, holding the weapon out for Nydia to see the brass plate in the grip.

She put a hand to her mouth, her face pale with shock.

"Something else just popped into my head," Sam said. "Wade Thomas told me one time my father sure could use a Thompson submachine gun. My mother gave him a look that would have fried eggs."

"What's a Thompson submachine gun?"

"An old-type tommy gun. Like the gangsters used to use."

"Are they any good?"

Sam smiled. "Up to about a hundred yards. If a Thompson won't stop what's coming at you, honey, with those big old slugs, it just isn't going to be stopped. I would love to have one of them."

"Have you ever fired one?"

"No, but it wouldn't take me long to learn." He looked at the pistol again. Somehow, and he could not shake the feeling, the weapon felt natural in his hand, almost as if he had held it before.

"What are you thinking, Sam?" Although she knew his thoughts.

He told her.

"Maybe that's what your father wants you to feel?"

"Yeah," he said softly.

A sudden sensation of being pulled into a dark force field enveloped them. "Sam!" Nydia cried, taking his hand. "What's happening?"

"Hang on! I don't know."

They sank to the ground. And they were speechless, immobile as the strange force took control.

Time took them mentally winging into darkness, spinning them wildly through multicolors. They watched a naked man fighting with a naked woman. The faces were blurred, but both Sam and Nydia knew who they were: Sam Balon and Roma.

Articles of clothing and pieces of equipment flew about the struggling couple, sailing in a slow circle. The man struck the woman with his fist, and her head snapped back, blood spurting from a suddenly crimson mouth. She slapped him, the force of the open-hand pop turning him in somersaults. He kicked out with a bare foot and she grabbed his ankle, her hand working upward to grasp his erect penis. She hunched and impaled herself on the phallus, howling with dark laughter.

He smashed a fist against her jaw and she slumped, the man pushing her from his penis. She flew at him, fighting him. He was growing weaker. Again and again she mounted his maleness, only to have him shove her away, each shove less forceful than the preceding one.

Then, shrieking her taunting laughter, she lunged at him and wailed her delight as the phallus drove to the inner depths of her. For what seemed like hours the couple fucked their way across trackless worlds of time, always in a slow circle, until their combined juices were leaking from her lathered cunt, leaving a trail as bright as the Milky Way.

The young couple, frozen in voyeurism, earth-locked, could see the man was nearly dead.

With one last supreme burst of courage and strength, the man threw out his arm, snagging something out of the maze of clothing and equipment that encircled the couple. The objects seemed to fire from his hand, through the years, straight toward the young man and woman sitting on the ground in Canada.

Nydia screamed.

Sam ducked.

They both jumped to their feet, looking around them. All was still and peaceful. Sam looked at the gun in his hand.

"He threw the gun at you," Nydia whispered. "And something else. But . . . how?"

"I think when we finally learn that, Nydia . . . we'll be dead."

"You know now what you have to do at Falcon House, don't you?" she asked him.

"I think I've known all along."

"It's Miles," Jane Ann said. "He wants to know how come the phones are still working when everybody else's don't?"

"They don't work in Whitfield," Balon replied.

"He says then maybe you would be so kind as to explain how it is he is talking with me on the telephone this very minute?"

"Tell him to think about it. The answer will come to him."

She relayed the message, then stood listening for a few seconds. She laughed. "He says he understands. He really doesn't, he said. But to please you, he says he does."

130

"Hang up the phone and come over here and sit on the couch," Balon said.

When she was seated in front of the only man she had ever loved, she smiled at the misty face and said, "All right, Sam."

"I will be able to protect you through most of what will occur during the coming days. But . . . in the end it will have to be your strength and courage that see you through."

"Can you tell me why?"

"Not yet. Most of it you will be able to guess. After . . . all is done, then you will know."

She smiled. "I love question and answer games."

"None of this is amusing, Jane Ann!" Balon fired the thought at her with such intensity it caused her head to ache. "Sorry," he said. "But enough is enough. Miles is treating this as some sort of comedy burlesque; Wade is his usual smart-ass reporter self."

"Sam! Angels aren't supposed to talk like that."

"I'm not an angel. Even if I were, it wouldn't make any difference. Michael has been known to loose some oaths that caused tidal waves."

"Do you two get along? You and Michael?"

Silence greeted her.

"Sorry," she muttered. "Conversing with the spirit world is not something I do every day, you know."

"There you go again, being flip. I can't seem to get through to you—any of you—the horror that is beginning . . . for all of you."

"Don't you think we know, Sam? We lived through it once."

"But none of you will live through this. None of you.

131

And your death, Jane Ann, is not going to be pleasant."

"I realize that, Sam. Last night I prayed for help."

"I heard you."

"Did He?"

"I am sure He did."

"*You* don't know!"

Silence.

"All right. Knowing Jean Zagone, I'm sure whatever is in store for me will be of a sexual nature."

The mist projected no reply.

"Rape, I'm sure."

Silence.

"Am I to be served up for the Black Mass?"

The mist gave no clue. Balon's unblinking eyes could not be read.

And then she knew what was in store for her; the culmination of the awfulness preceding the final hours of hideousness. She put her hands over her face and wept.

Balon could do nothing except silently watch, and invisibly weep with her.

A gentle rain began to fall over Whitfield.

Sam jacked a round into the automatic, eased the hammer down, and shoved it behind his belt. He glanced at Nydia. "Let's go see this hole in the ground. See the Beasts."

She grabbed his arm. "Why did you say Beasts?"

"Because I know, now, that's what they are. I don't know *how* I know. But they are the Devil's Beasts. My dad fought them—or some like them—in Fork. And now I know for certain I have been tapped—chosen, if you will—to pick up where Dad left off. Just another part of the country, that's all."

"And Roma, Falcon, Black . . . all those at the house?" she asked, almost running to keep pace with his long stride.

"I have to kill them," Sam said.

"Or try," she was forced to add.

"Yes."

"You won't run?"

"No."

Then they were at the hole in the earth, the ungodly fumes pouring from the blackness hundreds of feet deep almost making them physically ill.

"Bastards," Sam said, his voice low and powerful. "I know you're in there."

A growl ripped from the darkness and the stench to touch them.

Sam tossed his jacket to the ground, opening his shirt, exposing the angry red cross burned into his skin. The growling intensified, becoming louder as others joined in, swelling the howling and snarling to a fever pitch.

Sam pulled the .45 from his belt. "Why don't you come out?" he challenged them. "Let the light touch you?"

But nothing appeared at the mouth of the stinking lair of the Beasts. Only more howling and snarling sprang from the filthy cave.

Sam ignored the tugging at his sleeve. Nydia was so frightened she was trembling.

"Come up," Sam said. "Let me see you. Show me your evil red eyes." How did I know their eyes were red?

133

And one Beast did just that. A young Beast who lacked the caution of age leaped forward, just a few feet from the cave opening. It roared at the tall young man, its breath stinking. Sam shot it between the eyes, then stood smiling as the dead creature tumbled backward, falling with a boneless thud onto the first level of the many-tiered burrow. It would not be wasted: its relatives would feast on the cooling flesh and still-warm blood, sucking the marrow from the bones.

"One less," Sam said, then spat contemptuously on the ground, unaware his father had done and said the same thing years before, 1,500 miles to the west.

This time Sam allowed Nydia to pull him away from the rancid hole, leading him toward the house.

After the young couple had gone, a huge old Beast stuck his head out of the den. He had been on this earth for many years, hundreds of years, and had lived through purge after purge from both humans and the elements. He was old and he was wise, as Beasts go. He shook his great scarred head and snarled deep in his chest. He had never known a human without fear of his kind.

Until now.

And that primal sense of warning struck a resonant cord within his tiny brain. The Beast did not know he was evil; his brain could not distinguish between good and evil. He served his god because . . . well, it was the thing to do. He did not have the intelligence to question right or wrong. But he did understand courage . . . and something else: fear. And what he now felt was fear, and he did not understand why.

Growling, the Beast slipped back into the earth. He must warn the others of this human; tell them to stay

134

away. For this human was not like the other humans. This human had been touched by the Other Side. And the Beast feared the Other Side.

Black and Susan spun around as the echo of the shot drifted through the timber.

"That was close," Susan said.

But Black would only smile.

In Falcon House, Roma studied Falcon as the man stood speaking with Lana. He could be so charming. She wondered how long it would take him to get the panties off the little blond? Not long, if she knew Falcon, and she did. She would like to be there when he spread her legs and filled her with that enormous erection. Roma liked to hear screaming.

A thin line of perspiration broke from the skin on her upper lip at just the thought of sex. Damn that young man! She couldn't get him out of her mind. Roma knew, with a mother's sixth sense, that Nydia had slept with Balon's bastard . . . which was fine . . . no harm in that. But what Roma did not want was some puky little holy child to spring from the mating. That would be the height of humiliation.

A door slammed, and Roma looked around as Black and Susan strolled in. The girl looked rumpled. So her son had made it with the cunt. That was good. Better than his usual tastes: boys. Although the Master did not object to his subjects engaging in sex with the same gender. Roma noticed Susan now wore the medallion of the Master outside her shirt. Very good, Black. Falcon will want to sample her wares as well. How nice of you to break in a new pussy for him. She watched Susan touch her son's arm, smile up at him, then walk toward the steps to her quarters. Black came to his mother's side.

"All went well, I see."

"Very well, Mother. But we did hear a shot a few moments ago."

"Oh?"

"Yes. Seemed to come from around the circle."

"Of course, Sam would be armed. He is his father's son. Any ideas as to what prompted the gunfire?"

"He probably fired at a Beast."

"They would not have attacked with Nydia present." A frown creased her brow. "Unless . . ." she let the unimaginable trail off.

"Unless . . . what, Mother?"

"She became a Christian," Roma said sourly.

"If she did that, then that changes things considerably."

"Yes. But Sam Balon used to do the same thing back in Whitfield. Taunt the Beasts. No fear in either father or son." But still . . . could her daughter have been converted so quickly. It was possible. If so, Roma smiled, that opened up yet another can of wriggling worms, with more alternatives than ever.

Black looked at his mother. But unlike his mother, the young man was very familiar with fear. But he dared not tell her of that forbidden emotion, as forbidden as true love. She would be furious. Black had learned as a child how to keep his thoughts blocked from her.

But Roma picked up disturbing vibes from her son. "What's wrong, Black?"

Dark eyes met, held, with Black breaking off his gaze

under her hard look. He shook his head. "Nothing, Mother." He hoped he sounded convincing enough.

He didn't. But Roma said nothing about it. "Black, we have but one mission here on earth, and nothing must stand in its way. Nothing. Do you understand that?"

"Yes, Mother."

Scheming little bastard, Roma thought. Now you've added lying. "Our Master wants more converts, more churches. It is a very daring move they are taking in Whitfield, so soon after failure. If all succeeds, it will mean an entire town—everyone—worshiping the Prince of Darkness. That hasn't happened here on earth in more years than even I can recall. Nothing must stand in our way."

"Yes, Mother. But why simultaneously? Why here and in Whitfield concurrently?"

"Balon, dear. Both of them."

"But Sam Balon is *dead*, Mother. He is of the Other Side. He cannot be killed again."

She took his arm and guided him into the study, motioning him to sit. "Black, understand something, dear: Balon is very close to being chosen by . . . Him." She gestured upward with a carefully manicured finger. "Chosen to sit with Him."

"God likes His warriors," Black said.

"That is correct. But we don't want that to happen."

"Why?"

Roma sighed. Sometimes she felt she had birthed an idiot. "If for no other reason, son, to humiliate Him. To show Him He is not infallible."

Her son nodded his head, narrowing his eyes. "You think Balon will show up here?"

137

"Not necessarily. We'd rather he wouldn't. You see, if he stays in Whitfield, the temptation to help his darling beloved Jane Ann—that simpering little cunt—will be even more overpowering."

"I see." Black's reply was slow. "And if Balon tries to interfere, he will lose his seat beside God; come under much disfavor."

"Marvelous, Black," his mother's reply was edged with sarcasm. "There is hope for you yet."

The look the son gave was laced with hate. "I'm not a fool, Mother."

You'll be worse than a fool should you attempt to plot further against me, Roma thought. But her eyes remained cool. "I never suggested you were, Black. You're just young, that's all."

Black blinked, then vanished from the couch, to materialize in his room. How unimpressive, Roma thought. He can't even do that well. She sat alone in the study for a time, her thoughts many.

She wondered: When I was his age, was I that naive?

She ruefully admitted that it was difficult to remember. At that age, Louis XI was King of France and Columbus had a few years to go before conning the queen out of her jewels. And probably some pussy, Roma thought.

She thrust her eyes to the upstairs, to her son's room, grimacing as she watched him sitting in a chair, rubbing his shins. The fool had banged his legs when he materialized.

This will have to be my coup de grâce, she realized, not without some sadness. I am more than five hundred years old, I am tired, and have been everything from a whore to a nun; the former, she grimaced, much more preferable to the latter. If I can bring this off, I will assure myself a place by the smoking side of the Master. If I can somehow impregnate myself with Sam's seed—without cheating, too much—and if Nydia is a Christian and Falcon can plant his seeds within her . . . then we can leave the finest demons ever to walk the earth.

"Yes," the heavy voice cut into her head. "That would please me, assuring you a seat beside me."

Roma stiffened, asking, "How long have you been listening?"

"Long enough to realize that your son is a fool. Your son, not Balon's bastard."

"You know my son schemes against me?"

"My, how the plot thickens!" the devil howled with dark, burning laughter. "More and more curious, eh?"

The Lord of Flies grew silent. The room became warm. Roma remained still, waiting.

"Your foolish son is no match for Balon's boy-child of love, ancient one."

"I'm not that old."

"You're too old to be thinking of birthing any more children. You have many more years ahead of you on earth, serving me. You know to birth a demon at your age would mean death. It is written. And, Witch, remember this: there is no guarantee the demon would live."

Roma said, "He would—possibly *they* would—if you took a hand."

"Impossible."

"You mean you have given your word?" The question was put sarcastically.

The Lord of Foulness chuckled. "Not necessarily. In

139

part, perhaps."

"Nothing firm, then. So it is possible?"

"All things are possible, Roma-Nydia-Victoria-Adora-Zena-Ulrica-Willa-Toni-Sibyl . . . have I left any out?"

"Several," she said dryly, knowing the Master was reminding her of her age.

"All right, Roma: But what assurances do I have that you and Falcon *will* produce one of our own, and not some simpering, praying, puky Christian child?"

"If you take a hand, it is guaranteed. And then there is this: we can produce *true* demons."

"Nonsense! The last time that happened was more than a hundred years ago. Still . . ."

"It would be a coup against Him, would it not?"

"Yes." Just the thought of Him irritated the Master of Shit. "But you know to produce a true demon means excruciating pain; hours of unparalleled agony, and certain death for the Witch."

"I will do it for you, Master."

"Thank you. Very well, it is up to you, Roma. Do you remember the formula?"

"Yes."

"You may begin. I will help as I can."

Roma sat very quietly in the study as the roaring in her head changed from a howling, burning cacophony to a rush of colors, finally softening to a muted whisper before dying away.

Roma smiled. It was settled. She went in search of The Book.

In Sam's room, neither young person was surprised to see a large, canvas-covered object lying on the bed.

"Want to bet I can't tell you what's in that canvas?" Sam asked.

"No bet."

He opened the canvas pouch. A World War II issue .45 caliber Thompson submachine gun. A fully loaded drum and three fully loaded clips lay beside the weapon. A dozen boxes of .45 caliber ammunition made up the complement of lethal armament.

"Sam . . . ?"

"Don't ask. I can't answer your question. But you know as well as I where it came from."

"Your dad." It was not a question from her lips.

"Or one of his friends."

"I don't understand that."

Sam glanced at her while one hand rested on the old powerful Thompson. "God likes his warriors. Dad was a warrior. He would have warrior friends in . . . where he is. And, like it or not, I guess I'm a warrior."

"That gives me an eerie feeling."

"I'd hate to tell you what it gives me."

She read his thoughts. "Sam! Don't be sacrilegious."

He grinned boyishly. "I'm not. Just telling the truth."

She blushed, then gestured upward. "I'm not too certain what He would think about you having the . . . shits over a job you've been chosen to do—by Him."

"I'm sure He knows the feeling, Nydia. He made man in His image."

"You're a very lovely young lady," Falcon told Lana, smiling down at her. "I cannot imagine why the young men aren't chasing after you." And he could not rest the feeling that this young lady was hiding something.

141

"Are you really interested in knowing, Mr. Falcon?"

"Of course."

It was early afternoon at Falcon House, the sky gathering great dark clouds in advance of a storm. Falcon and Lana were alone in the downstairs study. The library room.

She gazed up into his dark eyes, eyes that masked the hunter's look. "Because I don't like what they do."

Falcon arched an eyebrow. "Oh? And what is it they do that is so repugnant to you?"

She walked to the great doors that separated the library from the study and closed them. She smiled as she became aware of the older man's eyes on her shapely derrière. She turned, walking slowly back to Falcon. "They practice Devil worship."

His laughter seemed out of place among the books that lined the walls. "Oh, my dear," he said, wiping his eyes. "Don't tell me you fell for that old joke? I thought Black had long ago given up that line."

"Joke?" Her eyes narrowed.

He placed a hand on her slender shoulder. "Just a joke, dear. Black has a rather . . . macabre sense of humor. But," he held up a warning finger, "don't let him—or anyone else—know I tipped his hand. Play along with the *bon mot*—excuse me, joke—right up to the end. It will be our secret."

"You mean that . . . you mean they don't practice Devil worship?"

"Oh, heavens no!" Falcon inwardly cringed at the hated word, hoping his Master would forgive him his blasphemy. "Oh, we'll have a fine old time with this, you and I. Just when Black thinks he has you convinced, we'll

142

jump up and turn the tables on him. He'll be hysterical; he'll see the joke. Black has a fine sense of humor."

"A joke," Lana whispered. She appeared to be relieved. "Just a joke."

Falcon chuckled and put his arms around her, gently pulling her to him. She rather liked the feel and the strength of the older man. Everything was going to plan. She pressed her face against the soft cloth of his smoking jacket, savoring the scent of his cologne. She had never smelled anything quite like it. It had just a touch of burning pine to it, mingled with a very pleasant scent of musk . . . and something else she could not define.

Falcon was equally enjoying the feel of the lush young lady against him. The feel of firm young breasts; the slight heat from her loins. Through centuries of practice, he kept his penis soft. "Oh, yes, dear. Just a joke. Oh, we'll have a fine time, you and I. It will be our little secret, right up to the culmination."

She looked up. "The culmination?"

"The height of it all, dear," he smiled, his dark eyes glowing with a hidden fire, "when we achieve the final summit."

"Of course," Lana breathed, her breath sweet.

"*Naturellement*," Falcon said. There was something very disturbing about this young lady.

After Lana had chosen a few books and left the room, Roma appeared in the center of the study, a slight odor of burning coals with her. "Well, Falcon, it seems you have assured yourself a place between her lovely legs. But what of the others?"

"All in due time, Roma. We have the time. But we must be careful not to *depasser les bornes*."

"I know the boundaries, Falcon. You just worry about your own perversions with pretty young things, *bon?*"

"*Oui.* I have missed you for several hours. Where have you been?"

"Speaking with someone not of this world, Falcon."

They both smiled, and the odor of burning sulfur seemed to grow stronger.

NINE

By midafternoon, the storm had struck, sending all its fury across the land: walls of rain hurled against the great house, the wind bending the trees in a grotesque dance of the elements, the silver liquid bullets of the Heavens hammered against the house. The storm intensified as Roma picked up a huge black book and began reading.

No mortal could have held the book's weight; no ten mortals could have held it, for the black-bound book contained the names of every human being who had ever been converted to the godless teachings of Satan. Every name, from the beginnings of time.

Roma hummed quietly as she flipped through the thousands of pages, the print so fine it would have taken a magnifying glass for a mortal to see anything other than a blur. She hummed a Faustian melody as she sought the page of her choice. It was not easy to find, for its words had rarely been investigated by those before Roma . . . those keepers of The Book. And it had been used even less. Then she ceased her humming as a smile creased her lips, the page and the evil words leaping at her eyes. Roma devoured the message, memorizing each ritual, each item needed. She closed the book as a satisfying sigh escaped her lips.

Falcon appeared in the center of the room, his face

145

dark with fury . . . and concern for the witch. "I cannot believe you are really contemplating this!"

"It need not concern you." Her reply was cold. "Your participation is minimal."

"Everything you do concerns me."

"Only to the point it gains some end for you."

"I'll not allow that remark to offend me, Roma. My dear, don't you realize this could well be your götterdämmerung?"

She shook her head. "Nothing quite that dramatic, I assure you. That is still in the future. But if you mean my death, yes, I know that."

"And still you persist?"

"For our Master, yes."

"I will try to be there at . . . the end. To help in whatever manner I can."

"No. That cannot be. You have never read the instructions?"

He shrugged. "Why should I? Birthing a demon is not the forte of a warlock."

"Only those women who are as we can be present. But you can help in the preparation."

"Tell me what I must do."

"I need the blood of a nonbeliever. That is where we must start."

Falcon sighed, walking to her, taking her hand. "I am really quite fond of you, Roma."

She jerked her hand from his. "Don't become maudlin. You know the only love we may experience is that which we feel for the Master."

"Yes. But I see now why you are doing this thing."

She looked up at him.

"You fell in love with Balon, didn't you?"

Her steady gaze did not waver.

"You don't have to go to this extreme in penitence, Roma. It wasn't that terrible a deed."

"It isn't atonement, Falcon. Put that out of your mind. I merely wish to leave a legacy—some part of me."

"Say it all, Roma," he urged her. "Share it with me—our feelings."

She shook her head. "No. That is past."

"That's not what I mean."

And the thoughts of the witch and the warlock were mingled: what if they failed here at Falcon House? What if all the plans of the Master came to naught? What then?

"I must say it," Falcon said. "You believe there is a chance we will fail?"

"Balon's love child has powers even he doesn't know about—yet. The young man might never have to bring them into play. Yes, he could beat us. So any demon child we produce is simply insurance against the future. I have the Master's permission to do this, so it is settled. And you will have to play a part with Nydia."

"We don't know she is Christian."

"I believe she is."

The witch and the warlock looked at each other for several seconds. Falcon then nodded his head. "I will do my part."

"Always remembering that right up to the last moment, we must attempt to convert them."

"Yes."

"But we may as well gather what we can—just in case. I need blood. The nonbeliever must not die, for we will have to return again and again." Their thoughts were shared. "Yes," Roma said. "She will do." She touched her neck. "Tonight, Falcon. Do it."

He vanished.

Everlasting life; eternal youth; beauty for the women, never-failing virility for the men; an orgy that would span time; an end to the mundane worries that plague mortals. That is what the Lord of Darkness had promised the Coven members of Whitfield in return for their pledge of service to him. For a nether world here on God's earth. Just one spot that would truly be the kingdom of the damned; of the Cloven hoof. Then, as time trudged on, the disciples of Mephistopheles could spread slowly outward, carrying the message born in the smoking pits to others, until the Prince of Filth ruled a county, a state, a country, or a world.

All was ready. The churches of Whitfield no longer held any trace of the Lord God: the crosses were hanging upside down; the altars were draped in black; the instruments of Holy Communion were filled with the vilest of liquids . . . all was in ready to receive the Prince of Darkness.

The word was received: Let it begin.

Falcon slipped down the quiet hall of the great house, pausing often to listen. But any slight sound he might have made was muted by the clashing of the storm as it battered the land. At a bedroom door, he stood for a time, a smile playing across his lips. He tried the door knob. Unlocked. He eased the door open and let his eyes play across the form of the girl sprawled in deep sleep on the bed.

Judy was a true Christian, Black had said, loyal to her God and His teachings.

She won't be for long, Falcon smiled, the lips pulling

back in a grisly leer, exposing the true direction of his long, bloody life. Fangs now marred the perfection of his ivory smile; his tongue was swollen, crimson as it throbbed with anticipation, mentally savoring the hot burst of living blood.

Falcon slipped into the room, quietly closing the door behind him, the noise of the heavy storm covering his soft footsteps. Standing over the bed, he began a low incantation, his deep voice soothing the young woman, edging her deeper into sleep, the slumber becoming a state of deep hypnosis as his voice touched her dulling senses. Falcon pushed her through the stages of induced sleep, until finally she was secure in the deep somnambulistic state of controlled sleep . . . and then past that into sleep controlled by the Master of the Black Arts, Ruler of the Netherworld.

Falcon gently slipped the thin cover from her body, licking his lips at the sight of her young beauty, his blood-red tongue bumping over the fangs on either side of his mouth, the points of the fangs arousing the engorged organ.

Judy was a dark-haired young beauty, the dark brown hair spilling over the whiteness of the pillow, shining with cleanliness and health. Falcon touched the silkiness of youth, entwining his fingers in the strands, loving the feel of her. For a moment he sat on the edge of the bed, a dozen emotions playing within his head. He recalled through the years that he had once done the same in Spain, centuries ago, with a lovely young lady who had a calling to be a nun. She had slept in a magnificent villa on the coast while Falcon had toyed with her, finally taking her. He smiled at the recall.

Judy lay on her side, clad only in the scantiest of bra

and pantie. The young ladies now, Falcon noted, no matter how pristine they pretend to be, do enjoy the loveliest of undergarments. He touched the softness of inner thigh, and the young woman stirred at his finger touch, sighing above the noise of the raging storm, stirring in her sleep. Falcon whispered a soothing phrase and she turned onto her back, her legs parting. He flipped the front clasp to her lacy bra, and young breasts sprang free, firm and rose-tipped, the nipples slightly erect from the rush of cool air.

"Lovely," Falcon breathed.

He bent his head and allowed his swollen tongue to touch one nipple, working at the tautness. She moved under the tongue play, her small hands clenching into fists at her side. He moved his mouth downward, between the young breasts, licking down her stomach, to the slight mound of her lower belly. He rolled the brief pantie from her, past the edge of pubic hair, uncovering the sweetness of her mons veneris. Bending his head, Falcon tasted the freshness of youth, his swelling, protruding tongue dipping into the sudden moisture of her.

He pulled away before his sensuality became too great to be controlled and he would have been forced to mount the sleeping beauty. That would have to wait. But it would be. Again, a smile played a macabre dance on his lips. Perhaps, soon, he could mount her as he sipped her life's blood, both of them climaxing just as life left her, just at that moment when her heart convulsed and died. That was one of Falcon's greatest thrills, and it occurred only too rarely.

Falcon put his hand on her soft belly, allowing his fingers to slide downward, to gently caress the mound of

Venus, one finger softly parting and entering the folds of her. She moaned under the digital intrusion, and Falcon placed his mouth to hers, her breath hot and sweet as she experienced a burst of lascivious pleasure, her juices wetting her thighs. In her deep mesmeric slumber, she began to move on the bed in approaching climax, Falcon's finger encountering no resistance of maidenhead as it plunged deeper into the satin heat of female.

He sensed she was very close to climax as her knees came up and her soft thighs closed, entrapping his hand and pleasuring finger, his thumb on her clitoris, rubbing the hard erectile of the vulva, swollen now in sexual enjoyment.

Just as Judy began to shiver in the throes of first climax, Falcon dipped his mouth to her neck and worked his fangs into the carotid artery just behind her ear. For a moment he greedily sucked at the flow of warm blood from her thrashing body. The liquid, thick and rich, filled his mouth and dribbled down his thirsty throat, the warm, slightly salty taste enriching him, flooding him with vitality. He removed a vial from his pocket and held it against Judy's neck, beneath his teeth, filing the small bottle with blood. She gasped as climax lunged through her, then sighed as the warm aftermath filled her with lingering contentment.

Falcon eased his fangs from her neck, licking away the last drops of crimson from the closing puncture wounds. He removed his finger from her and dressed her as he had found her, covering her with the sheet. The storm raged on.

"Sleep well, my dear," Falcon said. "For you are now one of us. Whether you will remain as such, only time

151

will tell. But I shall be back."

He returned to Roma, to give her the first of many ingredients, and to satisfy the aching in his loins. The storm beat on as the witch and the warlock coupled, Roma screaming out a mixture of pain and pleasure as she was impaled on Falcon's huge erection.

And while Sam and Nydia slept in each other's arms, content if not safe, and Judy slowly drifted out of her hypnotic state, dreaming of being tired, Adam kneeled in front of Lane's nakedness and took pleasure in homosexual love. Lana slept soundly, a slight smile on her lips. Linda dreamed of eternal youth and beauty, a dream she often materialized in sleep. Chad and Burt and Lester took their pleasures with Sandy and Vicky and Carol and Madge and Anne: a daisy chain of debauchery as the storm raged. Black caressed the nakedness of Susan prior to mounting her, her cries of pain-pleasure filling the room as Black's manhood filled her.

And in the caves beneath the land, behind the great house, the Beasts waited. The storm did not disturb them: they had seen many storms, and they knew they had nothing to fear from the elements. It was what walked above them, that human the old one had told them about they must be wary of.

Jimmy Perkins sat in a chair in his living quarters above the garage and slowly masturbated, his thoughts of Nydia. He fantasized of having sex with her; all sorts of sex, from the norm to the bizarre. He spilled his semen on the floor and leaned back in the chair. He felt better, but it was not enough . . . self-abuse never is. The time was growing near, and Jimmy wanted real sex and warm blood.

152

Nydia's blood.

He rose from the chair, zipping up his pants, letting himself out of the room. He slipped through the dark afternoon. Perhaps he could not have the daughter of the witch this day, but there was always one of the others. And if he could not have one of the young women, there was always one of the young men. Falcon had promised him—in a manner of speaking—he could take one of the young men.

"Any hole in a storm," Jimmy chuckled, proud of himself for his burst of human humor.

But five seconds later he could not remember why he had been chuckling.

Jane Ann looked across the street at the Cleveland house. The family had gathered on the front yard, staring at her house. The five of them stood in silence, staring. She turned to look at the mist of Balon.

"Why are they waiting?"

"For instruction," Balon projected.

"From Satan?"

"Yes."

"The others will be all right, Sam? Those at Miles's house?"

"Yes. The golem will protect them. But they will have to help. And they will."

"The golem can't be destroyed?"

"Not by a mortal. Not this one."

"Only by God?"

"Yes."

"How is that possible?"

"The golem is earth. He is air. He is water. God made

all those things. How is it possible to destroy something that God made without His permission?"

"We seem to be doing quite well with pollution and nuclear proliferation."

"The answer is contained within your statement."

"I . . . see."

"No, you don't. But you will."

"I'll have to be very strong, won't I?"

"Stronger than you have ever been before. The Prince of Filth will test your faith. He will tell you he will stop the pain, the degradation, the humiliation . . . if only you will renounce your faith in God. And he will not be lying."

"It will be terribly painful, won't it, Sam?"

"I cannot lie. Yes."

"But others have endured it."

"Yes. And so shall you."

Jane Ann folded her arms under her breasts and turned her attentions to the street. A crowd had gathered, with the Cleveland family leading the rabble. "They're coming."

"Yes."

"What must I do?"

"Let them attempt to take you."

"And then?"

"They will discover the awesome power of the Almighty."

"Through you?"

"Yes."

"He could stop all this, couldn't He?"

"With one gesture of His hand."

"Then why doesn't He?"

"Humankind must find their own way, Janey. He gave them a brain, the power to think, to reason. And He gave them compassion, if they will but use it. He gave them everything . . . all things to create a world of good. It is up to humankind to decide which path they will take."

"Hey, bitch!" the harsh voice rang from the yard. "I got about nine inches of cock I'd like to shove up your ass just to listen to you holler."

Jane Ann looked for the mist of Balon. But the mist was gone. She almost went into a panic. Then she saw the tenacles of vapor hovering over the Bible. The mist seemed to be drawing strength from the Word of God.

"Hey, Janey!" Tony's voice rang out. "How about comin' out here and givin' some of that good pussy to my buddies?"

"How can one man change so?" Jane Ann muttered.

"Very easily," Balon projected. "The Dark One offers much to those who are less to begin with."

"A caste sytem in Heaven? Really, Sam!"

"Step out on the porch, Janey," Balon told her. "Let them see you are not afraid."

"But I am afraid."

"You are afraid of what awaits you at the end, not of what confronts you now."

Jane Ann opened the door and stepped onto the porch. She looked at Steve Cleveland. "What do you want, Steve?"

"Some of your pussy, baby," he said, and stepped forward, reaching for her arm.

Steve recoiled backward, his face on fire, the bubbling and popping of burning flesh filling the late afternoon air. He began screaming, running from the house, dashing into the road, where he tripped on the curb and fell into the gutter, to lay screaming out his life as the fire intensified, his head engulfed in flames.

"You like the fire of your Master?" Balon's heavy voice cut through the afternoon. "Then enjoy it. Here . . . let me introduce you to God's power."

A woman erupted in flames, her body seeming to explode. A man standing beside her suddenly found his feet on fire, the flames spreading upward, engulfing him. The man and woman ran blindly down the sidewalk, howling in pain. They fell heavily, beating their feet on the concrete as they felt the pain of their brains cooking. Their wails soon diminished into low moans as life began to leave them. Steve Cleveland had already passed into the misty veil, slipping through, the wind sighing as he met his Dark Master's world.

"Whores and bastards!" Balon's voice sent waves of fear through the panicked crowd. "Leave. Get out! Your time for her will come soon enough . . . but not now. Get out!"

They needed no further urgings. They ran in all directions, Tony leading the pack. The Devil's spokeswoman, Jean, had not told them anything like this would happen. They ran to her.

And The Tempter watched all that was happening, watched it glumly. He simply could not believe his enemy had bestowed so much power in Balon. That was not at all like Him. Surely He did not believe that simpering whore, Jane Ann, was worth all this? Unless . . . the Dark One pondered, unless . . . He *knew* she would meet the challenge at the end. No! the Ruler of the Netherworld rejected that. No! Not even He would go so far. Or would He?

He shifted his never-closing eyes to the house of the Jew and Jewess. If that damnable lump of clay was with life . . . with breath from that . . . meddler in the sky . . . that would be an insult just too great for him to tolerate.

Satan saw half of what was once a human member of his Coven go flying through the air, the torso leaking blood and intestines and organs. The golem stood like a massive fortress in the center of the yard: a sentry against the forces of evil. The golem held one of Satan's people in one huge hand. Then, with no more effort than was required to open an envelope, the golem ripped off both arms and sent them flying across the street, where they smashed through a picture window.

The armless body screamed and flopped on the sidewalk, thick crimson gushing from empty arm sockets. He lay squalling in helpless agony.

Satan's forces scattered in fear and blind panic. The golem lumbered slowly up the walkway and sat down on the porch. A giant gray man, without features, without emotion. Here only to serve God's people.

"You son of a cosmic whore!" Satan screamed his message to the firmament. "We made a deal after Prague."

"I make no deals with you, Lord of All That Is Ugly." The silent voice filled the sky, heard only by the demon of all demons.

"Why here?" Satan howled his outrage. "Why for these five people? Why not in Israel?"

"The people of Israel can take care of themselves—as the world is rapidly discovering. And how do you know I haven't helped there?"

But Satan was in no mood for questions and answers. "All bets are off, you son of a bitch! We agreed twenty years ago, over this very spot, that I would leave Balon's bastards to their own wiles; in return, you would leave me this miserable village. You lied!"

"I do not recall any such agreement."

And while Satan howled and screamed his outrage at this supposed trickery on the part of God, the Almighty brooded among the thousands of worlds under His command.

Had He placed too much on the young man from Balon's seed? Was the young man mature enough to victoriously fight the odds against him? He had given the young man powers far beyond any He had given any other in many years . . . or rather, He smiled . . . Balon had.

The Heavens winked at the smile.

All right, He had done all He could do. Far more than He ordinarily did. It was time to withdraw. To think. Because there was the matter of His mighty ageless warrior, who was becoming restless, anticipating a fight between good and evil on earth, and wanting very much to be a part in any upcoming confrontation.

There was that to think about.

"The black mass that starts the ordeal will begin tonight," Sam said, startling Nydia. "Both here and in Whitfield."

She stirred in his arms. "How do you know that?"

"I just know," Sam replied in a whisper.

They lay on the bed in Sam's room, listening to the howl and rage of the storm as it slammed the mansion. They were fully clothed, and had not made love that day.

158

The impact of the knowledge that they were half brother and sister had finally hit home, sobering them, and, to some extent, frightening them.

"Your father told you?" she asked.

Sam's reply was a long time coming. When he did speak, his voice was hushed. "One of them."

TEN

Jimmy slipped through the huge house, knowing he was deluding no one of his kind, and knowing that, in all probability, he would be stopped before he could culminate his mission. But he had to try, for the urges rearing up in him had grown too powerful to suppress and too wild to placate with his hand and thoughts. He knew he was not as intelligent as he had once been, back when he was a policeman in Whitfield, so many years ago.

And as quickly as the thought came to him, it was removed from his mind, leaving the near zombie standing dumbly in the dim hallway, wondering what he had been thinking.

Jimmy heard a door open and ducked behind drapes in the hall. Peeking through the crack in the heavy drapes, he watched Balon's bastard son walk down the hall, past him, and into the stairwell leading downward. He listened to the footfall until they faded.

Quickly, Jimmy shuffled to Nydia's door. He stood listening for a moment, hearing the young beauty humming a soft tune. His erection was throbbing, his groin aching, his tongue swollen as he placed his hand on the doorknob and gently turned the brass.

Nydia was naked, all her beauty exposed to Jimmy's hot eyes: the full, mature breasts, rose-tipped; the heavy bush between her legs. He could not see her face for it was turned from him.

Jimmy pushed the door open a bit farther, ready to step inside and take her, by force if necessary, when a hand fell on his shoulder, hauling him bodily out of the door, the door closing soundlessly behind him, the loveliness cut off from view.

Jimmy turned to look into the fathomless eyes of Falcon. "Not her," the tall man whispered. "Never her, Jimmy. Not unless you wish to die ten thousand agonizing deaths a year for all eternity."

Jimmy dared to argue, so great was his need. "She is one of His now—what difference does it make?"

"Fool!" Falcon hissed at him, leading the man from the door, down the hall. "Your Master has other plans for her, and they do not include you. Now leave this wing immediately, and do not return—ever—without orders from Roma or me. Go!"

He watched as Jimmy shuffled off, his shoulders slumped in rejection. The man was becoming more and more a buffoon, his usefulness almost past. Falcon could not understand why Roma kept him alive. And then Falcon chuckled without mirth. Of course: he was the last reminder of her love for Balon. How typically female.

His eyes narrowed as the thought of the girl behind the closed door entered his mind. Falcon could understand Jimmy's desire, for Nydia was of astonishing beauty and very much worthy of any man's attention. Even Falcon had entertained thoughts of entering her; fantasizing of her moaning beneath him as he gave her more cock than mere mortals could ever possess.

And now he had that permission to do just that. But only when Roma gave the word. His smile became a thing

161

of ugliness as he thought of the girl's satin-smooth flesh, all hot beneath him.

He abruptly turned away, slipping quietly down the hall then up the stairs to his rooms. There he began to dress for the mass that evening. Once the mass was under way, and the true Master was called, no one would be allowed to leave this area, and only those who practiced the Black Arts could enter. Falcon House and the area surrounding it would be as unattainable as a lost planet in a black hole of space.

And then, Falcon smiled, hefting his penis, the party could really begin.

"We have no virgin for the ceremony," Roma said as she prepared to dress for the mass.

"Lana," Falcon corrected. "She has never been penetrated."

"I . . . am hesitant to use her," Roma said, slipping out of her gown, standing naked in the room. "There is . . . something about her that disturbs me."

"Yes," Falcon agreed. "I picked up on the same troublesome vibes. Pity. She is very pretty." Falcon thought no more of it as he became aware of a heating in his groin and a slight stirring of the massive organ that hung between his legs. Like Roma, he, too, was naked, very carefully choosing his robes for the ceremony.

"We can't use Judy," Roma mused, as much to herself as to Falcon. "She is now one of us. And I will need more blood from her."

"The pretty little Linda, then?"

"I . . . think not," Roma replied, glancing at the clock on the dresser. Their eyes met in reflection from the mirror. The mouths smiled. "She thinks she is fooling us, you know?"

"Yes," Falcon agreed with a smile. "But we know what she is."

"We'll let her play her little game."

Falcon looked at the witch, thinking how beautiful she still was . . . and how desirable. He stroked his penis, feeling it fill with hot blood under his touch.

Roma laughed at him. "Contain yourself, Falcon. Sometimes I believe your brains are located in your cock."

"I believe Wilder once said your brains were situated between your legs, Roma—did he not?"

She sat down naked at her dresser and began to brush her raven hair. Falcon walked up behind her to cup her full breasts, gently pinching the nipples, feeling them grow beneath his touch. She turned, kissing his penis.

"Wilder made a mistake," she said.

"Yes. Yes, I believe he did."

"We will defile one of the boys." Roma made her decision. "They have all had dinner and should be drugged by now."

Falcon frowned his distaste. "How droll, Roma. You know how I dislike pederastic sacrifices."

"Black rather enjoys them," she reminded him. "As you noted earlier."

"Yes, and I say again: Black is weak, and even for our standards, not quite normal."

Her face expressed her concern. "So the Master reminded me. Failure, failure," she shook her head. "I will not fail this time."

Falcon bent his head to kiss her, recoiling only slightly as he observed that her teeth were suddenly fanged. Their tongues touched gingerly, Falcon saying, "So that is how it will be?"

"Yes." Her smile was grotesque. "Howard will know the pain of our world at the point of my son's climax."

"Sometimes, Roma," Falcon said, pulling away from her, "your humor is hideous."

She shrugged. "I have never professed any desire toward becoming a comedienne, darling." She snapped at him playfully, laughing as he jerked away from her flashing fangs.

Nydia emerged from the bathroom looking pale. "That's the very first time in my life I ever forced myself to vomit," she said. "How do you feel, Sam?"

"A little weak." He opened a napkin and took out several rolls, handing one to her. "Eat this, it'll give you strength. You'll need it. I don't think they could drug the bread."

They sat on the edge of the bed, sharing their meager dinner, their stomachs accepting the bread after the self-induced vomiting.

Sam glanced at his watch. "What did you tell your mother?"

"That we were tired and were going to rest for a while."

"Her reaction?"

"She smiled and said that was probably a good idea. Sam? You seem to know a lot about what is going to happen—when will the mass take place?"

"Tonight. Full dark. That's what popped into my head. And we're going to be there, watching."

Her voice was filled with fear as she asked, "Do we have to?"

"Yes. I want to know just who is involved. Who I have

164

to destroy."

She trembled beside him. "Why did I suddenly get this feeling we have passed the point of no return?"

And just as Sam took her hand into his, some small thing touched him, touched him inwardly, striking with a hard but invisible force. "Because we have."

They had gathered.

Among the circle of dark stones, the worshipers of the Dark One had silently grouped. The servants, including Jimmy Perkins; the ten young men and women who wished to serve a new Master; Roma and Falcon and Black. Howard stood naked inside the inner circle, his eyes glazed from the drugs in his system. The torchlight reflected dully from the scarcely comprehending eyes of the young man. Outside the circle of people, the Beasts had gathered quietly, more than a dozen of them. They stood patiently, slobber leaking from massive jaws, their eyes glowing red with evil anticipation. For they knew should someone die at a high mass, they would feast well on that night.

Roma went among the new members, cutting off a small piece of hair from each head, then she walked to a stone where The Book rested. Their names were carefully recorded in that evil book, the hair placed beside the name.

Just as we have done for hundreds of years, Roma silently mused. As I personally have done for more than four hundred of those years, and those before me for thousands, all the way back to the caves . . . and beyond, before the first flood.

Roma cut her eyes to Howard's nakedness as a feeling of something very much amiss struck her. Something was all wrong. Falcon sensed it as well, walking swiftly to her side.

"What's wrong?" he asked, his voice low.

"The Master is here. And he is angry."

"What about?"

"I don't know."

The voice of the Ruler of the Netherworld boomed in their heads, thundering to them in a roar only they could hear. "Is this the best you can do? One shivering male?"

Roma thrust her thoughts to the Ruler of Hell: "We did not think you would object."

"You did not think!" Satan roared, causing them both to cringe. "That much is correct. Look at your idiot son, Roma. Look at him stroking his organ, practically drooling at the mouth like a Beast as he thinks about man love. Disgusting! And the son that should have been mine is crouched not a thousand meters from the circle, watching with your daughter. The daughter that should be taking part in this ceremony . . . worshiping me! You have failed me, Roma. Don't fail again. Wilder warned me you had a streak of decency in you; a very narrow streak, to be sure, but nevertheless . . . there.

"What in the name of all that is unholy have I *ever* done to deserve you two? This should be easy. The world is spinning about in utter chaos; wars breaking out everywhere; morals finally declining at a satisfying rate of deterioration; drugs and free sex and . . . oh, for pity's sake! Do I have to lecture the both of you? If so, I have failed miserably.

"Now, you hear me well, witch and warlock: the both of you will not fail this time. These are my commands: you will establish a Coven on these grounds; to insure that, I have ordered more members in, to reinforce this

166

group. They will be here tonight. You, Roma, will give me a demon son from the seed of Balon's bastard; you, Falcon, will give me a bitch demon from the womb of Nydia. But test them before you seduce them—as God is doing—see if they are worthy of my touch. You must offer them ample opportunity to leave, and allow them to do so if that is their choice. Of course," the Devil chuckled, "you can also ambush them on their way out."

The torches smoked for a few moments, the circle of stones silent in the flickering light. Then Satan roared.

"Do either of you really think I care how you accomplish any of this? I don't care how you go about it. I don't care if there is a sacrifice this night. I put the sacrifice business in the mind of that fool writer a thousand years ago . . . it's been repeated ever since. Why is *everything* I say constantly taken out of context? Can't I make a joke occasionally? After all, I was once an angel, and a goddamned good one, if I do say so myself. I'm not humorless. I gave the world Pilate, Hitler, and rock and roll music, didn't I?

"No, Roma, Falcon, you will not fail me. I want to hear the screaming of those puky holy people; I want to hear the wailing as their blood stains the ground, and I want to see a demon burst forth from your womb, and a matching bitch from the cunt of your *Christian* daughter.

"There are no rules—none! I have this precognition that I am going to be defeated in Whitfield. Very well. I can live with that; I can accept it. I will derive some satisfaction from it, however: the wailing and begging of Balon's Christian whore as she is ravaged and flogged and finally nailed naked onto my cross. And, no, you may rest your fears, Balon will not interfere here. He'll be much too busy back in Whitfield, with that impossible golem.

"No, that meddler from the firmament broke His word, even though He denies it, so I see no need for many rules. But you two hear me well: I want blood, pain, degradation, filth . . . everything *we* believe in . . . and more. Tell your fool son to mount the male if that is what he desires; he will never be anything other than a stooge to me. Failure, Roma. You failed with both your latest children. But at least, and it pains me to say this, Nydia did accept *something*; she is faithful to *something*. Which is much more than can be said of that foolish son of yours. He disgusts me. Scheming, plotting, foolish, foolish boy.

"It is doubtful I shall return here until you have completed your assignments. I must return west. That psalm singer broke His word, thinks He has *me* fooled; thinks I believe He has departed. Well, I don't trust Him. I know He's got something up His sleeve—I just don't know what. Be careful: Balon's goody-two-shoes son has tremendous powers, which is another reason I'm sending in help. So, good-bye. *And don't fail me!*"

"Something happened," Sam whispered. "I feel as if I was locked in some kind of time warp, where everything stood still."

"Me, too," Nydia said, returning the whisper. "Look! Roma and Falcon are moving now."

"They were speaking with Satan."

"How do you know that?"

"Some . . . one just told me."

She looked at him in the darkness, her eyes wide and scared. "Who?"

"I don't know."

Nydia suddenly gasped. "My God!" She grabbed at

168

Sam's arm. "Look at that."

Both of them grimaced their shock and horror as Howard was led to the dark altar by two servants and Black began his sodomy of the young man. Howard screamed his outrage and pain, fighting against hands that held him while Black laughed as he forced the ugliness.

Howard screamed again, his cries echoing around the small valley. Roma ran to the scene of rape, her black robe open, exposing her nakedness, the stones preventing Sam and Nydia from seeing what was taking place. They could but wonder what the witch was doing.

Kneeling in front of the altar, Roma sank her teeth into the femoral artery of Howard's thigh, the blood gushing from the fang bites, spilling over her face and lips. She drank greedily of the hot red liquid, biting him again and again, working steadily upward, until his thigh and groin area were pricked with the needle marks.

She drew away from him, her face covered with blood. Howard's cries tapered off into low moans as Black began shivering with approaching climax. The Beasts began dancing, a grotesque, obscene hunching, a debasement of any rhythm that needed grace or beauty. Soon all were dancing and chanting: "Prince of Darkness! King of the Night! Lord of the Flies and of Filth! Hear this one scream for you!"

Howard screamed as Black climaxed. The Coven members danced about the altar, tearing off their clothes. Howard lay unconscious across the altar.

Falcon pointed to the young man draped in humiliation across the flat stone altar. "Tend to his needs," he ordered.

Then, oblivious to the cold and the damp, the men and

women coupled like animals, their naked bodies gleaming in the torch-lit circle of stones.

The naked Satan worshipers began fucking like dogs, while the Beasts danced and howled and slobbered around them, their own erections starkly vivid in the flickering light.

Roma took Jimmy into her ageless cunt, while Falcon impaled a screaming Sandy against the damp ground, the young woman suddenly filled with his massive organ. She screamed her pleasure-pain and wrapped young legs around the older man's back, meeting him lunge for lunge, shrieking out her evil joy. She cried blasphemies, flinging the oaths into the night air, her shrill voice seeming to push the others into more profane, perverted acts.

"I've seen enough," Sam said, taking Nydia's hand, leading her away from the circle of flickering lights, back toward the house. They were dressed in dark clothing, blending into the night as they walked.

As they walked away from the blasphemous screaming and cursing, from the scene of Devil worship, Nydia said, "I get the feeling mother knew we were watching. You?"

"Yes. And I think Satan told her we were."

"That . . . feeling of being suspended for a time."

"Yes." They waited in silence for a time, Sam breaking the mood by asking, "I wonder what my mother is doing?"

"You should have seen Hershel do his stuff this afternoon," Miles excitedly told Jane Ann over the phone. The only two phones belonging to believers that

170

still worked in Whitfield, although the plugs had been pulled and the wires severed by phone-company personnel. "Those people who have been so crappy to us for the past year don't act so high and mighty now."

"Sam didn't do so badly himself," she replied. She looked around for the mist that was Balon. She could not see any evidence of the vapor, but she knew he was present.

"Janey? We're all right here. I don't understand what is happening; why this has to happen; why God just doesn't take us if that is His will . . . but you, are you doing all right?"

"I was afraid, Miles. But Sam comforted me. I prayed. You?"

"Like I haven't been away from synagogue for fifty years."

"Doris?"

"Like a mountain of faith. Janey? I don't understand any of this. It's so baffling. Are we being tested? Is that it? If so, why? What have we done with our lives that makes us so worthy . . . or unworthy, as the case may be? What does Sam say?"

"He says we will all understand someday."

"How like him." Miles's reply was dryly put. "Stay strong, Jane Ann. Our prayers will be with you, at the end," the last words were filled with emotion.

"You know what is going to happen?"

Her old friend's silence told her he knew only too well.

"I'll talk to you later," she said. She hung up the phone and turned to face the rear wall of the den as she sensed Balon's presence. "Have you been away?" she asked the forming mist.

171

"Part of me," Balon projected.

"I won't ask how that is possible."

"You're learning."

"Eight more days," she said, some of her fear returning, changing the tone of her voice.

"Put it out of your mind," Balon told her. "Think only of how pleasant it will be later."

"I wonder how our son is doing?"

The mist seemed to smile. Balon said: "Our son has more going for him than he realizes."

"What do you mean?"

"Exactly what I said."

"Do you always speak in riddles?"

"I do not speak in riddles. Those who are not yet a part of my world do occasionally interpret my words as riddles."

She sighed. "It's hours past full dark, Sam."

A scream cut the night, a wail of agony so intense it sawed at Jane Ann's flesh like a knife with a dull cutting edge.

"I thought we were the only ones who would be subjected to . . . whatever?"

"No. There are people in this town, this locale, who have professed to be Christians. Their lives were lies. Liars, cheats, hypocrites, imposters pretending to serve the Lord God. Many of them. Now they beg for His mercy. But it is too late. It will not come."

"I thought our God was a just God, Sam?"

"He is. But humankind must help. Humankind was not put here on earth with a blank book, Janey. The book is the Word of God. Humankind understands that; they just won't—many of them—follow His Word. Now they must pay for their sins."

"Sam? Answer this for me, if you can: isn't it true that God answers all prayers?"

"Yes. In His own way."

"Drop the other shoe, Sam. In plain English."

The mist seemed to sigh, then projected: "More often than not, the answer is no."

ELEVEN

Sam and Nydia made it back to the mansion just
seconds before the Coven members summoned by their
Master arrived, pulling up to Falcon House in half a
dozen automobiles and vans. The young man and woman
stood in their quarters, the lights out, the rooms dark,
watching the Devil worshipers leave the vehicles,
walking up the steps to the house. Not all of them were
willing participants: some fought the hands that held
them; some were crying; a few were little more than
children.

Nydia closed the drapes and stood for a moment, Sam's
arms around her. "Those poor little girls down there,"
she sobbed, pressing her face against his chest, crying
and trembling with fear. Finally, overcoming her terror
and horror, she pulled away from her young man and
turned on the bureau lamp. She looked at the bed,
gasped, one hand flying to her mouth. She pointed.

On the bed was Sam's Bible, open, two chapters circled
in red. And his beret, his Ranger beret he carried with
him in his luggage, whenever he traveled, lying beside the
Bible.

Sam was no longer shocked by the surprises that
occurred around him; his mind had accepted the
knowledge that there were some things that could not be

explained . . . so be it. He walked to the bed, looked at his beret, touched it, then answered Nydia's as yet unasked question.

"I worked and sweated my butt off to get this. I'm very proud of it."

He touched the red that outlined the chapter in the Bible.

"What . . . is it?" she asked.

"Blood. Marking Revelation, chapters twelve and thirteen."

"Blood! Whose blood?"

Sam shook his head. "I don't know. Let's read this."

They sat on the edge of the bed, reading in silence for a few moments, trying to comprehend the message contained therein.

"I've never read the Bible before," Nydia admitted. "Except for a few quick peeps at friends' homes. But it sounds absolutely fascinating."

"It is. Nydia, I don't understand any of this. What does the blood have to do with this?"

"There!" She pointed at a passage. She read aloud. "'And they overcame him by the blood of the lamb.' Could that be it?"

"I . . . don't think so. I just don't know. Mother said that my real father often told her the Bible was vague, given to many different interpretations. But look here . . . right there," he pointed, and read aloud, "'And I saw one of his heads as it were wounded to death; and his deadly wound was healed; and all the world wondered after the beast.

"'And they worshiped the dragon which gave power unto the beast: and they worshiped the beast, saying, Who *is* like unto the beast? who is able to make war with him?'"

They both read the remaining verses of the chapter in silence, Nydia finally saying, "It could mean so many things, Sam. Michael was a warrior, right?"

"One hell of a warrior."

"Sam . . . !" she gave him a disapproving look for his paradoxical statement. "Anyway . . . warriors fight. Blood is spilled . . . right?"

"Yeah," he admitted reluctantly. "Could be you're right."

"Is the beast the Devil?"

"I . . . guess so."

"You're a preacher's son, Sam. You're supposed to know these things."

"I'm a backslider, honey. Not a very good Christian."

She kissed his cheek. "I don't believe that, Sam. Not for a second. Michael cast out Satan, right?"

"That's what it says."

"So . . . of all the angels in Heaven, who would be the one most likely to help someone fight the Devil?"

Sam looked at her in the dim light. The look he gave her was of extreme uncertainty. "Are you . . . Nydia, are you saying that Michael is helping me? That he is *here?*"

"I don't know, Sam. Maybe he isn't here; maybe he doesn't have to be here, yet, to do these things."

"Yet?"

"Let me finish. Was your father a warrior?"

"A war hero. Yeah, he was a warrior."

"Who would he most likely make friends with . . . uh . . . up there?" She pointed upward.

"Honey, this is getting a little bit farfetched. When was the last time you recall any angels appearing here on earth?"

"Well . . . how would we know, really? I mean, people might not want to speak of the sighting, right?"

"You have a point. Yeah. For fear of being laughed at. I . . . seem to recall reading that Michael did appear to help—in some way—with Joan of Arc."

"All right. Your father had to have appeared to give you that envelope, didn't he? He's in Whitfield right now, isn't he?"

"Yeah. But my father isn't an angel."

"How do you know that?"

Sam shrugged. "I don't."

Before either could say another word, a light tap sounded at the door. Sam sighed heavily and stood up. "Put away the Bible, Nydia. No sense tempting the gods—from either end of the spectrum."

He opened the door. Roma stood looking at him, her dark eyes burning with a strange light.

"Mrs. Williams. Excuse me: Roma," Sam corrected. "It's late for a social call, isn't it?"

"Oh, I assure you, Sam Balon King. This is no social call."

He smiled. "All bets down, the pot's right, and time for the last card, right?"

She laughed. "Oh, my dear, you are your father's son. Yes, darling, time for a little chat."

"Between good and evil?"

She shrugged, the movement lifting her breasts, and she noted that Sam noticed. She had changed into a gown of dark blue, floor length, cut low, the *V* dipping far into the swell of her breasts. "Good and evil, Sam? Well, perhaps. Tell me: how far have you taken my daughter into the candy-coated world of Christianity?"

"I baptized her."

177

Roma grimaced, her nose wrinkling as if she smelled something bad. "How perfectly disgusting. Before or after you fucked her?"

Sam stood in the doorway. He said nothing.

Roma smiled. "You Christians—self-proclaimed—really want it both ways, don't you? You want on the one hand to mouth all those heavenly platitudes, but you still want to fuck whenever the mood grips you. Have you eaten her pussy yet, Sam?"

Sam returned her sardonic smile, sensing she was deliberately baiting him, trying to anger him.

She laughed. "Very good, Sam—I couldn't bait your father, either. Who, by the way, is also Nydia's father. And, of course, the father of Black. Just thought you might like to know that the next time you got an urge to screw."

"We know," Sam said.

"Fucking your half sister, Sam? My, my! What does your God have to say about that?"

"I don't know. I haven't asked Him."

She arched an eyebrow. "Well . . . how casual you are. That cosmic gnome you worship might take exception at your flip attitude toward sex."

"We'll take our chances."

Then, without explanation, her smile changed to one containing a trace of sadness. "Believe me, darling . . . we are *all* about to do that. I see no reason to stand here in the hallway discussing this. Why don't we behave as civilized human beings," she laughed aloud at that, "and adjourn to the den where we can be more comfortable? I assure you, no harm will befall either of you. We do have a great deal to discuss."

"Mac, Howard, Linda, Judy, Lana?" Nydia spoke from

her seat on the edge of the bed.

"They are sleeping soundly. Howard on his stomach, I should imagine. I have no doubt but what you will both rush to their sides upon their waking to tell them the dire news."

"Isn't Howard one of you now?" Sam asked, and wondered how he knew that.

"Ah . . . perhaps. Yes. You are a wise one, aren't you? Of course, he is."

"Then get him out of Mac's room and bunk him somewhere else. Give Mac a chance, at least."

Roma flushed. "*You*, young man, do not order *me* about."

Sam slammed the door in her face.

A short pause, a tap on the door. Sam opened the door, Roma's anger was under control, her face no longer flushed. "You're very sure of your power, aren't you, Sam Balon King?"

"As certain as I can be that my God will protect me against those who serve the Beast."

Roma turned her head and spoke in a language that Sam did not recognize. When she again faced him, he asked, "What language was that?"

"Ancient Gallic. I speak all languages known on earth, Sam—and many that have long since vanished."

"Considering how ancient you must be, I should imagine that would come in handy."

Roma howled her approval. "Oh, very good, Sam! Score one point for you. Oh, my, yes. You are a most worthy foe. I have instructed that Howard be moved into a room of his own." She smiled. "For all the good it will do Mac. Are you coming to the den?"

Sam glanced at Nydia. She nodded her head, her face

pale. "Yes," Sam said to the witch.

She vanished in front of his eyes, without a trace.

"Unusual activity tonight," the astronomer said to his colleague, his partner in sharing the lonely nights searching the Heavens from their earth-bound observatory in California.

"Oh? What type?"

"I . . . don't know that I can explain it."

His friend glanced at him. "Twenty-five years in this business and you give me an answer like that? Come on, Ralph: you can do better."

"Quick bursts of light; not connected with anything I know about. Strange. Almost . . . almost . . . like messages being sent from deep space."

"You been reading the Bible again, Ralph?" his friend asked, not unkindly, but with a slight sarcastic tone to his voice. It was something his partner had grown used to years before.

"I read the Bible every day, Glenn."

Glenn rose from behind his desk and climbed up the ladder to the huge telescope, actually a series of scopes, each amplifying the other, boosting the power to tremendous dimensions. The agnostic watched the Heavens for a few moments, pausing only to check his computations against those of his friend. They matched perfectly, verifying the location of the supposed sighting.

"Nothing, Ralph. You've been working too hard, that's all."

Ralph said nothing in reply.

"Did you shoot film?"

"You know I did." The reply was softly stated.

"Well . . . let's develop it."

180

But Ralph was strangely reluctant to do that, and that only peaked his colleague's curiosity even further. And when questioned, he would only shake his head.

"All right, Ralph." Glenn sat beside his friend. "Come on, give. We've been friends too long for this silent act."

Ralph looked at his friend and coworker for many, many years. Looked at him closely. Unlike Glenn, Ralph was a Christian—or tried to be—and he believed in the big bang theory about as much as he believed a duck could shit gold dust. "There won't be anything on the film," he finally said.

"Why?"

"Because what I saw can't be—won't be—filmed, that's why. So let's change the subject. Get some coffee."

Glenn put out a restraining hand. "I won't kid about your belief in God, Ralph. I can sense this is not the time. And I believe you did see something, and I stress 'something.' It will not go any further than this platform. I give my word. Now what did you see?"

Ralph's eyes appeared deep-sunk in his skull, and his face was pale. He ran nervous fingers through thinning hair. "I . . . saw the face of God."

Glenn sat quietly for a moment. "All right, Ralph. Is that all? What else? What did He look like?"

"Angry. Concerned. Worried. And . . . awesome. Oh . . . did He look awesome. Breathtaking."

"In human form?"

"In a . . . manner of speaking."

"What was He doing? Just skipping around the sky? And I don't mean that in an ugly way."

"He . . . was meeting with someone . . . something. Another being."

"Ralph! Have you lost your mind? Are you serious

about this?"

"Yes, I'm serious. He . . . was . . . well, it looked like . . . He had intercepted someone . . . something. A being, like I said. I've never seen anything like it. Glenn . . . it was . . . terrible. It was beautiful, wrathful. I hate to be redundant, but it was awesome."

"Explain awesome."

"I . . . don't know that I can. The figure was . . . holding something in one . . . mighty hand. It . . . oh, don't think me nuts, Glenn . . . looked like a sword or big knife. The figure appeared . . . I don't know. Exalted, I guess."

Glenn had worked with his friend for too many years to think he was pulling his leg, and to not take him seriously. Ralph Fairbanks was a highly respected man in his field, one of the top men in the world, constantly in demand for speaking engagements and classroom lectures.

Something very close to excited fear touched Glenn. He had not experienced it in a long time. "Go on, buddy . . . tell it all."

Somewhere in the vastness of the huge planetarium, a phone began to ring. It rang several times before someone stilled the jangling.

Ralph sighed. "It . . . seemed to me that the two . . . figures were, well, arguing, I guess is the right word. Almost violently. The one more . . . imposing figure, impressive, was pointing upward; the warrior-appearing figure was pointing downward, pointing with that terrible-looking weapon he . . . it held in his hand."

The blinker on the phone popped on. Glenn finally picked up the telephone. "Yeah?" He listened for a moment, his eyes widening. "No warning; no nothing?

Impossible!" He listened for a moment longer. "All in one night? This close together? Good God!" He hung up.

"What?" his friend asked.

"Small volcano in the Malay archipelago just blew its cork. Hell, it's been dormant for centuries."

"No warning?"

"None."

Ralph smiled. "What else?"

"How do you know there was anything else?"

"I know."

"Couple of small monsoons. A tidal wave or two. All without serious damage. No reported injuries or deaths. Earthquake in a couple of places. No major damage. People reporting some sort of . . . heavenly voices coming out of the sky. Their words; damn sure not mine. Large hail in spots. Tremendous lightning reported around Montreal."

"Where around Montreal?"

"Eighty-ninety miles north. Why?"

"And the temple of God was opened in Heaven," Ralph said, closing his eyes, "and there was seen in his temple the ark of his testament; and there were lightnings, and voices, and thunderings, and an earthquake, and great hail."

"What the hell is that drivel, Ralph?"

"Revelation, chapter eleven, verse nineteen."

"It was a fluke of nature, Ralph!"

"If that is what you believe, Glenn."

"Goddamnit, Ralph! Now listen to me: you're a scientist. You know as well as I there is a logical explanation for everything. I'm not going to argue fact and fiction with you; we've been doing that for a quarter of a century, and all it gets us is out of sorts with each other. I'm going to get that fucking film and see what's on it. I'll be back shortly."

When Glenn returned, Ralph had not moved from his seat. "Nothing on the film, Ralph. Nothing took."

"I told you there wouldn't be."

"I'm going to switch scope positions; take a look at that new star."

"All right."

"You don't object?"

"Why should I?"

"Maybe your . . . apparitions will pop up again. Don't you want to see your holy people?"

Ralph smiled at his friend's sarcasm. "I've seen them."

The red light on the phone glowed. Glenn answered it, listening for a moment. When he turned to his friend, the expression on his face was strange . . . tight.

"News?" Ralph asked.

"Some . . . stargazers up in Canada wanted to know if any of us had witnessed . . . something . . . some visions in the sky tonight. Said they shot film, but nothing developed. Said he didn't want me to think him a fool, or that he'd been boozing on the job, but it appeared to be two . . . *things* arguing."

"And?" Ralph prodded him, knowing there was more.

"He said," Glenn sighed, "that others had called in, from reporting stations all around the world. Said they all witnessed the same . . . whatever it was. Said they were all—to use his words—awestruck."

"Go on, Glenn."

"You really want to rub my nose in it, don't you?"

"No, old friend, I don't."

"Well . . . *I* didn't see it. If *I* had seen it, *I* probably

184

would have been able to identify the sighting without falling back on unproven superstition."

The two men glared at each other for a few seconds, Ralph finally breaking the silence. "What is it they claim to have seen?"

The astronomer stalked from the upper platform, carefully climbing down the ladder to the lower level. He walked to the door, his back stiff with anger. There, he paused, turning around. "They all claim to have seen . . . the face of God."

He slammed the door behind him.

Ralph looked upward, at the stars that twinkled high above him through the open roof. He said, in a voice that held the utmost respect, "I never had any doubts."

TWELVE

"Do you want introductions?" Roma asked the young couple.

"I imagine we'll all get to know one another very well before the next eight days are up," Sam answered.

The den was crowded with young people, and Sam knew Nydia felt as he did: somewhat edgy and very much alone. The young people, the kids they had seen being forced into the house were not present. Sam supposed they had been drugged and put to bed. Most of the men in the room were hard-looking types, with craggy faces and savage eyes. The women were attractive, in a sultry, evil way, with unreadable eyes. A couple were beautiful. Several young people no older than Sam were present, standing off to one side with the people from Nelson and Carrington College. They all wore smirky expressions, cocky looks, their eyes bright and shiny with depraved confidence.

"Members of the older Covens in this country and the United States," Falcon said, gesturing at the new group. "Your God broke the rules. We saw no reason to maintain our standards."

"Why are you telling us this?" Sam asked.

"So you can make your choice, naturally," Falcon replied. "Live or die . . . the latter being rather hideously, I might add, should you foolishly choose that course."

"The choice has been made for us," Sam said, glancing at Nydia.

"That was yesterday," Roma said. "I assure you both, you may leave this area if you so desire."

"Our God would prefer we remain," Nydia said, the words blurting from her mouth.

Falcon laughed as his eyes mentally undressed the young woman. Of all the females present, Nydia was by far the most lovely and desirable, and Falcon was looking forward to the moment when he would spread those lovely legs and position himself inside the wet heat of her. "My, Nydia, how brave you have become with your newfound religion. Are you looking forward to servicing half a dozen men—at one time?"

"I don't believe that time will come, Falcon," she told him, a set to her chin that was alien to him.

"We'll see," the reply was spoken softly, filled with menace.

One of the new men opened his trousers and brazenly exposed his penis, long and thick. He stroked his manhood and grinned nastily at Nydia. "I am certainly looking forward to the time."

"Put it back in your pants, Karl," Roma told him. She cut her eyes to Sam. "Don't you see your position is hopeless?"

"If that is the case, why not just take us now?" Sam asked. "What are you afraid of?"

The room filled with laughter. "Afraid?" Roma said. "My dear, *we* are not afraid. Put that out of your mind. If, or when, the time arrives, we shall take you both by force. But why so soon? Why risk personal injury when there is always the chance we can convince you—both of you—to come to our side?"

"You will be tempted." Balon's words in the letter filled Sam's head. "And you will fall to some of those temptations."

Sam remained silent.

"I'm Toni," one of the young women said. "And I have a question: why would you *want* to resist us? I don't understand. I was once a Christian; raised in the church. A few years ago my mother was dying of cancer. I prayed to her God—my God, then—to save her, spare her, or at least allow her to die mercifully. He did neither. She died a long, slow, horrible death—unforgivably agonizing. Don't hand me the bullshit of your God being a good and just God. Yet, after I joined the Forces of Darkness, my father was struck by a car and lay dying in a hospital. I asked our Master to save him, and he did." She moved to Karl's side. "This is my father. See, he is alive and well." She put her hand on his crotch and caressed his penis. She giggled. "Very well, I can assure you both of that."

Neither Sam nor Nydia had anything to say about the incestuous relationship. But both of them wondered about their own.

"Your God offers you nothing," Toni continued, her fingers rubbing her father's crotch. "The Prince of Darkness offers everything. And really, our Master demands so little, as compared to the rules your God expects you to follow. Don't you agree?"

"We serve our God," Sam said. "Our God serves us."

"Double-talk," Toni said. She looked at Nydia, open envy in her eyes as she gazed at her beauty. "I hope your man fucks with more conviction than he talks."

Nydia's smile was sweet, but tinged with hot anger.

188

"Odds are, dear, you'll never know. You'd better stick with dear old dad."

Toni flushed with rage, moving toward Nydia, her fists balled. No one made any attempt to stop her. When she got within swinging distance, Nydia, to Sam's surprise, gave the young woman a solid shot to the jaw with a hard right cross, sending her sprawling to the carpet. Toni landed on her rump and sat there for a moment, a glazed look in her eyes, her jaw beginning to redden and swell.

"You have all discovered," Roma spoke to the room, "that my daughter is very capable of taking care of herself." She gave Falcon a hot look. "Thanks to him. He insisted upon teaching her the rudiments of self-defense when she was a child."

Falcon had to smile. "Very good, Nydia. You remembered well."

Nydia rubbed her bruised knuckles and said nothing.

"Well?" Roma whirled to glare at Sam. "Your decision?"

"We're staying," Nydia and Sam answered in unison.

"A decision you will live to regret," Roma said with a smile, but thinking: all is working out very well.

The lights went out, plunging the room into darkness.

Nydia screamed in terror.

And from the firmament, the vault of Heaven, a figure ripped toward earth, moving at a speed untrackable by any machine known to man.

As the figure from the world behind the veil again made contact with earth, by the circle of stones behind the home known as Falcon House, a strange, unearthly sound was heard, and the creatures of the forest and the Beasts under the ground were still, as if frozen in motion

189

by the appearance of the near apparition. The figure, huge, pale, and ghostly, made no sound as it walked to the dark circle to sit on one of the dark stones. There, it appeared to brood for a moment, its eyes like lighted sparklers in the night, but to be seen only by those of his choosing.

The phantom traveler rose from the rock and turned its awesome bearded face to the great house, its eyes becoming as mysterious as its identity and mission. The eyes glowed for a brief time, then faded into hard tiny bits of diamond white. The traveler turned his back to the dark mansion, shook its great head, and walked toward the darkness of the forest. The ground trembled slightly as the manlike traveler walked, its feet clad in sandals, with leather thongs laced up the legs, almost to the knees. The dark robe was ankle long, belted at the waist with leather.

As the ghostly appearing man passed the rock altar, still stained with the semen from the man rape, a sword appeared in one mighty hand. The sword came down on the altar of defilement with a clash of sparks and a noise not unlike thunder. Where the sword had struck the stone a huge splotch of white appeared, starkly visible in the night, burned forever in the altar stone.

The awesome man snorted in disgust, and then spat on the ground beside the black altar, the spittle hissing and sizzling on the earth.

And then the cosmic traveler was gone, vanishing as quickly as it came.

Sam felt hard hands reach for him and grab him by the shoulders. Instinctively, he reacted as he had been taught: with extreme prejudice toward his attacker, with survival the name of the game. He jammed stiffened fingers into the throat of the man, spun, and ripped one hand loose from his shoulders, savagely twisting it until he heard the joint pop loose from the shoulder socket. The man screamed in pain and fell to the carpet just as the lights came back on.

Nydia had dropped to the floor when the room was engulfed in darkness. She was crouched behind a sofa on one denim-clad knee.

"All right?" Sam asked.

She nodded silently.

The man who had attacked Sam lay moaning on the floor, his face as twisted as his arm, which lay useless, out of the socket, the arm having been turned a full 360 degrees, something a human arm was not constructed to endure.

Sam spoke to the room of people, his voice thick with emotion, with all present knowing he meant every word. "I'll kill the next person who touches Nydia or me. Do you all understand that?"

His eyes touched each person, male and female, adult and teenager. Only a few eyes did not drop away from his savage gaze.

Nydia rose to stand by him. Sam took her hand. "Let's go."

"Wait!" Roma said, stopping them as they turned to leave the room. "Someone, drag that foolish man from the room," she ordered, then looked at the Christians. "That will be the last act of physical violence directed against either of you—unless you attack us first—until we have decided your decision to stay with your God is firm and irrevocable. I promise you that. And I further promise to personally punish anyone who tries to harm

191

you—physically—during that time." She quickly scanned the room with her dark eyes. "And the punishment will be severe. We will, however, attempt to sway you with words, deeds, and visual action or events. You have until midnight Thursday. After that . . ." She shrugged.

"THIS IS YOUR PERIOD OF TESTING!" the voice boomed in Sam's head. It was a voice he had not heard before, and it seemed to be near. "You were warned that you would be tempted. Fear not, for the LORD GOD is with you. Resist all you can, with all your might, and do not fear should you sometimes fail, for Christians are not required to be perfect, they are simply forgiven."

The voice faded into silence.

"Did you hear that?" Sam questioned Nydia silently.

"No. Hear what?"

"I'll tell you later."

Roma was conscious of something alien in the room, not physically present, but more a mental thrusting, and whatever it was made her flesh crawl with disgust. And something else crept its way up and down her spine: the first unfamiliar tenacles of fear. She fought the unfamiliar feelings until she had successfully driven them away, then stood quietly as her daughter and Sam left the room. She glanced at Falcon.

He pushed into her brain: "Did you feel that power a moment ago?"

"Yes."

"What was it?"

"I don't know."

She averted her eyes and looked at Karl, remembering his long, thick penis. She licked her lips and Karl smiled.

Falcon's eyes touched upon Toni, and she returned the

192

frankly sexual leer.

"I believe," Black said, speaking for the first time, "that we all should retire for a little fun and games. We have time, for we are many and they are but two puny Christians." He put his arm around a young girl and squeezed one breast, feeling her braless nipple swell under his palm..

Fool! Roma looked at him, knowing that her son would never survive any violent encounter with Sam Balon's Christian offspring. By all that is unholy, she mused, walking toward Karl, Nydia could probably whip him. She thought: I have given my word, and I must see to it that it is kept. Saturday through Thursday, no violent acts toward either of them . . . of course, she smiled, what is pudding to one person is poison to another. I will have the time to seduce Sam; to impregnate me, for that is not considered an act of violence if he agrees . . . one way or the other.

"You are truly a beautiful woman," Karl said to her when she reached his side.

"Yes, I know," she said smiling. "And that was a magnificent organ you displayed a few moments ago," she said returning the compliment. "For a bit of stimulation, shall we play voyeur for a time, watching Falcon work his way into your daughter?"

Karl licked thick lips. "Will she scream?" he asked, eyes bright with anticipation at the prospect of watching his daughter couple with the Master's agent on earth. There was always the chance she would be impregnated, and birth a demon. That would make the Master proud.

"They always do," Roma replied.

Sam and Nydia lay side by side in Sam's bed, but the

193

only thing touching between them was their fingers. Sam told her of the voice in his head, and of the message.

She was silent for a time, then said, "Despite that, Sam, and all that is happening around us, I want you."

"Yes," was his reply.

"But I don't believe we should, do you?"

"No."

"Sam?"

"Yes?"

"It may be wrong—I think it is, at times, that is—but I have to say it: I love you."

"And I love you, Nydia."

He could hear her silent weeping, and it cut at him. She asked, "Is it wrong, Sam?"

"I . . . don't know. We'll have to ask when this is over."

"Who do we ask?"

"I don't know that either. But I believe that somehow an . . . answer will be found. Here, I think. I get the feeling a moral question is not the . . . not going to be the main issue."

"I don't understand."

"Neither do I. Those words just popped into my head."

"Am I part of your temptation, Sam?"

"A little bit, I believe, and I am a part of yours."

"It isn't fair. God knew we would be thrown together, and surely He knew we would fall in love."

The words sprang into his head, then rolled from his tongue. "He had His reasons, Nydia. We'll know them when we face them."

She turned her back to him and cried herself to sleep, very much aware of him next to her . . . and wanting him.

194

*　　*　　*

"You're restless this night, Sam," Jane Ann said. She had abruptly awakened and automatically looked around the room for the mist that was Balon.

"In a manner of speaking, yes."

"Don't you sleep in your world?"

"Not as you know it."

"You're holding something back from me," she said, her tone not accusing.

"Yes."

"And you're worried about it." Not spoken as a question.

"To a degree."

"Can't you tell me about your concern?"

"A . . . friend; an acquaintance . . . a longtime resident of the world without end . . . has quarreled with God. He has found an exit and left the firmament. Against orders, I think. But I can't be certain of that. Even He . . . has moods."

"He made man in His own image, didn't He?"

"Yes and no. He made man and woman in our image."

"I don't understand."

"You will."

"Very well. Who is your friend that he would have the courage to quarrel with God?"

"A mighty warrior. The mightiest of the mighty. And a man who hates Satan and everything the Beast stands for."

"Does he have a name?"

"Yes."

"But you're not going to tell me, are you?"

Balon was silent.

"Is God angry with your friend?"

195

"I doubt it. No more than He is angry with me for leaving."

"Has your friend come to earth before?"

"Which earth?"

"Tricked you with that one, didn't I?" She smiled. "I got some information you weren't supposed to give, I'll bet."

"Jane Ann . . ." Balon seemed to sigh in exasperation. "All right. This earth."

"Many times."

"Where is he?"

"He is not here."

Jane Ann smiled. "Michael, the archangel. Has to be. It's reasonable to assume you would make friends with him. Both of you enjoy a good fight."

Balon projected nothing, but the mist seemed to stir.

Jane Ann giggled, the giggling startling Balon. He projected: "What in the name of all that is right and just do you find to giggle about? A woman of your age?"

"A woman my age? Oh? I didn't realize I was so unattractive."

"I didn't say that, Janey. I just . . . well, I can't seem to make you understand the seriousness of the situation."

"Oh, I understand, believe me, I do. I know all the pain and degradation that lies before me . . . that I have to face before I am taken home. At least I think I do. But my main concern was of and for Sam. Now I know that he will be all right."

"How like a woman."

"Chauvinism in Heaven? Really, Sam! How mundane."

"Go to sleep, Jane Ann. You're getting carried away

with this verbal cuteness."

"You're angry with me."

"That emotion is not . . . really displayed in my world."

"What emotions are allowed?"

"Allowed is not the correct word. But I'll let it be."

"Is love allowed?"

"Of course. Love is pure and good and just. You'll see, Janey."

"Love between two people?"

"In . . . a sense, yes."

"Sam?"

"What is it now?"

"I love you, Sam Balon."

"Go to sleep, Jane Ann."

"Chicken."

"Go to sleep!"

And she drifted off into a calm sleep, even though she felt she knew the horror that lay before her. She was not afraid. And when she had tucked herself into the comfortable arms of Morpheus, and her breathing had slowed, leveled, the mist that was Balon came to her, to hover over her.

And as the ever-living vapor wavered by her, Balon projected: "Oh, Jane Ann, you do not know how hard I fought to come here; you do not know how difficult it was; and you do not know the horror that awaits you. But I do. And I will suffer as you, but will be powerless to help until the end. When your time comes, Jane Ann, don't fight it; let life slip from you; let it ebb until I can take a hand and end your suffering.

"We sinned, Jane Ann, years ago, we sinned—just as our son and my daughter have sinned and will sin again, for Him. But God works strangely, sometimes, my love, and to enter His kingdom is not the easiest or the simplest thing to do. Have strength and faith, my love, for I will be beside you in all your trials, and He will be watching us both.

And I do love you, my darling. As much in this world of mine, His world, as I did as a mortal."

And the mist became a blanket that covered her with a gentleness, a love so pure, it could only come from above.

THIRTEEN

It was as if nothing evil had taken place, or was about to occur at Falcon House. The late breakfast was all smiles and cordiality, with everyone present speaking and smiling at Sam and Nydia, each group inviting them to sit and have breakfast with them.

Sam and Nydia declined each offer, electing to sit at a table by themselves, after serving themselves at the buffet line. Roma appeared at their table, assuring them the food was not drugged, and would not be again. Up until midnight Thursday. She added the disclaimer with a slight smile.

"Your friends will join you momentarily," the beautiful witch said. "And be assured, they are all right."

"The young girls who came with the new group?" Nydia asked.

"Alive and well," her mother assured her.

"Where are they?"

"In a safe place."

"Why aren't they allowed to dine with us?" The daughter held on to the subject like a bulldog.

"Why . . . they might decide to run away, hurting themselves in the process. They might run off into the woods, and get lost."

"Better that than what you have planned for them, Mother."

The two women stared daggers at each other.

"Drop the other shoe, Roma," Sam said, chewing slowly, reflectively, a thought just popping into his mind.

Roma helped herself to a piece of her daughter's toast, nibbling at it. "Why, whatever do you mean, Sam?"

"You know perfectly well what I mean. But it won't work, Roma. I won't come over to your side because of the kids."

"I see," she said, her smile suddenly very evil. "Oh . . . wait until you hear them screaming, Sam, dear, then make up your mind."

"You said no violence, Roma," he reminded her.

"No physical violence directed against either of you," Roma corrected. "And has anyone been ugly toward either of you this morning?"

"It won't work, Roma."

"I think I'll give one to Karl this evening." The evil smile became more malevolent. "Yes . . . Janet, I believe. The youngest one. Twelve, I believe she is. What a tight, tender cunt she must have. Oh, my . . . how she will wail."

Sam looked at her, the loathing for her blistering through his eyes. "And if I choose to interfere?"

"Why, darling . . . then we must defend ourselves. It would be only right and proper according to the rules. After all, *we* would not be assaulting *you*, would we?"

"You just have to be, Roma, the most despicable bitch I have ever encountered."

She patted his hand. "Of course, I am, darling. And I am so looking forward to you making love to me."

"Never!"

"Never say never, darling." She patted his cheek and laughed as he slapped her fingers away. "Ta-ta, ciao, and all that, dears."

She walked away, a regal bearing to her stride. She stopped at each table, chatting for a few seconds with each Coven member.

"She acts like this is some sort of fucking social gathering," Sam said.

Lana, Linda, and Judy appeared in the archway to the dining area, Black and Susan just behind them. "Judy looks very pale," Nydia observed.

"Take a look at her neck when she sits down," Sam said, the words popping from his mouth. As before, he wondered where they came from. Then he said, "Your mother is a vampire."

Nydia dropped her fork on the plate.

"Don't ask me how I know, Nydia. I just do."

"Then Black . . . ?"

"Must be the same. Falcon, too." And the vision came to him, numbing him: the events of the black mass replaying vividly in his mind. "That's what she was doing kneeling by Howard, hidden by the stones. Remember what I said to her in the room: Howard was one of them, now?"

"My mother drinks . . . blood!"

"Gross, isn't it."

"I don't believe it, Sam. I . . . just can't. That kind of thing . . . I mean . . ." She shoved her half-eaten breakfast from her. "Who is telling you these things, Sam?"

"The same person . . . thing . . . whatever, whose voice I heard earlier. The one I told you about. The message about the period of testing."

She gazed at the young man she loved so desperately. Something about him had changed. He seemed older,

201

stronger. "Your face has changed, Sam. It's . . . harder, somehow."

"I know." The reply was quiet but firm.

The trio of young women sat down with them, Lana and Linda bubbling and happy, Judy strangely silent, forcing a smile of greeting, picking at her food.

Sam looked at her neck; the fang marks were partially hidden by makeup, but the bites were visible if one knew what to look for. He lifted his eyes to Nydia, projecting silently: "She is one of them. Be careful."

Nydia nodded her head, a gesture so minute only Sam saw it.

"This is so wonderful," Linda gushed. "Isn't this the grandest house you've ever seen?" She looked around at the new arrivals. "Who are all these people?"

"Some friends of my parents'," Nydia said.

"Mr. Falcon is taking me horseback riding this afternoon," Lana said. "Going to show me the country. I bet it's just beautiful."

And I'll bet that's not all he's going to show you, Sam thought. He wondered how to tell her of what fate awaited her.

"You will not." The voice filled his head. "Neither of them."

Why? Sam silently flung the question to the unknown being or beings that seemed to hover invisibly around the estate.

And the voice came to him: "They were raised in the church and have been washed in the blood. They know their true God. The choice is theirs to make. There is nothing you can or will do."

"I don't understand," Sam said, projecting his reply. "But I will do what you say. Whoever you are."

Sam was very conscious of Nydia's eyes on him, unspoken questions in them. He projected: "Later."

"What are you two going to do this afternoon?" Linda asked Nydia.

"Read, relax, maybe take a walk. Would you and Judy like to join us?"

"Oh, I'd just love it!" Linda replied. "I . . . don't take this the wrong way . . . I just can't seem to get close to the others. You know what I mean?"

"I know the feeling," Sam said dryly. He looked at Judy. "How about you?"

The look in her eyes chilled the young man. The look was vacant, not of this earth. And he knew, somehow, she was gone from this world, his faith, his help.

"She is beyond help," the voice rang in his head. "She is one of them. Her thoughts have never been pure, although she pretended they were to others around her. She has denied her God many times. She is gone. Gone beyond our help."

"I'll find something to do," Judy said. She abruptly rose from the table and walked out of the dining area.

"She's changed," Linda said. "Changed so drastically in just a few hours."

"Oh, that's just your imagination working overtime," Lana said. "Maybe she's worried about something, or just tired." She hurriedly ate her breakfast and dropped her napkin beside her plate. "Well . . . gotta go. Mr. Falcon's waiting. See you kids later." Then she was gone.

Linda looked first at Nydia, then at Sam. She put her hand on Sam's arm. "Don't leave me alone in this house," she pleaded. "I mean it. Something is going on around here that's . . . I don't know . . . just don't leave me alone. Please?"

203

"Okay," Sam said. "You stick with us."

But preoccupied as he was with the seemingly impossible task that stretched before him, some of it still vague in his mind, Sam did not see Nydia's eyes narrow in suspicion, her dark eyes flitting across Linda's face, as the young woman slowly removed her hand from Sam's arm.

In Whitfield, the crowds began to gather in front of Miles's home in early afternoon. Anita and Doris tried to ignore them; Miles stood guard by the picture window, a shotgun across his lap; Wade totally ignored the silent crowd, writing furiously in a note pad. The pad would soon join the growing pile of legal tablets on the floor beside his chair.

"Maybe somebody will read them," he had explained.

"Those insane people out there," Miles jerked his white-maned head. "Those . . . Satanists, they don't bother you?"

"Not as much as your chattering does, old friend," the aging newspaper editor smiled, not looking up from his frantic scribblings.

Miles looked at his wife, looking at him. "Doris, do I chatter? Me?"

"Like a squirrel," she replied.

"Some friends I got," Miles groused, rising from the chair. "I think I'll go sit with the golem." He walked out onto the porch. "Hershel, you want some company?"

The Clay Man looked at him, nothing on his expressionless face. He pointed to the door that led back into the house.

"You don't want my company, either?"

The golem continued his pointing.

"Wonderful," Miles said. "I'm in such demand. I made you, you know?" he said to the huge Clay Man.

The golem shook his head.

"I didn't make you? My hands ached for a month after digging all that clay from the riverbank. Now you're telling me I didn't make you?"

The golem rose from the steps and lumbered toward Miles, towering over him by several feet. He turned him as one might turn a paper doll and gave Miles a gentle shove toward the door.

"You don't have to get physical," Miles complained. "I get the point already."

The golem shook his head, pointed to the shotgun leaning in the corner by the front door, and then pointed to the back of the house.

Miles's face brightened. "Oh! You want me to guard the rear of the house?"

The huge gray man nodded solemnly.

"Wade, too?"

Again, the nod.

"You're a good man . . . ah, thing, Hershel. I like you. You don't carry on a conversation worth spit, but I like you. And," he looked up at the expressionless face, "for all of us, I thank you."

The golem looked upward, toward the Heavens.

"Thank Him? Oh, I have, Hershel. A hundred times each day."

The golem nodded and walked back to the steps, slowly sitting down, his massive arms dangling by his side, daring anyone to enter the territory he was given life to protect.

Wade was on his feet, shotgun in hand, when Miles reentered the house. "You heard?" Miles asked.

205

"The golem is smart," Wade said. "To think about the rear of the house."

"Smart?" Miles looked startled. "How can he be smart? He don't have a brain. He's clay, from the river outside of town, and that's dry half the time."

"He's smart in ways we won't ever understand," the editor insisted. "You may have molded him, old friend, but the Almighty breathed life into him."

Miles smiled. "Least I get credit for something."

"This is going to be the most difficult part, isn't it, Sam?" Jane Ann asked. "The waiting, I mean?"

"You've asked me that before. No. I told you: the most difficult part lies near the end. And you are not prepared to face it. Not yet."

She smiled, and she was beautiful. "I try not to think about it."

"It's time you did; time you began preparing. Get my Bible."

She walked to the table, picking up Balon's Bible. "You want me to read the twenty-third psalm?"

Balon smiled through his mist, projecting: "Never anticipate a command."

"Yes, Sergeant."

"Read psalm three. Read how the Lord will sustain you. Read it again and again until you know it by heart."

She sat with head bowed, reading aloud, again and again.

Finally, Balon said: "Now read psalms five and twenty."

She read and reread those, then looked at the mist.

"Now the twenty-third," he told her.

Then he had her read 46 and 90, and of the 119th, she

read Nun.

Balon thrust: "Now read them again and again. Take comfort and keep the faith as you do so, for His words will sustain you."

She looked at the mist that was all she had ever loved on this earth and said, "I love you, Sam Balon."

"Read!"

"Isn't this lovely, my dear?" Falcon asked. "I find it so mentally refreshing to ride through all of nature's beauty."

"It is beautiful," Lana replied. "I feel . . . so peaceful here." She smiled at him. "And I'm glad I'm with you, Mr. Falcon."

"Thank you, dear. But just Falcon, please. I am too conscious of the differences in our ages as it is."

"Oh, that's silly, Falcon. You're the most handsome man I've ever met. Would you be offended if I asked a personal question?"

Would you be offended if I shoved this cock of mine in your pussy? Falcon thought. He smiled, riding behind her. And then in your mouth and up your ass? "Of course not, dear."

"Well," she turned to smile at him, "how . . . ah . . . old are you, Falcon?"

Four hundred and seventy-seven, he thought smiling. Or was it four hundred and seventy-eight? "I am forty-eight years old, dear."

She twisted her lovely ass in the saddle and said, "Oh, that's young, Falcon!"

"Really? I'm glad you think so, dear. Now I have a confession to make: I'm sorry I'm married. For if I were a single man, I'd ask you out."

With her back to him, riding just a few feet in front, Lana said, "What does married have to do with anything?"

Falcon smiled. It never varies, he mused. The dialogue is as old as time. From the grunting of the cave people to the causerie of modern humankind. The language varies from country to country, but the nuances remain the same. "Take the trail to your left, Lana. There is something I want to show you." Other than what is between my legs.

"Where are we going?" she asked, no alarm in her voice.

"A private place of mine. I had it built some years ago. It's a place I use to get away from it all; to be alone."

"I'll bet it's lovely and lonely."

"And very private."

"Good. It's getting crowded back at the house."

Not nearly as crowded as your cunt will soon be. "I felt the same, Lana. One of the reasons I asked you to come with me." Which you will soon be doing.

A mile farther and the cabin came into view: a picture-postcard dwelling; an idyllic setting for romance.

A perfect locale for evil.

"Oh, Falcon, it's so lovely!" She twisted and smiled at him, the push of her full breasts against the buckskin jacket he had found for her arousing him, bringing almost to the surface the brute heat and endless depravity that constantly lay smoldering within him, just beneath the surface.

"Yes." His words were soft. "It is. But not nearly as lovely as you." How many times have I said that?

"You're just saying that."

"No, dear. I mean it. I like to be with you." He

dismounted, loosening the cinch and looping the reins around a hitch post. He helped her from the saddle, and she deliberately rubbed against him, her hands lingering on his shoulders just a bit longer than necessary, her loins pushing against his crotch.

With her hands on his narrow waist, she asked, "Why do you like to be with me, Falcon? I mean, you have everything: wealth, charm . . . everything anyone could ask for."

"Everything except a loving wife."

"Oh, Falcon. But . . . Roma seems so . . . how do I say it? So . . . sexy."

"Outwardly, my dear. All that is but a show." He inwardly grimaced. *This dialogue is maddeningly droll. Soap stuff.* "She has not been a wife to me in years."

"That's so sad."

He pulled away from her and loosened the cinch on her horse, securing the reins.

"Why did you just pull away from me?"

"Because I did not wish you to get the wrong impression of me. I did not bring you up here to pour out my troubles or to seduce you. I like your company, and thought you might like to see my private hiding place. You're so lovely . . . I'm . . . afraid of my emotions."

Someday, Falcon thought, *I must ask the Master to allow me to pursue a career in writing.* Then he remembered he already had: back in the eighteenth century.

She walked to him, putting a small, soft hand on his arm. "There's no need to be afraid, Falcon. I know what it's like to want somebody; what it's like to be lonely."

He looked down at her, his smile sad and seemingly so very bittersweet. *Falcon,* he thought, *you are a perfect* son of a bitch. The tragic look on his face hid the evil that lay behind his obsidian eyes. "I have some truly excellent brandy inside, Lana. Shall we have a drink before we start back?"

She smiled. "We don't have to start back anytime soon, do we? After all, Falcon, we have all afternoon to . . . do whatever we choose."

"That's so true," he replied, and pushed open the door to Hell.

FOURTEEN

Somewhere in the depths of the great house, a thin wailing began. It could not be heard constantly, but rather only the high peaks of agony and fear, the thinnest shriekings at the zenith of pain.

"Can't you do something?" Nydia asked.

They were in Sam's room, Linda napping just across the hall, the door to her room slightly ajar.

"What would you have me do?" Sam asked. "I don't even know where the kids are being held. I can't go prowling, I'd be stopped before I got started. That's what your mother wants, honey. Me to start trouble."

"She isn't my mother," Nydia said. "And I will never again think of her as such. And don't you."

The awful wailing ceased abruptly, ending on a note of pain and terror.

"Maybe it's over?" Nydia suggested, a hopeful tone to her question.

"It's just begun," Sam said, shattering any illusions she might have had.

"What are they doing to her?"

"Use your imagination," he said flatly. "I'm sure you'll come up with something."

"The young girl mot . . . that bitch talked about at breakfast—the twelve- or thirteen-year-old?"

"I'm sure."

The screaming began anew.

Then Nydia asked the question Sam was dreading to hear, but knowing it was coming. "If your God—our God—is such a just God, why is He allowing this to happen?"

"I can't answer that question, Nydia. I don't believe any mortal could give you a satisfactory reply to that, and I'm equally certain it's been asked ten million times a day, since the beginnings of religion."

She looked at him, with Sam very much aware of the heat in her eyes, and the heat did not come from just her anger at what was happening somewhere in the mansion.

"No, Nydia," he said quietly.

"I love you, Sam."

"And I love you. But the answer is still no."

"What am I supposed to do?"

"Take a cold shower."

"I don't want to take a cold shower. I want you. What would be the harm?"

The words roared into Sam's head: "And when woman saw that the tree was good for food, and that it was pleasant to the eyes, and a tree to be desired to make one wise, she took of the fruit thereof, and did eat, and gave also unto her husband with her; and he did eat."

"Can't you see what's happening, Nydia? You're being tempted. The Dark One is everywhere in this house; in every room, in every object. Fight it."

"Sam!" she moaned. "I want you to fuck me!"

"Fight it!"

She came to him, tearing off her shirt, ripping the garment from her. She tore off her bra and grabbed at his hands, placing them on her breasts, the nipples hard

212

against his palms. She held his hands there, as she worked her loins against him. "Don't you want me, Sam? Please. Let me suck you, Sam. I want to take you in my mouth. I . . ."

He slapped her, slapped her open-handed, rocking her head back. He brought his hand back across her face, backhanding her, stunning her. A tiny drop of blood appeared on her mouth, where a lip had smashed against a tooth.

He laid her across the bed and ran to the bathroom for a wet towel. There was a strange roaring in his head, as visions so erotic they startled him began playing against the forces of good that reared up within him. Pictures of Nydia with her naked legs spread wide, her lushness open, waiting to receive him. Her hands worked at her erect nipples, pinching them, with her begging him to hurt her, bite her, fuck her.

Sam slammed a hard fist against the bathroom wall as the eroticism grew stronger, battling in his mind. A technicolor picture of him with his face pressed against her mons veneris, tonguing her into incredible wetness, while her hands wormed over his naked body. And then an invisible force slammed him against the wall, holding him immobile as the scenes of carnality grew wilder: Nydia with her long black hair fanned out over his belly, his penis in her mouth, her fingers caressing him as her tongue worked at his stiffness.

"Sam!" Nydia called from the bed, and he forced his head to turn and his eyes to open at her cries. "Oh, God, Sam—help me!"

She lay with her jeans wadded around one ankle, her panties ripped from her. Her fingers were busy between her legs, working in and out of the dark wetness.

Summoning all his strength, Sam pushed away from the wall and staggered into the bedroom, a wet towel in his hand. He washed Nydia with the cold, dripping towel, one hand forcing her fingers from her womanhood.

Her eyes were wild as she fought him, and she was strong in her fury, lashing out at him. When she found he was winning physically, she changed tactics, under the commands of a Master over which she had no control. She softened under him, her hands at her side, letting Sam gently bathe her nakedness with the cold, wet towel. She lifted one hand, placing the palm against his cheek.

"I'm sorry, Sam. I don't know what came over me."

"The Devil was tempting you. It's all right, now. It's over."

She slipped her hand from his face to his neck, gently drawing his mouth to hers, finding no resistance as their lips touched. Slyly, she slipped her tongue between his lips, working hotly into his mouth, and finding him responding to her.

Sam's hands found her breasts, caressing them. His hand slipped downward, to part her legs, to enter the wetness of woman ready.

Then, from the deep well within her, good burst forth, for the moment overpowering evil. She harshly pushed him away. "No, Sam. Get away. It's not over—can't you see?"

Almost violently, he pulled away from her nakedness. She covered herself with a sheet. "Read to me from the Bible, Sam," she hissed the request through clenched teeth. "Read to me."

Fighting back passions suddenly unleashed within him, emotions so wild and hot Sam was filled with fear, he grabbed for the Bible and flung it open.

"Read to me!" she screamed.

The book had opened to the General Epistle of James, and it seemed at first to be an odd place to begin. But as Sam read, a smile came to his lips as the text began unfolding on the source of temptation. Gradually, Nydia's breathing slowed and she rose from the bed and dressed, asking Sam to reread that passage about temptation. He did, and felt the room suddenly clear of all that is dark and foul and evil.

"It's over," Nydia said. "I can feel it, can't you?"

"Yes." Sam closed the Bible.

"I suppose we can expect more of the same?"

"Until Thursday night, at least."

She looked at him.

"That's when it'll really get rough," he explained.

She glanced at the still ajar bedroom door. "Linda didn't wake up, and we got pretty loud."

Sam shrugged it off. "She's probably a sound sleeper."

Nydia chose not to reply.

The young screaming began in the dark, evil depths of the mansion.

With the lighting in the room reduced to several flickering candles, and the fireplace popping and crackling, Lana held out her glass for a refill. Her third. "I've never tasted brandy like this. It's so good and smooth."

"It's rather expensive," Falcon admitted, tilting the decanter, filling her snifter past the point a brandy connoisseur would go.

"I like expensive things," she said, licking her lips.

"Oh?" Falcon arched an eyebrow expressively, the roguish gesture speaking volumes of understanding

215

garnered through centuries of inamorata.

"Yes. I think I'll look for a rich man."

"I wish you success in your quest. You're speaking in terms of marriage, of course?"

She shrugged. "Not necessarily. I have a lot to offer the right man."

"Your beauty, of course. And your intelligence."

"And my virginity."

Falcon chuckled unbelievingly.

"You don't believe me?"

"I didn't mean that, my dear. It's just that in this day of sexual promiscuity, a virgin would be a priceless item."

"Well . . . I am," she said, pouting playfully.

The brandy was taking its toll on the young woman, loosening her tongue, lessening any inhibitions she may have had. "I like older men," she said flatly. "Guys my own age are so dumb. All they want to talk about is how fast their stupid cars will run, or how bad they are. I think guys my own age are really gross."

Falcon sat beside her on the leather couch. "Well, I am certainly glad I am beyond that adolescent silliness of having to prove how macho I am to young ladies who really don't care."

"Oh, lots of girls like that shit."

Falcon winced.

"Did I say something?"

He made his move. "Well . . . if I am to keep you in pretty clothes, expensive automobiles, and a purse full of money, I think I'd better work on your grammar, as well."

"You're going to do all that for me?"

"Would you like that?"

216

"What do I have to do to earn it?"

He looked at her with his unreadable eyes, dark and hooded. "Only that which is usually required in any arrangement of that type."

"And that is?"

"You tell me, dear."

The gold digger in her sprang to the surface. "I don't mean to be crude, I really don't, but I'd want it in writing."

"Then you shall certainly have it, darling."

"Just like that?"

"*Oui.*"

"I don't speak much French. You'll have to teach me."

"I shall teach you many things, darling. Be assured of that."

"Why me, Falcon? You could have your choice of half the women in the world. I'm just a nineteen-year-old kid."

"You appeal to me. In many ways."

"Will I have to worship the Devil, too?"

That set him back. A grin creased his mouth, then he was roaring with laughter. He reached into his jacket pocket and removed a handkerchief made of the finest linen, wiping his eyes. "So, Lana, dear, Black badly misjudged you, eh?"

"Black is an idiot, and you know it."

"Only too well, my dear. I thought I had you convinced the other evening."

"You were wrong. A lot of people usually are about me. But that doesn't answer my question."

"I was under the impression you were a devout Christian."

"I still have my virginity, Falcon, but as far as me

being a Christian . . . I used to jack-off the preacher back home."

That startled Falcon, and the warlock was not easily jarred. "I beg your pardon?"

"Yeah, his wife didn't like sex, and he'd had the hots for me since I was about eleven. So we made a deal. I'd give him a hand job several times a week and he'd give me money. More money for a blow job."

"You might have difficulty doing that with me."

"Sucking you off, you mean?"

"Crudely put, but correct."

"Nobody's that big."

His smile told her she was wrong.

"May I see?"

"By all means."

She opened his trousers and hissed at the sight, wrapping her soft fingers around the organ. "You'd make some of those porn stars look like babies. You really expect to stick all that into me?"

"That I do, my dear." He reached into an inside pocket and removed a medallion and gold chain. "This one is a bit different from the others. Much more intricate in detail. If you'll be so kind as to release your grip from my penis, dear, I'll get a magnifying glass and you can see for yourself."

She removed her hand from his penis. "I'll take your word for it, Falcon. But you still have not answered my question."

"I think you know the answer, Lana. Let's not be coy. After this half-hour of conversation, I feel I know you rather well. I don't believe your thoughts have been pristine and Christian for years. I don't believe you give one whit for any Christian God; so what does that

218

leave you?"

"You're pretty sharp, Falcon."

"More than you know, Lana. And were I you, I'd bear that in mind."

"What do I have to do to get into your church . . . whatever you call it?"

"Put this medallion around your neck, renounce your God, and take the oath."

"That's it?"

"It's a one-way trip, my pretty."

"No returns, no exchanges," she stated.

"That's how uncomplicated it is. The Christian God is very unyielding about other gods, Lana, and quite specific about worshiping the Prince of Darkness."

"Big deal. I won't have to attend that stupid fucking college anymore?"

"No."

"I get a car of my choice, money, clothes, a place to live—a nice place?"

"All those things, dear."

"But it really means nothing to you, does it. Me, I mean?"

His shrug was noncommittal.

"And you're not the only one I'll have to screw, right?"

"You'll understand once you become one of us, Lana."

She slipped the gold chain over her head, around her neck, the medallion gleaming dully between the mounds of her breasts. "Oh, what the hell," she said. "Tell me what I have to say."

The wailing had begun anew, with an added note of

pain and horror that was increasingly difficult for Sam and Nydia to ignore.

Roma appeared at their open door, a smile on her red lips. "Her name is Janet," she said. "Such a pretty little thing. And Karl is holding up quite well for a man his age. He introduced himself to her pretty little pussy at first, now he is experimenting with the back door. I don't believe she's enjoying it very much, do you? Pity. I always have."

"I'll try it that way with you, Roma," Sam said, ignoring the sudden look of fright of Nydia's face.

"Oh?" the witch's face brightened.

"Yeah. But you're probably so wallowed out I'll have to tie a two by four on my ass to keep from falling in."

Pure evil hate flickered in Roma's eyes. "You'll pay dearly for that remark, Sam."

"Yeah," Sam said, the word coming out slow and soft. "You're probably right. But my payment will not be the way you're thinking of it."

Roma grinned wickedly. "You see, Sam Balon King: already you are thinking about your sins against your Master and how you will be punished. Oh, Sam! Why are you fighting what you know you truly want in your heart? Sam, Sam. My Master doesn't disapprove of a brother-sister love affair. And you two are in love; that's evident for all to see." She walked across the room, sitting down in a chair. "What does your God offer you— either of you?" she looked at her daughter. "You want me to answer for you? I can assure you both, I know the Bible far better than either of you. I can quote you book, chapter, and verse." Without waiting for a reply, she said, "Read Leviticus, Chapter eighteen. Read it . . .

both of you, and see what His wrath will be."

Sam and Nydia sat quietly, listening to her.

"But my Master, children, oh, he is a far more forgiving Master than your God. And so much easier to obey.

"I won't bore you or tempt you further, children. All I ask is that you both think about my words. Think about them while you two are lying in bed this night, close to each other, wanting each other, but fearful to touch. Fear, children, that's what your Master offers you . . . and nothing else."

She was gone, simply vanishing before their eyes.

Nydia and Sam looked at each other, the unspoken question in their minds hanging like a shroud between them.

"Incredibly tight," Falcon muttered hotly. "I don't believe I've ever had a woman this tight." He seemed oblivious to the moanings of the young woman beneath him. He worked in another inch.

Lana screamed, attempting to push him away . . . anything to ease the pain. But she succeeded only in aiding the man in his onward and inward conquest. Bright spots of blood dotted the whiteness of sheet beneath her nakedness.

The medallion between her sweaty breasts glowed faintly.

Falcon bent his head to touch his lips to hers. "Only a bit more, my dear, and then you will begin to enjoy our afternoon's tête-à-tête."

He hunched and she screamed.

There is, Falcon mused with a smile, nothing so lovely

as a young lady receiving her first taste of cock . . . especially if the cock is large enough to produce wails of pain.

Lana bit her lip and wept in pain.

On his knees, Falcon's hands on her hips, he pulled her to him, savoring her pleas for mercy. With one savage hunching motion, he finally pulled her to him, impaling her to the full extent as his eyes drank in her nakedness, enjoying her pain. He allowed her to rest for a moment as he viewed her.

Her once shiny blond hair was now matted from perspiration-induced pain; a trickle of sweat ran from her pulsing throat between her breasts. And such lovely breasts, he thought. High and firm and tipped with delicate roses. Ah, youth, he mused, fleeting and fickle in its brevity. Such a pity it is wasted on the young.

He said, "Did you know, my dear—of course not, how could you—that I had the largest cock in all of Paris?"

"Take it out!" she screamed.

"Is it hurting you?" Falcon smiled.

"Yes!"

"Good." His smile widened. "It has been said that pain serves to enhance pleasure."

That said, Falcon withdrew from her and with one brutal thrust, rammed his thick length home.

Her screams echoed about the cabin in the woods.

That done, pleasured by her pain, Falcon began making love to her, gently, allowing her cunt to adjust to him, allowing the juices within her to flow, and it was not long before pleasure overwhelmed pain, and she began to whimper under a shivering climax.

"Do you love my Master?" Falcon asked.

"Yes!" she hissed.

Falcon settled into the rhythm that has become the oldest introduction of the species . . . and the most pleasurable, and Lana groaned her welcome.

"Any other God but mine is shit, Lana," he said.

"Yes," was her reply. "The Christian God is shit!"

At his promptings, Lana repeated more damning words, the medallion between her breasts glowing its approval as more blasphemies rolled from her mouth, the words becoming filthy in content, raw obscenities from the lips of youth, from a heart now blackened forever by the soot from the ever-smoking pits of Hell. Her hands rubbed his naked flesh, taking pleasure and comfort from the hot flesh, working their way down his flat belly, into his hairy crotch, her fingers gently touching the beginnings of his thick root, now slick from her own juices.

And as he drove into her, each thrust a hammer blow of male density, roughly caressing the silkiness of female inner heat, the words from her mouth increased in number and profane impiety, until the room filled with the radiance from the medallion.

They thrashed on the damp sheets, each seeking release, while Falcon encouraged Lana's verbal garbage, prompting her, pushing her past the point of no return, searing her flesh and filling her heart with painless invisible burning coals from his Master's kingdom in the netherworld.

"Fuck God!" she screamed, as Falcon's meat of the Devil, a gift from the Dark One plummeted home. "All praise the Lord of Flies."

"I am his," Falcon urged.

"I am his!" she screamed.

And Falcon gently sank his teeth into her neck, painlessly sipping a few drops of her.

And she was his. Not of this world.

An event that Falcon had discreetly failed to mention would occur.

FIFTEEN

"We'll have a full twenty-four hours to gather strength for the ordeal facing us," Sam said, the words seeming to leap from his mouth, as if a separate brain had taken full control.

"Why?" Nydia asked. "How do you know that?"

"Someone is telling me these things. And I don't feel inclined to question the source. Sunday is the one day the forces of Black Magic, Od, Satanists, whatever you choose to call them, can't move. Supposedly," he put a disclaimer on that. "That is God's day, and we'll probably be left alone." He fell moodily silent for a few moments.

"What are you thinking, Sam? I can't quite read you."

"Probably the same as you: how we're going to get out of this mess; how we're going to win it."

"You mean, *if* we're going to win it."

His eyes became alive with a fever she had never before witnessed. "No, Nydia, not *if*. We can't have doubts— ever. The instant we start doubting, and really dwell on those doubts, we're finished. If we start doing that, we may as well hang it up."

"I'm . . . not as strong as you, Sam. I'm a newcomer to all this."

"What do you think I am?" His words were spoken much more harshly than intended.

Tears touched her eyes, rolling down her cheeks. "Don't be angry with me, Sam—please? I'll do whatever you tell me to do, but you've got to help me."

He sighed, taking her hands in his. "I'm sorry I snapped, honey. I'll die for you if I have to." And she knew he meant it. "I love you, Nydia. Even though I know it's wrong, and I'll—we'll—pay for it someday. I can't deny my love for you any more than I could deny my love and faith for the Lord God."

"Roma was right, you know. Our love is wrong, and God won't have it; He won't allow it to go unpunished."

"Let's get out of this . . . mess first," he said grimly. "Then we'll worry about that."

"Worry about that tomorrow?" She forced a smile. "But where is Tara, Sam?"

"Wherever we choose to make it, honey. And we will make it—together."

"Promise me?"

"Yes." He spoke with renewed faith, renewed hope. "Yes, I promise."

They wanted very badly to kiss, but both held their emotions in check. She pulled her hands from his and stood up, walking across the carpet to her room, picking up the Bible along the way. "I'm going to study this for a while, Sam."

He could but nod his approval.

The crowds of Devil worshipers in Whitfield paraded up and down in front of Miles's home, shouting filthy words and making obscene gestures. But no one dared to violate the space guarded by the huge Clay Man, and the golem would not venture past the front yard. It was a stand-off.

226

"Around back," Jean Zagone suggested to her foreman. "We'll keep that fuckin' monster occupied here; you take some people around to the back of the house. Quietly now. Try to take them alive for some fun."

The foreman, Jake, nodded his approval. "I'll get in my pickup, pretend like I'm leavin'. That ought to throw 'em off some. Then I'll circle 'round back, pickin' up some guys I know along the way."

"Go. Get some men you can depend on, Jake."

"You can depend on me, baby."

Jean watched his slender ass as he walked away. Jake was one of the heaviest-hung cowboys she had ever known, and she reckoned she had fucked about half the men in the county. But Jake was pure randy, and wasn't nothing he wouldn't do; nothing too kinky for ol' Jake. And he was mean and about half crazy, to boot. And he sure liked to fuck.

Jake had told her any number of times over the years, 'way back when they was just gettin' this Coven started, that he sure would like to shove the meat to Jane Ann; either end, didn't make no difference to him.

Jean had promised him he could have Jane Ann. That had got him so turned on she had to suck him off right then and there. Damn cock so big she couldn't hardly get it in her mouth. Cummed all over her.

Jake located several of the Coven's good old boys and together they eased around to the back of Miles's house, as furtively as possible. The golem was standing impassively in the front yard, making no move toward the street. Jake knew that to attempt to shoot the goddamned thing was useless: he had personally pumped a full clip of .308s into the fuckin' thing and hadn't even

227

staggered it; the slugs just bounced off, one of them hitting one of his own people on the ricochet. Jake didn't know where the Clay Man had come from, but he damn sure didn't want any truck with it, not after seeing it rip off both arms of man with no more effort than if he'd been lifting a soft titty to squeeze.

Jake shook his head; have to quit thinkin' 'bout pussy, he cautioned himself. Ain't had none in two days, and that wasn't good for a man: man ought to wet his dauber every day—twice a day if he could find a hole to stick it in. He sneered as he thought of Jane Ann. Now that was gonna be some prime fuckin'. Prissy little psalm-singin' bitch. So damn high and mighty when everybody knew she was fuckin' that preacher fellow, Balon, 'way back then, and them not even married, or nothing. Bet her eyes will pop when I shove my meat to her, Jake thought, grinning. Got to be close to 45 years old and still looks good enough to eat.

They were back of the house, squatting down behind a line of hedge, watching for anything out of the ordinary. They saw nothing to alarm them.

"Jew boy so sure his God's gonna take care of them they ain't even guardin' the back," Boo said.

"Stupid fuckers," Clint agreed. "Come on, let's take 'em. I wanna see that Jew bitch squall when we pour gasoline on her and set her afire."

But Jake was too old a hand to be sucked into something this obvious. And since he didn't particularly care for either Clint or Boo, he said, "You boys git on up there. Me and Link'll stay back a piece, keep a good eye on your back trail."

The two overanxious members of Zagone's Coven nodded their heads in eager agreement. They ran across

228

the yard. They made it to the back porch steps before two shotguns blasted, the slugs from one catching Boo in the face, blowing his head apart. The other blast hitting Clint in the center of his chest, flinging him backward. He died as he hit the ground.

"I didn't figure they was that dumb," Jake said, fingering the medallion that hung around his neck. "Come on. I got me an idea."

Jean wasn't surprised to hear their attempt to rush the house had failed. Things were not going as planned. Not at all. "What's your idea, Jake?"

"Simple," the foreman said. "Burn 'um out."

Gasoline was found, Molotov cocktails made. The first firebomb exploded in the hands of its preparer; the second and third ones bounced off the house and went out. The fourth and fifth bombs were picked up by the Clay Man and hurled back at the crowd, badly burning one man and blinding another.

"Enough!" the Prince of Darkness hurled his command into the brain of Jean Zagone. "It is as I thought: useless. Let them be."

And the Dark One knew then his attempts to wrest the town of Whitfield from the hands of God and build a Coven there were doomed to failure. The Almighty Meddler had allowed him to waste his time here for more than twenty years, knowing all along He would not allow the final act.

The Dark One brooded, his thoughts more savage than usual. He searched the Heavens for some sign of his lifelong foe, but He was not to be found.

Could it be, Satan mused, could it be true, that He really did retire into His firmament? But why would He do such a thing?

The Dark One could find no logical reason for such silly behavior on His part. There were reasonably innocent people in this miserable village . . . well, not really innocent, he amended that . . . but He had not—so far—interfered with their taking; their torture; their rape; their degradation.

Why?

Why would He save only the Jew and Jewess, and those silly Gentiles? Satan could not believe He would allow the torture and rape of Jane Ann simply to test Sam Balon . . . or would He? No, that might be it in part, but there was more to this. The Prince of Rats knew that God sometimes acted in mysterious ways, but this was erratic even for Him. It made no sense.

And Satan knew something else: he was having to work too hard here to accomplish so little. If he accomplished anything at all, he added.

No . . . something was amiss. There had to be more to it for Him to behave so strangely.

The Lord of Pus looked upward and roared: "Star-Wart? Answer me, you bastard!"

But there was no reply from the firmament.

The King of Shit howled and screamed his displeasure, vending his anger, fouling the Heavens with profanity, daring the Mighty of the Mighty to give him a reply. And the Beasts around The Digging huddled in their caves, shaking with fear, for they sensed doom. They had been the first to sense it, for they were much more animal than human, and could feel with a perception that humans did not possess that it would rain, snow, the ground tremble, the sky produce hail, and when things were going badly for their kind.

230

And they were afraid.

Jane Ann looked at the mist of Balon and asked, "Will they come for me this night, Sam?"

"No. It will be near the end."

"And they will have me . . . ?"

"About thirty hours."

"And then?"

"It will be over for you on earth."

"And we will leave together?"

"Yes."

"Miles and Doris, Wade and Anita with us?"

"Yes."

She rose to get his Bible and opened it to one of the psalms she had been reading. "I wish it was over," she said.

"We can't get out!" a Coven member told Jean, near hysteria in her voice. "Everywhere we turn, we're blocked."

"'At's right," another member said drunkenly. "We done been ever' where in this part of Fork, down ever' road. We blocked in and shut out."

"Blocked by what?" Jean almost screamed the question.

"Nothing."

"*Nothing!* Damnit, that doesn't make any sense. What the shit do you mean: nothing?"

"There's something there, but you can't see it. It's invisible, but it's solid. Like a big bubble. You can feel it, but you can't see it. And it slopes upward, real gentle like, just enough where you can't get no purchase on it. And we seen two or three out-of-staters drive right through it, but when we run over there, it was closed to us. And them people in the cars didn't pay us no mind at all. It's like we was invisible, or something."

"That's right," the mayor of Whitfield said. He, like the others, was filthy, his clothing reeking from sex and sin and death. He was unshaven, and his breath and body stank. "We're trapped in here, Zagone, trapped like rats in a barrel. What's going on?" he screamed, his fear becoming contagious, touching others of the Coven.

"Now, just calm down," Jean said soothing them. "The Master will take care of us. He promised he would; hasn't he always?"

So far, they all agreed.

"All right, I'll speak with him. For now, you people relax. Go get one of those not of us and crucify them — have some fun. Everything will be all right. You'll see."

Her smile and words seemed to placate them, and they went into town, to find another luckless, hapless so-called Christian; they had all had such fun listening to them scream while they tortured them, raped them, nailed them to roughmade crosses. Selected areas of the town were dotted with crosses, with naked tortured bodies dangling from the towers of pain.

The men and women who still screamed out their lives were dying wondering why . . . just because they had cheated a little bit in business, here and there; just because they had professed to be Christians and had secretly or openly held hate in their hearts for niggers, Jews, spics, greasers, Indians . . . that shouldn't mean they should have to die this horribly . . . should it? Just because they had lied in their hearts while they prayed to

Him, knowing they were lying all the time . . . that wasn't enough to warrant this . . . was it?

Just because they had enjoyed browbeating employees and cheating on income tax and palming a few bucks a day from their employers and every now and then getting in a quick fuck from their neighbor's wife or husband or secretly getting together with the boys to watch a fuck movie. . . . That wasn't enough of a sin to warrant this awfulness . . . was it?

After all, hadn't they gone to church every Sunday, just like the Bible instructed them to do? Hadn't they tithed like He asked them to do? Well . . . maybe not ten percent, but shit, in this day and time, that's just not reasonable. I mean, a fellow has Country Club dues and the whole family has to have a new wardrobe every year for every season and everybody's got to have their own car and bass boat and RV and all that, right? I mean, it's tough about all them starving kids in the world, but . . . that ain't my problem. Is it?

And didn't we pray for forgiveness every time we fell from grace and fucked the secretary or screwed the boss? Sorry it was an every week arrangement . . . but a guy or a gal's got a right to get a little strange cock or cunt every now and then . . . right?

But I guess, looking back over our lives, we really didn't try very hard to maintain His standards, His way, His rules, His teachings.

Maybe we did deserve all this.

The invisible barrier around Whitfield and parts of Fork County didn't upset Mephistopheles; there was no barrier he could not penetrate—except Heaven, and he

233

certainly had no wish to go there. And the fact that he knew he was going to lose in this locale did not bother him very much . . . not really: he had lost before and would again. These ignorant, stupid, greedy, vain, petty, grasping mortals were all his anyway . . . no matter what took place during their short squirt of breathing life . . . most of them were too ignorant to understand that. No, what really bothered the Prince of Foulness was that he just could not understand why He was doing this. It was almost as if He had made up His mind to give up on the human race . . . end the game.

But Satan knew that wasn't true, knew they had a few more years in contest ahead of them. No, He wasn't yet ready to end the game and sear the world with nuclear fusion. This world. The game, the Foul One knew, had many millennia left; other worlds yet to experience his and His warfare; thousands of creatures left to yet develop into thinking beings, for now, though, as yet undeveloped enough to make the choice between darkness and light. Truth and lies. Beauty and ugliness.

No, Apollyon sighed, the sigh producing a great wind that raked the barren rolling hills around Fork County . . . no, that was not it. And then the Dark One decided, as he had done so many times in the past, that he really didn't know what motivated Him; what caused Him to accept one human being and reject another. His philosophy was so complicated . . . so simple, Satan corrected his thinking, to make it *appear* confusing.

Well, the Foul One concluded: so much for Whitfield. His enemy had won again. But, his smile was all things evil, there was still Falcon House, and even should I lose there, I will not lose entirely, for the witch was ready to make her move, to give him a demon child; the warlock

234

ready to make his move, to give him another demon child, and he had more souls for the pits. So, all in all, it had not been an entirely fruitless pursuit. No, not at all. I'll leave these fools and twits to their own cunning here in this wretched village. Go to Falcon House, see how I may be of assistance there.

There was always tomorrow.

SIXTEEN

Neither Sam nor Nydia encountered many Coven members on this, the Lord's Day. Those they did see walked with quick, furtive steps, shifty, hurriedly averted eyes, and slumped shoulders, as if expecting a sudden blow from behind.

"Sam?" Nydia asked, as they had breakfast alone in the large dining room. "Wouldn't this be the day to defeat them?"

"It would seem so," the young man replied. "But the feeling isn't right. I'm not supposed to start yet. I don't believe the period of testing is over . . . for me."

She accepted that without question. "Why . . . are they so . . . I don't know . . . afraid, I guess is the right word?"

"You mean today?"

She nodded.

"God's day, honey. We're safe, comparatively speaking, that is. But some warning voice . . . no, that's not true, not a voice, a sense, I guess, deep inside me, tells me to be on guard, for this is their territory, not ours."

"Or His," Nydia said.

"Yes."

She looked up, sudden fear in her eyes.

"What's wrong?"

"Falcon and Roma coming toward us."

"Hell with them."

"Apt choice of words," she said, smiling.

The witch and warlock stopped at the buffet line to fill their plates, then walked to the table, Falcon smiling, saying, "I know you young people won't object if we join you."

"Not at all." Sam returned the smile. "We were just about to say a morning prayer for thanks." He pointed upward. "To Him."

"How disgusting!" Roma said.

"Go right ahead," Falcon said. "But you will understand if we don't join in?"

Sam bowed his head and Nydia followed suit, not knowing what her young man was going to do. She didn't even know if Sam knew a morning prayer of thanks.

Sam, with his head bowed, hiding his smile, said, "Dee Dee, Ta Ta."

Falcon and Roma looked at each other. "Is that some kind of a joke?" she asked.

"No," Sam said. "When I was just learning to talk, really before I could pronounce words, after Mother or Dad would say the prayer, I'd always say that. Our God is listening, and He knows what I said, and meant."

Roma sat down. "And you people call us weird." She buttered a piece of toast, nibbled at it, then said, "Have either of you given any more thought to what we discussed last evening?"

"The answer is no, Roma," Nydia said, and she was conscious of Sam looking at her through eyes of love and respect.

"Nydia," Falcon said, "have you considered this: how do you know you will be accepted into His flock; His hand

237

of protection? Think about it. You have not been properly baptized; you do not know the Bible and nothing of His teachings. Aren't you taking a chance, my dear?"

"Yes," she surprised him with her reply, "and I've given that a great deal of thought. But our answer is still no. I've been reading Sam's Bible, and it says: 'God so loved the world, that he gave his only begotten Son, that whosoever believeth in him should not perish, but have everlasting life.' Now . . . I don't know, really, how that should be interpreted, but I read it to mean that if a person believes in Jesus and the Father, and tries real hard to do what is right, to be a good person, well . . . everything's going to be all right. I may be wrong. I hope not."

Sam gently squeezed her fingers in support.

"How touching," Roma said dryly, observing the gesture of love.

"Shut up, darling," Falcon told her, and this time she heard a distinct note of warning in his voice. She closed her mouth. Falcon said, "Is there no way we can reach a compromise?"

"No," Sam said, flatly rejecting the offer.

"He's just like his father," Roma blurted. "Hardheaded as a goat."

"And very proud to be," Sam said, smiling.

Roma nodded her head; the extent to which she agreed with Sam was impossible to tell from the curt gesture.

Falcon's eyes were hard as he looked at Nydia. "My dear, you can make this enjoyable, or very unpleasant . . . when the time comes. I suggest you think about it."

"I don't know what you mean," she replied.

Falcon's smile was evil. He pointed to his crotch. "You and I, dear."

She shook her head slowly.

"The same applies to you, Sam," Roma said.

"Sorry," the young man told her. "I think I'll pass." He had no way of knowing his mother had spoken those same words to Roma more than twenty years before, referring to Black Wilder's offer:

"A lot of your mother in you, too, darling," Roma said with a nasty grin. "And your mother is going to have a lot in her before all this is over. Do pardon the slight pun, won't you?"

Sam shot visual daggers of hate at the witch.

"Do either of you realize," Falcon said, "how hopelessly outnumbered you are? How puny your powers are compared with ours? And how foolish you are to reject this offer of compromise?"

Sam and Nydia merely looked at him, saying nothing.

"We really are not obligated to abide by any rules," Falcon confided in them. "Believe that. The only reason we are here is to give you young people a chance to come to your senses."

"He is not lying," the heavy voice said as it sprang into Sam's head. "You may accept the offer from the devil's agent and become one of the undead. There will be no more trials and tests should that be your decision. The choice is yours."

"Tested by both God and Satan?" Sam flung the silent question. "How much is to be placed on my shoulders, and when does it end?"

But the mysterious voice was silent.

Both Roma and Falcon were once again aware of the strange power in the room, neither of them understanding it.

"Your decision, young man?" Falcon urged.

239

"Go to hell!" Sam told him.

Both Roma and Falcon laughed, Falcon saying, "Oh, we've been there, many times. Even at its best, it is a dismal place."

"Then we'll do our best to avoid it." Sam locked eyes with the man.

"Very well," Roma said. "I would suggest the both of you enjoy your . . . day of rest." Both she and the warlock laughed.

The witch and the warlock vanished before their eyes, leaving behind them a foul odor of sulfur.

Nydia's hand covered Sam's fingers and he gently squeezed it. "It'll be all right," he said.

A different odor covered the departing smell of Roma and Falcon. This one was hideous, stinking of stale blood and rotting flesh, of the grave and beyond.

Nydia looked up, her nose wrinkling at the smell. Her eyes widened, face paling. She began to scream.

Sam started to turn around, to see what Nydia was viewing. Something savage smashed into his head and he fell, tumbling into painful darkness.

"They have all withdrawn from sight," Wade said, putting down the shotgun. He was very tired, and he had left his bifocals at home, having to make do with an old, inadequate pair of glasses he kept in the glove compartment for emergencies.

"They have withdrawn—period," Miles said. He put his shotgun on a table, Doris frowning as the front sight scarred the polished wood. But she said nothing to her husband of oh-so-many years. Good years . . . all of them. No regrets.

And she was sorry she had called him a klutz so many

times over those years. But even with that feeling of love and penitence, she had to smile. Miles was clumsy . . . always had been. She said prayers even when he tried such a simple task as changing a light bulb. Especially if he had to stand on a stepladder. For if he didn't fall off the ladder, he would always manage to drop one of the bulbs; usually the good one.

But she loved him, loved him with all her heart: he was such a good, decent man. Just like Wade, but in a completely different way. Both of them were honest, decent, and Godfearing, helpful to people in need, no matter what race or religion. She sighed in remembrance.

She turned her attentions back to the men, who were, as usual, arguing.

". . . in hell do you know that?" Wade was saying.

"I know. I feel it. Something drastic has happened. You wait, you'll see. Sam will tell you I'm right."

"He is right." Balon's voice jarred them all.

They still could not accustom themselves to Balon's sudden appearances.

Balon said: "They will not be back here. Ever. They will come for Jane Ann on the night before their final night on earth."

"And us?" Miles asked hopefully. One could always keep a bit of optimism that The Man might change His mind.

"We will exit this life together."

Miles muttered something inaudible to human ears.

"I heard that," Balon said.

"So sue me," Miles replied.

"What about him? It?" Doris pointed toward the front steps, at the golem sitting hugely, impassively.

"He requires no aid, no comfort, no food or water—he

241

is all those things. He will sit thusly until he is needed. When he is done with here, he will return to the river."

"I feel sorry for him," Anita said.

"Oh, for heaven's sake, honey," Wade said. "He's made of clay; he has no emotions, no feelings, no concept of what a human experiences. And I still don't believe he's really here."

"Don't blaspheme," Miles said quickly. "Now is not the time. Just accept."

Balon spoke to Wade: "You are wrong. God breathed life into him, so he does have feelings. He has feelings of protectiveness toward the four of you. But since he has no tongue, he cannot express them. Since he has no eyes, he cannot see you—as you know vision—so you cannot see his feelings. But that is just as well. Doris would probably have had him in for coffee and cake."

"And didn't I have *you* in often enough for cake and coffee?" Doris challenged the mist. "I committed some sin by doing that? You ate like a horse, Sam Balon."

"Doris!" Miles was appalled. "You hush up that kind of talk. Don't you know who you're talking to?"

"I'm talking to Sam Balon the same way I always talked to Sam Balon. And I'll speak the same way when we get to . . . wherever it is we're going."

"I never heard of such disrespect for the . . . excuse me, Sam . . . dead," Miles said. "Sam—why? Why did they pull back?"

"Because Satan knows he is beaten here."

"But people are still being raped and tortured and tormented and dying," Wade said.

"That is true."

"Why?"

"I do not question the will of God."

"Will we get a chance to ask Him?" Wade persisted.

The hollow voice that was Balon chuckled, then projected: "I think you're in for a surprise, Wade."

"What do you mean, preacher?"

"You'll see."

"Janey?" Anita asked.

"She is well."

"That's not what I meant."

"I know. She has an ordeal ahead of her. A terrible one. But she will endure."

"You can't know that for certain, Sam," Doris said.

"I know."

Then the voice faded and the house was still.

Sam's head hurt, throbbing with pain. The side of his head was sticky. He put his fingertips to his head and gingerly touched the aching. His fingers came away sticky. He touched his head again, exploring the wetness, finding a small cut just above his ear.

Groaning, he attempted to sit up in the darkness. He made it on the second attempt, rested for a moment, then got slowly to his feet, swaying in the darkness of the . . . he looked around him . . . of the what? Where was he?

As his eyes began to penetrate some of the gloom around him, he could tell he was in a large room. A damp basement, he concluded. He stood very still, attempting to get his bearings. He was confused: Roma had assured them no physical action would be taken until Thursday night.

"And of course you believed her." The mysterious voice ripped into his aching head. "Words from the Devil's whore? How typically mortal."

Sam's temper flared. "Sermons I don't need. If you knew she wasn't to be trusted, why didn't you tell me?"

"You are your father's son."

"I'm getting a little tired of hearing that, too, Mr. whoever-you-are."

The powerful, awesome voice chuckled, and Sam could hear the rumblings of nearby thunder.

"Nydia!" He remembered her screaming. "Where is she?"

"Never take anything for granted," the voice said.

"What!"

"Do not trust them further. For as it is written: he knoweth that he hath but a short time."

"All I asked was a reasonably simple question. Why are you giving me such a bad time with all these riddles?"

"Oh, but I don't speak in riddles. It is only that you interpret my words as puzzles. But bear this in mind: remember your father's words at the airport."

Sam's sigh was more exasperation than frustration or anger. "What words?" he asked wearily. "More riddles?"

" 'I cannot guarantee she will not be hurt. If anything, it was blessed by the Dark One.' Now go to her."

A wind blew cold through the darkness; a door banged open, dim light beyond it.

"Through that door, huh?"

"You have reservations?"

"Yeah. How do I know you're one of the good guys and not Old Scratch pulling my leg?"

And again the powerful voice chuckled. Once more, thunder rumbled overhead. "You are learning, young warrior."

Sam felt the mysterious force move away. He was alone.

He looked toward the dim light of the open door. "Oh, what the hell . . . heck. No! I meant hell!" He walked out of the dampness into the cold of the Canadian night. And it struck him: night! How long was I out? Hours, at least. That had to have come from more than a knock on my head.

"Witchery." That almost overpowering voice cut into his head.

"Thanks." Sam's reply was dry. He spoke as he walked around the huge mansion, searching for a door. "Tell me: Are you here to help me, or just to bug me?"

"Bug?"

"Annoy; harass; needle."

"Ah. I haven't as yet decided."

"You will let me know?"

"Oh, you will know, young warrior. I promise you that."

Sam stopped at a back door. "I'm going through that door; so I'll be looking forward to hearing from you again. When you decide which side you're on."

The chuckling, thundering. "Oh, I know which side, young warrior. Of that you may be certain."

"Riddles," Sam muttered. "Riddles. I don't know what I'm doing here; don't know what I'm supposed to do—not really; and don't know how I'm supposed to accomplish what it is I'm not sure I'm supposed to do. If that makes any damn sense."

Thunder rolled.

"Yeah," Sam said. "Real cute." He opened the door and stepped into the warmth of the house.

*   *   *

The speaker of mighty words and the producer of thunder appeared in the circle of stones behind the mansion and once more sat on a boulder. He folded his massive arms across his chest. The manlike traveler appeared to be waiting for someone.

It was not a long wait.

"Why didn't you tell the young man his young woman saw the face of the Hooved One?"

"I think he has to be tested further. But . . . perhaps I should have. Is that what you wish me to do?"

"A test? A painful, wicked one, Warrior. What I want you to do? I didn't want you here to begin with."

"But I am here."

"Obviously. And instead of listening to the pleas of mortals and attempting to keep shaky fingers off of buttons that would ruin the earth, I am with you, wondering why my most powerful ally is sitting on a rock in a circle of stones, erected to worship Satan."

"The Foul One does not know of my presence."

"He suspects."

"Am I supposed to tremble with fear at that knowledge?"

The Heavens rumbled with laughter. "Hardly. But at the risk of being redundant, this is not your place. I should order you away."

"If you do, I shall obey."

"Yes," the most powerful voice in all the thousands of worlds seemed to sigh. "But have I ever?"

"No."

"And so I shall not this time."

And with a rush of wind, the voice faded, leaving the mightiest of God's warriors sitting on the rock, thoughtfully stroking his beard.

Sam wandered through the huge mansion, making his way to his room, hoping he would find Nydia there. Their rooms were empty; the great house silent. As a grave. He shook that thought away.

He washed the cut on his head and applied some antiseptic to the small wound, then took several aspirin and changed clothes. He debated several moments over whether to take the .45 pistol, then shook his head and left the weapon where it was. He went in search of Nydia.

He stopped at every door, carefully looking in every room. He found no one in either the east or west wings of the mansion, on either floor. The dining area was deserted, as were the servants' quarters. That left only one place. Sam stood very still in the foyer, listening for the sound that had stopped him in his search. There it was again.

Organ music.

He listened to the faint but unmistakable sounds of funeral music, somber and low, coming from up above him.

"Funeral music?" he said. "Who died?"

And then panic hit him hard. What was it the voice had said, speaking in riddles, repeating his father's words: I cannot guarantee she will not be hurt.

"Nydia!" Sam said, running toward the curving stairway, taking the steps two at a time, running for the third floor of the mansion, the music becoming louder with each step, heard over the hammering of Sam's heart and the blood rushing hotly through his veins.

"Nydia," he whispered. "Nydia!"

He flung open each door he came to, with each room

247

yielding the same: nothing. He stopped in the center of the dimly lighted hall, staring at the open, yawning door at the end of the hall. Flickering candlelight danced deceptively from the room, and a heady, not unpleasant East Indian essence drifted from the gloom. The music became louder, but this time it was accompanied by the sounds of soft weeping, from a number of people.

Sam walked toward the open double doors, the scent of incense growing stronger with his faltering reluctant footsteps. He stopped just inside the door, just as the gloom and the music and the sweet odor of musk and jasmine enveloped him.

He cut his eyes to the candlelit scene at the end of the long narrow room. A coffin, lid open, rested on a bier, on deep black velvet. The body that lay with its hands folded across its stomach was pale, the lips bloodless. It took but one look to tell there was no life left within the beautiful corpse, or who it was lying there.

Nydia.

SEVENTEEN

Sam's fragile world spun madly for a few seconds, almost dropping him to the carpet. He maintained control, rubbing his face with shaky, sweaty hands. He took several steps closer to the casket, nearer to the dreaded sight, hoping all this was some awful joke. It was not. Nydia was dead.

Roma and Falcon came to his side. He looked at them closely: their faces were pale and drawn, with real worry lines creasing their brows.

Sam touched Nydia's hand. Cold and dead. He withdrew his fingers.

"We are sorry," Falcon said, his voice deep and sepulchral.

"Yes," Roma echoed his sentiments. "Even though we . . . are worlds apart in worshiping Masters, she was my daughter, from my womb, and I loved her, in my own strange way."

"How . . . ?" Sam started to ask.

"Time enough for that," Falcon verbally restrained him. "But suffice to say, we had nothing to do with Nydia's . . . untimely demise. And we both beg you to believe that."

"But you were going to kill us both!" Sam protested, once more touching Nydia's cold flesh. He shuddered.

"So how can you expect me to believe you had nothing to do with . . . this?"

They gently led him from the scene of tragic young death. "Oh, no, no," Roma objected. "No . . . those were hollow threats . . . only that, nothing more. We wanted you both on our side . . . worshiping our Master, but by all that you believe in, do you think I would plot the death of my own daughter? My own flesh and blood? How ghastly, Sam! Cajole, threaten, bluff . . . and yes, I will admit it, even rape . . . but death? No, Sam . . . no."

"Ridiculous!" Falcon's look was both stern and filled with sorrow, perhaps even a touch of outrage at such a suggestion.

Across the room, and on both sides, the chairs were filled with Coven members, but they did not at all resemble the men and women Sam had witnessed prior to this; none of them wore the arrogance previously exhibited on their faces. Jimmy Perkins broke into wracking sobs; soon others joined him, the sounds of weeping almost drowning out the soft, sad music.

"You look exhausted, Sam," Falcon said. Roma put a soft, perfumed hand on the young man's arm. "Let my wife get you some coffee, something to eat, perhaps, and you can tell us where you've been for hours."

"You don't know?" Sam asked.

"No," her reply was open and honest. Sam searched her face for a sign of a lie, but could find none. "How could we know?"

"But you people did that!" he almost shouted the words, pointing toward the open casket.

Her face registered her shock. "No, Sam . . . we didn't. Falcon was telling the truth. We did not. But our

250

Master did."

"Satan?"

"That . . . pig!" Roma spat the word with such venomous hatred Sam was stunned. She spoke it as if clearing her mouth of something nasty.

"But he is your God, your Master," Sam said. "How can you call him a pig?"

"He may or may not be our Master," Falcon injected. "That is something we both want to speak to you about. But first," he sighed, "I must go offer my apologies to Nydia. Whether she can hear them or not, it is something I must do." He walked to the casket and gazed down at the face of death. There were tears rolling down his cheeks. Genuine tears.

"I . . . don't understand," Sam said.

"Is it too late for us?" Roma asked, all the while gently leading the young man to a room off the large mourning room. There she sat him on a couch and shut the door behind her, blocking out all sounds of the weeping, the sad melodious notes of the organ; only the soft scent of incense remained.

"All that," Roma flung her arm toward the door and the scene behind it, "has come home to us, Sam. Reluctantly, at first, I have to admit it, but finally with more conviction than I have felt in . . . well, might as well be truthful, hundreds of years. I began to admire your God."

Sam stood up. "This is a trick!" He turned to leave the room.

The sounds of Roma's weeping stopped him. He turned, real tears were streaming from her eyes. "Oh, Sam, I'm so confused. I don't know what to do, where to turn. None of us do. Do you think we would be, to a person, weeping and mourning if we did not feel a terrible sense of loss and of guilt over this tragedy? We have spoken of nothing else for hours: repentance, the coldbloodedness of the creature we worshiped, yes, even admired for centuries. We want," she sighed, ". . . out."

Sam returned to his seat on the couch, beside Roma. "I don't know what I can do."

"Nydia said you took her into the arms of your God. Can't you do the same for us?"

"Baptize you?"

"If that is what it takes, yes."

"You would have to renounce all other gods, and you would have to be sincere in that renunciation, for my God can see into your hearts."

"I know," she said softly. "And for Falcon and myself, and a few of the others, it would mean instant death. We are willing to do that."

"Death?"

"Yes, Sam Balon King. The instant holy water touches the flesh of a witch, warlock, or the undead, we die."

"You're willing to go that far?"

"Yes," the softly spoken one-word condemnation touched him as might a velvet-encased hand gripping his heart.

He cut his eyes to the door. "You've discussed this with all the people out there?"

"Every one of them, Sam. That is how severely this . . . tragedy has touched us all."

"I just can't believe it," Sam leaned back in the couch, closing his eyes. "This is just too much . . . too much in one day." Test her, the thought came to him, but it was his thought, and not spoken from any outside source. He rose from the couch. "I'll be back in ten minutes. Who wants to be baptized first?"

Her smile was warm and sincere. "Anyone in that room."

"The line on the east wall, the third person from the end."

"As you wish, Sam."

He went to his room and filled a small bottle with blessed water from a church in Montreal. A member of the Coven sat beside Roma when Sam returned to the room, one of the newer members from New York. He smiled at Sam.

"I don't know all the right words," Sam told him. "But maybe this will work. You're sure you want to go through with this?"

"I am certain."

"This is no guarantee you'll get into Heaven," Sam told him.

"It's a guarantee that I will die, however," the man said gently.

Sam glanced at Roma. She smiled sadly. "I told you we were all sincere." She rose from the couch to stand beside Sam.

Sam looked at the man, sitting quietly before him. Sam sighed, and said, "Lord, I believe this man is sincere, and I'm asking You to help him. I . . . don't know what else to say." He wet his fingers with holy water and touched them to the man's forehead.

The man recoiled backward in pain, his flesh bubbling as the blessed liquid ate into his face. The man began a series of regression, as his body flew back in time. A

253

horrid stench filled the room. Soon there was nothing but a pile of rotting rags on the floor in front of the sofa.

Sam stood, stunned by it all.

Roma gently led him across the room, to another couch. "This is going to be a terrible ordeal for you, Sam. I think you had better have some coffee, a sandwich before you continue."

"Yes," he said. "You're right. Please, that would be nice."

He must have dozed for a few moments, for when he opened his eyes, Roma was beside him on the couch, smiling at him. Sam thought he had never seen such a sad, tender smile in his life. On a coffee table, a small steaming pot of coffee, two cups, and a thick sandwich.

"Eat," she urged him, pouring the cups full of rich-smelling coffee. "Then we'll talk about your God."

"This is not a dream?"

"No, Sam. It's very real. And in case you think the food or drink is drugged, choose what cup you want and give me any part of the food."

He shook his head. "I believe you." He looked at the pile of rags across the room. "After that."

The sandwich was delicious, the coffee as good as the first cup he'd had in the dining area of the mansion—it seemed so long ago. He listened to Roma speak, her words tearing at him as he suspected they were to her.

"Satan broke all the rules, coming here, speaking to us. He told us he would no longer abide by any rules of the game."

"The game?" Sam questioned.

"Of course, it's a game, Sam. A game between the two mightiest players in all the universe. This universe and

254

all the others. A game they have been playing for thousands of years."

"A game," Sam said dully.

"A very ugly game, and a very profane one. The Foul One returned, appearing behind you. He is seldom seen in his natural form—even by us. He is . . . grotesque, hideous. His very presence often kills should human eyes fall on his ugliness. Nydia's did."

Sam touched the side of his head. "Who hit me?"

"The Dark One. He is everywhere at once, as is your God—my God, I hope. Sam?" she leaned forward until her face was only a few inches from his. "Will you teach me how to pray to your God before you baptize me?"

"If . . . you would like that, sure."

"Oh, yes, I would like that. More than anything in this world, for I know my time remaining is very short, and growing shorter."

"My God might . . ."

"No," she shushed him, placing a soft finger to his lips. "I know things you do not. Now finish your sandwich, Sam, and then teach me how to pray."

Sam finished the hefty sandwich and drank another cup of coffee. "I feel so guilty, Roma, sitting here eating while . . . she is . . ." He could not bring himself to say the word: dead.

"Don't be," she slipped a bit closer to him. "Do you think Nydia would want that?"

"No, I suppose not. You're right, of course. She would be happy for you. Is Satan still here?"

"He is everywhere."

"That's not what I meant."

"I know. Yes, I can feel his presence. He is furious, but

unable to do anything about his anger—at this time. You see, Sam, by merely talking with you about . . . our decision to reject Satan and accept your God . . . well, that puts the Dark One in a very bad position. Now he *can't* make any moves against you; all his earthly allies— that is, we at Falcon House—have switched sides, and the Prince is fearful of your God's powers should he break any more rules."

"It's all very confusing, Roma. But I'm happy for you, if you're sincere, and I believe you are." Sam waited for the mysterious voice to hammer at his brain, but his head remained free of any silent vocal intrusion.

"I don't resent your doubts, Sam," she said, moving a bit closer to him. He was suddenly very much aware of the woman heat of her. "Of course you have suspicions, why shouldn't you?"

The perfume she wore was a scent Sam had never smelled before: very pleasant, not too heady, not too light. And as it assailed his nostrils, the essence seemed to relax the young man, wrapping him in fragrant invisible arms.

"You're very tired, Sam," he heard her say. He nodded his head in agreement as fatigue hit him hard. "Why don't you sleep for a while? The rest will do you good."

Sam struggled to remember why he was here, but his mind drew a blank. He could but vaguely remember soft music and the scent of lighted candles and incense. Everything was blocked out of his mind. What does it matter? he thought, as arms of incredible sweetness and softness slipped around him, cradling him gently.

"Here, Sam," Roma whispered, amid the rustling of clothing, the soft snick of a clasp opening. "Rest your head here." She pulled his head to her breasts.

Somehow, Sam thought, I knew they would be bare and beautiful. He opened his eyes, no more than a slit, and found the breasts to be more than beautiful: the nipples were stiff and erect, set amid half dollar sized rose-colored circles. And it seemed only natural his lips would find the papilla, encircling it.

Her hands were at the back of his head, gently holding his mouth to her breast, silently encouraging the young man to suckle her as a child.

Sam felt feverish. Not the unnatural heat of sickness, but that his clothing was an encumbrance he did not need.

"Here," she said, "let me help you." Her fingers worked at the buttons of his shirt, and Sam quickly felt the coolness of air on his bare arms. Pillowing his head against her breasts, he could not think of one single reason why he should object as she worked at his belt buckle, loosening the snap at his waistband. The snick of the zipper followed, and he moved his legs, assisting her in the lowering of his jeans.

She held him close to her for several moments, one hand resting on his flat belly, where his T-shirt had pulled up, exposing just a few inches of bare skin.

He heard her say: "It will be wonderful, Sam. You and I, together."

"Yes," he replied, in a voice that seemed strange to him, alien, not from his larynx. He added, "At last." Although he did not know why he said that.

She moved slightly, and her skirt was gone. She was naked. Sam started to protest that this was wrong, but that strange perfume stiffled any objection forming

257

within him.

Why is it wrong? he asked himself.

"It isn't wrong," she said.

"Yes," he said. "It isn't."

Sam was conscious of cool air on his groin, but he felt it wasn't worth the effort to open his eyes and look. Then he realized his underwear shorts had been removed and that seemed all right, as well. Everything seemed all right. Natural. Perfect. A man and a woman together. He moved his head to the satiny smoothness of her naked belly and kissed the indentation of navel, aware of the woman scent of her.

She moved her hand, fingers encircling his growing thickness, stroking him into surging hardness, bringing him, through the manipulation of her skillful touch, almost to the point of ejaculation.

Then, with one swift movement, she mounted him, laughing as she did so.

Everything returned to Sam . . . coming in such a rush it almost overwhelmed him with its magnitude: his father's warnings, the warnings of the mysterious voice. Nydia! her memory leaped into his brain. Where he was; what had happened; what was happening. He recalled the vision he had shared with Nydia: the scene of his father fighting with the witch . . . this woman who now had impaled herself on his maleness, driving her way frantically toward completion.

He began fighting the witch, attempting to dislodge her from his erection, but her strength was incredible. Despite his feelings of revulsion and self-disgust, knowing he had been tricked like a schoolboy, Sam was very close to exploding his semen into her wetness.

She held his hands to her waist with no more effort than if she were pinning a helpless baby to its crib. And despite himself, Sam felt his juices boiling. They began to spill over, then exploded. Using her inner muscles, Roma milked the last drop of precious semen from him, pulled away from him, and padded naked to a table. There, she picked up a vial of dark red fluid, opened the small bottle, and drained it into her mouth.

Sam was too weak to move as she began speaking in a language he did not understand, the incantation evil as it rolled from her tongue. Lightning licked around the mansion, as thunder ripped the countryside, the smell of burning sulfur strong in the stormy air.

Laughter reached Sam's ears, spilling from the other room. Hot, wild rage filled him, causing his blood to run strong, giving him the strength to claw on his clothing and stagger from the room where he had been seduced into an unwilling paramour.

The scene that greeted him was of the vilest imaginable: a grotesque real-life panorama more vivid than anything Hollywood could ever produce in its most brutish moods. Nydia had been lifted from the casket, pillows placed under her. She was naked, her lifeless white arms hanging over the sides of the brass entrapment. Her lovely legs spread apart, knees to feet hanging out of the casket. Falcon was between her thighs, his gross maleness erect, pumping in and out of the young woman.

Shouting his rage, Sam charged the sickness before his unbelieving eyes. He was tripped, sending him tumbling to the floor, where he was kicked and beaten into semiconsciousness. He lay bloodied on the carpet, unable to stop the hideousness taking place.

Falcon's hardness became slick with blood, and Sam could not understand that, for Nydia was dead. Then he decided in his near delirium it was not blood, merely the way the candles cast their dubious flickering light.

Nydia's head was thrown back, her mouth a black gaping hole, eyes closed in surrender on her voyage to the stygian shore.

Falcon continued to ram his maleness into her.

"Why don't you pray, mother-fucker?" a female voice screeched at Sam.

He looked up through his pain into the wild eyes of Lana, squatting half naked beside him.

Sam shook his head as the taunts began, profane and loud, exhorting him to call on his God for help. He fought to get to his feet, but hands turned into fists, pounding him back to the carpet. He watched as the ugly act of necrophilia drew closer to completion, Falcon lunging in earnest, burying his long thickness into the dead flesh of Nydia. The man howled like an animal as he ejaculated, spilling into the young woman.

Falcon arrogantly rose from the satin-lined casket like some monster from the grave, and stepped onto the floor, wiping his softening penis with a towel handed him from one of those as lost as he.

Sam put his head on the carpet and wept.

"Oh, don't be such a crybaby, Sam!" Roma's voice cut at him as a cat-o'-nine-tails would rip the flesh of its victim. "You may have her now." She raised her hand and performed a ritual that was too quick for Sam to follow.

He shifted his eyes to the sounds of someone suddenly

weeping and thought he was going utterly mad as Nydia's eyes opened and she looked around her, a bewildered expression on her face, as if she not only did not understand where she was, but why she was crying. She looked down at her nakedness, then at her temporary home, and screaming joined the tears.

Roma laughed. "There is your darling, Sam. Take her, and witness what marvelous parturient pops from her womb. You won't have a long wait, for when my Master takes a hand, events such as the one now growing within Nydia's womb develop rapidly, such wonders to perform. Take your darling, Sam, and both of you carry your sniveling selves from this room. So we lost a member from your application of holy water," she answered the puzzled look in his eyes. "No great loss—it is an honor to die for the Master." She cackled like the witch she was. "How does it feel to be beaten, young man and woman of God?"

The room of lost and damned souls howled with laughter.

Sam pulled himself to his knees and wiped blood from cuts above his eyes. When he turned to look at the witch, she hissed with fright and drew back from the sight of his burning eyes. "We're not beaten, you whore. I'm whipped for now, but I'm not down for the count. I don't understand what has taken place here, for I know Nydia was dead; no one could look that dead and not be dead. I don't know if I'll ever understand it. But I know this: for some reason you can't or won't kill us . . . yeah," he said slowly, his eyes shifting to Nydia. "She's got to be kept alive, right? Sure. I see that. Me . . . I don't know why you didn't kill me after you screwed me . . . maybe I'll never know. But I'm going to beat you, bitch." His eyes lashed at the witch. "Some way, somehow, I'll win this battle. Bet on it."

Sam rose to his feet and walked to the candle-lighted bier, helping Nydia to the floor. No one tried to stop him, no one attempted to interfere. Sam ripped a drape from behind the bier and wrapped it around Nydia, covering her nakedness. They walked from the room amid the jeering, ugly sounds of the Unbelievers. Party music began playing, a loud raucous noise as the people began dancing in a hunching fashion around the room, the dancing more a lewd profanity than any type of graceful movement of partners.

"Sam?" Nydia spoke in a whisper, even though the room and all the evil of its occupants was farther behind them with each step. "I was . . . dead!"

"I know, honey. And don't ask me to explain it, 'cause I can't."

"Sam?"

He looked at her, taking her offered hand.

"I know what you have to do."

They were on the second floor of the great house, walking down the corridor to their rooms. "What, Nydia?"

"You have to make love to me, as quickly as possible."

"I . . . don't understand."

"Yes, you do," the voice boomed in his head. "And may your seed be strong."

"I heard the voice that time, Sam," she told him. "And that's why you have to make love to me."

"You *remember* Falcon raping you?"

"Every awful, ugly second of it. I can't explain it, for I

couldn't move—not even my eyes. But I could feel pain. It's . . . I was dead, Sam, but I wasn't. I know my heart stopped when I looked up and saw that thing . . . what in God's name was that?"

"I didn't see it, but Roma said it was the Devil. I guess that much of what she said was true. Your heart stopped?"

"Yes. I came back when Falcon . . . began raping me. Something else, Sam."

"What?"

"I . . . saw you and Roma."

"But you were . . ."

"I know. But I could still see you both. I was so proud of you when you fought through the drug and began to resist."

"The food was drugged?"

"No. The perfume she was wearing. An ancient aphrodisiac. She stayed within the rules of the game in using it."

Sam shuddered. "A game. Like no other game in the world."

"While we're here, Sam, we're not of this world. We're kind of in limbo."

Sam was conscious of that mighty presence near, but no voice sprang into his head. The force withdrew.

At the door to their rooms, Nydia stopped him. "You go take a shower, Sam. You smell like . . . well, like her. I've got to do something; maybe it will help."

"What?" Sam asked innocently.

She looked at him and shook her head. "Douche," she said flatly.

* * *

Sam tended to his face after the shower, applying antiseptic to the small cuts. One eye was puffy, the area under it turning a shade of greenish-blue, and there were numerous smaller bruises on his face and chest and legs. But he concluded he would live.

"How long and what for is the question," he muttered.

"How skeptical you are," the voice spoke to him. "Weren't you warned you would be tested? And wasn't it I who told you not to fear should you sometimes fail?"

"I did a pretty good job of failing this night, didn't I?" Sam said glumly.

"So did your father, but he found a place beside God."

"Am I right in doing what I'm . . . we're about to do?"

"I cannot answer that. That is something only you and the young woman can decide."

"What if Falcon's seed takes hold?"

"She would birth something truly awesome and terrible. Your seed within Roma was strong, and she will please her dark master."

"So I have to try and overcome Falcon's seed?"

"I told you: I cannot answer that for you."

"Why do I feel that what I'm about to do is right, but with a nagging feeling of guilt that it is somehow wrong?"

But the mighty force had gone, Sam feeling the invisible presence fade from his brain. He looked up as Nydia entered the room.

"You said we'd know His reasons for throwing us together like this, Sam. And it wouldn't be a moral question . . . or issue. Are we facing the real reason; doing what is right?"

"I . . . think so, Nydia."

She smiled. "I hate to quote an old line, Sam, but

264

please be gentle with me. I hurt."

And he was, and they both felt their lovemaking was somehow pure, somehow sanctified. And when it was over, and they were asleep, lost in exhaustion, something entered the room, something awesome in its righteous power, and it guarded the two as they slept.

And they were truly not alone.

EIGHTEEN

Miles and Wade stepped out onto the front porch, both of them wincing as the sickly sweet odor of death struck them again, assailing their sense of smell. They had just been around to the back, dragging the bodies of the Coven members from the backyard.

"I wonder why we can't smell it in the house?" Wade asked.

Miles smiled through the awful permeation. "I would guess this house is off limits, Wade. Protected."

The golem stared mutely ahead of him, unseen eyes never leaving the perimeter it was created to protect. It took no notice of the two men.

Somewhere in the distance, a thin yowl of pain could be heard, at first only a faint howl, then gradually building into a flesh-crawling shriek that wavered its way to the ears of the two men. The painful howling would then fade into a low moan, only to build again.

"Let's go back inside," Wade suggested. "I don't believe I care to leave the house again."

"Not until Saturday night," Miles said.

The editor glanced at his lifelong friend. "And where do we go at that time, pal?"

"Home, old friend."

*   *   *

Nydia was the first to notice the slight odor in the room. She lay watching Sam sleep, wanting to cry at his torn and bruised face. Then she noticed the faint odor. It was not unpleasant, not at all; it was . . . a male odor, she concluded. But not a sexual pungency. It was more a scent of supreme strength, of confidence. And she wondered how that could be, and how she could so easily identify the aroma of it? And she wondered, too, how or why the odor would fill her with an inner calmness, a peace she had not experienced in all her life?

And she knew with only the knowledge that a woman possesses that something else had occurred, but she decided she would keep that a secret for a while longer.

She lay very still, inhaling the strength of the man scent that lingered in the room. But, she frowned, it was more than that . . . it was, and she hesitated to use the word . . . almost holy, but yet, she decided, it was not pristine in its consecration: there was a touch of the warrior with it, a tinge of worldliness, as if whatever had left the scent was not only marking territory, but telling those within that region that it knew what they were experiencing . . . and what they would experience in the days to come.

And Nydia thought it very strange she would know all that.

And there was something else she detected: sadness. Just a very slight trace of that, but there nonetheless. Odd, she thought: I have never been so frightened in my life, but neither have I ever felt so secure in a . . . what? She struggled for a definition, a word, finally settling on faith.

Yes, she smiled. Faith.

Sam stirred by her side, and she had another thought

267

as she moved close to him, putting one arm across his bare chest, just above the burn that signified the Everlasting Cross on his flesh.

"Sam?" she whispered, her mouth close to his ear.

"Umm?" he stirred, pulling out of sleep, opening his eyes to look at her through eyes of love.

"I have an idea."

"Now?" his eyes widened.

"Oh, Sam! Not that. I want us to get married."

It took a moment for that to register with him. He finally cocked his head on the pillow and blinked rapidly several times. "Say again."

"You heard me." She lifted herself up on one elbow and stared down at him, thick strands of long silken hair shading one side of her face.

"Nydia . . . I mean, how? Who would perform the ceremony? I really doubt we could leave this house . . . or at least the immediate grounds. We'd have to leave . . ."

She shushed him with a soft kiss. "They have JPs in your country that marry people; judges and the like. They aren't ministers, so what makes them any better than you?"

"Me! This is weird, Nydia. And certainly illegal."

"I'm not concerned with moral law, Sam. And I'm really not sure it would be acceptable in the eyes of God—probably not. I just want the words, from you and from me . . . from out of our hearts. So let's get cleaned up, get dressed, and go into the timber and get married. Now!"

Sam knew, with only the knowledge reasonably intelligent men possess concerning their limited understanding of women, that it would be best not to argue.

Just get up and follow orders.

"He is pleased," Roma spoke to Falcon over coffee in her quarters. "Our Master said he was most happy with the way matters are proceeding."

"Are you with child?"

"Yes. I can feel the demon growing."

"When will you birth?"

"On the sixth day of the sixth week, precisely on the sixth hour."

"How prophetic. The Mark of the Beast. 666. And your chances, my dear?"

"None. I will die for the Master; the demon will live forever. As Black was meant to be and do. But I failed there."

"I am . . . admittedly unknowledgeable on such matters; they occur so rarely. How is 'forever' possible?"

"A demon . . . have you never seen one, Falcon?"

He shook his head. "Not on earth."

". . . They are of and for the Devil. Protected by him. Only a holy child, born in the same time frame, from the same father can kill the Master's son. And since you battered Nydia's cunt so well, the odds of that happening are infinitesimally minute."

"The same time frame?" Falcon looked confused.

"666. Day, week, month, or minute."

"But not necessarily at precisely the same moment as your birthing?"

"That is correct."

Falcon was thoughtful for a few seconds. "It is reasonable to assume Balon's boy-child of love coupled with Nydia last night?"

"I would think so. But your seed is much more

269

powerful, Falcon; older, with the strength of the Master. No . . . I think she is with a demon child."

Falcon was not so certain, but he hid his doubts. He changed the subject. "There was an . . . intruder in the house last evening. I am very much surprised you did not sense the presence."

"An intruder, Falcon?"

The warlock's only reply was to lift his eyes upward.

"You are certain?"

"As certain as I know Nydia's cunt was tight."

The mother took no umbrage to his statement. "Male or female?"

"Male. A warrior."

The witch and the warlock looked at each other, gazes all knowing, holding. "So he has slipped out again." It was not a question from Roma.

"It's been many years since that one took any direct action on earth," Falcon said. "Jeanne d'Arc."

"That we know of," Roma corrected him. "I don't like this; that one has bested our Master on more than one occasion."

"Don't let him hear you say that. You know how our Prince hates the warrior."

"There can be no mistakes this time, Falcon. I must get Nydia and leave this place. The demons must be birthed. We can't take a chance on staying."

Falcon's face showed his concern . . . and something else. Roma read the silent worry lines.

"What, Falcon?"

"My dear . . . I don't believe we *can* leave—any of us—until it is concluded. The Master might make an exception for you, taking into consideration your condition. But the rest of us . . ." He left it at that.

"What *are* you babbling about?"

He shook his handsome head. "Not babble, Roma. I spoke with the Dark One's emissary early this morning, just before dawn. She told me that Whitfield is cut off; no escape. All is lost except for the taking of Balon's whore. That is why our Master returned here."

"Then . . . he is here?"

"Nearby. Angry. Brooding."

"But I spoke with him last night!"

"He is not angry with us. He knows the warrior is here—or at least suspects it—and is furious that his enemy would allow such a breach of the rules."

Roma laughed. "Those so-called 'rules' are unimportant; for the most part a myth."

"But our Master believes his enemy should abide by those rules—since He professes to be so holy."

Roma quietly picked up on the reversal of roles between herself and Falcon. "You have suddenly become quite knowledgeable, darling."

"Your time is short, Roma, and growing shorter with each tick of the clock. He has elevated me to a more lofty position here on earth."

"Congratulations, Falcon. It was only a matter of time."

He nodded his acceptance and appreciation of her felicitation. "He is mulling over a suggestion of mine."

"Oh?"

"That we breach all rules of the game; kill the young warrior now, just after we call out the forces present invisibly at all black masses."

"How did he receive that suggestion?"

"Well, I think."

"It's dangerous, Falcon, and could easily get out of

control. Have you ever seen the calling out of the forces?"

"Truthfully . . . no. But Black Wilder told me once, oh, back in Germany, three centuries ago, back when I was a young buck, racing willy-nilly about, that he witnessed it once. Said it was quite spectacular, in a bell, book, and candle way. He was quite young when he saw it . . . about two hundred, I believe he said. In this life, that is. Said it came very close to frightening him."

"It is frightening, Falcon. And in my condition, I could not witness it; too dangerous." She was thoughtful for a moment. "While it is dangerous, calling out the spirits, you must have done some research on the subject."

Falcon smiled.

"I thought as much," she returned the devilish smile. "If God's warrior is here, that would infuriate the ancient warrior, and he would have to fight, for it is his nature to do that. Our forces might win—and I stress might—but if they lost, it would seriously deplete our od forces on this planet."

"I took that into consideration. We would call out only those within a certain, prescribed distance of this locale, and only every other one, thereby insuring us a reserve."

"Wise. When did our Master say he would reach his decision?"

"An hour before dawn, tomorrow. If our Master's reply is yes, a special mass will be called for tomorrow night—midnight."

"You will need two virgins and another young one for the altar, to cut out her heart."

"We have them. The children from the city. Black will have to take part, and that is the only stumbling block that I can see."

She shook her head. "My son is weak; not to be trusted. But I think perhaps a visit from the Dark One might put some steel in his backbone."

Falcon arched an eyebrow expressively.

"I will speak to the Prince if his answer is yes to the calling out."

Falcon nodded and turned to leave. "Oh," he said, "I saw Nydia and God's young warrior leaving the house a moment before I came here. They were practically beaming with love. I found it disgusting."

For a moment, Roma was flung back in time, to Whitfield, Fork County, to a little creek, beside which two lovers lay, performing a marriage ceremony without benefit of legal entanglements. She smiled, a bittersweet movement of her lips, the smile touched with evil.

"Why are you smiling?" Falcon asked.

"I was thinking about a marriage I witnessed back in '58."

"Whitfield?"

"Yes. I think Sam and Nydia are about to do the same."

"It must have touched you, Roma. For you to remember something so trivial all these years."

Her returning gaze was hard. "In a manner of speaking. I puked after they left."

"Here," Nydia said, looking at the familiar surroundings. "Where you made me a Christian."

"I didn't make you a Christian, Nydia," Sam replied.

"You made yourself a Christian. I just dropped a few sprinkles of water on your head." His face changed after saying that, hardening.

"What's wrong, Sam?"

"I was thinking about holy water, and how quickly it killed that man last evening. Last evening," he said softly. "So much is happening so fast."

"We must have picked up several quarts of holy water in the city," Nydia reminded him.

"We'll probably need every drop before this is over." And he smiled mischievously, one hand dropping into his jacket pocket.

"Why are you smiling, Sam?"

He pulled out a tiny vial of water. "I think we can spare this, don't you?"

Sudden tears sprang into her eyes. "Oh, Sam, I love you."

"I love you, too." He gently kissed her mouth. "You got the Bible?" He did not notice the tiny marks on the side of her neck, right above the vein.

"Yes. Where do I open it?"

"I haven't the vaguest idea. Let's sit down and look at it."

They sat and read for a time, reading various verses of different books of the Bible. Then Sam turned to the beginning. Together, they read parts of Genesis, neither of them knowing that Sam Balon had done the same thing when he married young Sam's mother in that impromptu ceremony, witnessed only by God and a tiny singing bird.

"I like this," Nydia said, pointing to chapter two, verses 23 and 25.

"Then that's what it will be," Sam said.

They read the passages aloud, and then solemnly anoinfed each other's head with a tiny bit of holy water. They kissed tenderly, gently, Nydia saying, "I guess we're married."

"In whose eyes is the question," the strong voice came to them both.

"Did you hear that?" Nydia asked.

"Yes." Sam looked around him, and when he spoke, it was directed at the mysterious voice. "What do you mean: in whose eyes?"

But the voice was silent.

"I sensed his presence in the room this morning. Strong and male and fearless. I was going to say something about it, but the marriage idea came right on top of it."

Sam smiled. "Interesting choice of words. The voice speaks in riddles, I'd better warn you of that."

"Not this time. The hooved one has made his decision. You, young warrior, are marked for death. A special black mass has been called for tomorrow night. They will attempt to call out the forces of darkness. If they succeed, I will do battle with them. You will know at midnight tomorrow night if their calling has been successful. If so, you must take your . . . wife and leave the house immediately. Do not attempt to fight them alone, they are too wily for your young age. You both must run and hide in the timber. But, a word of warning: you cannot travel past the set boundaries. You will know them, for they are easily seen. Remember, young warrior, your sole purpose is to destroy this coven, and the tablet, if possible."

"Tablet? What tablet?" Sam asked.

"The Devil's tablet. It is here. Hidden."

"And if I destroy it, what happens?"

"That is an unanswerable question, for it has never been destroyed."

"Wonderful," Sam said sarcastically. "How will I know this tablet?"

"It will know you, for the tablet is evil, and you represent good."

"May I ask what may appear to be a foolish question?"

"Ask."

"Why me? And who are you?"

"That is two questions. Which do you want answered?"

"The first one."

"Because you are who you are."

"Thank you so very much!"

"Sam!" Nydia touched his arm. "Don't be ugly to . . . him."

"You are . . . good," the voice rumbled in their heads. "Both of you. Not perfect, but no mortal is. And I have made my decision: I will help you."

They both felt the force withdraw. They sat on the log, by the little creek, staring in amazement at each other.

"Sam?" Nydia said, her voice low. "Is all this a dream? Are we both going to wake up back at school and laugh about this?"

"No. But I wish that were true."

"Sam?"

"Umm?"

"I'm getting cold."

"I brought two blankets and a ground sheet."

"I wonder whatever on earth for?" She grinned shyly, then playfully but gently tickled his ribs. Gently because

276

she knew how bruised they were.

"You really don't know?" Sam grinned.

"Oh, honestly, I don't!"

He showed her, both of them a bit timid and embarrassed, wondering if the face behind the voice was watching.

He was. And was both amused and concerned for them.

MONDAY AFTERNOON

While Sam carefully inspected the two backpacks he had put together, and oiled and cleaned the .45 pistol and the old Thompson SMG, Nydia went unmolested to the kitchen, where she put together enough food to last them several days, carrying it back to their rooms. She encountered several people on the trips, but they ignored her, not looking at or speaking to her. She felt like a stranger in a strange land, unable to speak the language, and fearful of the inhabitants. She saw Jimmy Perkins, and he openly leered at her, rubbing his crotch as she passed him. She kept her eyes straight ahead.

She saw Mac in the study, speaking with Black and Falcon. The look she received from the young man was not friendly, and she suspected he had been swayed into accepting the Other Side. When she returned from the kitchen, she saw Vicky sitting on Mac's lap, the young man openly fondling her bare breasts, and she knew her suspicions were correct. She did not know how he had been so easily converted, only that he had.

Sam did not seem surprised at the news. "Mac's weak," he said. "And he hasn't made many friends at school. The others told me he was a jack-off artist; couldn't get a date with anyone. That's probably one of the reasons Black invited him up here; knew he'd be an

278

easy convert."

"Then we're alone, except for Linda, and I don't like her," Nydia said. "Jack-off artist, Sam? That's sad."

He shrugged. "Nydia, what is it between you and Linda?"

She shook her head. "I . . . hope I'm wrong about her—the way I feel. But I don't know."

"Come on, Nydia: the truth. Why don't you like her?"

She smiled, an obvious effort on her part. "You're thinking I'm jealous . . . and in part, you're right. But only a very small part is jealousy, Sam. Hear me out," she raised a hand as he started to interrupt. "It's time. You remember on the way up here, that first day, the three of us? I told you I knew more about you than you thought? Well, Linda was my source of information. For the first few weeks of school, we roomed together."

"Sure, now I remember: Black had a few dates with her."

"My brother, in his eloquent manner of speaking, told me Linda didn't put out. That's why he stopped dating her. But he told her enough about you to get her interested, and she talked about you almost nonstop; almost as if she were desperate to get with you. I had to get out, move into a different room. But that's not the main reason, Sam. I don't trust her. I think she's one of . . . them," she averted her eyes to the door. "And they don't know it."

"I . . . don't follow you, honey."

"All right, then hear this; tell me what it means: There is a . . . peculiar mark on Linda's chest, just under her left breast. She saw me looking at it and told me it was a birthmark. But that's no birthmark, Sam. I've seen others like it, on people visiting here at Falcon House.

279

One time that same mark was on *all* the people here. I saw it when they were swimming. I sneaked out of my room to a place just off the pool area. I was just a little girl at the time, but I've never forgotten it. They frightened me. I ran back to my room and stayed there the entire time they were here, pretending to be sick."

"What does this mark look like?"

"A five-pointed star."

"Pentagram. I know from watching horror movies that has something to do with black magic, the occult. Why didn't you tell me about this before, Nydia?"

"I never gave it much thought, Sam. Things were happening so quickly around here it just slipped my mind. Then all of a sudden, the other day, when she was sitting with us at the table, it came to me . . . like a sixth sense in my head." She sighed, "Maybe I'm paranoid."

"And maybe not," Sam said thoughtfully. "We'll just have to play it by ear while we're getting ready to run."

She came to him and put her arms around his waist. "Hold me, Sam."

She was trembling, and Sam could sense, with the recently acquired powers of perception and silent communication, that the trembling had nothing to do with fear.

"What's the matter, honey? I know something is wrong, but I can't read you."

"Don't ask me how I know, Sam; I've read and heard that some women just sense when they're pregnant. And I'm pregnant. I know it."

Sam thought, forgetting that she could read his thoughts, I wonder if the baby belongs to me, or to Falcon?

"That's the problem, Sam. I don't know!"

*　　*　　*

"You are to remain close to Sam Balon King," the burning voice scorched into the brain of the receiver. "If all fails here, and he dies, then your *only* mission in life will be to stay with Nydia and make certain of the well-being of the child growing within her womb. Accept whatever comes your way, be it feigned faith in their God, or the life of poverty or prostitution, only the child's welfare is important—do you understand?"

"Yes, Master," her voice was full of strength and awe.

"You are a good actress. Your show to date has been superb. I compliment you."

"Thank you, Master. It was all for you."

"Don't become gushy, bitch! I cannot tolerate such behavior. You are a woman, your only purpose in life is to fuck; receiving maleness in whatever hole they choose to stick it in. Don't forget what I told you."

"I shall not, Master."

"For your sake, I hope not. Now go to them."

"Sam? Nydia?" the knock on the closed door as timid as the voice.

Nydia looked at Sam. "Your sweetie, darling," she said, her voice as warming as an arctic breeze in the dead of winter.

"Retract claws, dear," Sam told her. "We don't know anything for certain."

"I know one thing for sure. No . . . make that two things."

"And that is . . . ?"

"She's got the hots for you, and if she tries to come on, I'll snatch her bald-headed."

Sam nodded his head as he moved toward the door,

281

remembering Nydia's right cross in the den. He opened the door cautiously, tensely, expecting anything to come leaping at him. But Linda stood there, looking pale and frightened and really, Sam thought, real pretty.

"I read that!" Nydia projected.

Damn! "Come in, Linda." He closed the door behind her.

"Wow," she said. "What happened to your face?"

"Little accident," Sam said, not really lying to her. "Tell you about it later."

"I . . . uh . . . just wanted to be with you guys for a few minutes, that's all. Maybe have dinner with you all this evening, if that's okay?"

"Of course," Nydia answered for the both of them, thinking, Where would you like to start eating—on Sam?

"And I read that, honey."

"You're going to read a lot more before this evening is over."

"You guys went off somewhere this morning," Linda said. "I got a little panicky."

Nydia was hammering mental thrusts at Linda, attempting to enter her mind. She could not. Her attitude softened a bit toward the young woman, as she detected truth in her statements. Still, there was something about her . . . some little vagueness Nydia could not pinpoint.

"We went for a walk in the timber," Sam said.

And got married, Nydia thought. So hands off, babe! And, she mentally tallied up the events of the past twenty-four hours, where were you when I was getting raped by Falcon's baseball bat.

"It's not that big," Sam projected.

"It wasn't sticking in you, dear."

"True. Thank God."

Linda said, "I don't know what's been the matter with me lately. I sleep so soundly . . . even when I lie down just to nap. I've never done that before . . . sleep so much, I mean."

"It's the cold clean air," Sam suggested.

Linda solemnly shook her head. "No, Sam. It's much more than that. And I think you two know it. This place is weird! No offense, Nydia, but it's true—it is. I'd like to leave; go back to Carrington. Would one of you take me?"

Sam sighed, cutting his eyes to Nydia. She shrugged. "Sit down, Linda," he said. "I guess we'd better talk."

Jane Ann stood at her picture window, gazing out at the quiet street. It was ominously silent in Whitfield. For a time there had been the faint sounds of hammering. Now that was gone.

Jane Ann looked down at her hands and was reminded of a TV commercial: Hands of a twenty year old, she smiled. But not for long. That hammering was meant for me. They wanted me to hear it. She again looked at her hands. It's going to hurt when they drive the nails.

The mist that was Balon hovered silently, watching Jane Ann, knowing every thought in her mind and unable to help, for what she was thinking was true. And if a being from the Other Side could sigh, Balon did, knowing she would have to endure almost unbearable pain for a time . . . before he could step in to end it. She would be humiliated, sexually assaulted, tortured . . . tested. Only then could he end it. And after Balon did that, He would really end it, and Whitfield would be no more.

283

Miles and Doris, Wade and Anita sat in the growing darkness of the living room, discussing the Bible. They knew they should turn on some lights, but they did not want to break the feeling of closeness they were sharing.

"Let's pray for Jane Ann," Wade suggested.

The Clay Man sat motionless on the porch steps, knowing his short time in a form resembling human conformation was ticking away. The golem knew degrees of the human emotion, picking them up from osmosis. He rather liked these humans he protected, but he had no desire to be like them. He did wonder what would happen to him when it was his time to return to the earth. Would he still be aware of his surroundings? He didn't know. Then, that thought was pushed from him with such swiftness the golem was not aware of ever possessing it.

You are all things, he was told. And will always be such.

And the Clay Man was at peace with himself, feeling new strength enter his form.

Just outside of town, the Beasts had gathered to feast on the bodies of those who had died in Whitfield. They snarled and growled and ripped the dead meat from the bones, stuffing their fanged mouths as the drool dripped from their jaws, leaking in slimy ribbons to foul the ground. The males found a human female among the piles of bodies, a female who had only pretended to be dead, who was suffering from only minor injuries. And as was their custom, they dragged her screaming to the oldest male among them, the leader.

Her shrieks as they tore the clothing from her changed

to wails of pure terror as the big male pushed her to her bare knees and mounted her under the cool moonlight of western fall. When the oldest male had finished, the other males, according to age and rank in the pecking order of things, took their turn with the woman, each biting her on the neck as they lunged deep within her.

Within hours her body would be covered with thick, coarse hair, her face would change, the jaw enlarging, and she would be as them. She would be able only to mumble and snarl and growl, and the Beasts would understand her, and she them. She would not remember any worshiping of the God she thought she was deceiving as she prayed and lied.

And she would be happy in her new form.

In another part of Fork County, Jake rubbed his crotch and thought of Jane Ann. Jean had told him, since he was the largest of the men, in one particular department, certainly not mentally, he could have Jane Ann first—in any fashion Jake chose. Just make the prissy little bitch holler. Jake grinned. He figured he could damn sure do that, all right.

Jean came to him in the night, opening her shirt so he could fondle her breasts, pinch the nipples in play-pain. "You want me to suck you off, Jake?"

"Yeah," he dropped his filth-encrusted jeans to the ground, around his boots. "Yeah, you do that."

And she kneeled between his naked legs.

Nothing came close to Whitfield; no cars or trucks traveled the single ribbon of highway to or from the small damned community. There were no birds, except for the scavenger and carrion type, which wheeled and circled and called. Any animal that could leave the area, had left, a precognition in their tiny brains telling them to stay would mean death.

It was as if the physical elements that made up the town of Whitfield: the brick, the stone, the mortar, the timber, had but one single thought: they were going to be destroyed.

Soon.

MONDAY NIGHT

"Black magic? Devil worship? Roma and Mr. Falcon are witch and warlock?" Linda looked first at Sam, then at Nydia. "Vampires? You're both putting me on—right?"

"No," Sam insisted. "It's all true."

"Your . . . real father left you a letter? You've been in communication with the . . . spirit world?"

"That is correct, Linda," Nydia said. "I know it's hard to believe, but it's true. Believe it."

She looked at the pair for a long moment. Finally a slow smile began pulling at her mouth. "Now I get it! Oh, boy . . . you two had me going for a minute. It's all a big joke, isn't it? Yeah. There's gonna be some sort of . . . costume party here, right? Spooks and monsters and things like that. Okay, I won't spoil it for you guys. I . . ."

"Linda," Nydia leaned forward, taking the young woman's hands into her own, "it isn't a joke. It's deadly serious. I was raped last night—by Falcon. In a casket! Sam was beaten after my own mother—Roma—seduced him. Judy is one of them."

"Lana?" the question was asked in a soft voice.

"Yes. Most definitely."

"Then . . . everyone here is . . . one of those people?"

287

"Except for the young girls the new members brought with them. We're alone," Sam said. "In human form that is."

"And I don't trust you," Nydia said, still holding Linda's hands. The young woman tried to pull back, away, but Nydia's grip was strong.

"What . . . what do you mean: you don't trust me?"

"Nydia," Sam cautioned her. "I . . ."

"No, Sam! Let's get it in the open." She gave the entrapped young woman a dark look. "You're one of them yourself, Linda."

"No!"

"The pentagram on your chest."

"That's a birthmark, Nydia. I swear before God it is. You've got to believe me."

Somewhere in the house, a wailing began, containing a familiar note of pain and terror.

"What in God's name is that?" Linda asked.

"You've never heard it before?" Sam asked. "You don't know?"

"No, Sam—I swear it."

"That's one of the young girls brought in—kidnapped from God knows where. She's being raped . . . from both ends, probably; passed around among some pretty heavy-hung guys. She's not enjoying it very much, is she?"

Tears sprang into the blue of the girl's eyes. "I don't want that done to me. Ever! Oh, God, believe me, both of you, I'm a Christian. I go to church every Sunday. I worship God, not the Devil. Please, help me, believe me."

"Get the Bible, Sam," Nydia said. "Let's see."

The Bible was placed next to Linda. Nydia released her hands. Linda grabbed up the Holy Book and clutched it to her, her tears dropping onto the leather of the Book. "As

288

God is my witness," she said. "I love only Him. I swear it."

"Holy water," Nydia said, still not convinced of Linda's sincerity.

Sam put a few drops of holy water on the young woman's forehead. Nothing happened.

Nydia leaned back in her chair, nodding her acceptance. "All right, Linda. I guess you're telling the truth."

The young woman fell to the floor and began weeping uncontrollably. Sam glanced at Nydia and shook his head, silently projecting: "I told you so."

Her reply was a shrug. She said, "Linda, move your things into my room; stay close to us. We'll make it out of this . . . mess."

Linda stayed on her knees, on the floor, for several moments, alternately weeping and praying. Finally, she rose to her feet, wiped her eyes, and apologized for her behavior.

"It's understandable," Nydia said, warming more and more toward her. "It's gotten next to both of us, several times. Go on," she gave her a gentle push, "get your things and come right back."

After she had left, Sam said, "But she could still be one of them. Roma told me the Holy Water only affects a witch, warlock, or the undead."

"What a performance." The burning words seared into the girl's head. "You almost had me weeping over your dilemma. But water and I don't mix very well. Such a pity it wasn't Oscar night."

"Thank you," was her reply.

"Well done." The voice cut into her brain. "Spoken

289

without being gushy. You're learning quickly. I'll be in touch."

"Yes, Master."

And the evil force was gone from the room.

"Your mother must bear me the demon," the hot words penetrated into Black's brain. "She must be taken care of with the utmost of delicacy. Do you understand?"

"Yes, Master."

"You had better understand, young man. I will not tolerate any further backbiting from you. No more plotting against the female who birthed you. She soon will have served her purpose on earth and will be called home . . . to me."

"I understand, Master. Falcon?"

"Oh, you are a schemer, aren't you? Not a drop of loyalty in you."

"Only to you, Prince."

"Bah! Only to me because you are afraid of me. You shit your pants each time we communicate. Do you really believe, young man, that you can best your mentor?"

"Sir, Falcon is not my mentor. Falcon is an idiot."

"Perhaps he is that, to a point. But he has loyalty, and that is something you do not possess."

"What can I do to prove my love for you?"

"Obey orders, for one thing." The voice had a tinge of dryness to it. "Have patience, young schemer, for you are but a child in the order of darkness. You have this life to live before anything of any significance is placed into your greedy hands."

Black was pouty. "I should have been born a true demon."

"Yes, but you weren't, and there is nothing even I can

do about that. Have patience, those are my orders, and I expect to have them obeyed."

"I will obey you, Master. But now you hear me. . . ."

"Oh? Perhaps there is some hope for you after all. I detect—for the first time, I must add—a touch of courage in your usually whiny voice."

"I will rule this Coven, Master. Perhaps not today, or tomorrow, but someday. And if Falcon gets in my way . . . I will kill him."

The Prince of Darkness was silent for a moment. "Very well, young man, you have made your desires known. Fine. I admire and respect courage. Perhaps there is more of Balon in your blood than even I suspected. We shall see. I will tell you this much: should Falcon fail, and should you have the opportunity and skill to destroy him . . . well, that would be points in your favor."

Black wanted to ask more of the Prince, but with a rush of stinking winds, the Master of the Profane was gone, and Black knew better than to push the issue. But, the young man smiled, the King of Terror had not rejected his words or chastized him for them. So there was a glimmer of hope.

Ruler of the Coven. Black rather liked the sound of that.

ONE HOUR BEFORE DAWN TUESDAY

"He has spoken," Falcon said. "We will attempt to call out the forces this evening."

Roma lay on her bed. She did not feel well, for the demon within her was growing as a cancer in her womb, and she was in pain much of the time. "I wish you a great deal of luck, Falcon," she whispered. "But I must add this note of warning: watch Black, for his plottings now include you. The Master has warned him that I must be protected, but you have no such assurances from the Prince. Be careful."

"Then Black is a fool. He underestimates me, Roma."

"Grossly."

"I may be forced to kill him, or have him killed."

"He should have died at birth," the mother said, turned her head away, and bit her lips as waves of pain struck her, cramping her.

Falcon watched her twist on the sheets. "Is there nothing I can do?"

"Only tell me that Nydia is in the same agony."

"I am afraid she is not."

"That does not mean she is undergoing a normal gestation period. The sperm may be in combat within her. It could be days, even weeks—before the matter is decided. It is entirely possible it will not be decided until the moment of birth, or even weeks afterward. It depends upon who is present; if one of our kind is there, and has the power from the Prince, it could even take months . . . years. I know of such cases. In any event, I will not know the outcome for some time."

"Why, Roma?"

"Because I will be gone."

"Roma?" He walked to the bed of Devil-induced pain. "What of the demon?"

"If it is a true demon—and believe me, I know that it is—it will need very little assistance after birthing. Only a week or so of suckling. Then the metamorphosis is so rapid it is not only unbelievable, it is also utterly terrifying in its majesty."

"I . . ." Falcon struggled for words.

"Go, Falcon, you have much to do and I do not wish you to witness my suffering. Go."

He moved away from the bed, walking to the door. He paused. "I will tell you how things went this night, Roma."

She laughed, and her laughter chilled him. "If you live through it, darling. Many of those called will be rabid from the pits."

TUESDAY MORNING

They had slept unusually late. Sam awakened the young ladies roughly, no gentleness to his touch. He spoke the same message to each young woman: "Get up. Get dressed. Boots, jeans, heavy shirt. Keep a jacket close by. It's only a matter of hours before we have to run for our lives."

"What's happened, Sam?" Nydia asked, rubbing the sleep from her eyes.

"I . . . think we're about to witness the most awesome event to ever occur on the face of this earth." He smiled. "Other than that fellow who was born in Bethlehem, that is." He sobered again. "Remember what the voice told us: the calling out of the forces of darkness? It's going to happen tonight."

"He came to you? He told you?"

"No. I just know." Sam shook his head. "I don't know. Nydia—maybe he did come to me in my sleep. I have no recall of any conversation between us. I just woke up and knew it was going to happen."

"I am scared half out of my mind," Linda said.

"That makes it a club of three," Sam replied.

In the lush timber behind the great house, a shadowy figure drifted in and out of the tall trees. While his movements seemed vague and uncertain, the tall warrior was actually deep in thought, his musings troubled and sometimes dark with fury. Of all things that held sway outside of the firmament, the warrior hated Satan with a passion that borderlined on disobedience to the teachings of God the Father. Indeed, the warrior had come close to admonition from Him on more than one occasion for his passionate hatred of Satan. The warrior had pleaded with Him for millennia to destroy the Beast once and for all. Have done with the Filthy One. End it. Call His people home.

But the Master of All Things would merely shake His great head and say, "Not yet."

And the warrior knew that "not yet" would apply to this blinking in the span of all things, as well. He was not afraid of the od forces; he knew no fear of the demons and the other grotesque creatures that would soon be called to appear. He had destroyed their kind many times in the past, and would this time. No . . . what troubled the old warrior was the mystery in the great house of the Evil One, and should he alert the young Christian offspring of Balon to that mystery?

No, he finally decided. No, I can do only so much without overstepping the boundaries. Really, he concluded, I have probably interfered too much as it is.

He stopped by the filthy, sin-encrusted circle of dark stones and looked toward the mansion. No, young warrior, you must cope with that mystery by yourself. I will help in other matters, but in this, your strength must be all powerful; your faith all-believing and never wavering; and your cunning at its zenith.

God be with you.

TUESDAY NOON

The wailing had stopped. The great house was silent. It seemed to the trio seated close together in Sam's room as if they were alone: the only ones left in the mansion.

"The only humans," Nydia said.

Linda shuddered with fear. Sam had a brief fleeting thought of putting his arm around her shoulders, but gave up that idea when Nydia read his thoughts and gave him a look that would fry bacon.

"Sam?" Nydia asked. "What is an od force?"

"Beats me. Where'd you hear that?"

"It just popped into my head."

"It has to do with the supernatural," Linda said. "Sorcery . . . stuff like that."

Eyes swung toward her. Nydia stiffened on the day couch.

"My little brother got all involved in that stuff for a time, until my parents made him stop it," Linda explained. "He was—right there at the end—trying to get in touch with the dead; all that junk. I heard him mention that od force thing several times. My uncle, Uncle Homer, really used to kid Billy—that's my kid brother—about it. It got to the point my brother hated . . . really hated Uncle Homer. He'd go in his room at night with a doll he'd made—called it Uncle Homer—

and read and light candles and chant all those weird incantations, trying to get something to happen to Uncle Homer. Finally Dad made him quit; said Uncle Homer didn't mean anything by it. But Billy hated Uncle Homer until the day he died. Billy refused to go to the funeral."

"The funeral?" Nydia asked.

"Yes. Uncle Homer was killed one day; strangest thing, too. Just walking along the street in Buffalo and a small piece of steel fell from up where some workers were doing repair work—really high up on a building. Split his head wide open. Died right then and there."

"What was Billy's favorite way of killing his Uncle?" Sam asked.

Linda blinked, paled, then said, "Hitting the doll on the head with a . . . hammer."

TUESDAY NIGHT

Sam had taken the heaviest pack and distributed the weight of the other materials evenly among the young women. He had looked for his father's picture, literally tearing up the room in his search. But the picture was gone. He gave up the search, turning as Nydia slipped something into his pocket.

"What's that, babe?" he asked.

She smiled. "I thought they might come in handy. Little pills you can buy on campus—if you know the right person—just before you have to start cramming for an exam."

Amphetamines. Sam returned the smile. "I heard that."

"How are we going to get out of here?" Linda asked. "Won't they stop us?"

"They would if they saw us." Sam grinned. "But I'm betting they won't."

"How do we manage that, Sam?" Nydia asked.

"You remember complaining about all that rope we took from the storage area that night?"

"Yes. So?"

"We're going to climb down, ladies," Sam said, pointing to the window. "Right through there and down."

"Sam! . . . that's fifty feet."

"Not really. It just seems that far." He smiled mischievously. It was about forty feet down, though, but he wasn't going to tell them that. He pulled a knotted rope from under the bed. "I did this while you two were napping this afternoon." He secured the rope to a bed post and then opened the window, removing the screen. "You two go, then I'll secure the rope from that drain bracing just outside the window, crawl out on the ledge, and close the window behind me. The doors are locked to both rooms, so with any luck we'll be able to fool them 'til morning." He took a frim grip on the rope. "You first, Nydia. Easy does it."

She hesitated only long enough to kiss him on the mouth and then was gone down the rope, scampering to the ground. Sam looked at Linda. She shook her head.

"I . . . can't. I'm afraid of heights, Sam."

Sam was painfully blunt with her. "How would you like to be gang-screwed, Linda? Passed around among ten or fifteen guys? And then positioned on your knees and fucked like a dog—right up the asshole?"

She looked at him in shock, then without any further comments, she went out the window and down the rope, fear making her strong.

Sam watched the two women gather together on the ground, then untied the rope from the bed post and secured it to the drain brace. He lowered the three packs, then the other equipment, finally the weapons. He slipped out onto the ledge, feeling the bite of the suddenly cold winds of November as they came singing down from the north.

He was halfway to the ground when he felt the rope begin to give in his hands and the bracketing spikes pull away from the brick and mortar. But Sam was a veteran parachutist, young and in excellent physical shape, and a fifteen foot drop was no more to him than stepping off a curb. He hit the ground rolling and sprang to his feet.

"Better this way," he said. "The rope won't be dangling for anyone to see. Besides, we might need the rope before we're through."

Sam struggled into his backpack and the others did the same, Nydia asking, "Which way do we go, Sam?"

"North, to the high ground," he said, pointing through the darkness. "That ridge about three-quarters of a mile from the stone circle. I want to see this calling out of the forces." He turned and took the point, leading the way, three who refused to bow to the whims of Satan; three who chose to fight rather than surrender; three who maintained a strong belief in their God.

But as they walked through the night, toward the deep timber, one among them looked back at the great house . . . and smiled . . . oddly.

Since he had first noticed the unusual activity in the Heavens, the astronomer at the observatory in California had been quietly working overtime. On his own time and with his own equipment. He had asked for and received permission to take two weeks of his vacation and Ralph was now deep and high in the rugged mountains of California, maintaining a vigil, sleeping during the day, working from dawn to dusk.

He had discovered another area where unusual activity was periodically occurring. And he spent his nights alternating his powerful telescope between east and west. His wife, Betty, although not a professional stargazer, did have enough experience in the field to be more than an amateur, and, like her husband, was a Christian. If Ralph said he saw the face of God, then he saw it. Period. Now Betty would like to see His face. Or she thought she would.

"Why are you changing scope position tonight?" she asked, watching her husband reposition the small but extremely powerful scope, shifting it to the east.

"Hunch," he replied. "You ought to know after all these years of putting up with me that I'm a hunch player."

"What do you feel is going to happen?"

He shook his head. "I . . . can't really answer that, honey." He glanced at his watch. Seven o'clock, PST. Ten o'clock over most of Quebec Province. He didn't know how he knew, but he felt time was growing short. Two more hours, maximum, until . . . whatever it was would occur. Unless he was all wet in his hunch playing. "Make us a fresh pot of coffee, honey," he said. "Maybe some sandwiches, too, if you will, please. Come midnight, or thereabouts, we'll be too busy for anything else."

"Ralph! You're being deliberately vague."

"No. No, really that's not true. I just don't know . . . what we're going to see. And . . . I'm a little afraid of it, I think."

She shivered beside him.

He put an arm around her shoulders. "Cold?"

"No," the reply was softly given. And he asked no more questions, just held her to him in a loving embrace. They clung together for a few seconds before she pulled away. "Ralph! Now don't you get any funny ideas."

"Why not?" He grinned at her. "We have two hours."

She returned the grin and took his hand. As they walked to the solid little cabin they had built—working side by side—more than twenty years back, she said, "Ridiculous! And at our age, too."

The mist that was Balon's shape on earth shifted almost nervously. He sensed something was building, far to the east, and he was worried, wanting to go to his son, but knowing he could not. His place was here, with Jane Ann and the others, and young Sam would have to work it out alone. The mist seemed to smile. Well . . . not quite alone. The warrior was there . . . he knew the warrior was there, and knew, too, that the mighty one would help Sam all he could. But if Balon's suspicions were correct, the warrior would have his hands full combating the forces that would soon leave the netherworld, trekking their way past the smoking veil and into present life and form.

It would be an awesome sight, Balon felt. And one hell of a fight.

"Here." Sam dropped his pack to the ground. "We can see it all from here and still have time to run if they spot us."

"Run where?" Linda asked.

"Run and run," Sam answered the edgy question. "Run. Hide. Then run some more. Until it's time to make a stand and fight it out."

"When will that be?" Again, the questioner was Linda.

"When it's time," Sam told her, patience in his tone. "I'll know."

"How?" she pushed him for a firm answer.

Nydia gave him a look that said all her past suspicions were returning.

"I can't give you a flat, firm answer to that." Sam

looked at the flat plain that contained the dark circle of stones. The altar, although Sam could just barely make it out, held a vivid white slash across its top. "But I'll know."

His answer did not satisfy the young woman, but she shut up.

"I wonder what their reaction will be when they discover we're gone?" Nydia asked.

"Rage and hate," Sam said, shifting the Thompson from left hand to right. He looked at Linda. "Can you fire a weapon?"

She shook her head. "My dad never allowed them in the house. He said guns kill people."

"People kill people," Sam said, rebutting her statement. He glanced at Nydia, and she picked up the unspoken question from his thoughts.

"I can shoot. Rifle, shotgun, pistol."

"All right!" Sam smiled.

"But I've never had to shoot at a human being," she added.

"These aren't human beings," Sam reminded her.

Linda shifted her butt on the ground.

Nydia put her hand to the side of her neck, touching the tiny bite marks. They itched. She wondered what had bitten her. "What time is it, Sam?"

"Eleven-thirty, Eastern time," Ralph said to his wife. "We'd better get into position."

She grinned at him.

"Old lady," he returned the grin, "you are a wanton woman."

"I'm a-wantin' you," she aped a southern accent. "Again."

"See me next week, some time." He zipped up his jacket.

"Getting old, eh?"

Ralph waggled his eyebrows and grinned lewdly at his wife. He stepped out into the cold mountain air of the Sierra Nevada range, striding purposefully to the small observatory he had built on one of the highest peaks of that range. His wife was only seconds behind him.

"Wait up," she called, and he stopped, holding out his hand.

"What's the matter, old woman—did I wear you out?"

"Dream on, stud." She squeezed his hand. They walked for a few seconds in silence, his wife breaking the mood by asking: "Ours has been a good marriage, hasn't it, Ralph?"

"Any better and I couldn't have stood it," he joked.

"No, I'm serious, honey."

"It's been the best, and I mean that. Why are you asking that at this time?" He stopped, looking at her in the brightness of starlight. Stars that seemed close enough to reach out and touch.

"It's just . . . well, we enjoy . . . it so much. You know what I mean? Sometimes I think we enjoy it too much."

He laughed aloud, pulling her to him. "Honey, you worry about the darnedest things. Nowhere in the Bible—that I can find—does it say a married man and woman can't enjoy all the slap and tickle they can handle. And I think if I ever find that passage, I'll just ignore it; pretend like I didn't see it. I might even petition . . . someone to get it thrown out."

She smiled. "They have been good years, Ralph. I wouldn't trade them for anything. I mean that."

"You're in a very reflective mood this evening. Why?"

"You know I always get that way when we come up here. It's . . . a feeling of being so close to all things that really matter."

"A feeling of being closer to Him?"

"Yes," she said softly.

"Well . . . so do I, honey. That's why I love to come up here."

She kissed him and said, "Let's go view the Heavens."

"What time is it now, Sam?" Nydia asked.

"'Bout three minutes later than the last time you asked me." He grinned, white teeth flashing against the tan of his face.

She squeezed his hand. "Anybody ever tell you you're a handsome fellow?"

The look Linda gave her, hidden in the gloom of the timber, was of hate.

"Oh, dozens of girls. Hundreds. And one guy."

"Are you serious?"

"About the guy?"

"Yes," she laughed.

"Sure am. Never ran so fast in all my life. Fellow tried to kiss me . . . right on the mouth."

Linda did not share their humor, sitting glumly on the ground behind them, her eyes full of hate.

Nydia laughed softly. "I don't believe you, but tell me about the girls."

"Oh . . . they all lusted after my body. Nearly drove me crazy. I finally had to get a big stick and carry it around with me. One time I started a riot; all the girls

305

started chasing me and fighting over who got to keep me. Why . . ."

"Sam," she stopped him, "that is the biggest lie I have ever heard."

"Yeah," he grinned, "I guess it is, at that." He put an arm around her shoulders just as Linda got to her feet and walked to the crest of the ridge where they stood.

"Oh, my God!" she said, pointing to the dark circle of stones. "Look down there. Past the stones and stuff. Over by the house."

A long wavering line of torches smoked the night, casting trembling evil flickers of light into the sky. The line marched toward the circle of stones.

The trio on the ridge above the sin-stained circle of stones watched for a few moments. The line came to the barren plain and slowly began to circle the stones.

"What time is it?" Linda asked.

Sam glanced at his watch. "Eleven fifty-five."

MIDNIGHT

"You are too close," the voice boomed into Sam's head. "It is dangerous where you are. And it is not advisable for mortals to view this awfulness."

"I have to see what I am to fight," Sam replied, as Nydia and Linda looked at him in surprise.

"Stubborn. And young. Very well. Have it your way, young warrior."

The mighty voice faded.

"Who were you talking to?" Linda asked.

"The Other Side," Sam replied.

"The other side of what?"

"Life." Sam thought for a few seconds, then added, "As we know it."

Linda pulled her attention back to the torches. She shook her head in disbelief. Neither Sam nor Nydia knew if the almost indiscernible movement of her head was meant for Sam or the scene before them.

On the fringe of the torch-lit circle, the trio on the top of the ridge watched as shadowy figures moved closer to the light, walking in a peculiar, hunkered manner. Even at this great distance they looked grotesque . . . not human.

"The Beasts," Nydia said.

"I wonder where they came from?" Sam mused aloud.

"I mean . . . what was their origin?"

"Hell, I suppose," she replied. "I don't know, Sam. You know as much about them as I do."

Linda was strangely silent.

God's failures! The phrase leaped into Sam's mind.

And the young man questioned that statement: but how can . . . could God fail at anything?

He wished for the mighty voice to return: to answer his questions, but the voice was silent. Then he remembered something his mother had told him, something his real father had told her: nobody knows how many times God tried to make man in His own image . . . and failed.

Sam pondered that for a few moments, thinking: were the Beasts God's failures? What happened to cause the failure?

"I can't answer that, either, Sam," Nydia said. "Only He can answer that."

"I forgot you can read my thoughts. I wonder if we'll always have that power?"

"I . . . really hope not, Sam."

"Yeah, me too."

"You two can read each other's thoughts?" Linda asked, astonishment in her voice.

"Yes," Nydia said. "And sometimes other people's thoughts as well."

Sam glanced at her. "You know something I don't?" he projected.

Nydia refused to reply.

"There's something going on down there," Linda said. "Look."

The participants in the calling of the forces had gathered in circles, several rings of them, each growing progressively smaller inward, the Beasts forming the larger outer circle. The circles began moving, the first clockwise, the next counterclockwise, the third circle clockwise, the inner circle counterclockwise. It was a grotesque form of dancing, the women dancing back to back, the men front to front. They hummed lowly, the faint humming only occasionally reaching the ridge. Standing by the dark altar was Falcon, his face whitened with makeup, in stark contrast to his black robe.

Sam stood with Nydia by his side, both of them watching through binoculars. "Hideous," was her only comment.

The humming changed into a chanting, the dancing becoming more profane. The chanting changed into a low roar as three young girls were dragged screaming through the dancing, leaping, chanting circles of worshipers. One was stripped naked, her clothing ripped from her. She was secured to the altar, her legs spread wide, bent at the knees. She could not have been more than eleven or twelve.

"I don't want to watch this," Nydia said. She lowered her binoculars and turned her face from the scene of depravity and sin.

"I want to see it," Linda said.

"I suspected you might," Nydia said, just loud enough for Sam to hear.

Sam's face remained impassive. He said nothing. He knew something was going on between the two young women, but did not know what. Linda took the binoculars, lifting them to her eyes. Nydia turned her back to the obscenity below her and sat down on a log, zipping up her jacket to her throat for protection against the strengthening wind.

"Call the hyenas!" a voice screamed, and the chanting

grew thunderous.

"Dogges, Dogges," the circles screamed. "Hear our cries, O, Dogges."

"Call the centaur!" the voice commanded.

A bleating young lamb was dragged into the circle. Its throat was cut and the blood sprinkled around the altar, encircling the naked, weeping girl.

"Centaurs, centaurs, those who prance for the Prince of Darkness. Ixion and Nephele, Kentaurus and Magnesian. Come to us now."

"Call the satyrs!"

"Diomedes! Dionysus! Flesh eater and Lord of all that is pleasurable. Come join us."

The flesh of the lamb was ripped from its body and passed about the circles, the dancers gnawing at the bloody strips of meat.

"Call the griffin!"

The chant went up.

"Call the owl and the raven!"

And Sam heard the beating of wings overhead. Something beat close to his head. Instinctively, he ducked, the talons just missing his head.

"Call the Great Rukh!"

The dancers began flapping their arms and shrieking hideously.

"Bring me the basilisk!"

"Where is Sirius?" the circles called.

"Sirius is in place," Falcon answered, lifting his arms skyward.

"Bring to us the double amphisbaena."

The circles hissed ominously.

Falcon threw a great caldron of water into the air, calling: "The hydra—come, hydra, those of you who know the Master.''

"Come, hydra," the dancers chanted.

Another dark caldron of water was hurled into the cold air, Falcon shouting, "The Demon Merman."

The circle of leaping, hunching, chanting dancers began a movement that vaguely resembled a huge fish swimming.

"Bring the bats and the rats!"

The forest surrounding them became eerily silent. Then a faint scurrying sound was heard, and something furry and evil brushed Sam's boots. He kicked it away just as Nydia muffled a scream. Sam whirled: a bat was entangled in her hair. She finally slapped it free and the furry filth went flapping and screeching off into the night, toward the torches and the stones.

"Black!" Falcon shouted. "Now!" he pointed to the terrified girl bound naked to the altar.

Black jumped upon the altar. Like Falcon, he was dressed in a dark robe. He lifted his robe, exposing his erect maleness. Lunging at the girl, he tore her bloody as he bulled his way inside her, laughing at her pitiful screaming.

The circle of dancers laughed with Black, howling their glee at the child's wails of pain. Falcon ran to her, his teeth shining brightly in the torchlight. Fanged. He bent his head and tore at the vein in her neck, sucking her blood just as Black began his ejaculation.

Rats, the lower form of creatures that they are, began running and squeaking around the dancers, they, too, taking a joyful part in the evil ceremonies. Bats wheeled and cut the night, squeaking their contentment to be free of the darkness in which they had been confined.

"The merman!" Falcon looked up from the girl's

throat, blood leaking from his mouth. He pointed to the sky as a horrible creature sluggishly made its way through the darkness.

Others of the Coven rushed forward to drink at the dying girl's fountain of gushing blood. A male member of the Coven took Black's place between the girl's legs, lunging at her as her body began to pale from the loss of blood.

"I don't believe I'm seeing this," Sam muttered.

"What is that thing?" Linda asked. "It looks like it's half man—or monster—and half fish."

"And part goat," Sam muttered, looking at the horned head of the merman.

"Call the little people!" Falcon shouted. "Come, imps. You have our Master's permission. Come!"

At first, Sam began to sense, more than see, the change in the sky. The change was very gradual, the flush in the sky above the circle of stones changing little by little, from a dark amber, through the color patterns, until finally it settled into a dark, bloody red, the glow transforming the scene before them and around them, their own faces and exposed hands now an ugly red.

"What is that smell?" Nydia asked, still sitting on the log behind Sam and Linda.

"Sulfur," Sam whispered.

"It's more than that," Nydia said. "It's . . . evil."

Linda looked at her.

The sky was now a color of Hell, the flames—real or imagined—licked the area above them, dancing down out of the sky to touch and mar the earth. The stink from the pits stung the eyes of the three on the ridge, wrinkling their noses against the smell.

As Falcon began another incantation, the sky was

suddenly filled with bats, hundreds of them, their excrement falling to the ground with soft plops. The ground around the circle wriggled with rats, their red eyes reflecting dully in the torchlight and the strange coloration of the sky.

"Hear me, O Lord of Filth. Hear my cries, O Prince of Darkness. Hold us close to your chest, Apollyon. Let us taste more of your foulness; touch us with your lips; let us hear the sounds of your cloven hooves. For we, to a soul, are yours. Send the forces of all that is evil to aid us. Send the serpents and the demons, the denied and the defiled. Come to us, little people!"

And as if Merlin had suddenly waved his wand, the ground around the altar was filled with satanic imps, dancing and leaping and laughing wickedly.

The wind picked up, slamming its strength and coldness over the land, blowing first cold, then hot, confusing the elements. Falcon's voice grew stronger, ringing over the night-draped, red-tinged, evil-enveloped countryside.

"Asmodeus! Belial! Beelzebub! Mephistopheles! We who serve you implore you to rip away the veil and send all the forces to us. We are in need of the help only you can send. We stand in awe of your majestic power, Great One, and pray through the blackness you hear our cries."

Falcon turned, signaling for the second girl to be brought to the altar. She was dragged, screaming, to the dark flat stone, her clothing ripped from her, exposing her nakedness to the cold-hot winds and the hungry eyes of the worshipers of filth. Her breasts had just begun to bud, and only the lightness of down touched her apex. The dead girl, pale and bloodless, ghostly white, was rudely tossed to the ground. A Beast ran forward, grabbed the girl, and raced back to the outer circle. There, she was devoured, the flesh stripped from her, stuffed into drooling mouths.

The screaming girl, no more than a child, was positioned on the altar, legs spread wide apart. Falcon leaped upon the altar, lifting his robe, exposing his maleness, jutting and throbbing with power.

"For you, Master," Falcon said. "Only for you." He positioned himself and hunched savagely.

The girl's wailing echoed around the stones and the barren earth as Falcon split her, blood leaking from her torn vagina. Falcon pushed deeper.

"It's cold," the girl shrieked. "Cold! God—help me!"

Members of the Dark Coven laughed at her pitiful cries for help, shouting profanities and blasphemies at her, their hooting and laughing sullying the red night.

The laughter and the cursing increased with each lunge from Falcon, each push that brought wails of pain from the child. The flickering flames from the torches seemed to join and mingle with the bloody red of the sky.

Sam then noticed the third girl. She had gradually slipped back from the men who had brought her, moving no more than an inch or two each time. They had not noticed her, all their attentions riveted on the scene of rape and defilement on the now bloody altar.

"She's going to make a break for it," Sam muttered. "I'll bet you that's Janet. I've got to help her."

"Sam . . . !" Nydia protested.

"No. It's something I have to do. She's suffered enough."

The look in Linda's eyes was strange: a mixture of loathing and respect.

"I'm going down to that second ridge," Sam pointed,

checking the Thompson. The full drum was fitted in the belly of the SMG, the canvas pouch filled with clips on Sam's belt. He turned to look at Nydia.

"I will be back," he said.

"I know," she said, then stood and watched him slowly make his way down the gently sloping hill until he was lost from view, the red darkness swallowing him.

The circle of dancers pushed forward as Falcon began his climax, withdrew, and stepped from the altar, wiping his bloody penis on the rag that was once the young girl's shirt. Janet did not move with the crowd, staying in place, half hidden just outside the limit of the torchlight.

A huge wooden cross was carried to the altar, driven upside down behind the dark and bloodied stone. The girl was jerked from the altar and dragged to the cross. Strong hands held her upside down as hammers and spikes began their gruesome work. Her screaming as she was crucified seemed to fill the small valley. She was left hanging upside down, spikes in her hands and feet, to wail out what life was left in her.

But it was not yet over for the girl. They would return to her one more time.

"Send us the demons!" Falcon said, his voice carrying full and strong. "Send them, O, Great One."

The sky became entirely red, its bloody hues casting slick shadows over the grounds. The rats and bats ceased their scurrying and flapping, the imps were silent, and the only sound to be heard was the moaning of the girl behind the altar. Nailed to a cross.

Janet slipped deeper into the shadows. She looked toward the ridge where she had seen a flash of light reflecting off metal. She moved toward the high ground, moving slowly, attracting no attention.

315

Sam waited.

Linda moved up silently behind Nydia, her fists balled.

"Now!" Falcon screamed the one-word plea.

"Now!" the crowded circle, one massed ring of evil, echoed.

The sky seemed to split wide open. Great stinking clouds of evil-smelling gas settled over the estate of the Devil. Janet edged deeper into the dark red of false night, moving faster now, her youth giving added strength to her legs.

Great grotesque creatures filled the sky: two-headed amphisbaena were flung out of the gaseous mist; reptilian basilisks coiled and hissed and rolled to earth; winged, clawed griffins flapped and settled on the ground, fire and filth snorting from the demon head; the deformed and monstrous su, with its feathered tail and horned head suddenly appeared around the circle, its mighty claws digging into the ground; the gulon, a creature so hideous as to be indescribable howled as it came to earth from behind the hot curtain of Hell; the clawed, many-headed hydra came to rest on earth, its hideousness only slightly less than the Great Rukh that beat its way to earth, its feathers still smoking from the pits; the owls and ravens and centaurs and satyrs and hyenas joined the now crowded circle, all gathering around the cross where the girl hung in torment, spikes holding her upside down, the blood leaking from the wounds, dripping into her eyes.

"Black!" Falcon called. "Come. It is time for the final act."

The young man stepped forward, a sadistic gleam in his eyes, a sharp curved knife in his hands. The girl began wailing as the blade cut strips of flesh from her body,

316

cutting tracings of vulgar images in her skin. Black chanted as he worked, with Falcon beside him, calling on all the dark forces of the netherworld. The rite, as old as this world, was finally concluded. Then, with no thought of mercy, Black cut out the girl's heart and he and Falcon ate the still trembling muscle.

The warrior was near, watching, trembling with dark rage and hate swelling within him. But the mighty warrior from the firmament was powerless to interfere. He had to turn away from the bloody scene of sacrilege, for his eyes and thoughts could kill . . . and as much as he wanted to do just that . . . it was not his place to do so.

Yet.

Janet lay beside Sam on the ridge overlooking the scene of outrage. Sam had fought back the temptation to raise the Thompson and blow the Devil worshipers back to Hell. But the range was far too great, and besides, he knew it was not yet time for that. He would have to wait.

"Come on," he whispered to the girl. "Let's go."

"Are we going to be all right?" Janet asked. "I'm in . . . kind of hurt from what they did to me, you know?"

"I think we're going to make it," Sam took her small hand in his. "Come on."

On the far ridge, Nydia turned just as Linda's hands reached for her. Their eyes met. "I know what you are," she said. "And I'll knock the shit out of you if you try it."

WEDNESDAY MORNING DAWN

Sam had led them several miles from the site of depravity, camping deep in the thick timber. They had slept in sleeping bags, on ground sheets, no canvas over them. Sam had sensed there had been trouble between Nydia and Linda, but when he asked Nydia about it, she would merely shrug.

When Janet had learned of Nydia's true identity, she shrank back from her, not wanting the daughter of Roma to touch her . . . and for some reason, unexplained, Linda did not want to go near Janet.

Sam lost his temper. "What in the hell is wrong with you?" he asked Linda. "Do you realize this kid has been through hell, literally? Damnit, she doesn't have some . . . social disease."

Linda didn't back away from the angry young man. "And have you considered this: she may be one of them."

"You're crazy!" the young girl cried. "Do you have any idea what they did to me? What it was like?"

Linda shuddered and for some unexplained reason, moaned softly.

". . . I'm still bleeding from what they did to me. What's wrong with you: are *you* one of them?"

"How dare you!" Linda drew back her hand to slap the

318

child. Sam's quick hand stopped the blow. Janet darted behind him, peeking around his waist. She stuck out her tongue at the older woman and made a horrible face at her.

Nydia laughed at the girl's antics.

"None of that, Linda," Sam warned her. "I won't have it."

Linda spun around and stalked away, back to her bedroll. Sam turned, putting his arm around the child. "I think I can understand how you feel about Nydia, honey, but you're wrong about her. Flat out wrong." Then he told her what Roma had done to him, and what Falcon had done to Nydia. The girl could only shake her head in horror.

"Where did those other girls come from?" Sam asked.

"One from Montreal, the other from New York. They grabbed me in Montpelier. I was on my way to school." She looked at Linda, sitting with her face averted, a pout to her lips. "I'd like to slap her. She doesn't know what it was like . . . back there. And I hope to God I'll be able to someday forget it." She looked up at Sam, tall and strong.

"We'll get out," he assured her. "Go on to Nydia, now."

The child smiled, the first time since joining the group. "Can I wait just a little bit longer before I do? I mean, Roma *is* her mother, and Roma watched some while that Karl was . . . doing it to me. I mean . . . she even came over to us once and . . . and held his . . . thing. She did something to make him . . . ready. Then she laughed while he . . . put it in me. I just can't go to your friend now. Please understand."

Sam could sense the child was very close to tears. "Okay," he said gently. "Sure. Want to stay with me for a time?"

She hesitantly put her slender arms around his waist. She looked very much like a ragamuffin, for she had been half naked when she slipped away from the circle of worshipers. She was not a large child, and Nydia's shirt was far too large, as were the jeans from Nydia. The jacket sleeves were rolled and pinned back, the hip-length coat hanging past the child's knees. "Yes," she looked at him through soft eyes, "I think I'd like that."

"My time is growing short, darling," Jane Ann spoke her thoughts aloud.

"I will be with you all I am allowed to be," Balon projected his reply.

"Even . . . there?" She tilted her head, indicating the outside.

"Especially there. But I am not permitted to be with you constantly."

She did not ask why that was. "It will not be easy for you, will it, Sam? Watching me, I mean."

"Not easy."

"I . . . will try to be brave."

"They will want you to scream, to beg for mercy, to weep."

"I will not give them the satisfaction."

There was no response from Balon.

"Sam?"

"I'm here."

"Should I?"

"Should you what?"

"Scream, beg, cry?"

"I cannot answer that. That is your decision alone."

"Was my sin so great that I must endure this?"

"Perhaps, Jane Ann, sin has nothing to do with it. Have you thought of that?"

"I don't understand."

"Millions of people, for thousands of years, have died for God. Do you think all of them were hopeless sinners? Beyond saving?"

"But didn't most of them die because of their *belief* in God?"

"Not necessarily. Many of them died because of their strength."

"Sam! You're speaking in riddles."

"No, I'm not."

Jane Ann was thoughtful for a moment. "Strength? Are you saying that . . . because I'm the youngest of the . . . survivors I am better able to endure the pain and humiliation of what lies just ahead of me? If so, I still do not understand why it has to be."

The mist that was Balon was steady, with no thrusting reply.

"All right. But tell me this, if you can: part of . . . this does have something to do with sin—right or wrong?"

"In part."

"Whose sins?"

"Yours, mine . . . others."

Her last question was asked softly, and it was filled with love. "Why do I get this feeling I am dying partly for you, Sam?"

The mist could not lie. It stirred, then projected: "Because you are."

Jane Ann smiled. "Then my dying will be so much easier."

"Let me tell you something, Janey. This does not have to be. You, Wade, Miles, Anita, Doris . . . all are assured a place in Heaven."

"I know that, Sam Balon."

"Then . . . ?"

"I love you."

WEDNESDAY NOON

"Sam?" Nydia spoke from the rear of the short column. "How far are we from the main house?"

"Five or six miles, I'd guess."

"You said we would encounter boundaries. Where are they?"

"Honey," there was an edge to his voice. "I don't know. We'll know them when we see them."

"I'm tired," Janet said. "And I'm hurting real bad."

Linda looked at her, a strange light in her eyes. Then unexpected, she walked to the child's side and put her arms around her. Janet smiled up at her.

"We're all tired and edgy," Nydia said. "Let's take a short break, Sam."

But the rest was to be a very short one. Sam had just eased out of the straps of his heavy pack when he heard a sound to his left, slightly behind him. He tensed, thumbing the Thompson off safety. He spun, throwing himself to one side, coming up on one knee, the SMG leveled, on full auto.

What he saw numbed him momentarily.

A demon griffin, a winged horror that, until now, had been only a part of mythology. Its ugly head lowered, the creature charged Sam, howling as it came.

Sam pulled the trigger, a one second burst of heavy,

.45 caliber slugs. The griffin screamed, humanlike, and fell to its knees, blood gushing out of the holes in its chest and throat. It kicked on the cold forest floor for a few seconds, then, with a terrible shrieking, it beat its wings and died.

"What in the name of God is that thing?" Sam asked.

Only one among them knew the answer to that, but she had no intention of explaining.

Nydia screamed, Sam whirling around. Rats had encircled the young girl, and Nydia was beating at them with a stick. Linda stood with her back to a tree, her face pale with terror. The rats, much larger and bolder than their earthbound cousins, seemingly had no fear of humans, and no interest in attacking anyone other than Janet. The child was kicking at them with her tennis shoes. One of the rodents leaped at her, yellow teeth snapping.

Sam slapped it to the ground and stomped on it with a heavy jump boot, smashing the guts from the devilish rodent. He looked up, and only then did he see the white slash on the bark of a tree about fifty yards from their rest stop.

Fifty yards behind them.

"Run!" Sam yelled, grabbing up his pack. "Get the weapons and the packs and run. Toward that big oak," he pointed. "Get past it."

Nydia grabbed Linda and shoved her into action, literally forcing her to stop and pick up her pack and the shotgun she was carrying.

The rats pursued them to the slash-marked tree, but would not attack them once they had passed the line. The rodents raced back into the forest.

Janet looked at the slash on the tree. Whatever, or

whomever had marked the tree had done so with a mighty sword or knife, wielded with awesome power. "Those boundaries you people were talking about? I think we found them."

Sam lay on the ground sheet, his head resting on his pack. His thoughts were many. It was late afternoon, and turning colder. Already a few flakes of snow had fallen, and it felt as if it might start snowing in earnest at any moment. If that happened, he would have to build a fire and a lean-to. The lean-to didn't worry him, but a fire might bring some unwelcome visitors.

Why are they waiting? he mused. We are few and they are many, and with their powers, they must know where we are. Surely they can't be that afraid of me?

"Do not flatter yourself so, young warrior," the voice boomed into Sam's head. "It is I they fear."

"I wondered where you had gotten off to," Sam spoke, oblivious to the others looking at him, listening to the one-sided conversation.

"I have been busy. Now hear me, young one: you must be on guard, but you need not fear the evil forces as much as you believe. I will take care of those spawns of hell. They will harass you, worry you, but they won't harm you—if you remain careful and maintain your faith."

"You mean, I can kill them, but they can't kill me, or us?"

"I didn't say that."

Sam sighed, an exasperating expulsion of breath. "Riddles again, huh?"

"Only if you believe they are riddles."

"Study your words, huh?"

"That is correct."

325

"Is it against the policy of . . . Him for you to come right out and say things in an understandable fashion?"

"How like your father you are."

"You hedged the question."

"Correct. Young warrior," the voice held a slight note of puzzlement. "I have spoken to many mortals over these thousands of years, but you baffle me."

"How?"

"You aren't afraid of me."

"Why should I be? You're on my side, aren't you?"

And if that force that sits by the right hand of God, that force of all this is good and pure and just, could chuckle, it did. "Confidence is good, of course, all great warriors must possess it, but don't allow it to cloud your judgment."

"I don't intend to do that. But I will tell you this much: as soon as I get some sign from you, or the feeling is right—whatever—I'm goin' to Falcon House and kill every swinging di . . . uh . . . everybody in there."

Again, Sam got the impression the mighty voice was laughing.

"With the jawbone of an ass?"

"Did that really happen?"

"In a manner of speaking, certainly."

Sam held up the Thompson. "I'll start with this . . . no telling what I might end up with, though."

"Live a good, strong, healthy, productive life, off-spring of Sam Balon. And when your time on earth is over, I will personally welcome you home."

"My time on earth could very well be short."

"That is entirely possible."

"Tell me something."

"If it is permitted."

"Am I really speaking with you? Are you Michael? And will I remember any of this—if I get out alive, that is?"

"You ask probing questions, young warrior. Inquiries I am forbidden to answer."

"I won't ask why."

"Wise of one so young."

"Instead I'll ask this: when do I start my mission?"

"You have wards to look after, lives in your care. A flock, if you will. But remember this: sometimes a wolf may disguise itself to enter the flock. And a cabin of evil may sometimes be turned into a fortress of truth. If you so desire, you may begin whenever you are ready."

The voice faded away.

"Sam?" Nydia said, watching the young man she loved get to his feet. "What are you going to do?"

"Start a war," he said quietly.

THURSDAY MORNING

The weather had held for the good, and they rested and slept on ground sheets, in sleeping bags. Sam had talked long into the night with Nydia, with her asking all the voice had said.

"There is only one cabin on our land," she told him. "That I know of, and I think I would know of any others. That's several miles north of the house. Falcon had it built. It's quite cozy."

Sam glanced at the sun peeking through the tall timber. "If we head due west, we should hit the cabin. With any luck," he added.

"You think that's what the voice was saying?"

"Honey, I just don't know. I've studied his words, over and over. That's the only thing I can think of. As for that bit about a fortress of truth . . . I don't know."

"Well . . . I'm ready anytime you are," she said.

He grinned at her.

"No way," she said, verbally tossing cold water on him.

"Ever since we witnessed that . . . display in the Heavens, Ralph, you've been moody. Out of sorts. What's the matter, honey?"

"You remember I went into town the next morning?"

"Yes."

"Well, I made some phone calls; I made about a dozen phone calls. Charged them on our credit card." He grinned ruefully. "Our phone bill next month should be a real doozie. I called four stargazers in America, one in Canada, the rest overseas and in South America." He looked at his wife. When he again spoke, his words were soft. "All that activity we watched: the sky changing colors, the plumes of dirty . . . smoke—whatever it was; those odd, unexplainable occurrences . . . everything. Betty, we were the only ones to have witnessed anything unusual that night. The only ones in . . . this . . . world!"

"That's impossible," she protested. "Ralph, it went on for more than an hour! Somebody, somewhere, has to have seen it."

He solemnly shook his head. "No one I spoke with. And I talked with the best people in the business."

"I . . . don't understand, Ralph. We certainly didn't dream what we witnessed. That was a heavenly phenomenon unequalled . . . well, by anything I've ever seen or read of. I'm sorry the camera malfunctioned and we didn't get it."

"If the camera malfunctioned," he said. "Remember, the film I shot back at the observatory came out blank, as well."

"The people you talked with . . . could they be holding back? Deliberately holding back? Maybe to do a paper on the sightings?"

"I thought of that with the first two I spoke with," he admitted. "But a dozen people? No." He sighed. "So, that brings it right back to us."

She sat beside him, taking his hands in hers. "You

weren't alone in seeing that . . . sighting several days before this one."

"No."

"Why then and not last evening?"

Ralph was silent for a moment; reflective in his quiet musings. "Don't think me a fool for saying this, Betty, and rest assured you will be the only person to ever hear this from my lips, but . . . all right, charge ahead and get it said.

"Betty . . . we're Christians. Maybe not the best in the world, but we do try. We're believers, let's call it. So perhaps what I witnessed previously . . . no, not *perhaps*—I know I saw the face of God. It was magnificent . . . holy . . . even though He appeared to be quarreling with . . . somebody . . . something. What we witnessed the other night . . . well, have you given any thought to that being . . . from the other world?"

"What other world, Ralph?"

"Hell."

By noon, Sam had brought in enough wood to last the women several days. There was plenty of oil for the lamps, candles should they need them, and ample fuel for the portable stoves and lanterns. He took a can of that for his own use. There was plenty of canned food in the cabin. There was no more Sam could do, but he was hesitant to leave the warmth and safety of the cabin . . . even more hesitant to leave Nydia. Looking at her, sitting quietly in a chair by the fire, Sam realized just how much he loved her, and knew that that love—right or wrong, morally—was growing each day.

She met his tender gaze. "It's time for you to go, Sam."

"I know."

"We'll be all right," she said. "We have weapons, and I know how to use them. And," she blinked away sudden tears, "you have a job to do. Time is growing short, I believe."

"Yes," he agreed, still reluctant to leave.

"I packed the holy water as carefully as I could. You're sure you have everything else you'll need?"

He nodded his head.

"I love you, Sam."

"And I love you, Nydia."

"Go with God," she said, her voice breaking.

Without looking back, Sam opened the door and stepped out into the cold air. He quietly closed the door behind him, jacked a round into the chamber of the old Thompson, slipped the SMG on safety, and walked down the path, heading toward Falcon House. The young man had a mission few would envy.

To meet the Devil.

A thousand miles away, the Coven was resting in and around Whitfield. The members, hundreds of them, were, to a person, exhausted after a night of debauchery, torture, and depravity. Their clothing reaked of filth and sin, for none among them had bathed in a week. The stink of the Devil worshipers and the smell of rotting flesh hung over the town like an ominous cloud called into being from the drum and cannon of a depraved rainmaker. The Coven members lay in sleep where they had fallen in exhaustion, stinking breathing heaps of wickedness . . . who would soon learn the awesome furious power of God's retributive wrath toward those who serve another Master.

In the Lansky home, the four people sat quietly. They

listened to the almost too loud ticking of the old grandfather clock.

On the porch steps of the Lansky home, the Clay Man was immobile. He waited.

Jane Ann sat, reading from the Bible, reading the verses the mist that was Balon had directed her to read. She read, gaining inner strength for the ordeal that faced her. Soon.

And in the firmament, the Ruler of All Things, all planets, gave a rumbling command. A dead star sprang into life, billions and billions of miles from the planet known as earth. The bit of rock began to glow and smoke, and it began its journey slowly.

A creature from another time, another world, sprang onto the path Sam trod. It roared and clawed the earth. But Sam had studied the words of the warrior and understood at least part of them. He stood his ground, glaring at the gulon, a hideous mixture of the hyena and the lion.

"You can harm me only if I cease to believe in God's word, God's love, God's power, and God's protection," Sam said to the creature. "And I will never stop believing in Him. So get out of my way and get back to Hell where you belong."

The creature turned its tail and slipped back into the timber, afraid of this mortal with God's protection against its kind.

"Personally," the voice came to Sam, "I would have fought the ugly beast of Hell."

"To each his own." Sam continued walking.

"The house, the few acres around it, and those who live with evil in it are yours. All else is mine."

"Going to destroy the Devil's spawn?"

"Yes. Those that were called."

"There are more of those . . . things?"

"As many as a nonbeliever wishes there to be."

"Someday—not soon, I hope—I'm going to have a long talk with you."

The mighty warrior could have told Sam when that time would be, but that was forbidden. Not that the warrior always obeyed the rules, for he did not. But . . . most of them.

The warrior faded and was gone from Sam's consciousness. But he watched the young warrior stride purposefully down the path. He could not tell him of the pain that awaited him; could not relate the horrors that would confront him. But the warrior felt the young one could cope. He would be bloodied, but with his head not bowed in subservience to that filthy rabble of the Hooved One.

A mile from the cleared ground of the mansion, Sam stopped for a rest, and to prepare some equipment. He carefully checked the old Thompson and his father's .45 pistol. He tested the edge to his knife. He bloused his jeans in his jump boots, retying the boot laces, securing them. He had filled half a dozen small bottles with the highly flammable portable stove fuel, and he checked them for breakage, repacking them carefully. He stood up, reached inside his jacket, and pulled out his black wool Ranger beret, with his old unit crest attached. He settled the beret on his head, took a deep breath, and walked down the path.

He was as ready as he knew how to be.

"He's coming," Karl spoke to Falcon, utilizing a hand-held handy-talkie.

Falcon stood in front of the window of his quarters; Karl was hidden in the timber, waiting with other men to ambush Sam.

Falcon knew where Nydia and the others were, just as he knew his Master had instructed the bitch to watch out for Nydia's well-being, in case Falcon's seed had overpowered Sam's weak flow of semen and she was with demon, as Roma felt her daughter was.

Falcon also knew the fight that Sam was bringing to the grounds was to the death. And the young man was without fear. He was cautious, but not fearful. Falcon had observed, with the help of his Master's all-powerful eye, the young warrior face down the gulon, the creature slinking off into the timber, back to its hiding place.

And the old warrior, the Mighty One's favorite archangel was here, rubbing his hands together, looking forward to a good scrap, spoiling for a good fight with God's most hated enemy.

It had not gone as planned, Falcon sighed. We have a good chance of winning this fight; the odds are still in our favor, but . . .

He chose not to think of the alternative.

"Be careful, Karl," he spoke into the handy-talkie. "The young man is dangerous, and he has been well trained for battle. And something else: he has been tested in actual combat; he has killed, and he will not lose his courage."

"Bah!" the man dismissed Falcon's warnings. "He is too young to be that dangerous."

Fool! Falcon thought. "Sam Balon's offspring is a combat-tested, ex-Army Ranger, you idiot. With several

334

special warfare schools behind him. Don't underestimate him."

"We lost him!" Karl's excited voice belched from the speaker. "He was in sight just a moment ago. Where'd he go?"

"Probably coming up behind you, you clod! The young man is a trained guerrilla fighter." Falcon opened the window facing the woods just in time to hear the sounds of gunfire. "Damn!" he muttered.

Sam had been expecting an ambush and had been watching closely for any signs of one. He had spotted the movement of bushes ahead of him and darted off the path, coming up softly behind the men. The young man had been well trained, and terms of surrender was the last thing on his mind. He raised the SMG and blew the men into the arms of their chosen God.

Sam eased his way up to the fallen men. Blood, bits of bone, and gray matter were splattered on the trees and the ground beneath the men. One man was alive; he raised his hand and groaned.

"Help me," he pleaded.

"Certainly," Sam said. He shot the man between the eyes.

The Old Warrior smiled grimly, thinking: I have no need to worry about this young warrior. Then he was off, searching the timber, sword in hand, looking for a fight with the forces of evil.

Sam picked up a rifle lying beside one of the bodies and inspected it for damage. The bolt action was a Winchester model 70, .338 magnum, in good shape. He rolled the dead man over and removed a cartridge belt from him, then searched his pockets for more cartridges, finding another boxful in his jacket pocket. Sam left a short-barreled lever-action carbine, and picked up a bolt action .308. The fourth man had been carrying a Weatherby .460.

"Elephant gun," Sam muttered, grinning as he stood among the carnage he had wreaked. "I think I'll find me a nice vantage point and do a bit of sniping."

The first round went through a rear window of the great house, hitting a young woman in the stomach, knocking her backward over a coffee table, the mushrooming slug slamming a hole in her stomach as big as her fist. She lay on the floor, screaming her life away, wailing for her chosen Master to help her . . . stop the awful pain.

He did not.

"Jimmy!" Falcon roared. "Come here."

The zombielike living dead shuffled into his earthbound master's quarters.

"What is all that noise?"

"Young Sam Balon on the ridge northeast of the house, sir. Got a rifle."

Another slug came whining through the mansion, ricocheting off a brick of the fireplace and knocking a jagged hole in the wall.

"That son-of-a-bitch!" Falcon cursed him, all the while feeling admiration for the young warrior. "By all that is unholy, why couldn't Black have turned out like him?"

"Because young Black is a schemer and a plotter, sir," Jimmy said.

Falcon turned deathlike eyes on the man. "You know something I need to know, Perkins?"

"He plots against you, Master. With some of the younger members. I heard them talking. I was listening and they did not see me."

"What did they say, Jimmy?"

"Young Black said—told them—he had been in communication with our True Master, and the Master had said young Black could have the Coven should you fail."

"Thank you, Jimmy. Thank you very much. For once your snooping and spying was of service. I have a task for you: go to Roma's quarters. Put her in the center room that is free of windows. She must be protected at all times."

"She is with Demon child, sir?"

"Yes, yes," he said impatiently. "Then, Jimmy, as a reward for your information, tell Judy to come to me. I will instruct her that you are to have her at any time you wish."

"Thank you, Master," Jimmy drooled, the slobber dripping in slick ropes to the floor. "You are kind."

"Yes, yes. Now get moving, you cretin."

Falcon stood arrogantly at the open window, waving at the ridge where Sam lay sniping. He felt the tug of the lead as it passed through his body. He howled with dark laughter, making an obscene gesture toward the ridge.

Sam watched Falcon through the scope on the .338. The young man was a qualified sniper, having shot for qualification at more than a thousand meters. He knew perfectly well if the weapon was adequate and sighted in. Using the right ammunition—which he was—he could hit anything he could see. And he knew he had hit Falcon.

"Sure, dummy!" he berated himself. "Don't you

remember all those monster movies? You can't kill a vampire with anything other than a stake through the heart or a silver bullet, and I sure don't have any silver bullets." There on the wind-swept ridge, cold in the winter sun, Sam chuckled, then wondered about his sanity, laughing at a time like this. "Where are you, Lone Ranger, now that I need you?"

He again laughed. "That's me, a lone Ranger." He shook his head, wondering if the stress was getting to him?

No, he thought. No, it's just like my instructor said about me, back at Fort Benning. "The kid is a natural-born killer."

The remark had gotten back to Sam, and the young man had accepted it. He knew he was different from most; knew that, discovering it early, 'way back in grade school, when an older, larger boy had jumped him for no reason other than the bigger boy was a bully. Sam had picked up a club and bopped the bully on the side of the head with it, dropping him like a felled tree. "He started it," Sam told the principal. "I don't believe in fair fights. I believe there is a winner and a loser . . . and he lost."

"You're not sorry for what you've done?" the principal questioned. "The boy is in the hospital with a fractured skull."

"No, I'm not sorry. That's his problem."

Sam had taken his licking from the principal without flinching. But he thought it unfair, and told his parents his thoughts.

"Just like his father," Tony had snorted, then walked from the room.

That was about the time, Sam remembered, lying on

the cold, windy ridge, that Tony began to change, young Sam hearing rumors about his stepfather's sexual antics. And that was the time a lot of other people began to slowly change. Sam let his thoughts drift back in spurts, short bursts of remembrance, then back to the present, keeping alert. The ministers began complaining of a lack of attentiveness among many of the churchgoers. Some of the churches closed their doors, others got ministers that Christians whispered about, questioning the men's faith.

But his mother had told him, "Just watch your temper, Sam. You're a lot like your father, Sam Balon."

"Is that good or bad?" Sam had asked his mother.

She had smiled, and Sam remembered how pretty she was. "Oh, honey—I think it's wonderful."

Sam pulled his attentions back to the present and chambered a round in the .338. He would have to move just at dusk, changing positions, for he knew they would be sending people in after him. Then he smiled. He'd have a nice surprise waiting for them.

He slipped from the ridge and set about cutting off small limbs, sharpening them. He whistled as he worked.

THURSDAY NIGHT

The hoarse bellow of pain drifted over the darkness of the land. Again and again the screaming spiked the night. Before the echoes of the first howling had died away, another yowl of pain ripped the gloom cast by the shadows of the tall timber. The line of men stopped and backtracked to the clearing behind the mansion, one running for the huge house, fear hastening his feet.

"What is all that screaming and howling?" Falcon asked.

Gulping for air, the Devil-worshiper gasped, "The Christians, sir. He's . . . put out traps for us. Awful things. Like they used in Vietnam. Punji pits. And he's got swing traps set all over the place; and wire stretched ankle high, too."

"He has what!"

"The wire or rope, sir, is stretched tight, ankle high; man trips, falls forward onto sharpened stakes driven in the ground. The swing traps, sir . . . you take a stick and tie half a dozen smaller, sharpened sticks to it, about six inches apart. Then you bend a limber sapling back and fix your trap with rope or rawhide. Man triggers the trap, the limb pops forward, coming real fast. King's got them rigged stomach high. It's bad, sir. I never seen nothing like it. You told us this would be easy. You said . . ."

340

"All right, all right," Falcon waved him silent. "Stop your babbling and whimpering, man. Get control of yourself. Pull the men back. We won't do anything until morning."

"No, sir, Mr. Falcon," the man stood his ground, "I'm going to have my say on this."

Falcon almost sent him scorching his way to Hell, in the form of a roach, but he held his temper in check. Things were going badly enough without a revolt among the ranks. "Very well—speak."

"All them monsters and demons and things we helped call out? Well . . . they're runnin' around like scared chickens. In a blind panic. And do you know why? Well, I'll tell you: 'cause something is after them. There's some . . . thing out there in the deep timber. I never seen nothing like it in my life."

Falcon suspected what *it* was. "What do you mean? Speak more descriptively, man. What kind of . . . thing?"

"Well, it ain't human. I don't know what he is. Wears a gown or a robe; carries the biggest sword I ever seen. Damn thing's five feet long—glows. This thing . . . laughs; and when he does, it thunders. He's killed a hundred or more of them big monsters. The imps are hiding, so are the satyrs. The centaurs have stampeded, or whatever those stupid-looking fuckers do. Everybody is getting uptight, sir. You gotta do something."

Falcon stared the man down, until the frightened Devil-worshiper dropped his eyes. "I shall do something, Earl. But for now, pull your people back to the house. We all need a good night's rest."

When the man had gone, Falcon allowed himself the first taste of fear, of failure, and it was bitter on his tongue. Ugly. He could understand the fear of the forces in the timber. Even the Beasts had refused to leave their caves. While no mortal could kill Falcon with any conventional weapon, the warrior could. And would. If Falcon was foolish enough to leave the house and go traipsing into the timber. And Falcon dared not call on the Master for more help, for that would be admitting failure, and he would be sent back to the netherworld.

Oh, how Black must be enjoying this! Falcon's thoughts were foul, his mood savage and bitter. Grist for his cunning, scheming mill.

Somehow, Falcon mused, I must draw Sam into the house. Once in here, I have a plan, and I will win.

But how to draw him in?

Falcon decided to rest on the matter.

But no one got much rest that night. Every fifteen minutes, on the dot, rifle slugs would pock the house, seeking entrance through the darkened windows. Then Sam would change the timetable, and every five minutes his rifle would roar. And then he would be silent for a half hour. Then firing every minute. One man was hit through the stomach when he recklessly exposed himself in front of a window, light behind him. One young member of the Coven took splinters of wood into his eyes, blinding him. Another was shot through the head as she tried to peek over a windowsill.

On the ridge above the house, Sam smiled grimly, knowing full well the nerve-rattling psychological game he was playing.

In the deep timber, the once tranquil forest floor began to resemble a bloody, stinking battlefield as the Warrior wielded his mighty flashing sword as if God's fury was controlling each devastating swing of the blade.

The creatures of the evil calling were running and flapping and scurrying and lumbering and galloping in all directions, fleeing the awesome sword in the hands of the warrior they knew they could not best.

The mightiest of all God's warriors strode through the forest, shouting in a voice only the godless could hear. He roared at them to stand and fight; he insulted their courage with oaths that made God cringe in the firmament, thinking: *I* will have to speak to the old warrior about that . . . again.

The warrior rained down slurs upon the od forces' master. But still they ran in fear. Roaring his rage, the sky thundering from the echo of the mighty voice, the warrior stamped the evil life from the rats that scampered in fright beneath his great feet; the bats swirled overhead, screeching their fear, not understanding this manner of man who roared at them, disturbing their inner radar, causing many to slam into trees. Those that were left went flapping back to the warp in time that had allowed them entrance to this place.

And when the forest was quiet, rid, for the most part, of the forces of the netherworld, the old warrior rested, quite pleased with his work this night.

He did so enjoy a good fight.

FRIDAY MORNING

Sam catnapped from four in the morning until the first red streaks of dawn filtered through the timber. He cautiously moved a mile from his resting place before he squatted down and ate a sandwich Nydia had fixed him, washing it down with cold water from his canteen. With that in his stomach to soften the blow of the diet pill, Sam took one of Nydia's amphetamines, knowing he had to be alert, and knowing he had not had the rest to maintain the vigil he must keep . . . in order to stay alive and win this fight.

He smiled at the carnage that lay on the soft blanket that was the forest floor. The warrior had indeed meant his words when he said he was going to destroy the Devil's spawn.

Sam inspected the dead creatures, and found them to be as hideous in death as they were in life. So there was some truth to what is mistakenly called mythology, he concluded. The scientists and the professors and the arrogant atheists aren't as wise as they profess to be.

"So what else is new?" he muttered.

He left the dead ugliness of the Devil to rot and made his way back to a ridge, this one on the east side of the huge mansion. It was by far the best vantage point he'd found, for his shooting distance was shorter, and he would be able to see if anyone tried to slip from the house and circle around behind him.

Smiling, he noticed a bell hanging from the rear of the house. Nydia had said it was very old, an antique her mother had picked up in Europe—Holland, she'd said. Sam jacked a round into the heavy, .460, braced himself for the recoil, and sighted in the bell. "Ring my bell," he muttered, then gently squeezed the trigger, allowing the weapon to fire itself.

The bell clanged, then jumped from its bracings, blown from the brackets by the force of the heavy slug. But the men and women of the Coven, trapped inside the mansion, were ready for Sam this time. From every window came an answering volley of shots, forcing Sam to scamper back below the lip of the ridge. He crawled to the slight protection of a small clump of trees and carefully eased his way forward, until he could see the house. He sighted in one man, firing from the third floor, and eased the trigger back. The butt pounded his shoulder. But Sam had been shooting downhill, the scope adjusted for that angle, and his shot was high, not catching the man in the chest, but in the throat, almost decapitating the Coven. The .460 slug flung the man backward, his bubbling scream cut off before it could reach his lips.

Sliding backward, Sam changed positions, running several hundred feet before dropping to the earth and easing his way up to the crest of the ridge.

He spent the morning harassing those in the mansion, but taking no great personal risk in doing so. He knew he would have to go inside the mansion, and he was not looking forward to that, for that would put him on Falcon's territory, and the warlock would then have the advantage. But as long as he could, Sam intended to cut the odds . . . down, at least make it fifty/fifty, even-up, the scales tilting in no one's direction.

NOON, FRIDAY

Jane Ann heard the clock chime its chilling message. Noon. Odd, she thought, I've always loved that old clock. Now, I hate it. Then from the outside, she heard a low chanting coming from the center of the small, doomed town, growing stronger and louder with each heartbeat. She listened until she could make out the words.

"Praise him that is our Master," they chanted. "Now the Christian whore dies. Praise the Hooved One."

The chant was repeated, over and over, until it became a maddened drone in Jane Ann's head. She looked for the mist that was Balon, and was not surprised to find him gone. He had warned her she would have to face some of the ordeal alone. She stood up, moving to the front door. She had taken a long hot bath, fixed her hair, and done her nails. She had put on her best dress, her best jewelry, and now stood facing the door, her Bible in her hand.

Waiting.

"Why does this have to be?" Miles asked the misty face of Balon.

The mist stirred but projected no reply.

"I will, if not gladly, certainly willingly take her place," Wade said. "And I know I speak for all here. We've all talked about it."

"That cannot be."

"Why, for God's sake?" Anita asked.

"Precisely the reason."

"Sam, you're speaking in riddles," Miles accused him.

"No. You are perceiving them as puzzles, that's all."

"She's dying for us, isn't she, Sam?" Doris asked.

"Yes."

"But there is more to it than that, isn't there, Sam?"
Wade asked.

"Yes."

"She's dying for you, isn't she, Sam?" Miles's words
were softly spoken, and not accusatory.

When Balon thrust his reply, the one word was
charged with emotion: "Yes!"

The long filthy line of Satanists stopped in front of the
house. The chanting ceased. The town grew quiet.

"Hey, bitch!" a man's husky voice called. "Get your
ass out of that house. It's your time."

"Yeah," another called. "And you might as well step
out of them panties 'fore you do, 'cause you gonna be out
of them damn quick."

Ugly laughter rang in Jane Ann's ears.

The petite lady stepped out of her house, onto the
porch, facing the ugly crowd. She was jerked from the
porch, seized by dirty, rough hands, manhandled
profanely. As if envious of her neat appearance, a woman
reached out and quickly mussed her hair. Hard male
hands roamed over her body.

"Take her to the circle of stones," Jean Zagone
commanded. "The Digging." She stood in front of Jane
Ann, hate shining from her dark eyes. She spat in Jane
Ann's face, the spittle dripping from the smaller woman's

cheek. "It's going to be fun listening to you beg, Christian cunt."

Jane Ann's reply was calm. "That will never happen. I can't say I won't scream. But I can assure you, with the Love of God in my heart, I will never beg."

Jean slapped her, her hard hand rocking the woman backward. "Take her."

Laying on the ridge facing the house, something very cold touched Sam's heart. His big hands gripped the rifle until his fingers ached from the strain. "Mother," he whispered.

The scene in Whitfield was suddenly played before his eyes, a five-second burst of reality. Then it vanished as quickly as it had appeared.

Sam put his forehead on the ground and allowed himself the denied luxury of tears.

A rifle shot from the house, spitting dirt onto his face brought him back to his own reality.

The young man cut his eyes upward. "I guess You have Your reasons."

She wondered how long she had been here. Wondered if it was hours, or days. Another man fell on her bruised nakedness, spreading her legs, forcing his way into her, grunting his dubious pleasure as he worked in and out of her. Jane Ann had learned early on that to fight them only meant more pain, with the end result being the same. Better not to resist.

She opened her eyes, watching the last of the sun's rays fade in colors beyond the western horizon. She had stopped counting the men assaulting her when she reached twenty, and there had been many more after that.

Jake, Jean Zagone's foreman, had been the first, and he had been furious when she did not cry out as he assaulted her.

"Come on, bitch!" he had yelled, plunging his maleness into her. "I bet you ain't never had this much meat before."

And she had made a mistake by saying, "My first husband was bigger."

That had gotten her a hard fist on the jaw.

Jake had then proceeded to tell her—in great detail, with many four-letter words—what he would do to make her beg . . . later. This was bad enough, Jane Ann thought; she was not at all looking forward to Jake's promise.

The man lunging at her shivered as he ejaculated, and she felt the wetness of him on her thighs, and then the coolness of approaching night fanned her nakedness. Still abnormally warm for this time of year, she thought, then fought to keep a smile from her lips. How ludicrous, she thought. I am lying here on the ground, naked and sore from the assault of . . . only God knows how many men, wondering what is next for me, and thinking about the weather. I must be going insane.

But she knew she was not losing her mind; knew she had been, as so many prolonged rape victims, learning to detach herself from reality.

She was left alone for a time, lying on the ground next to the dark altar. Someone tossed a stinking rag of a blanket over her, and she closed her eyes.

She must have dozed off, for when she opened her eyes, returning to her world of pain, it was fully dark, the circle of stones torch-lit. Someone kicked her on the buttocks with a sharp-pointed boot. She looked up into the hard, evil eyes of Jake. She let her eyes drift downward to his erect maleness. He held the throbbing organ in one hand, stroking it.

"Get up," he ordered. "And bend over that altar, whore. I'm gonna shove this meat up where I think your God lives. This'll make you beg to Him."

Painfully, stiffly, Jane Ann rose to her feet, looking around her. The crowd had swelled to several hundred men and women, with more arriving each minute. But it was a silent, sullen gathering watching her.

Jake reached out, fondling Jane Ann's breasts, brutally twisting the nipples. She flinched, but made no sound. "Real gutsy gal." He grinned nastily.

He pushed her face down on the altar, her body bent at the waist. Male hands grabbed her wrists, holding her firm. She felt the smaller hands of a woman parting the cheeks of her buttocks, then something hot and hard pushing at her anus.

A moment later, her screams were echoing over the circle of stones, mingling with the dirty laughter of the now huge crowd. She screamed out her pain and humiliation.

But she would not beg.

FRIDAY NIGHT

"You have twenty-four hours, young warrior," the heavy voice boomed into Sam's brain. "Forget the tablet, for it is gone."

"Where is it?"

"Taken by the Dark One."

"Then he must know he is going to lose here?"

"He never loses entirely. Something of importance to him will have been gained here, delivered elsewhere, bursting forth on this earth. Perhaps twice. But time is growing short. Twenty-four hours, young warrior. But you must be gone from this place by the twenty-second hour. Do not ask me why that must be. You have a task before you. Good luck, young warrior."

The force of good was gone.

Sam leaned back against a tree trunk, his mind racing, tossing out ideas and plans almost as soon as they formed. Only one course of action was certain: he had to go inside the mansion.

Sam needed sleep, but was afraid to doze for fear they would find him and kill him. His eyes closed, resting for a moment. Exhaustion quickly overcame anxiety and the young man slept.

The mightiest of all warriors was amused as he watched over his young charge. Sleep for a few hours, young warrior, he thought. I will bend the rules a bit and watch over you. Bending the rules is not that uncommon for me.

Jane Ann lay on her back on the dark alter, blood from her torn anus staining the dark evil stone. She shifted position, softly whimpering as pain cut through her.

"Beg for mercy from your God!" Jean and the others had screamed at her while Jake anally assaulted her.

But Jane Ann had shaken her head no, all the while biting her lips against the pain being forced in and out of her.

When Jake was finished, another took his place, then another . . . it seemed never to stop.

Jane Ann wept when Tony stepped forward. "I always wanted it this way," he said. "But you never would let me—remember?" His words had been barely audible over the waves of pain washing her. He mounted her brutally, laughing at her cries of pain. "Good, isn't it, baby?" he shouted.

The rape had finally stopped . . . for a time. Then someone brought a huge artificial penis to Jean, the Coven leader laughing as she strapped it on. "It's better to give than to receive," she said. "Well, baby, receive this."

Jane Ann had passed out from the pain.

And now the words Jane Ann feared were spoken, "Let the black mass begin," Jean said. "Bring the virgin child to the circle."

Jane Ann was jerked from the stone altar and shoved naked into the hands of Coven members. Still their fingers would not stop the seeking of openings to her body. Finally, they tied her hands behind her back, the rope cutting into her flesh. They forced her to kneel before the altar as the black mass began. The Coven members sang their praises to the Dark One. Jane Ann, with a smile on her lips, sang God's hymns in a soft sweet voice. Even when a Coven member urinated on her, she continued to sing praises to her God. Her small soprano voice seemed to carry above the chanting of the hundreds of voices. Her singing infuriated Jean, the woman running to the naked, kneeling Christian, slapping her across the mouth, back-handing her, attempting to still the voice singing praises to a God Jean had rejected years before. But even with blood from smashed lips leaking down her chin, dripping onto bare, bruised breasts, Jane Ann sang to her God.

Jean became wild with fury, striking at Jane Ann with balled fists. Jane Ann slumped to the ground, bright lights popping like painful flashbulbs in her brain. "Shut your goddamned filthy fucking mouth, Christian whore!" Jean screamed. "One of you men come up here and stick a cock in her mouth!"

One did, ramming his maleness into Jane Ann's mouth.

Jane Ann bit him . . . hard, clamping down like a bulldog, hanging on with her teeth with all the tenacity of a Mississippi River snapping turtle. The man screamed and howled in pain. Jane Ann spat out part of the man's pride and joy.

Jean kicked her in the stomach. Jane Ann fought for breath, gagging and retching on the ground.

A small girl was led crying and whimpering to the black altar. Jane Ann recognized the child as the daughter of a friend. Carol. She was eleven. Jane Ann struggled to her knees. Speaking around the blood in her mouth, she told the child, "I can do . . . I can only pray for you, Carol."

The man who now possessed only half a penis was still screaming in pain as he was led away.

"Oh, no, Carol," Jean said, patting the girl's head. "She can do so much more than that. She can save you all the pain and hurt. Yes, she can. Just ask her."

The child turned anguished eyes to the bound, naked woman kneeling in the dirt. "Do it, Miss Jane Ann. Please?"

"You rotten bitch!" Jane Ann cursed Jean.

The woman laughed and spat at her. "Ball's in your court, now, Miss Prissy Pussy. All you have to do is renounce your faith in your God and the kid goes free. And that message comes straight from the Dark One's lips. How about it? Want to see Big Jake and his friends split this little cunt wide open with those peckers of theirs?"

"I will not deny my God," Jane Ann said. "And He will not deny me."

"Listen to the little cunt scream for a few hours, bitch. You might change your mind."

"No," Jane Ann said quietly. "I will not."

"Tell me this, Miss Christian Cunt: you people are taught that your God is a just and merciful God. Why then, would He allow this to happen? The rape and torture of a child? Come on, pussy, tell me."

"You know I can't answer that, except to say that after the pain there is a home where there is no pain. Where His people can live in . . ."

Jean kicked her in the stomach, silencing her. "Oh, don't hand me that mumbo jumbo. I'm sick of hearing all that shit!" She raised her hands into the air. "Let the mass begin."

And the crowd surged forward, all straining to see the girl raped and tortured and offered up to their Dark Master in sacrifice.

Jane Ann had thought the pitiful weeping and screaming of the child would never cease, and she knew she had never before in her life prayed so fervently. Certainly she had never prayed for the death of a child. Until now.

Selected men of the Coven had assaulted the child in every conceivable manner, until her blood dripped from the altar. And Jane Ann had been forced to stand by the altar and watch. She had prayed with her eyes open, for when she shut them a fist would bruise her battered flesh until she opened them.

Just before the hideous sacrifice was to begin, when a chosen member would literally slice strips of flesh from the girl, the child shuddered, gasped once, and died, the blank empty eyes staring at nothing.

"No!" Jean screamed her outrage at this denial.

Jane Ann looked to the Heavens. "Thank you," she said.

Jean spun around, glaring at the smaller woman. "You . . . you had something to do with her death, didn't you?"

"I certainly hope so," Jane Ann said.

Jean's smile was grim, filled with all the evil within her. She looked at Jake, standing by her side. "Break all her fingers, Jake. One at a time. Do it slowly. Make her beg."

"You must prepare to leave," Falcon stood over Roma's bed. "We cannot risk harm coming to you. I have

356

spoken with the Master, and those are his wishes. He told me you are very susceptible to mortal injury while you are with Demon child."

"True," Roma said, looking up at him. "But where will I go? And how?"

"Use the tunnels. It will be difficult for you, but it is the only way. Now the other thing I must do. I have a plan, but it will mean the death of Black."

She shrugged. "He is worthless. He has plotted against me; plotted against you. Only a few hours ago he gathered some of the ones from school to scheme against you. As Nydia is no longer my daughter, Black is no longer my son. Do with him as you must."

The witch and the warlock locked gazes, their thoughts exposed.

"No," she said. "No, I cannot allow it, Falcon."

"There is no other way."

"I will not permit it. You are a good man, Falcon. A bit vain, perhaps, but all good men are. I will not permit your dying for me."

"I fear I must. For I am the only person in this house capable of besting young Sam. My plan will surely mean my death."

She sighed. "I seem to have played out this scenario before." Her words were ruefully spoken.

Falcon could but shrug. "I have instructed Jimmy and two of the other servants to go with you . . . see you to safety. We won't see each other again, darling . . . at least not on this earth."

"Nydia?"

"One of ours is with her, on direct orders from the Master."

"Kill Balon's Christian bastard for me, Falcon. Only

357

for me."

"It will be my pleasure," he said, smiling wickedly, then turned, walking from the room.

Jane Ann lay on the ground, her useless hands by her side. She had never in her life felt such intense pain as when Jake calmly broke her fingers, laughing at her screaming. She had passed out several times, only to be brought back to searing consciousness and harsh awareness by buckets of water being hurled on her nakedness.

She had screamed and she had wept.

But she had not begged.

She had been dragged to the darkness of the outer circle, forced to watch as the Beasts ate the body of the young girl.

She felt hands pulling her to her feet, and someone spraying her with cold water. The nozzle was jammed between her legs. "Got to clean up the pussy," Jean grinned at her. "Get you all ready for another round." She turned to Jake. "Stick the nozzle up her ass, too."

Jane Ann was positioned on the altar.

And the defilement began anew.

The Coven members laughed at her screams, the Beasts howled and danced.

Jane Ann silently prayed for forgiveness.

THREE A.M., SATURDAY

The voice awakened Sam.

"This will be our last communication, young warrior. For I must leave now."

"Are you going back . . . ah . . . home?"

"By a wandering route, yes."

At a loss for anything else to say, Sam said, "Well . . . been good talking to you."

The voice chuckled, the sky thundered. "How like your father you are. Good luck, young warrior."

Sam felt the force pull away, and knew that he was now truly on his own in this fight. Alone, he reminded himself, amending his thoughts, as far as physical assistance, that is. I still have . . . Him, he cast his eyes upward toward the twinkling Heavens.

"I hope," he muttered.

He ate the last of his food, then catnapped until dawn split the east with hues of awakening colors. Sam returned to his sniping war of nerves. At full dark, with only a few hours left him to complete his task, Sam would enter the house.

He didn't know how he would accomplish that, but he felt he would find a way, since he didn't really have a choice in the matter.

He also felt those in the house knew he would be coming in. And they would be waiting for him.

DAWN

There was grudging respect in Jean's eyes as she prodded Jane Ann awake with the toe of her boot. It had suddenly turned cold in Fork County, the temperature dropping into the mid-thirties during the night. Satan had pulled away his presence. Jane Ann lay shivering, naked on the ground. But she had neither complained nor begged.

"You think you've won, don't you?" Jean asked, her lips pulled in a sneer.

"Yes," Jane Ann managed a whisper, pushing the word past swollen lips. "My God always does."

Jean squatted down beside her, the stench of her unwashed body unbearable. She pulled a hunting knife from a sheath. "What I think I'll do, bitch, is cut off your tits and feed them to the Beasts."

Jane Ann said nothing.

"You wouldn't beg even then, would you?"

"No," the suffering, ravaged woman said.

"You know what we're going to do, don't you, cunt?"

"Yes."

Jean stood up, looked at Jane Ann for a moment, then savagely kicked her in the face with a booted foot. "Get the cross," she said to Jake. "And the hammers and spikes. Do it. Now."

*   *   *

"Is it almost over, Sam?" Miles asked. "Please God, let it be."

"A few more hours."

"Then you'll stop the suffering?"

"It will be stopped."

"I still don't understand why it had to be," Anita said. "Not entirely."

"It will be explained. I promise."

"You left us several times last night," Miles said. "I felt your presence leave."

"I went to the scene of ugliness several times. Once I let the spirit of a child depart her body."

Doris asked, "You could do that for her and not for Jane Ann?"

"Yes."

"There is so much I do not understand."

"It will be explained. Behind the curtain of life and death."

Wade sighed. "I never thought I'd hear myself say this: but I'm ready to go."

"He said it, Sam," Miles pointed to Wade. "Not me."

Soon, the mist that was Balon told them. "Only a few more hours."

"Ohh," Miles moaned.

She had screamed when they drove the spikes into her hands, her feet, her sides, losing consciousness only momentarily. Then, awake, she found the strength to cope. They had jammed a crown of thorns on her head, the blood dripped down her face, streaking her bruised beauty. She hung naked from her wooden tower.

"Tell me your God is shit!" Tony yelled up to her.

361

Her eyes found him. "My God is love," Jane Ann whispered.

"Say it," a man urged. "Tell us you renounce your faith in your stupid God and we'll get you down, tend to your wounds."

But Jane Ann managed a smile, shaking her head no.

Some in the crowd, a few, grew restless, worried, for this was not going as planned. They had beaten and raped and tortured this woman nailed to a cross and still she could smile and keep her faith. Some began to openly question what they had done. Others began questioning their minds: could they, under the same circumstances, retain their faith for the Hooved One? Many doubted it.

"I want out," a woman sobbed. "Oh, God—help me get away from here."

A few others joined her. "Take Janey down!" a man called out. "She's suffered enough. Set her free and tend to her wounds."

Those few were seized and killed. One was spread-eagled on the ground, a stake driven through his stomach. He lay screaming for hours. Another man was given to the Beasts; they ate him alive. Two of the women were raped, then given to the Beasts for breeding purposes. The woman who first cried out to leave was given to Jake. She screamed out her humiliation as he took her in various ways. Then she was stoned to death.

"Anyone else want out?" Jean demanded, shouting at the huge crowd. "If so, just step forward."

No one did, but the thoughts of some were confused and troubled.

Jane Ann watched them, sensing the mood of many shifting. She wanted to tell them that if they confessed their sins and accepted God as the only True God, they could be saved. But the words would not form on her tongue. And she wondered why?

"Don't concern yourself with them!" Balon's words cut through the horrible pain in her body. "They are filth—rabble, body and soul belonging to the Dark One."

"You are a warrior, Sam Balon," she whispered, her voice not carrying three feet from her lonely tower. "And you will always be so." The crowd gathered ten feet below saw her lips move, but could not hear her words. They assumed she was praying. "Those are human beings," Jane Ann told the invisible spirit of Balon. "Some of them used to be my friends. And obviously, some of them still have good in their hearts. They were tempted, Sam, and you know how delicious Satan can make sin."

Balon was firm. He projected: "They are sinners of the most evil sort. Knowingly, willingly, lovingly violating all of God's Commandments."

"I want to help them if I can." Jane Ann was just as stubborn as Sam Balon.

And the mist that was Balon, invisible as it circled around the scene of pain and degradation, projected: "You are certain? Even after all they have done to you? All the pain, the humiliation—you wish to help them?"

"Yes."

And in the firmament, the Total Being knew He had been right, choosing well.

Balon said: "Very well. That choice is entirely up to you."

Jane Ann felt Balon's presence fade. Once more, she was alone, looking down at her tormentors from her nailed position of pain and faith. She gazed at the assembled throng of Satanists, and many looked back at her, most with open hatred and defiance, but a few with concern and pity. Her eyes touched those, holding for a few seconds. When Jane Ann had their attention firm, she said, "I can promise you nothing except what help I might be able to give . . . offering my prayers for you. The rest is up to you."

"What the fuck are you mouthing about now, bitch?" Jake yelled up at her. He laughed hoarsely. "The silly cunt is losing her mind."

But a few among the many knew better. About thirty moved to the base of the pain-wracked tower. The numbers equally divided between men and women. They stood defiantly before the crowd, many of whom were old friends and lifelong acquaintances. The few looked at one another, then began to sing, softly at first, then with gathering power as the faith they had lost once more filled them with the strength they knew they would soon need. Many openly wept as their love of God returned to them, overwhelming them with the feeling that at last, long last, they were doing something worthy with their lives.

No one among the large crowd watching them attempted to interfere, for those gathered under the bloody, starkly vivid cross were all armed.

"Throw down your guns," Jane Ann told them.

All but one did. He walked back into the crowd that encircled the Cross of Faith and the few who, at the last, had seen the True Way.

The powerful strains of "Faith Of Our Fathers" rang over the site of rape and defilement and slow, agonizing death.

Shouting profanities, the Coven members surged forward, with Jean shouting orders to build more crosses, and do it quickly.

FIVE O'CLOCK, SATURDAY THE LAST DAY

Sam darted across the grounds, toward the mansion, only faintly defined in the growing darkness. No lights showing. Dark windows like evil, watching eyes. Stopping at the back door, he paused to catch his breath and to ponder his sanity at doing this. Putting an ear to the door, he listened, but could detect no sound from within. He drew back, extending his arm to the door knob. Just before his hand touched the brass, the door swung open, and Falcon stood smiling at him, his fanged teeth glistening wetly in the darkness of the room.

"My dear Mr. King," the warlock said, his smile hideous. "So good to see you. Please come in. We've been waiting."

"Stay away from me," Janet warned the older girl. "I mean it. I don't trust you," she whispered.

Linda smiled, her smile both evil and wanting. She returned the whisper. "Why don't you scream? Nydia will come to your aid."

"I will if you don't leave me alone."

Nydia lay on the couch before the fire, deep in sleep. Her stomach was hurting. She moaned in her sleep.

Linda was steadily backing the child into a corner, her face holding a strange look, eyes burning. "Really thought you could get away with it, didn't you?"

"I don't know what you mean," Janet whispered. "I thought you were my friend."

"I am your friend, and you know what I mean."

Janet's hand closed around a poker, her back to a wall. "Leave me alone."

"Open your shirt," Linda commanded. "I want to see if you're marked."

"You're bananas!" the child hissed her fear.

"I want to see if you're marked!"

"Marked?" the girl questioned. "Is that all?"

Linda nodded, running her tongue over her lips and teeth.

"All right," Janet said. "But I still think you're nuts." She fumbled with the buttons of her shirt. Her breasts were bare, the buds tipped with tiny nipples.

Linda's tongue snaked out of her mouth, wetting her lips. Her tongue was unusually red. "I knew you were one of us."

"I'm not one of anybody! I'm not marked." The child pressed her back against the wall.

"I can see it in your eyes. You're really one of us." She held out her arms. "Come to me."

"You touch me and I'll bop you with this." Janet lifted the poker.

"Don't be afraid, child of ours, our God understands," Linda said.

Janet raised the poker. "Don't take another step," she warned.

Linda moved toward her, eyes shining, lips wet.

The poker swung. A dull splatting sound filled the room.

Nydia awakened to screaming.

*　　*　　*

"It's good," Jean spoke to the Coven. "We have been assured a long, exciting life on this earth. This act guarantees it."

Behind them, all around the circle of stones, around and slightly beneath the height of Jane Ann's lonely perch, a low moaning, sobbing sound was heard, the anguished sounds of pain and prayer audibly mixing with the silent flicker of the torches that lit the scene of awfulness. Some of the men and women who had repented to the True Way had been crucified; some had been stripped naked and the skin peeled from living bodies; others had been sexually mutilated and left to bleed to death; all of the women and some of the men had been sexually assaulted . . . hideously.

But not one had renounced the Lord God.

"Good-bye, Sam," Jane Ann spoke to her son. "Remember that Mother loves you."

The words slammed into Sam's brain as he stood poised in the open doorway of Falcon House. "Good-bye, Mother," he said, flinging his thoughts with all the mental strength he could muster.

"I heard," his mother's voice was faint in his brain. "Be careful."

Sam's head was once again clear of voices. He felt new strength enter him. He looked at Falcon.

"You can save yourself a great deal of pain, young man," the warlock said. "With just one simple act."

"And that is . . . ?"

"Renounce your God."

"I have something to say to that." Sam returned the mocking smile.

"Yes, young man?"

And just before Sam hit the warlock smack in the mouth with his leather-gloved fist, dropping him to the floor, momentarily stunning the man, he said, "Fuck you!"

Sam was past the dining area and into the den, running hard, before Falcon could pull himself up from the floor, vile-smelling blood leaking from his bruised mouth. The young man charged the room full of satanists, startling them. Holding the Thompson SMG firm, swinging it left to right, Sam blew a half dozen of them into the arms of their Master, then charged through the house, running up the first flight of stairs, heading for Roma's quarters. He had several sharpened stakes shoved behind his belt.

Turning at the landing by the second flight of steps, Sam ended the life of several more, emptying the drum into them as they charged recklessly behind him. A wildly fired shot pulled at Sam's left arm, gouging a bloody path. His arm burned from the lead, but it was slight and not serious. He ran up the stairs.

Lana confronted him, hissing at him, teeth fanged, fingers turned into talons, reaching for him, her breath stinking. He fired into her body and she flopped on the floor, screaming oaths at him. But she would not die. She crawled to her feet, mouth and tongue blood-red just as Sam tore the top off a vial of holy water and flung it at her. The water bubbled and hissed as it burned her face, searing and smoking as acid, eating into her living but dead unholy flesh. She screamed and thrashed on the floor, beating her feet to a macabre dance of pain and death.

Furious footsteps sounded behind him. Sam spun, ejected the drum and rammed home a clip, jacking a round into the chamber. He crouched, at the ready, as several youthful members of the Coven, all from Nelson or Carrington College came rushing at him. Sam pulled the trigger back and held it, starting the hard burst waist high. One slug caught Mac on the hipbone, flinging him backward, over the railing. He screamed as he flailed through the air, the screaming abruptly halted when he hit the marble floor. He splattered with an ugly sound.

The hallway was littered with dead and dying and undead. Sam doused them with blessed water and raced to Roma's quarters, the screaming smoking flesh fouling the air behind him.

Roma was gone, her quarters empty. Sam ran through the three room suite, pausing to look at a picture on a dresser by a rumpled bed. It was the 8 x 10 of his father. Sam stood for what he thought was only a moment, but he had a feeling that time was spinning past him, and he did not understand that. The picture seemed to hold him mesmerized; he was conscious of a strange stillness in the great house. Nothing was moving. Then, he shook his head. Noise once again drifted to him. And before his disbelieving eyes, the photograph melted into nothing.

He spun at a noise behind him. Black stood, a dueling sword in each hand. "I will guarantee my position of greatness by your death at my hands," he said smiling. "We will fight fairly, you and I. With these," he held up the slim swords. "You mortals have a streak of justness inherently bred in you. So I know we shall have a fair fight. Shall we begin, half brother?"

"If you'd ever gone through Ranger school, Black, you'd know better than to ask a stupid question like that." Sam lifted the Thompson and blew a dozen holes into Black.

Black was flung backward, slamming against the wall, the bullet holes in his chest smoking pocks. But he would not die. He slowly rose to his feet, laughing insanely. "You don't fight fair, half brother," he said, flicking the tip of the sword at Sam.

"Ain't that the truth?" Sam said, then cut off Black's legs at the knees with another burst of lead.

Black shrieked and thrashed on the floor, unable to get up. Sam heard loud voices and the faint sounds of boots, running, a door slamming, then another door opening and closing. He jerked a stake out of his belt and drove it into Black's chest. A filthy liquid poured from his half brother's chest and mouth, the color and odor of stinking pus.

As he lay dying on the floor, Black said, "One point I must make, dear brother," he gasped, as unlife ebbed from him. "Have you taken into consideration that one day you may have to do this very thing to your wife?"

With pus and foulness rolling in streams from his body, Black closed his eyes and died.

Sam pulled out a small bottle of fuel. He doused the drapes and carpet with it, then tossed a match onto the floor, the extremely flammable fuel going up with a whooshing sound, the flames jumping around the room, spreading into the hall carpet.

Picking up a sword, Sam ran from the room, literally knocking Judy down in the hall. She hissed at him, teeth fanged. Sam ran her through with the rapier, leaving her pinned to the floor, flopping and screaming, foulness staining the carpet beneath her thrashings.

Sam ran from room to room, setting the drapes, beds, and closets, full of clothing, blazing.

"Fire!" someone yelled. "The house is on fire."

Sam ran to the balcony and opened fire on the panicked Coven members, knocking several of them spinning and howling to the marble floor. He ran down the hallway, setting rooms blazing, quitting only when he ran out of fuel and matches. He looked up at the top floor, it was blazing, smoke pouring out in oily plumes.

It can't be this easy, he thought. I can't have won this easily.

"Quite right, young man," Falcon's voice reached him from the floor below.

Sam spun, the Thompson at the ready.

"Oh, for pity's sake," Falcon said. "Put that foolish weapon away. It can't harm me in any manner—unlike your half brother. I've been shot by more jealous husbands than you have cartridges for your weapons."

Falcon's face was only slightly bruised from Sam's hard punch. He was dressed in a smoking jacket, his right hand in his pocket.

Sam looked at his watch. He was shocked to find it was eight-thirty. He had ninety minutes to get to Nydia and the others and get away. Where had the time gone? It must have had something to do with his dad's picture; that odd sensation he experienced.

"Are you taking some sort of medication or expecting company?" Falcon asked.

"What?"

"Your watch, and the expression on your face when you consulted your timepiece. Ah!" comprehension flooded his features. "I see. The ancient warrior gave you a timetable, did he not?"

Sam chose not to reply. He shifted the Thompson from right to left hand and stepped onto the stairs, the bannister hiding his right hand from Falcon's eyes. He hoped. His fingers closed around one of the two vials of holy water he had left.

"Ah, God's young warrior." Falcon smiled. "You are really going to fight *me?*"

"I don't see that I have any choice. Where are all the others?"

Falcon laughed, rather bitterly, Sam thought. "What others? You've been charging around here firing that weapon and driving swords and stakes into people. We were not that many to begin with."

"You're a liar."

Falcon merely shrugged. "I have been called much worse, I assure you. No, a few ran away into the night."

"Roma?"

"Gone. Safe."

"You set Black up to die, didn't you? Giving him that silly sword?"

"Very astute of you. Yes."

Sam was only a few steps from the bottom. He slowly removed the bottle of holy water.

"You can't win by fighting me, Sam," Falcon told him. Then, quite unlike him said, "I set you up, too."

Sam flung the holy water at the warlock, deliberately aiming at the spot just in front of his feet, so the bottle would break and splatter its contents.

The blessed water splashed on Falcon's legs and a few drops hit his flesh, burning him. The warlock screamed in pain. Sam jerked the last vial from his pocket, smashed the top against the railing, and threw it into Falcon's face.

It had the same effect as acid, producing holes in the man's face, smoking pits. One eye turned to ooze, running down Falcon's face.

"You lose, young man," Falcon managed to hiss, the

words like a gurgle from the smoking holes in his throat.

"I lose?" Sam said.

But Falcon could no longer talk, his throat a burning hole, emitting putrid odors of the grave and beyond. He slowly pulled a flat automatic pistol from his jacket pocket and pulled the trigger twice, both slugs hitting Sam, in the chest and stomach.

Sam tumbled forward, down the steps. He rolled next to Falcon's rapidly metamorphosing body, his blood mixing with the slime oozing from the warlock's rotting burning flesh.

Sam tried to get to his feet, but strength was leaving him. He collapsed as darkness enveloped him, falling into the oozing slime.

THE FINAL MOMENTS

"Get into Wade's car," Balon projected. "Everybody! Don't ask questions. Do it. I will bring the Clay Man."

"You?" Miles said. "That golem weighs half a ton. Ask me. I almost gave myself a hernia fooling with it."

"Don't argue with me!"

"Yes, preacher," Miles sighed. "What do we do when we get into the car?"

"Go to The Digging. We will be waiting for you there."

"This is it then?" Doris asked.

"Yes."

"Ohh," Miles said, putting one hand to his mouth. "Already I feel strange."

"Miles," his wife said. "Be quiet. All right, Sam, I'm ready. Let's go."

"Doris!" her husband said. "Don't be in such a hurry. You got to be so pushy!"

"Don't be afraid," Balon projected. "When you get to The Digging, get out of the car and walk toward the crosses. You won't be seen or bothered."

"Why?" Miles asked, stalling for a little time.

"I'll tell you when you get there. If I told you now, you wouldn't go. Move it, people."

"You were a sergeant, weren't you, preacher?" Miles asked, Doris pushing him toward the door.

"That is correct."

"Once a sergeant, always one. Must be something in the food they serve you guys."

His wife shoved him out the door.

No one noticed that when they walked under a bright street lamp on the way to Wade's car . . . none of them had a shadow.

Sam felt hands on him and he tried to fight them off, finally giving up. He was too weak. He opened his eyes and looked into the beautiful face of Nydia, and eyes of pure love.

"You'll have to help us, Sam," she said. "Try to get up, honey—please?"

"Us?" Sam asked, painfully struggling to get to his feet.

"Janet is with me."

"Where's Linda?"

"Dead. She was . . . one of them. I told you there was something about her I didn't like. Come on, we'll talk later. Move your legs, Sam, one step at a time."

"Don't forget Dad's Thompson. I want it."

"It isn't here, Sam," Nydia told him. "And neither is the pistol with your dad's name on it."

"Where'd they go?" Janet asked, on one side of Sam, helping him toward the door.

"I don't know," Nydia said.

Cool air hit Sam as they reached the front door of the burning mansion. "I do," Sam said.

When Wade and the others drove up to the old dig site, they witnessed the end of the Coven. The golem was indestructible and awesome in his fury. Not even when

375

dozens of Devil-worshipers charged the Clay Man could they move him, stop him, or even slow him in his killing frenzy.

"We're supposed to walk through all that and not be harmed?" Miles asked, looking around him. "Dear God, how?"

But Wade had already guessed. "We're not here anymore, old friend."

They glanced at him, Doris saying, "You mean . . . we are . . . ?"

"Yes," Balon's voice came to them. "You are free of this earth. Walk toward the crosses."

They walked across the digging site, littered with the broken bodies of those who chose to live with the Dark One. No one seemed to notice them. Miles stopped by one Coven member who was paralyzed with fear, unable to move or tear his eyes from the sight of the golem in its fury. Miles tapped him on the shoulder.

"Hey, you *shnorrer**, you still owe me for that living-room furniture you bought ten years ago."

But the man paid him no attention.

"You hear me, you crook?"

The man ran screaming into the night. He ran right through Miles and Doris, Wade and Anita.

Through them.

"So send the money to the JDL, you *goniff!***" Miles called after the fleeing, frightened man. Miles turned, once more facing the starkly outlined crosses behind the circle of stones. "Oh my," he said, his eyes finding the tortured form of Jane Ann. "Oh no." He began prayers in Hebrew, his wife joining him.

*Chiseler

**Thief

376

"Hideous," Anita said. "How could a human do that to another human?"

"Easily," Wade told her. "Ever looked at pictures of Nazi concentration camps?"

The four of them walked through the scene of blood and pain, past the golem who was occupied solely in tearing both arms from a shrieking Devil-worshiper. They paid no attention to him, for the Clay Man was still earthbound, still a part of a world to which they could no longer relate. They walked to a petite figure standing beside the tallest cross, under the ravaged pale naked body of Jane Ann. Beside the figure dressed in a white robe, her hair shining in the glow of the torches, her complexion unmarred by bruises, beautiful and radiant, was the tall rugged form of Sam Balon. The four of them ran the last distance, Wade holding out his hand in greeting.

"No, don't touch," Sam Balon cautioned them gently. "Not just yet. It takes a little time."

"You're speaking . . . normally," Miles said.

"Yes. Come, old friends. It's over."

But no one wanted to move. Anita smiled at Jane Ann. "I've never seen you looking lovelier, Janey."

Jane Ann returned the smile. "I'm fine, Anita. At last."

"Come," Sam Balon said, motioning them forward.

"This is the part I ain't real thrilled with." Miles looked nervously around him.

Sam Balon laughed at his old friend, a hearty, booming laugh. "You'll never change, Miles."

Miles put his hand on his left forearm, the hand going through the arm as if moving through vapor. "This is not a change?" He looked at Sam Balon.

Balon smiled at him. "Come, we must go. Time is growing short."

Far down a strange-appearing road that angled softly, gently upward, they could see a line of people walking. They were happy, laughing and talking.

"The ones who stood beside me at the end," Jane Ann explained.

Miles took his wife's hand. Together, hand in hand, they walked up the road, Sam and Jane Ann in the lead, Wade and Anita following.

The six of them walked the strangely lighted road, a road with no ruts, no holes, no obstacles; a smooth nonsurface. All around them a misty blue light illuminated their way.

"Don't look back," Balon cautioned them. "Look straight ahead for a time."

"Toward home," Wade said, his words almost a sigh of relief.

"Yes," Reverend Sam Balon said, his big hand seeking and finding the soft hand of Jane Ann.

And the two were together, forever, at last.

When the golem's work was done, he began his lumbering walk to the river, miles from the scene of defilement. At the river, the Clay Man stepped down the bank and stood on the clay that was him. He slowly melted into the earth and became once more that which he was: all things of this earth, a creation of God, with the Almighty once more reclaiming him.

The fireball seared the land, leaving nothing but smoke and fire and desolation. The land would one day grow again, bits of grass popping forth, flowers springing upward, seeking the warmth of the sun. But it would be a

378

long time. Years. And when the first flower would appear, pushing out of the earth toward God's sun . . . it would be a blood-red rose.

The doctor in the small French settlement finally came out of his small operating room, a smile on his lips. "He's going to be all right," he told the young woman standing beside the young girl.

"Thank God," Nydia said, tears streaming down her face.

"He'll need lots of rest and care," the doctor told Nydia and Janet. "But," his smile was gentle, "I think he'll be in good hands."

EPILOGUE

In a small French settlement in Eastern Canada, a woman died giving birth. No doctor was in attendance. The baby did not birth normally. It literally exploded from the womb in a gush of blood and mangled flesh. Roma screamed for the last time as the gaping wound in her belly tore the life from her. She saw only a glimpse of the infant before she finally died, but that one quick look was enough. She died with a smile on her lips, knowing she had served her master well.

The child fought the hands that cleaned it and bathed it and held it. It had enormous strength. It howled and snarled and snapped. And then, as if spoken to by an invisible force from some far-off world beyond human comprehension, the child became docile, losing its monsterlike features.

The child allowed an old woman to hold it for a time. The old woman's daughter, who had just birthed a child, was brought in to nurse the infant. The nursing mother, like her mother, and all the others in attendance, wore a strange-looking medallion around her neck.

The child, after nursing, played with the medallion.

In the caves behind the charred remains of the once great mansion called Falcon House, the Beasts settled in

380

for a long sleep. They had kept a very low profile during the battles between the evil forces and the old warrior. They knew when to fight and when not to fight. Now they slept. With only a single sentry on guard. They would be called again. They always were.

And on the sixth day of the sixth month, at precisely the sixth minute of her pregnancy, Nydia gave birth to a tiny premature baby. The doctors were astonished at the baby's condition, for the boy was in perfect health. A beautiful child.

"Amazing," the doctors said.

Mother and father could but look at each other in silence . . . and wonder.

"I'll help you take good care of the baby," Janet told Nydia. "I promise I will."

Janet's parents were fond of Sam and Nydia, and delighted their daughter had been returned to them unharmed.

"I know you will," Nydia said, patting the child's hand.

The bite marks on Nydia's neck had healed and vanished without scarring months ago.

"Janet just loves babies," her father said, smiling.

"I don't know what we would have done without you," Sam said.

Janet walked to a window in the hospital room, away from Nydia and Sam and her parents. She stood for a few seconds, looking at her reflection in the glass. She smiled, the parting of young lips exposing teeth suddenly fanged, the points glistening sharply, blood-red. Her eyes were wild, that of a person possessed.

The wild look vanished, the teeth were again normal.

The young girl turned around, facing the adults. "I don't know what I would have done without you and Nydia," she said, looking at Sam. "I owe you both my life. And I promise you both I'll look after the baby. Forever and ever."

Janet smiled. Very sweetly.

THE BEST IN SUSPENSE FROM ZEBRA
by Jon Land

THE DOOMSDAY SPIRAL   (1481, $3.50)

Tracing the deadly twists and turns of a plot born in Auschwitz, Alabaster — master assassin and sometime Mossad agent — races against time and operatives from every major service in order to control and kill a genetic nightmare let loose in America!

THE LUCIFER DIRECTIVE   (1353, $3.50)

From a dramatic attack on Hollywood's Oscar Ceremony to the hijacking of three fighter bombers armed with nuclear weapons, terrorists are out-gunning agents and events are outracing governments. Minutes are ticking away to a searing blaze of earth-shattering destruction!

VORTEX   (1469-4, $3.50)

The President of the US and the Soviet Premier are both helpless. Nuclear missiles are hurtling their way to a first strike and no one can stop the top-secret fiasco — except three men with old scores to settle. But if one of them dies, all humanity will perish in a vortex of annihilation!

MUNICH 10   (1300, $3.95)
by Lewis Orde

They've killed her lover, and they've kidnapped her son. Now the world-famous actress is swept into a maelstrom of international intrigue and bone-chilling suspense — and the only man who can help her pursue her enemies is a complete stranger . . .

DEADFALL   (1400, $3.95)
By Lewis Orde and Bill Michaels

The two men Linda cares about most, her father and her lover, entangle her in a plot to hold Manhattan Island hostage for a billion dollars ransom. When the bridges and tunnels to Manhattan are blown, Linda is suddenly a terrorist — except *she's* the one who's terrified!

Available wherever paperbacks are sold, or order direct from the Publisher. Send cover price plus 50¢ per copy for mailing and handling to Zebra Books, 475 Park Avenue South, New York, N.Y. 10016. DO NOT SEND CASH.